THE VAMPIRE'S BARGAIN

EMPIRE OF ETERNAL NIGHT: BOOK ONE

JASMINE WALT

DYNAMO PRESS

COPYRIGHT

THE WORLD OF
VALENTAERA

GRIMCREST

T

VALE
OF MISTS

CAELUM
CREST

ELYSIUM VALE

NOXALIS

GRAVITON
HEIGHTS

CRIMSON
CLIFS

IMPORTANT NAMES AND PLACES

THE GODS:

RADIEL: God of Light and Order. He is one of the two creation gods of Valentaera.

ATHANASIA: Goddess of Darkness and Chaos. She is the second of the two creation gods of Valentaera, and the consort of Radiel, God of Light. Together, the two of them created Valentaera, which served as a model for the hundreds of other worlds they have spawned since. The two of them have three children: Phaeros, Hecate, and Astellion.

PHAEROS: God of Dawn and Father of Humans. He carries the sun across the sky every day in his flaming chariot, bringing light and warmth to the world of Valentaera.

HECATE: Goddess of Twilight, and Mother of Witches. Her lunar energy bestows incredible blessings on her children, allowing to perform powerful feats of magic.

ASTELLION: God of Night and Father of the Nightforged. He once ruled over the celestial heavens, and gifted his children with starborn magic that allowed them to tap into the mysteries of the universe, but he was killed by Phaeros.

TENEBROS: God of the Underworld and Father of Vampires. Formerly Astellion, his mother Athanasia tried to bring him back to life after he was killed, only to accidentally reincarnate him as the undead ruler of the underworld.

THE WORLD:

VALENTAERA: The world this story takes place in. It is a continent made up of three realms: Heliaris, Trivaea, and Noxalis.

HELIARIS: The human realm. It is made up of three kingdoms —Aetherion, Ferae, and Maris.

TRIVAEA: The witch realm. It is divided into five clandoms— Grimcrest, The Vale of Mists, Crescent Cove, Stonewatch Basin, and Greenwarden.

NOXALIS: The vampire realm. It is sectioned into four house territories—Caelum Crest, Elysium Vale, Graviton Heights, and the Crimson Cliffs.

THE FOUR VAMPIRE HOUSES:

HOUSE INVICTUS: The most militant of the four houses. Vampires born into this house have the gift of Unyielding Might, also known as super-strength. They are known for their harsh discipline and iron will, and their house symbol is an iron sword stabbed through a blood-red heart.

HOUSE STELLARIS: Also known as the dreamers. Stellaris vampires are attuned to the stars—they are master astronomers, and also wield Shadowfire—a dark flame that has the power to burn through anything. Their house symbol is a flaming orb circled by seven stars.

HOUSE PSYCHOROS: Masters of the mind, Psychoros vampires are known for their telekinetic abilities, which allows them to manipulate matter itself. Their house symbol is the astral web.

HOUSE SANGUIS NOCTIS: Occasionally referred to as bloodmages, Sanguis Noctis vampires are the most savage and bloodthirsty of the four clans. Their culture is primal and rooted in ancient rituals and traditions. Their house symbol is a red rose dripping blood onto a black field.

THE THREE HUMAN KINGDOMS/RACES:

AETHERION: a technologically advanced kingdom of humans with the ability to manipulate aether, a type of magical energy that exists in the atmosphere. Many of their inventions are powered using aether.

FERAE: a tribal kingdom of humans with the ability to bond with and draw power from animals. There were once three tribes: the Wolven, The Equinox, and the Aerie.

MARIS: a seafaring kingdom of humans with the ability to manipulate the tides and commune with sea creatures.

THE FIVE WITCH CLANS:

THE NOCTURNE CLAN: the original race of witches created by Hecate, Nocturne witches are blessed with the ability to wield both lunar and shadow magic. Their power waxes and wanes with the phases of the moon. Crescent Cove is their territory.

THE NECROSPIRE CLAN: necromancer witches who commune with and reanimate the dead. They prefer to spend their time in graveyards or battlefield sites. Grimcrest is where they make their home.

THE STONEHEART CLAN: earth witches who specialize in crafting enchanted objects made of stones and crystals. The Stonewatch Basin is their home.

THE WHISPERWEAVE CLAN: masters of illusion magic and interpreters of dreams. They reside in the Vale of Mists.

THE VERDANTIA CLAN: greenwitches who specialize in herbal/plant magic. Greenwarden is their territory.

For the romantasy girlies who thrive in the shadows, yet never allow their inner light to go out.

PART I

THE AWAKENING

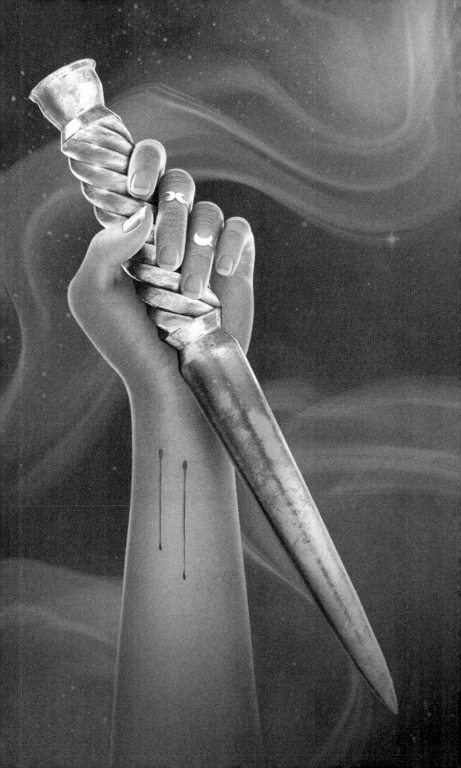

1

I was scratching a tally mark into the lid of my sarcophagus when the vampire entered my tomb.

Well, tomb wasn't the right word. *Technically* this was a temple, or at least it had appeared to be when my ex had lured me in here under false pretenses nearly fifty years ago. Or was it eighty? Thirty? The tally marks, which I etched into the lid every time I found myself conscious, were the only way for me to keep track, and I hadn't been consistent with them. Not to mention I couldn't even see them, only feel them by tracing the grooves with the pads of my fingers.

Anyway, even if this had been a temple, it had been decades, probably even centuries, since anyone worshipped here. The only people who ever stopped by to visit were lost travelers, and only on the night of the new moon, when the illusion spell that cloaked this place grew weak enough to allow passersby to see it.

The sound of the temple door opening, the scuff of leather shoes on stone, the rustle of a cloak in the otherwise still night, were a welcome interlude from the usual interminable silence that filled this place. My nostrils flared as I tried to scent the intruder, but all I inhaled was the stale odor of dust and decay that had been my close companion for as long as I could remember.

Once upon a time, I would have been able to smell the vampire long before they'd entered my prison. Would have been able to get a rough sense of their age, when they'd last fed, which house they hailed from. Would have also heard them coming far before they'd opened the door. But starvation and captivity had blunted my senses so badly, I couldn't even tell if my intruder was male or female. Time had worn me down to a shadow of myself, a skeleton wrapped in skin and leather, able to neither live nor die.

A subtle wave of power rippled through the hall as the vampire ventured farther in, sending goosebumps shivering across my skin. Automatically, I reached for the silver stake lying next to my thigh, allowing myself to trace the cool metal with my fingertips. A macabre security blanket, and wholly unnecessary. None of my midnight visitors had ever successfully opened my prison. The warding spells built into the sarcophagus violently repelled anyone who tried.

Spells that, ironically, were fueled by my own fucking magic.

"Sparrow was right, Sire," a male murmured. The voice was deep and gravelly, the rougher undertones at odds with the formal way he spoke, and I stiffened as I realized there were not one, but *two* vampires in the chamber. "This is the place."

"Of course he's right," the other vampire said. His soft voice echoed through the chamber, a rich, velvet timber that smacked of upper crust sophistication. "And even better, she's still alive. I can hear her heartbeat." A hint of amusement lightened his tone. "She knows we're here."

The stake was in my hand in an instant. Sweat slid down my spine as my heart beat faster, and my blood thrummed in my chest as I prepared for the worst.

These vampires weren't some lost, drunken fools looking for shelter in the rain.

They had come looking for *me*. Specifically.

"Sire, are you sure this is a good idea?" the throaty-voiced vampire asked. "Perhaps Sparrow was wrong about the nature of the spell, and—"

"Sparrow has never let me down before, Lucius, and time is of the essence," the other male said. "We do this now."

I braced myself for the barrier spell surrounding the coffin to blast the two vampires across the room. Instead, the stone lid of the coffin scraped back from the box in one swift, fluid motion. It clattered to the floor, and I gasped as a gust of fresh, icy air whooshed in, caressing my skin like the long-lost touch of a lover. Faint threads of starlight shimmered through the windows of my divine prison, illuminating the stylized figure of a goddess looking down at me from where she'd been etched into the cracked stone ceiling. She gazed at me with hollowed out eyes, hair rippling out from her oval face in waves, her sweeping cloak depicting a multitude of nocturnal creatures.

I hadn't noticed the stunning relief when I'd been shoved into this sarcophagus. Had no idea that Athanasia, Goddess of Darkness and Chaos, Divine Mother of the Universe, had enjoyed a prime viewing spot of my suffering.

A split second later, I was on my feet, my chest heaving as I faced the vampires. I cursed as my bandolier of silver stakes dropped straight from my hips to the bottom of the coffin—I had wasted away to nothing during my imprisonment, my clothes barely hanging onto my bony frame. But there was no time to crouch down and collect them—the stake in my hand was my single shot to freedom, and I had to make it count.

The two vampires stared at me, vastly different expressions on their faces. The one on the left—an umber-skinned male with long, black hair woven into braids and secured at the nape of his neck with a black ribbon—stood with his arms over his broad chest, his lips pressed into a thin line as he studied me. The look of obvious disapproval in his amber eyes would have rankled me if I gave a shit about vampiric opinions. Beneath his cloak, he wore a fitted charcoal-grey tunic and trousers, and in addition to the blades he'd hidden on his body, he wore a steel gauntlet on his right arm I was pretty sure concealed a retractable blade.

In contrast, the other vampire bore no visible weapons, save for the claws that tipped his ivory hands. He wore a high collared black shirt paired with a sleek, midnight-blue vest and matching trousers tucked into knee-high black boots. Unlike his companion, he hadn't deigned to lower the hood of his cloak, so I could make out little of his features save for cold blue eyes, a sharply defined jaw, and a full, unsmiling mouth. His perusal of me was far more clinical, as though I were a horse he'd come to market to inspect... and had found lacking.

"So," he said in that midnight voice of his. "This is the infamous Kitana Nightshade. The most feared vampire slayer in all of Valentaera. Now reduced to little more than a bag of bones."

The corner of his mouth kicked up, a taunting smirk that broke the dam on my pent-up rage and sent it shooting straight to the surface. "Sire—" the other vampire warned, but I was already halfway across the room, my teeth bared in a snarl as some hidden scrap of energy burned through me. The arrogant bloodsucker made no move to defend himself, and I raised my stake, aiming it for the center of his chest—

Every muscle in my body seized, and I froze in mid-air, my stake a hairsbreadth from his chest. His smirk widened as I struggled, displaying just a hint of fang, but my withered muscles could do nothing against the invisible hold.

"Not bad," he said, his breath ghosting against my cheek. We were inches—fucking *inches*—apart, and I couldn't do a damn thing as he slid a clawed fingertip beneath my chin and lifted my face to meet his. "Your movements are impressive considering the length of time you've spent trapped here. Once you've gotten some meat onto your bones again, you'll be quite formidable."

"Formidable?" I spat, my muscles trembling with rage and fatigue. "The word you're looking for is cataclysmic, vampire. You're lucky that I'm a 'bag of bones', as you said, or you and your friend would both be dead right now."

"I have no doubt." The vampire's smirk widened. "In fact, that's what I'm counting on."

I frowned at that, and peered into his face, trying to figure out what in all the hells he was talking about. Up close, his eyes were stunning. The irises were a cold, galaxy blue, with the faintest ring of fiery red around the pupils that radiated outward. It was as though the gods had taken strands of starfire from the celestial heavens and woven them into his undead soul, and I'd never seen anything like it before.

How many humans had he enthralled with those other-worldly eyes? And how many had he killed?

"You're a Psychoros vampire," I said, the gears in my brain turning now that my body was forced to a standstill. The bastard hadn't been taunting me for the fun of it—he'd deliberately provoked me to see how I would react. What I was capable of, even in this weakened state. A quick glance into his pupils confirmed how haggard I looked—my square face reduced to skeletal proportions, my black-brown hair limp and scraggly, my violet eyes nearly as hollow as those of the dark goddess who watched us from the ceiling.

Anyone else would have died of starvation a long time ago.

It was only the curse of my blood that has kept me alive.

"I am." He removed his hand from my chin and inclined his head. "Maximillian Starclaw, at your service."

I stared at the vampire, my mind whirling as I struggled to

comprehend what was going on here. Psychoros was one of the four houses of Noxalis, the vampire realm. Each house had its own special ability, gifted by Tenebros, the dark ruler of the underworld and the god of vampires. To House Invictus, he gave the Unyielding Might, a terrifying super-strength that could crush bones into dust with the flick of a finger. To House Stellaris, the everlasting burn of Shadowfire. To House Sanguis Noctis, the Blood Covenant, which allowed them to weaponise blood of any kind. And to Psychoros vampires, the Psychic Shift —otherwise known as telekinesis.

My memories were muddled after decades of imprisonment with only dreams and nightmares to keep me company, but from what I could recall, the Starclaws were the ruling family of House Psychoros. And judging by this vampire's haughty, aristocratic demeanor and the fact that he had a vampire servant with him rather than a human thrall, I assumed Maximillian held a prominent position in his house's hierarchy.

"What do you want from me?" I hissed through gritted teeth. If I'd had the full might of my magic, I could have fought back— after all, the vampire could only hold me physically. But after decades of being drained repeatedly by that sarcophagus, I didn't have a drop of magic left to defend myself with. If this vampire or his lackey wanted to kill me, there wasn't much I could do to prevent it.

"Are you here to use me as a blood bag?" It wouldn't be the first time. The only thing vampires loved more than human blood was witch blood—the magic in our veins was a lot more compatible with theirs than human magic, and gave their own powers a significant boost. It was the reason they had hunted us when their race had first been cursed with vampirism, and the reason humans and witches had formed the Midnight Accords to protect us from their endless hunter.

To my surprise, the vampire curled his lip. "A blood bag?

How unimaginative." He turned away, as though I'd disappointed him. "Take her, Lucius. We need to be on our way before Highlord Lysander finds out we're trespassing in his territory."

"Yes, Sire." Lucius stepped forward, and the invisible force pressed hard against the sides of my neck, cutting off my oxygen. I tried to fight it, but darkness crept into my vision, and the hard look in his eyes was the last thing I saw before I passed out.

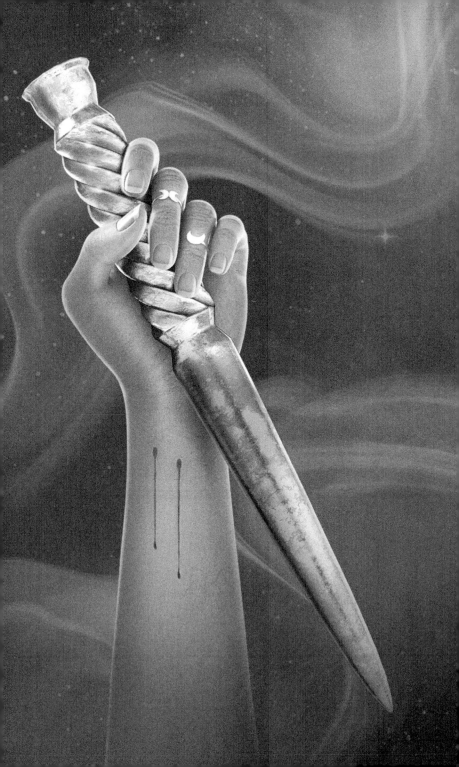

2

"W*ake up, child.*"

A silvery whisper penetrated the thick, suffocating blanket of sleep, and I blinked my eyes open. A black silk tapestry embroidered with a sparkling network of crisscrossing silver lines hovered above me, and below, a plush mattress cradled my body. The crackling fire to my left threw shadows across the dark chamber, and a strange humming sound emanated from somewhere to my right.

Confusion swamped me, and I tried to sit up. A slight tug at my right wrist halted the motion, and I glanced down to see a fine glass tube poking out of my vein. The tube spiraled upward, connecting to an ornate mechanical device sitting on a table to my right—the source of the strange humming. Golden liquid swirled in the bottom of a crystalline canister in the center of the device, flowing out of the machine and down the tube leading into my body.

Panic seized me, and I yanked the device out of my body. I didn't know what in all the hells that thing was, and I didn't want it pumping any more of that mystery fluid into my body. Crimson and golden droplets sprayed across the bedspread, but

I ignored the mess as I threw the sheets back, desperate to free myself from the tangle around my legs. My feet sank into the thick pile of carpet covering the floor as I stood, and I wobbled a little as a wave of disorientation washed over me.

But my legs held, and my body felt strong.

Stronger than it had any right to feel after an untold number of decades in captivity.

I knew I should move, but as my weight settled into the ground, the sheer novelty of the position struck me. I was standing—*standing*—on my own two feet, something I hadn't been able to do in the long decades I'd been trapped in that accursed sarcophagus. My toes curled into the carpet, and I hesitantly stretched my arms out to the side, then over my head. A simple movement, but one that had been denied to me for so long, I genuinely couldn't remember the last time I'd done it.

Memories of the two vampires who had entered my temple and freed me from my prison trickled into my mind's eye, and I gripped one of the bed's wooden posts for support as it all washed over me. Had that vampire with the starfire eyes brought me to this place? Why had he put me in such a well-appointed chamber instead of his dungeon, and without even chaining me to the bedpost? Did he really think I wouldn't try to escape?

Letting go of the post, I took one cautious step forward, then two, allowing my body to re-familiarize itself with the concept of walking. It felt strange, being able to move my limbs so freely— I'd been confined to a box made specifically for my proportions, with barely enough room to wiggle, never mind stretch or use my limbs. By all rights, they should have atrophied, yet here I was. Walking.

Once I was reasonably confident my legs weren't about to collapse beneath my weight—scant as it was—I moved around the bed so I could explore the room. The bed was massive, its luxurious frame chiseled from ebony wood, the blanket a midnight blue velvet with matching silk sheets beneath. A black marble fireplace crackled to my left, the fire within burning brightly enough to tell me it had been tended to recently. The black and burgundy patterned wallpaper and the crimson velvet curtains hanging on the windows definitely pointed to vampiric tastes.

But my eyes narrowed on the chandelier hanging from the ceiling, and the handles of the wardrobe on the other side of the room. They were made from sunsteel, a metal favored by the Aetherions—one of the three races of Heliaris, the human realm. And the machine that had been hooked up to my arm was of Aetherion make too—one of their advanced medical devices, no doubt.

That was strange. Vampires didn't use aetheric technology. They shunned human inventions as a rule, even going to so far as to reject the Aetherion king's offer to develop a device capable of transmogrifying animal blood to make it more palatable to vampires. The bloodsucking bastards acted like their immortality made them better than everyone else, but they were just a bunch of prettily dressed corpses stuck in their archaic ways.

I was just about to reach for the heavy brocade curtain covering the windows when the door opened. Turning, I watched as a petite olive-skinned woman entered the room, a glass cannister with the same golden liquid from the machine tucked under one arm. She wore a pair of navy blue coveralls that were zipped open to the waist, revealing an orange shirt underneath, her short, golden curls tucked beneath a matching blue cap.

The woman's mouth fell open as she sighted me, and to my shock, her green eyes filled with delight. "Phaeros's beard, you're awake!" Her cheeks flushed as she nearly dropped the cannister, and she fumbled it back beneath her arm. "Max is going to be—"

I was behind the woman before she finished speaking, my arms wrapped around her neck and underarm in a sleeper hold. She struggled as I squeezed, cutting off her circulation in a way very similar to what Lucius had done to me, and the cannister crashed to the floor, glass and liquid puddling at our feet. I gave an apologetic wince as she sagged in my arms a few seconds later, knowing she'd probably be blamed for the mess.

But if she was a human in House Starclaw's service, that meant she was a thrall—a brainwashed servant blood-bound to follow her vampire master's commands. I knew from experience that thralls viciously defended their masters, no matter how badly they were being abused. It didn't matter how nice or friendly she appeared to be—she was still the enemy.

Careful not to step on broken glass, I carried the unconscious woman to the bed, then searched her body for anything that could be used as a weapon. The belt around her waist was stuffed with a variety of tools—helpful for a mechanic, but useless against vampires—and her pockets were empty except for a pencil and a grease rag. Frustrated, I abandoned my search in favor of the closet. At the very least, I needed to get out of this flimsy nightgown and into something better suited for running.

I opened the closet door, then jerked back in surprise. An array of colorful gowns and tunics hung from the rack, but on the floor beneath them were my clothes, my armor, and my stakes. I snatched them up from the floor and put them on, cursing as my black leather pants sagged around my bony hips. My armored corset refused to stay on at all, so I abandoned it for a white cotton blouse hanging in the closet. My bandolier was also too wide for my hips, so I slung it over my shoulders, then shrugged my black duster on over it. Lastly, I fitted my vambraces over my forearms. Everything smelled like it had been freshly laundered, and the stakes even looked like they'd been polished.

Why in all the hells would the vampire lord leave my weapons here where I could easily reach them?

I shoved my feet into my leather boots, then stalked over to the curtain and yanked it away to reveal a pair of glass doors. I sucked in a breath at the glittering view beyond, but before I could adjust to the sight, I heard footsteps coming up the hall, and caught the unmistakable scent of a vampire.

"Eliza? Where are you?"

Fuck.

I yanked the glass door open, then vaulted over the railing and out of view. The cold metal bit into my skin as I hung off the balcony railing, and I glanced upward to see I was suspended from the side of a massive tower. The sunsteel edifice climbed toward the night sky, its golden surface shimmering faintly in the scant moonlight. Wrought metal balconies and crystal falcon heads jutted out from the walls, which were smooth aside from the sun motifs etched into the metal. A circular construct crowned the structure, and I didn't need to see the top of it to know that it was a magnificent sundial. I'd heard the stories of this place, even if I'd never set foot here in my life.

I wasn't just hanging off any old tower. This was the Tower of Dawn, the architectural crown jewel of Lumina, Aetherion's capital city.

The enormity of that realization hit me like a hurricane, along with the fact that there was so much *space* around me. Hundreds of feet between me and the ground, and an endless expanse stretching above and around me. The night wind shifted, and I flinched against the icy caress on my cheek. My breaths came faster, tighter, my palms growing slick against the cold metal. The sky seemed to press in on me from all sides, and—

"Eliza! Are you ok?"

The shout snapped me out of the panic closing in on me,

and I let out an explosive breath, as though I'd been sucker punched. Before I could think too hard about it, I swung myself along the balcony railing, toward the tower wall, then leaped for the nearest crystal falcon.

I landed on the massive head, then nearly slipped right off the slick surface. Swallowing curses, I wrapped my arms around the crystal bird's neck, then swung myself toward the next balcony railing.

I rinsed and repeated this insane maneuver, sticking to the shadowed side of the tower to avoid the attention of the guards posted on the compound walls. I kept one eye on the ground as I descended the six stories separating me from the earth, noting the alarming number of people moving about the paths between buildings despite the late hour, and picking out the guards posted along the top and outside the entrances of the stone wall that surrounded this place.

Getting out of here was going to be an absolute bitch.

Before my imprisonment, I would have been able to rappel down the tower in a matter of minutes. But my movements were rusty, my muscles weak from disuse, and I had to take breaks between each jump to make sure I didn't fall. By the time I reached the bottom, sweat dripped from my forehead, and my body trembled with exertion. I pressed myself against the wall of the tower, sucking in gulps of air as quietly as I could as I tried to catch my breath.

A guard walked around the corner of the nearest building, and I stilled, my nose twitching. There was no mistaking the icy scent that was both earthy and metallic, reminiscent of the deep chill of night air, of cold stone and metal, punctuated with the faint but persistent note of dried blood.

This guard was a vampire.

Which meant the other guards on the wall were likely vampires as well.

And if that was true, that meant the Tower of Dawn, home of Aetherion's royal family and one of the most important monuments in this kingdom, had been taken over by vampires.

The thought was unfathomable. How had vampires managed to conquer the city? Aetherion had the most advanced weaponry of all three human kingdoms—the aetheric cannons they shot from their airships could vaporize an entire battalion of vampires. If they'd had those airships during the Chaos War when the vampires first attacked the rest of Valentaera, we could have wiped them from the continent back when this all started. But they had them now, or at least they had when I'd been imprisoned. So why hadn't they used them?

The guard turned my way, sensing movement, but I whipped out a stake and flung it in his direction before his eyes could settle on me. He let out a pained gurgle as the silver weapon found its mark, straight through the chest to puncture his undead heart. I barely paused to yank it out of him as I dashed past, making for the compound's southern entrance, which appeared to be the least guarded. I felt for my inner well of magic, trying to gather shadows around me to cloak my movements, but there was hardly anything to draw on. And with only the barest sliver of moon hanging in the night sky above, there was no way for me to draw magic from my goddess, either.

Shouts rang out behind me as I cleared the southern wall, killing the two vampires guarding the entrance as I went. Arrows whizzed past me as my feet hit the cobblestones, and I zigzagged to avoid them as I raced into the crowded city streets.

The city blurred around me as I ran, phosphorescent lamps casting an eerie glow against the swirl of sleek structures. The metallic tang of the air mingled with both the frosty, death-laced scent of vampires and the warm, vibrant aroma of human life. I pumped my legs as hard as I could as I plowed through humans and vampires alike, breath sawing in my lungs as I worked to put as much distance between myself and the compound walls as possible. But I knew the longer I ran, the more people would notice me. So I ducked around a corner, cut through an alley, then casually strolled into a market square, taking deep breaths to slow my heart rate as I attempted to blend in with the crowd.

I stuck to the shadows as I walked, staying alert for any signs of pursuit as I took in my surroundings. Vendors, both human and vampire, peddled their wares from the stalls—produce, leather goods, clothing, mechanical devices. But also vials of blood, pumped directly from humans hooked up to a strange contraption. Horror curdled in my gut as I stared at the man, who in turn stared vacantly into the distance as his master pulled a fresh vial from the machine and handed it to a waiting vampire. The bloodsucker licked his lips, then slapped a coin into the vendor's hand before disappearing into the crowd.

This can't be real.

A nearby clock tower began to ring, drawing my attention away. I glanced over at its crystal face, noting the hour hand was set at two o'clock. But the bell kept ringing... three, four, five... six...

A sense of dread began to form inside me, growing heavier and heavier with each gong I counted. Twelve... thirteen... fourteen... then a silence that made me feel like the entire world had slid out from beneath my feet.

It wasn't two o'clock in the morning.

It was two o'clock in the *gods-damned afternoon.*

"This has to be a mistake," I muttered. I glanced up at the pitch-black sky, as if I might find the sun hiding in the black spaces between the stars, or peeking out from behind the sliver of moon. But that turned out to be a fatal error. That sense of vastness opened up around me, and I felt exposed, vulnerable, like I was a mouse crouching in an open field, and the stars were the twinkling eyes of some avian predator. Sweat broke out across my forehead as the feeling worsened, creeping up my chest and into my throat until it had a chokehold on me.

Vampires turned their heads in my direction as my heart pumped faster, and I struggled for breath. Recognizing the danger, I retreated, disappearing into the crowd and away from their predatory gazes. I had enough wits left about me to duck into an alley, and as the shadows closed around me, some of the panic receded. The sounds of the city faded a little, and I was able to take in a full breath.

"Well, well. What do we have here?"

I spun around to see a vampire leaning against the brick wall, a pipe dangling from his fingers. He was well-built and handsome, dressed in a black-collared shirt and suspenders, his trousers cuffed at the ankles and his sleeves rolled up to expose his forearms. A wicked scar slashed over his left eye and across the bridge of his nose—a relic from before he'd been Turned, or a wound from a silver weapon, as vampires didn't scar otherwise. His dark eyes gleamed with curiosity as he looked me up and down, taking in my attire. "Unusual clothes for a slave. Who do you belong to?"

"I don't belong to anyone." I palmed one of my stakes, clenching it tight so my hand would stop shaking. I took a step toward him, angling my back toward the mouth of the alley so he couldn't escape. Even if I wanted to let him go, I couldn't, not when he might grab some of his cronies and come back to finish me off.

The vampire's eyes widened as he took in the stake in my hand, and then he laughed. "I don't know where you found that toy, but put it down, little human. Only a real silver stake will work, and you—"

I lunged for him, determined to prove just how real my silver stake was, but the vampire was faster. He darted out of the way, and my weapon gouged a deep line into the brick wall, right where he'd been standing. I tried to spin around, but I was off balance, and my movements were rusty. A vicious kick landed on my ribs, and I swore as I sprawled across the ground, my stake rolling beneath a dumpster.

"You bitch!" The vampire tried to kick me again, and I rolled the opposite way, cursing my weakness. My flight from the Tower had drained a lot of my strength, and captivity had dulled my once-lightning-quick reflexes. The vampire grabbed me by the hair and yanked me on my feet, then banded an arm around my waist and pulled me against his body.

"Where did you get those stakes?" he growled. His fangs scraped against my neck, sending a rush of anger through me. "Vampire hunters haven't been sighted in decades, not since the witches closed their borders!"

The witches closed their borders? I almost asked the question out loud, but I didn't want to reveal my ignorance. Instead, I snapped my head back and stomped on the vampire's instep at the same time. His nose crunched on impact, and as his arm loosened, I grabbed his other arm and flipped him over my shoulder. My stake followed him to the ground, and his death scream echoed off the alley walls as it found its mark in the center of his heart. Blood burbled over his lips, and his skin sagged around the bones of his face. As his immortality faded, so did his body, his muscles withering away until he resembled nothing so much as a mummified husk.

Probably similar to what I looked like right now, honestly.

The back door to the building on my left burst open, and two more vampires spilled into the alley. They'd obviously heard the commotion, because one of them brandished a sword, and they both looked like they were out for blood. I sprang to my feet, a stake flying from my hand, but the swordsman knocked it aside it with a slash of his blade. The second one flung a hand out, and I cursed, dodging to the left as the air rippled with invisible energy. Still, I wasn't fast enough, and the telekinetic blast clipped my shoulder, spinning me the opposite direction and causing me to stumble.

"Take her alive," the telekinetic ordered as the swordsman advanced. "The boss will want to hear about this one."

Rage surged through me, and I palmed two stakes. I'd just tasted freedom for the first time in what felt like eons—I wasn't about to let these bloodsuckers put me in a cage. The swordsman rushed me, and I dropped low to avoid his strike, then stabbed him in the thigh with my stake. The vampire roared as his dark blood spurted into the night, but it wasn't a fatal blow. His crony tried to hit me with another telekinetic blast, but I gathered my legs beneath me and leaped into the air before he could connect. The icy wind caught my duster as I soared into the air, fanning it out behind me, and I threw my second stake at the telekinetic. His eyes bulged out of his skull as the silver weapon pierced his heart, and he dropped to his knees as his body disintegrated.

But the second vampire had followed me into the sky, and I was too slow to avoid his strike. I twisted in mid-air as he brought his sword down, and raised my forearm to block. My vambrace absorbed the powerful blow, but the force of it sent me flying. Pain exploded through my entire body as I crashed to the ground, a cloud of dust kicking up as the pavement cratered beneath me.

The vampire's boots hit the pavement, and I rolled to my side, struggling to rise as he stalked toward me. "I'm going to rip your throat out and feast from your neck right here in this alley," he growled, his eyes burning with fury.

So much for taking me alive.

I made it to my knees by the time he closed the distance between us, but my hands were shaking so badly, I could barely draw my next stake. A wave of hopelessness washed over me, and despite myself, my shoulders began to sag.

Was this really how I was going to die? Finally free after untold decades spent trapped in a tomb, only to meet my end in a filthy alleyway at the hands of a low-life vampire grunt who couldn't even use magic?

The vampire reached for my throat, then stopped, his hand inches from my skin. His eyes widened, and my breath caught as his arm trembled, refusing to obey him.

"I think that's enough for tonight," a familiar voice said.

A clawed hand punched through the vampire's chest, tearing a hole straight through the center of his body. This time, it was my turn to stare, wide-eyed, as that pale fist clutched the vampire's undead heart, then pulled it back through the hole in his body. My would-be murderer collapsed to the ground, revealing the other vampire standing behind him.

But comparing the vampire towering above me to the one on the ground was like comparing a cute little firefly to a comet streaking across the sky. While the vampire bleeding out in front of my knees had been lethal, he was little more than a typical vampire grunt, possessing heightened strength, speed, and senses, but no magic to speak of.

The vampire standing before me practically radiated power. It shimmered in the luminescent glow of his skin and hair, in the subtle shift and hum of the air surrounding him. His aura filled the alleyway, taking up far more space than his lean frame warranted.

"Hmm." Maximillian studied the heart in his hand for a moment, then crushed it in his fist. Blood ran down his muscled forearm, staining his sleeve before he lowered it so the blood could drip onto the cobblestones instead. He studied me beneath lowered brows, his starfire eyes gleaming. "Sorry to interrupt, but it looked to me as though you required assistance."

I pursed my lips, not sure how to respond to that. I definitely *did* require assistance—still did, in fact, as it was taking every ounce of strength I had just to stay on my knees. But I'd be damned if I thanked a vampire for anything.

"Why did you kill him?" I demanded.

Maximillian's eyebrows rose. "Is it not obvious?"

I huffed out a breath. "He's a vampire. One of your own people. I'm a witch. Your enemy. It's not obvious at all."

Maximillian's lip curled with disdain as he glanced down at the dead vampire at his feet. He kicked the body aside as if it were a piece of garbage, then crouched before me. Even squatting, he was still a head taller than me, and I scowled, cursing myself for being so short. The clouds drifting across the sliver of moon above us cast his face in shadow, but his eyes glowed with an inner fire as he studied me.

"It's very simple," he said, sliding a finger beneath my chin and tilting my head up to look at him. "You are under my protection. Which means that so long as you remain in this city, you are mine. And anyone who touches what's mine, dies."

He spoke softly, but the intensity in his voice rattled me. "I'm not yours," I hissed at him, affronted by the very concept of being owned by a vampire.

He chuckled. "Not yet," he agreed, rising to his feet. He held out a hand toward me, but I made no move to take it. "You fought well, Kitten. I can see why your name still strikes fear into the hearts of vampires, even all these years after your presumed death."

"*Kitten?*" My mouth dropped open, so shocked by his audacity that I couldn't even bring myself to be angry. Was this soft-spoken, cold-as-ice vampire actually calling me by a *pet name?*

He shrugged. "You're all of what, five feet tall? Even shorter when you're on your knees." He smirked, and my face grew scalding hot. "You're pint-sized, adorable, and a whirlwind of chaos. Kitten is the perfect nickname for you."

"I'm five-foot-three," I seethed, seizing his hand. I'd be damned if I was going to spend even one more second kneeling before a vampire, even if that meant I had to accept his help.

Maximillian's fingers—strong yet elegant—wrapped around mine, and he hauled me to my feet in one fluid motion. My head spun, and I instinctively tightened my grip on his hand to steady myself. An unexpected wave of emotion swept through me at the contact, and I blinked in shock as a lump formed in my throat.

It took me a second to realize that I was reacting this way because I was experiencing my first non-threatening touch for the first time since I'd been imprisoned. Not at the hands of a witch, or even a human. But a vampire.

Maximillian's eyes flickered, and perhaps I imagined it, but I could have sworn his expression softened just a touch. Coming back to my senses, I yanked my hand out of his and stepped away, doing my best to look down my nose at him. Which was not an easy feat, considering that he was at least six-foot-four. But when you're a short girl, you work with what you've got.

The vampire lord raised his eyebrows, seeing right through my poor attempt at posturing. "If we're finished here," he said, crouching to retrieve something from the ground, "I'd like to return to the Tower and get cleaned up."

Anxiety tightened my chest, and I took a step back. "I won't be your captive." Pain radiated up and down my spine now that the rush of battle had faded, but I stood firm, refusing to give into the pain. I would sooner drive a stake through my own heart than allow myself to be locked up again.

Maximillian straightened, shaking his storm cloud hair from

his eyes. "You aren't my captive," he said, and extended his hand to me again. I blinked at the sight of my stake in his outstretched palm. The silver metal had to be burning the fuck out of him, but he acted as if the pain didn't bother him at all. "I didn't break you out of that prison just to put you into a new one."

I snatched the stake out of his hand before he could change his mind, then brandished it between us as if I was in any condition to fight him off. To his credit, he didn't scoff or laugh or show any other sign of disdain. He simply met my stare and waited, my chest rising and falling rapidly as I struggled to regain control of my breathing.

I didn't want to believe him, but I couldn't deny that he hadn't treated me like a prisoner so far. There had to be some kind of trick to this—altruism wasn't exactly a vampiric trait—but I couldn't figure out what his agenda was, why he'd gone through so much effort to help me.

"Why should I agree to go with you?" I finally asked.

"Because you need answers about what's happened over the past fifty years," he said. "Answers about why it's full night at two o'clock in the afternoon. Answers about how and why vampires have taken over one of the most powerful human cities in Heliaris. And answers about why a vampire broke you out of your prison, put you up in a comfortable room in his stronghold, and gave you full freedom to run about his city in weapons and armor."

I opened my mouth, then clamped it shut. Because he was right. I did need answers. And though I trusted Maximillian about as far as I could throw him—which, at the moment, wasn't very far at all—he was my best source of information right now.

So when he turned away from me and headed toward the mouth of the alley, I followed him back to the Tower.

Keeping my stakes clutched in my fists the entire time.

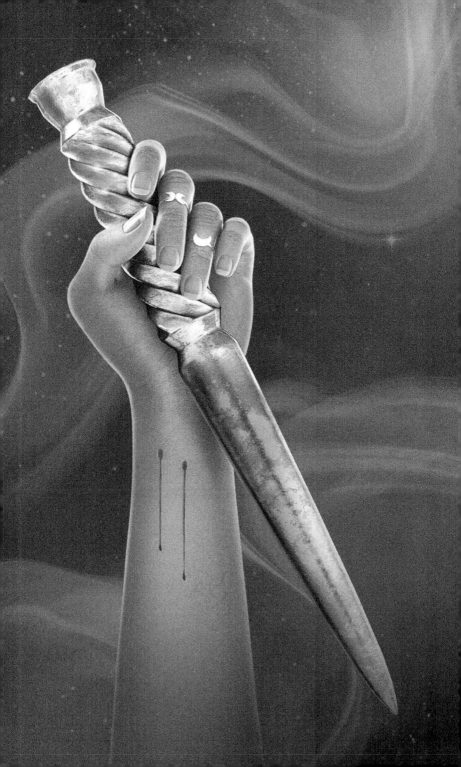

3

I f looks could kill, I would have been dead the moment I approached the compound gates.

"My guards aren't too happy you killed three of their own," Maximillian murmured as we passed through the gate and into the compound. The two of us had to be quite a sight—the vampire lord disheveled, his arm drenched in gore, and me hobbling beside him like a cripple. At least my blood-spattered weapons and armor were hidden—Maximillian had leant me his cloak, informing me that while I was a guest under his protection, it would raise far too many questions for me to be running around the city looking like I was about to slaughter every vampire in sight. He suggested that on future excursions, I keep a lower profile.

I couldn't even wrap my mind around *future excursions*, never mind the one I'd just returned from. The truth was, I'd pulled up the hood of Maximillian's cloak the moment we'd left the alleyway, and stuck as close to the vampire lord as possible. That overwhelming desire to curl up into a ball in the darkest corner I could find and hide from the world had returned, and the relief

I felt as we passed through the gates was so palpable, it filled me with disgust.

"Oh, and Eliza will be upset with you as well," Maximillian added. "She was very excited about your arrival, so I imagine you crushed her hopes quite thoroughly when you choked her out on your very first meeting."

His tone was conversational, but I detected a hint of accusation beneath it that made my spine stiffen. "You can't blame me for that," I said, even as a stab of guilt pierced my gut. I remembered how excited she'd looked when she'd seen I was awake. But why in the hells did I even care about that? It wasn't like I knew her. I'd been as gentle as I could with her under the circumstances, rendering her unconscious instead of injuring or killing her. "Or for killing the guards. You should have known I would try to escape."

"I did," he admitted. "That's part of the reason I had Eliza tend to you instead of sending a vampire. I knew you wouldn't kill her."

"How could you know that?" I asked, affronted on her behalf. That her master would so callously put his thrall's life in danger like that… it took everything in me not to stake him on the spot.

"I made it my business to learn everything I could about you."

I pursed my lips, not knowing how to respond to that. He clearly *did* know a lot about me—enough to figure out the location of my prison and the exact night that the spells protecting it were weak enough to be breached. And I knew almost nothing about him, except that he was a powerful telekinetic and a high-ranking vampire noble.

I stewed about that as we approached the Tower entrance— a grand archway, flanked by two slender obelisks of burnished sunsteel. The vampire lord raised a hand, and the door, a work of art adorned with etchings of sun symbols and iconography, swung open of its own accord. Beyond, a vast foyer awaited, bathed in an enchanted, muted glow emanating from veins of aetheric crystal embedded into the walls. A vaulted ceiling set with an array of crystal stars arched above us as we crossed the threshold, and sunstone floors gleamed beneath our feet, reflecting the crystalline light so that it almost appeared as if we were walking on water.

Or, it would have, if not for the deep blue runner that stretched from the foyer entrance and through to the main hall. Embroidered across it, in gold thread, was an intricate design displaying a large eye that sat smack dab in the middle of a web-like constellation. I knew that symbol. This was House Psychoros's crest—The Astral Web.

A female vampire stepped forward to greet us. Her auburn hair was styled in loose waves that cascaded around her slim shoulders, and she wore a high-collared dress with a narrow skirt that flared out just below her knees, paired with pointed, low-heeled shoes. Gold panels were sewn into the sides of the figure-hugging garment, highlighting her tall, willowy frame. She held a notebook in one hand and a pen in the other, and I noted her claws were retracted, and that she'd painted her nails a deep crimson.

"Welcome back, Sire," she said, dipping her head. Her hazel eyes glittered as she surveyed me, her brows pulling together into a faint frown. "I see you've retrieved our guest. Would you like me to send for a healer?"

Our guest?

"Yes," Maximillian said dryly. "She's done an excellent job of sabotaging Eliza's efforts over the past few days. Nothing another night hooked up to the Elinfuser won't fix, but at the very least she should take a painkiller tonic."

"Elinfuser?" I thought back to the crystal-and-sunsteel

machine I'd been hooked up to. "Is that what that thing is called?"

"Yes," the redhead answered for him. "It's a special device that delivers elixirs directly into the bloodstream, and Eliza used it to pump you full of *vitraya*, a serum that has the power to bring most humans back from the brink of death."

"Or in your case, restore you from decades of atrophy," Maximillian added.

"Sunlight is a key component to its creation," the redhead went on, "As you can imagine, it's a valuable resource."

Her tone was razor sharp, but I barely paid any mind to her disapproval as I thought back to the clock tower. "You say that as if sunlight is scarce," I said, looking between them.

The two vampires exchanged a loaded glance. "I think this conversation is best continued over dinner," Maximillian said smoothly. "Nyra, please show our guest back to her room so she can get cleaned her up, then bring her to me when she's ready."

I opened my mouth to object, but he stepped past me, and in the next second, he was embroiled in conversation with another vampire in the entrance hall.

"Come along," Nyra said as I glowered at the back of the vampire lord's head. "We'll get you a hot bath and a change of clothes."

"I don't need you to mother me," I protested.

The vampire wrinkled her nose. "There's nothing motherly about it. You reek of vampire blood and human piss. I'm tempted to dunk you into the river after the trouble you've caused, and I doubt you could fight me in your condition. So come along."

Nyra turned on her heel and strode off, her heeled shoes clicking purposefully against the marble floor. I bristled at her high-handed tone, but swallowed my pride and followed her, trying not to hobble even though my legs were begging to collapse beneath me.

I would suffer through this vampire's hospitality for another evening. Just long enough to find out what he wanted, and what had happened to my world while I'd been rotting away in that sarcophagus.

And then I would seek the vengeance I'd been dreaming of for the last fifty years.

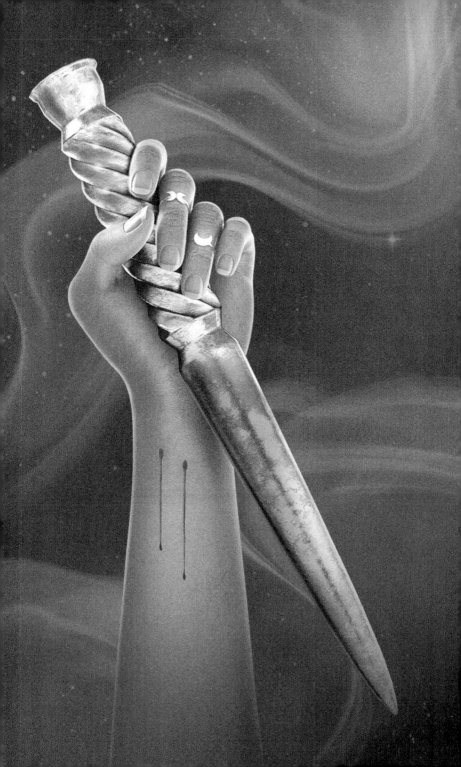

4

The moment I shut the bedroom door, the hair raising prickle that had been crawling across my skin for the past hour vanished. I let out an honest-to-gods sigh of relief at finally being alone, and the knot in my stomach loosened in response.

"Pathetic," I muttered, shaking my head.

I was Kitana Nightshade. Daughter of witches. Wielder of shadows. Slayer of vampires.

And I was afraid of the fucking sky.

Blowing out a frustrated breath, I lifted my head and glanced around the room. It had felt too big when I'd first awakened, but after nearly melting into a puddle of terror from being exposed to the outside, it felt like a refuge. A place where I could hide from the watchful eyes of the world.

I hated that I felt this way. I hated that I preferred this room, given to me by a vampire, over the freedom awaiting me beyond these walls.

But is there truly freedom out there? a voice in the back of my mind whispered. *You saw the city. Vampires crawling everywhere, humans little more than slaves. And you have no magic. What would you become if you go out there, other than a slave yourself?*

I clenched my jaw. I would never be a vampire slave. I'd rather fling myself from the balcony than subject myself to that kind of degradation.

Grinding my teeth, I tromped into the bathroom, then stripped off my clothes. As promised, a hot bath waited for me, steaming with fragrant oils. I paused at the sight of leaves floating atop the water, then carefully plucked one out of the tub and sniffed.

Esaleaf. An herb used to ease muscle stiffness.

I briefly wondered how Nyra had arranged this between the time Maximillian had handed me off to her and the time we'd arrived here. The vampire female was waiting for me in the sitting room—she had told me not to dally, or bother trying to escape using the balcony doors again. Her keen vampire hearing would detect any attempt to escape via the balcony again, and there were guards posted around the base of the tower now to catch me should I make it down to the bottom.

So much for not being a prisoner.

Still, even if I wanted to escape, I didn't have the strength for it. My limbs were so heavy with fatigue that I had to drag myself into the bath, but it was worth it. I moaned as the hot water enveloped my body, easing the tension from my muscles and filling me with a floaty sensation. It was so sublime that despite my better judgment, I let my guard down and leaned my head against the back of the tub. My eyelids slid closed, and I drifted into the darkness, allowing sleep to drag me under.

"You can't go back to him! I won't allow it!"

Holding tight to the doorframe, I watched Mama argue with the lady who visited our little cabin lots. Her name was Elna, and she was important in the Wolven Tribe. She often brought yummy treats and her granddaughter, Vaya, who was really fun to play with.

"You don't understand, Elna," Mama said. Her voice was full of worry as she walked around by the big fireplace, her black hair all

tangled. I really wanted to go give her a big hug, like she does when I'm sad. But I was meant to be in the shed, making herb poultices, so I just peeked, not making a sound.

"The dream I had... it was a vision, I know it. I can't just sit here and do nothing," Mama said, sounding really sure but also kind of scared.

"And what of your daughter?" Elna asked, looking really serious. "Are you going to take her back there too?"

"I've taken the necessary precautions," Mama answered, trying to sound strong. But her voice shook a bit, and she played with her silver ring like she always does when she's nervous.

Elna took Mama's hand, her face all worried. She's tall and looks like a queen from the stories, with her skin like the earth and her long, black hair.

"I don't understand, Lyria," Elna said, looking sad. "Why would you do this now, after everything you've done to keep Kitana safe?"

Mama sounded just as sad when she said, "Because he is the other half of my heart. I thought I could leave him behind for her sake, Elna. I really did. But if I don't go back for him, his fate will haunt me forever. And I will never be whole."

"Kitana!"

I sat up with a start as Nyra pounded on my bedroom door. Water sloshed over the sides of the tub and onto the floor as she flung open the door and stalked in, her hazel eyes sparking with impatience.

"I've been waiting outside for nearly an hour," she said, grabbing a fluffy bathrobe hanging on a hook. "What are you doing in here, trying to drown yourself?"

"You wish," I snapped. I reached out and snatched the robe from her fingers, then shrugged it on as I climbed out of the tub. I hadn't meant to fall asleep, nor take that very unexpected trip down memory lane. I tried to cling to the details of the dream, but Nyra dumped a towel on my head, interrupting my concentration.

"Hey!" I yelped as she began to roughly towel-dry my hair. "What are you doing?"

"Getting you ready, since you seem to be incapable of doing it yourself." She whisked the towel off my head, then plucked a brush off the bathroom counter and moved to attack my hair.

I snatched the brush out of her hand before she could make contact with my scalp. "I can brush my own hair," I said firmly.

The two of us stared at each other for a long moment before Nyra finally lifted her chin. "Fine. I'll select an outfit for you. But hurry up. Lord Starclaw doesn't like to be kept waiting."

I opened my mouth to tell her that I didn't give a damn about what 'Lord Starclaw' did or didn't like, but she disappeared back into the bedroom. Sighing, I reluctantly approached the mirror with the brush in my hand, afraid of what I might find looking back at me.

To my surprise, I didn't look nearly as bad as I thought. Sure, my face was a little gaunt, and the robe hung far too loosely on me given that I'd tied it as tight as I could. But my hair had a thick, lustrous shine, and there was healthy color in my cheeks. The shadows dogging my violet eyes were something I could do without, though. I hoped they would go away as I continued to recover.

I dragged the brush through my hair a few dozen times, then abandoned it on the counter and returned to the bedroom. A burgundy dress with matching undergarments had been laid out atop the bedspread for me, and a pair of simple black satin slippers waited by the foot of the bed.

"Good, you're finished." Nyra moved away from where she'd been standing by the balcony doors. "Dress."

I picked up the heavy velvet garment, then held it up to my chest. "Absolutely not," I snapped as I looked at it in the mirror.

"I'm not wearing anything with an off the shoulder neckline around a vampire."

Nyra laughed, the sound a masterclass in elegance and disdain. "Do you really think a collar would stop Lord Starclaw from feeding on you?" she asked, her upper lip curling into a sneer. "Your naivety is astonishing."

"Of course not." I scowled as I tossed the garment back on the bed. "But that doesn't mean I need to parade myself like a buffet around him at dinner. I'll find something else."

I turned toward the closet, but Nyra's scathing voice stopped me in my tracks. "There is nothing in there that's suitable for your skeleton frame. I've already checked."

To my horror, my lip began to wobble. I knew I was painfully thin—my clothes had barely fit me, and the blouse I'd borrowed from the closet had billowed around me. But for Nyra to actually say it out loud was a blow to my already battered ego. My body had once been strong and powerful, with just the right amount of curves, honed from years and years of warrior training. To hear that I'd lost all that progress, that I was small and weak again—

Stop it, I told myself. *You'll get it back. One day at a time.*

Woodenly, I reached for the ties on my bathrobe and slipped it off my shoulders, letting it fall to the ground. Nyra's expression shifted as she glimpsed my naked form, the antipathy in her gaze giving way to curiosity as she beheld the spray of nightshade flowers in the middle of my torso, just beneath my breasts. But to my relief, she didn't ask about them, and I quickly put the undergarments on and stepped into the dress. Nyra did the buttons up in the back, the ran the brush through my hair one more time before arranging it around my shoulders.

"You'll do," she said as we both gazed at the reflection in the mirror in front of us.

I nodded. The dress was a little loose at the waist, but it

molded nicely to what little cleavage I had left. I ran a hand over one of my collarbones, hating the way they jutted out so sharply.

Nyra's eyes tracked the movement. She disappeared into the closet, then returned with a black wrap. "Here," she said, thrusting the garment at me. "To protect that delicate swan neck of yours."

I snorted, but took the wrap and swirled it around my shoulders. I knew it was silly, but the scrap of fabric really did make me feel more protected. Not as protected as my armor and coat would have, but it was better than nothing.

After tucking two stakes into my dress pockets—which Nyra rolled her eyes at, but didn't object to—I followed the vampire out the door, then down the hall to where a metallic box with a wrought metal cage waited. She pressed a button on the wall, and the double doors slid back to reveal a closet-sized room with padded green walls.

"Come on," she said, stepping inside.

Apprehension filled me as I eyed the box, wondering if this was some kind of trap. "What is this thing?"

"It's called an elevator. It's an aetherion invention." When I stared blankly at her, she added, "It takes you up and down the floors so you don't have to climb the stairs."

I frowned. "Is there something wrong with climbing the stairs?"

Nyra sighed. "No. But sometimes I don't feel like it. Now are you getting in?"

Aware that I had no idea where we were going or how to get there, I begrudgingly followed her inside. She reached past me to a panel on the wall with an array of buttons, and pushed the second one from the top.

The cage doors closed, and I slapped my hand on the wall for support as the elevator lurched into motion. I held my breath as it creaked and groaned, waiting for something to go wrong, for it to get stuck and leave us trapped in the middle of the tower, or worse, for something to break and send us plummeting to the ground.

But none of that happened. The elevator clanged to a halt, and I let out a breath of relief as the metal doors whisked open.

"See? Perfectly safe." Nyra exited the elevator, and I hurried after her into a grand foyer. The space was expansive, with crystal chandeliers dangling from a high ceiling. Soft, ambient light poured from them, casting elongated shadows that danced along the walls, which were adorned with paintings depicting both portraits and landscapes. One portrait in particular, placed directly across from the elevator, drew my gaze, and I let out an audible hiss as I realized who it depicted.

Nyra turned back to see what I was looking at, and her eyebrows rose. "Ahh," she crooned as I stared at the painting of Vladimir Invictus, King of Noxalis, the vampire realm. Long, golden waves of hair cascaded around his shoulders and framed his harsh, angular face. He wore a spiked iron crown tipped with black diamonds as hard and cruel as the line of his mouth, and his citrine eyes glittered as I stared into them, almost as if the actual king were watching me through the painting. "I see our beloved emperor has caught your eye."

I whipped my head around to look at her. "Emperor?" I demanded. "Of what, exactly?"

"Of all of Valentaera, or so he proclaims." Maximillian's voice drifted from beyond an open door on our right. "Now won't you come in so we can eat? It's been a long day, and I'm starving."

The word *starving* sent a shiver of apprehension through me, and I hastily checked my pockets to make sure the stakes were still in there. Nyra opened the door and stepped through it, then moved to the side and executed a quick bow as I entered.

"Your guest, Sire," she said.

My gaze swept past the bay of windows to my right—mercifully curtained off—and to the head of the long dining table, where Maximillian sat. He'd changed out of his bloodstained outfit, and was now dressed in a dusky blue waistcoat with a swirling, silver-grey pattern, a simple white shirt beneath it. A goblet filled with blood dangled from his hand as he surveyed me, and before were two covered plates—one for him, the other, I assumed, for me.

Those full lips of his curved, his eyes trailing down the length of my dress, then back up to my face. "You clean up well."

My cheeks heated in response to the praise, and I scowled. "Flattery won't get you anywhere with me," I said as Nyra made herself scarce, the door clicking shut behind her. "Especially when you two have already declared me to be little more than a walking skeleton."

"But a magnificent one." Maximillian waved his hand, and the chair to his left slid back from the table, beckoning me to sit. "And nothing that a few square meals won't fix."

I ignored the gesture and surveyed the room, cataloguing anything that might help in case the vampire lord decided to try his luck at dining on me. Aside from the door I'd entered through, there was another behind Maximillian and to his right —a servant's entrance, most likely. The windows to my right might be another option, if I could scrounge up the courage, though since they were covered, I had no idea if they opened and whether they led out to anything. As for weapons, the fireplace poker would do in a pinch, as well as the cutlery and glasses laid out along the table.

"There's also a pair of swords hanging over the door behind you," Maximillian drawled. "In case you'd prefer something with a little more finesse."

"How did you know I was looking for weapons?" I demanded, folding my arms over my chest.

He raised his eyebrows at me. "It's what any hunter would do when walking into a predator's den."

I stared at him, unsettled by how easily he seemed to be able to read me. If I didn't know better, I'd say he was eavesdropping on my thoughts.

Don't be ridiculous, I told myself. *Vampires can't read minds.*

Still, it was better to be safe than sorry. Ignoring the chair he'd selected, I pulled out the chair at the opposite end of the table and sat down.

The vampire lord raised his eyebrows. "There's no need for such theatrics. You're perfectly safe with me."

"You say that," I said, folding my arms across my chest, "but I don't even know who in the hells you *are*."

"Ahh." His lips curved in an expression that was somehow a sassy smirk and an apologetic smile all at once. It was oddly disarming, and I had no idea what to make of it. "I suppose that unlike you, my name does not precede me in your realm. I am Maximillian Starclaw, son of Callix Starclaw and heir to House Psychoros. At present, I also serve as the Viceroy of Lumina, at the pleasure of Vladimir Invictus, king of Noxalis and emperor of Valentaera."

He waved his hand again, and the entire place setting that had been arranged in front of the chair he'd selected—food, cutlery, glasses, and all, floated down the table to settle at my end. A pitcher of water followed behind, tipping to fill my glass before setting down along the center of the table, but still within reach in case I wanted it.

I made no move to touch any of it, frozen stiff as I stared at my would-be host. I'd been right that Maximillian was a ranking noble, but he wasn't just *any* ranking noble. He was the son of a vampire highlord, which made him the second strongest vampire of his house.

And somehow, he had seized control of a human city, and was now ruling it on behalf of his king.

"Eat," Maximillian said. "Before your food gets cold."

I opened my mouth, a gaggle of questions on my tongue, but Maximillian lifted the cover off his own plate, revealing a grilled fish fillet on a bed of greens. My stomach growled at the sight of the food, and my mouth watered as the scent of the meat wafted across the table toward me. Anticipation bubbled up inside me at the thought of eating food—real, solid food—and despite myself, I whisked off the plate cover, eager to see what lay beneath.

That excitement deflated in an instant as I took in what appeared to be a bowlful of mush.

"Is this..." I picked up a spoon and poked at the unappetizing looking mash, "... gruel?"

"Root vegetable mash," Maximillian supplied. I looked up to see me watching me with an unreadable expression on his face. "Gruel would have been a better choice for you, but we're in short supply of grains these days."

I shook my head, bewildered. "I don't understand. You had me dress in these fancy clothes, and come all the way to your fancy dining room, to eat mash?" Did all humans eat this way under vampire rule? Or was this an attempt for Maximillian to assert his superiority over me? I would have found it insulting if I hadn't been caught so off guard.

"When you put it that way, it does sound rather cruel," Maximillian said. He propped his chin on his fist as he stared ruefully at my meal. "I'm sure you would prefer a more exciting meal than this after being locked away for fifty years, Kitten, but I'd rather not watch you projectile vomit all over my dining room. I'm told it's best to reintroduce food slowly after a period of starvation."

"Oh." I glanced down at the bowl of mash again, deflating.

Of course. That aetheric machine may have restored most of my wasted body, but that didn't change the fact that my stomach had been out of commission for a very long time. "I hadn't thought of that."

I braced for some kind of sneering retort from the vampire lord, but he only nodded. "I'm not surprised. The realities of recovering from starvation would be the last thing on your mind, given all that you've seen."

I scooped up a spoonful of mash, trying not to scowl. I hated that he was being so understanding, so *reasonable.* I wanted someone to fight, someone to take my frustration out on, and since I couldn't set foot outside this building without having a meltdown, he was my only available target.

But when I shoved the spoon of mash in my mouth, every single thought evaporated as my tastebuds came alive. I expected the mash to be bland, but it had been so long since I'd eaten anything that the subtle flavors were a symphony on my tongue. I closed my eyes, savoring not just the sweet, earthy taste, but the warmth spreading through the cavern of my mouth. The creamy texture was a welcome weight on my tongue, and an eternity seemed to pass before I remembered to swallow.

A ravenous hunger rose inside me as the mash slid down my throat, entering the cavernous pit of my stomach. I shoved another spoonful in my mouth, then another, and then—

"Slow down," Maximillian said sharply. I ignored him, stabbing for the bowl again, but my spoon scraped against the table instead as the bowl slid away from me. Annoyed, I reached for the bowl, but it scooted farther back, out of my reach.

"Give it back." I glared at him.

"No."

I opened my mouth, prepared to threaten him with bodily

harm, but a wave of nausea rolled through me, and I clamped it shut.

Fuck.

I sat back in my chair as the weight of the food—so little, only a few bites—suddenly made itself known in my stomach. It pitched, railing against the inconsiderate assault I'd launched at it, and I pressed a hand against it, taking in slow breaths through my nose to steady myself.

Maximillian raised his eyebrows, the '*I told you so'* look written across his face plain as day. A hot prickle of embarrassment washed down the back of my neck, but he said nothing, taking a sip from his goblet as he waited patiently for me to regain my composure. My mouth went dry as he licked the blood from his lips, and I glanced away, staring into the hearth instead.

"I think I'll save the rest for later," I said, once I was certain I could speak without vomiting.

"A wise decision. I can have it sent to your room later, if you prefer."

I looked back at him, my lips pursing. "I don't understand why you're being so nice to me."

"Conventional wisdom suggests that when you want something from someone, they're far more likely to give it to you when you treat them with kindness and respect." Maximillian leaned back in his chair and studied me over the rim of his goblet. "But aside from that, I find you fascinating, Kitana Nightshade. You have an interesting past, to say the least."

"What is that supposed to mean?"

"Well, you rose to be one of the most fearsome warriors in your clan, despite the fact that you are a no-name orphan with no real family background, and that you lack the ability to wield lunar magic—one of the two signature abilities of your clan. Yet it was your shadow magic, stronger than any witch who has come before you, that made you so formidable before you were imprisoned. Your ability to shadow travel, appearing like a wraith in the night to hunt down unsuspecting vampires, is what made you a household name in our realm. Yet despite your magical prowess—or perhaps because of it— the heir to your clan decided to lock you away just as you were beginning to make real headway with your movement against us."

I clenched my hands beneath the table as the memory of Sebastian's face flashed in my mind. The regret in his ochre eyes as he shoved me into the sarcophagus. The hot lance of betrayal that speared my chest as he'd slid the coffin lid over my face. The rawness in my throat after screaming his name for hours, and the yawning pit of despair I'd fallen into when I realized that, after everything I'd done for my people, no one was coming for me.

I wasn't a particularly vengeful person, but I'd spent the past fifty years dreaming of all the ways I'd kill him. Slowly, painfully, bringing him back from the brink again and again until he begged for death.

"I can help you get your vengeance," Maximillian said softly. "Help you make him pay for his betrayal."

"I don't need your help." I smoothed the skirts of my dress again, striving for calm. "The only reason he was able to imprison me is because he caught me off guard. He won't be able to touch me again, not once I'm at full strength."

"Ahh, but what will you do until then?" Maximillian flicked his gaze toward the windows, and the curtains swished open. I flinched as they revealed a bay of windows offering an unob-structed view of the city skyline, and more importantly, the cres-cent moon hanging above it. "You'll need to perform the Twilight Communion beneath the full moon in order to refill your magical reservoir, and that celestial event won't occur for another three weeks. Where will you go until then? Who will you find shelter with?"

"If you think I'm going to shelter with you, you're an idiot," I snapped. "I have allies amongst the other witch clans. I'll go to one of them."

"You could," Maximillian agreed. "Except that your beloved Sebastian erected a magical barrier across the entire length of Trivaea's land border. No one can pass, not even witches. You might be able to shadow travel, but again, you'd have to wait until you can recharge your magic to do so."

My stomach plummeted, but I shook my head, refusing to believe that. "Sebastian couldn't have sealed off the border. A spell like that would require an insane amount of magic—all five clans would have had to combine their powers to pull it off."

"And so they did." The vampire lord gave me a grim smile. "I'm not sure how he managed it, but your former lover executed quite the coup. Although he is not officially the king, all five clans bow to his whim. Which is another obstacle you'll have to overcome if you return to Trivaea. Your allies may not be as accessible or as willing to aid you as you think."

"You're lying." I clenched the edge of the table. "The clans barely agree on anything—that's why there are five of them. There's no way they would have united under one clan's banner! And especially not if a man was trying to get them to do it."

"The same thing could have once been said about the four vampire houses," Maximillian pointed out. "And yet here we are, united by Emperor Vladimir's iron fist."

Right. "You and Nyra told me earlier that he's the emperor of Valentaera. What do you mean by that, exactly?"

"Well, self-styled is more what I meant," Maximillian admitted as he forked up a piece of fish. I'd never actually seen a vampire eat food before, but I knew that while blood was essential to keep their undead hearts beating, they still needed solid food like the rest of us for energy. "But while he has made great headway in his plan to conquer the continent of Valentaera, he has not yet accomplished that. He only holds the human kingdoms, at least for now."

My mouth was suddenly dry, and I reached for my goblet of water. "What do you mean 'only the human kingdoms'?" I said after I'd gulped down the last of my water. Had the vampires taken more than just the city of Lumina?

Maximillian flicked his finger, and the pitcher of water rose again to refill my glass. "About a week after you disappeared, the sun stopped rising. We don't know precisely what happened, but Vladimir seemed to be expecting it, because he had already positioned most of his troops near the border Noxalis shares with Heliaris. He waited two days, giving time for the chaos to fully set in, then attacked. It took us six months to take all three human kingdoms."

I froze, my body going still as my mind churned, trying to comprehend the magnitude of what the vampire had just said. "The sun disappeared... completely?" I finally asked. "And it hasn't returned since?"

Maximillian nodded, and I forced myself to glance at the windows again, at the spangled blanket of darkness that covered the sky despite the afternoon hour. The sun should have been halfway toward its descent to the skyline, the city's spires gleaming brightly in its wake. Instead, they were shrouded, illuminated faintly by what I assumed to be aetheric crystals.

As a witch, I generally preferred the evening, when the goddess Hecate showed her face and blessed us with her gentle lunar glow. But humans were children of the sun god Phaeros— their power came from their connection to the sun, and therefore to him. For the sun god to cease pulling his chariot through the sky, bringing light and warmth to the human race... a catastrophe like that would have had devastating consequences to their magical abilities.

I scrubbed a hand across my face, trying to wrangle the chaotic thoughts whirling through my mind. If I wasn't careful, I could easily follow them into a spiral of doom, and while everything the vampire lord had told me was dire enough to warrant that kind of reaction, the only thing I'd verified from his story was the sun's disappearance, and the vampire occupation of the city. I had no idea if King Vladimir had actually conquered all three kingdoms, or if this supposed magical barrier cutting off Trivaea from the rest of Valentaera was real.

"You've gone through a lot of trouble," I finally said, raising my head to look at Maximillian. "Uncovering my past, breaking me out of my prison, and bringing me here. Why do all this? What do you want from me?"

Maximillian leaned forward, bracing his forearms on the table. "I'd like to offer you a bargain. My help in enacting your vengeance against Sebastian Nocturne, in exchange for the use of your professional skills."

He spoke casually, but there was an expectant gleam in his eyes that sent a warning thrill through me. "My professional skills?" I repeated, confused. "Do... do you mean my vampire hunting skills?"

"Precisely."

I scoffed. This seemed too easy. "And who is it you want me to kill, exactly?"

The gleam in his eyes intensified, and I froze as the last name I expected to hear dropped from his mouth.

"Vladimir Invictus."

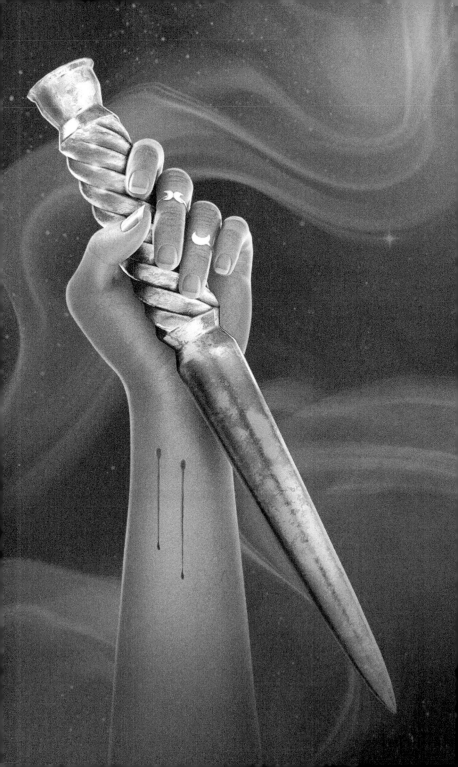

5

I stared at the vampire lord for several long seconds, my jaw hanging open.

And then I threw my head back and laughed.

"Is that a yes or a no?" Maximillian propped his chin in his hands as he watched me, a droll look on his face. "Mortals laugh for all kinds of strange reasons, so I can never tell."

I clutched at my belly as I laughed even harder, trying to get a hold of myself. I had no illusions about the state of my psyche —being trapped in a magical sarcophagus for half a century would leave anyone with at least a touch of insanity. Part of me still wasn't convinced that this wasn't another dream.

But not even in my lowest, most desperate moments, where I envisioned all kinds of scenarios in which I gained my freedom, had I ever conjured up a fantasy as wild as *this*.

"This has to be a joke," I finally said, wiping tears from my eyes. "There is no fucking way that you went through all this trouble to break me out of that prison, just so you could hire me to assassinate your king."

"And why is that?"

I scoured Maximillian's face, searching for any hint of

subterfuge, any sign that this was some elaborate prank or scheme. But he watched me steadily, those starfire eyes of his glittering as the firelight cast flickering shadows across his pale, elegant features. Ire rose inside me when I found nothing in his expression, not even the slightest tell.

"Because," I said, sweeping a hand toward the city view behind me, "King Vladimir gave you all of this. He's the reason you rule this city, the reason you vampires now *own*—" I spat the word—"the human race. Why in all the hells would you stab him in the back like this? Is this some hairbrained scheme to take the throne for yourself?"

"My reasons are not your concern," Maximillian said coolly. "Nor are they relevant to the bargain."

"Like hells they're not," I snapped. "If I'm about to help one despot replace the other, I think I have the right to know what your intentions are!"

"All you *need* to know," Maximillian countered, "is that in seven weeks' time, the Emperor will be hosting the Sanguine Summit. I plan to be there, with you in attendance as a member of my house. And on the night of the full moon, when you are at the height of your powers, you will help me put an end to Vladimir Invictus's reign."

"Have you lost your ever-loving mind?" I gaped at him. I wasn't an expert in vampire politics, but I'd heard of the Sanguine Summit. It was an annual event held in Umbral, Noxalis's capital city, and attended by nobility from all four vampire houses. "Vladimir will be surrounded by his most powerful supporters. Trying to assassinate him during the Summit is suicide!"

"It will be risky, yes," Maximillian agreed. "But the presence of those vampires will keep Vladimir's court and his guards pre-occupied, and as a high-ranking noble, it will be easy for me to lure him into position for you. You will attend as a candidate for the Descendency, which means you will have access to most of the same events and sections of the castle as the vampire guests."

"The Descendency?" I choked out. "Isn't that the vampire turning ritual?"

"Yes." Maximillian's lips thinned. "It is now a requirement for all female candidates to be brought before the court, in case you happen to be an *amorte*. But given that you are a witch, not a human, that shouldn't be a problem for us to worry about."

"This is absurd," I seethed, shoving up from my chair so I could pace in front of the windows. The view barely bothered me anymore, not with everything else occupying my mind. My skirts fluttered around my ankles with every step I took, and I resisted the urge to rip at the cumbersome length of fabric. *Amortes* were rare humans blessed—or cursed, depending on how you looked at it—with the ability to bear the children of natural-born vampires. The idea of spending a week surrounded by hundreds of vampires who would be sniffing at my heels, trying to determine if they could plant their seed in me, was so abhorrent, it made my skin crawl. "I'm not going to allow you to parade me in front of the entire vampire court like some prized breeding horse, just so you can get your shot at the throne."

Maximillian snorted. "I'm not 'parading' you. You'll be by my side the entire time and under my protection. So long as we prepare you, there's nothing to fear."

I didn't believe that for one second. "If my choice is between spending a week in a castle full of bloodthirsty vampires pretending to be a defenseless human, or blindly striking out into the world on my own, I choose the latter." I turned away from the windows, heading for the door. "Thanks for breaking me out of that hellish prison, but I'm leaving."

A gust of wind ruffled my hair, and suddenly Maximillian

was in front of me. I gasped as he crowded me against the window, the cold glass biting into my skin through the thin fabric of my dress, and involuntarily inhaled a lungful of his scent. The heady blend of mahogany and leather immediately went to my head, and he took advantage of the opportunity to brace a hand against the glass, blocking my path to the door.

In the next breath, I had my stake drawn, the tip pressing into the center of his chest. But the vampire lord paid the threat no mind. He cocked his head as he looked down at me, then used his other hand to brush a stray wisp of hair from my face, as if we were two lovers having a clandestine moment instead of the enemies we were destined to be.

"Are you scared of me, Kitten?" Maximillian murmured, his eyes glowing faintly as he traced the side of his finger down my cheek.

My breathing hitched, and it took everything I had in me not to lean into the vampire lord's hand. After fifty years of being trapped in a coffin without a single soul for company, my touch-starved body was desperate for more, and I hated how easily he brought this shameful weakness of mine to the forefront.

"No." I dug my stake into his chest a little more, puncturing the layers of his vest and shirt. His blood laced the air between us, and we both inhaled sharply, but he didn't move away.

"Good." He let his hand fall to the side, a lopsided grin tugging at his cheek. "I would hate for you to be afraid when we're about to spend so much time together."

I scowled. "Didn't you just hear what I said? I'm lea—"

"Stay." He took a step back, giving me the space to leave if I wanted. "You don't have to agree to the bargain, not yet. But stay here as my guest, at least until the full moon comes and you can perform the ritual. You can take your time to explore the city, verify if what I've told you is true, and regain your strength."

"And if I decide to leave?" I challenged.

"Then you're free to go." He took my hand, which still gripped the stake, then brushed his lips over my knuckles. I shivered as the slightest hint of fang scraped across my flesh. "But I hope you'll stay, Kitten. I have grand plans for us. And you may even find them fun."

I opened my mouth to retort that there was no way I would find *anything* to do with him fun, but he was already gone, the door clicking shut behind him. I stared at the empty space where he had been, chest heaving as I tried to regain control of my breathing.

And wondered if I was insane for considering this.

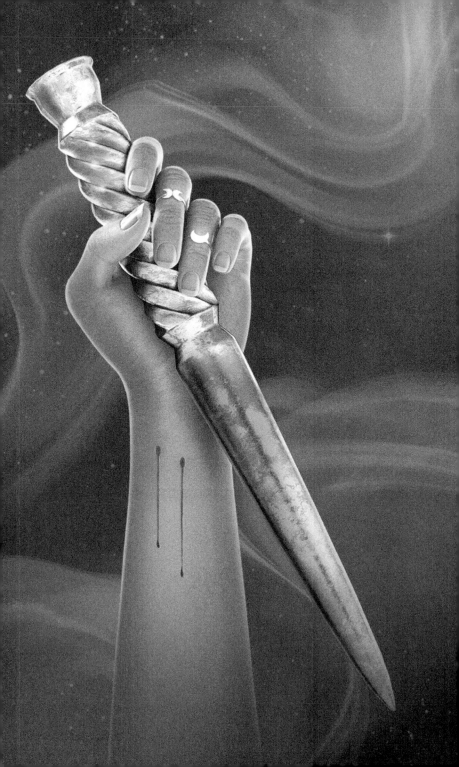

6

My head was so crowded with thoughts when I left Maximillian's penthouse, I was sure I'd spend the rest of the night pacing in my room while I mulled over everything I'd learned this evening.

But when I sat down on the bed, a wave of fatigue swept over me, and before I realized it, I was sinking back onto the pillows, my eyes drifting closed as my body dragged me into a deep, healing sleep.

I didn't know how long I was out, but I came back to the awareness of a heavy weight settling on my chest. At first, I thought it was just the exhaustion, but as I tried to fall back asleep, a sharp pricking sensation pierced the haze of my mind.

Claws, I realized with sudden clarity.

My eyes flew open, and I found myself staring into a pair of large, bottle-green eyes. A cat perched on my chest, regal entitlement oozing from every inch of her furry body as she stared back at me. Her paws continued their rhythmic dance on my chest, heedless of the tiny stabs of pain they produced, and her black fur seemed to absorb the scant light in the room, making her appear as if she'd been sculpted from the darkness itself.

In a way, she had been.

"Jinx!" I shot upright, and the cat yowled, back flipping through the air and landing on the windowsill. Her back arched, fur spiking along the length of her spine as I pressed a hand to my pounding heart. The two of us looked at each other for a long moment, the cat glaring balefully while I stared at her in shock.

"Is this real?" I finally said. "You... you're not a figment of my imagination?"

The cat promptly turned her back on me, then lifted her tail to show me her asshole.

Well, that definitely seems like something Jinx would do. She was my shadow familiar—an animal I'd created using my own shadow magic when I was only seven years old. I'd been jealous of Vaya and her wolf familiar, and since I wasn't Ferae, I'd decided to create one of my own using magic. My mother had expected Jinx to fade after a few hours since shadow constructs were temporary, but for reasons no one really understood, Jinx had stuck around. She'd been my faithful companion throughout my life, right up until Sebastian had locked me away.

Hesitantly, I swung my legs over the side of the bed, then approached her. The cat sat down on her haunches and began grooming one of her paws, ignoring me. I sighed as I sank to my knees, reaching out for her.

"Oh, come on," I said a little crossly when she shifted away from my hand. "I didn't mean to send you flying. And besides, you knew waking me up like that would freak me out, especially since you've been gone so long. You did that on purpose!"

Jinx lifted her head at that, her paw falling back down. A tiny growl rumbled in her chest as if she were chastising me, and then, as if deciding that was punishment enough, she stretched her neck out and butted her forehead against my nose.

Tears welled in my eyes, and I ran my hand down the sleek length of her back. Jinx purred, nuzzling harder, and I scooped her into my arms, cuddling her against my chest. She might have been made of shadows, but she felt real and solid in my arms, and I held her tight, finally giving into my need for physical touch. My tears soaked her fur, but she didn't seem to mind. She just tucked herself against my chest and allowed me to take what I needed.

Finally, once the tears had stopped coming, and my trembling eased, she butted the top of her head against the underside of my chin, asking me to release her. As soon as I did, she scampered toward the door, then started meowing insistently.

I frowned, getting to my feet. "Hang on. I can't go anywhere like this." I glanced down at the nightgown I was wearing. Apparently, I'd been out long—and hard—enough that someone had undressed and tucked me into bed. Reaching up, I pulled on the cord attached to the crystal chandelier, and a soft, yellow glow illuminated the room, allowing me to see the clock on the wall.

"Ten a.m." I walked over to the closet and pushed it open. To my surprise, a different set of outfits awaited, all in varying shades of blue and black, with Maximillian's house crest stitched on the breasts and lapels.

"You'll need to blend in if you plan to stay here," Nyra had told me as she'd escorted me back to my room last night. *"Running around dressed like a vampire hunter will only attract the same kind of trouble you ran into last night. I'll have your closet outfitted with garments appropriate for a human thrall in Lord Starclaw's service."*

Well. Either she'd made quick work of that, or I'd been out longer than I thought.

I riffled through the outfits and eventually settled on a pair of black trousers and a blouse with a ruffled collar. A few jackets also hung on the rack, but I ignored them in favor of my duster. I didn't care if it wasn't typical—the fabric was reinforced with amurel thread—a rare silkworm found exclusively in the Vale of Mists whose threads could be spun into a stab and slash-proof fabric. An absolute necessity around vampires, as far as I was concerned.

I slipped four stakes into the pockets, shoved my feet into a pair of soft black boots, then followed Jinx out the door. But I paused again at the sight of a covered basket sitting on the low table in the room, and my stomach growled at the delicious scent wafting from it.

The basket turned out to be filled with fresh bread rolls. They smelled of potatoes rather than wheat flour, but they were soft and buttery when I bit into them. My stomach didn't revolt the same way it did when I'd eaten the veggie mash, so I tucked one roll into my pocket, then slowly munched on another while I followed Jinx out into the hall.

Aether crystals set at intervals along the wall bathed the corridor in their ambient glow, revealing a series of doors. Interspersed between them were paintings showcasing a variety of landscapes—some from the human realm, others from Noxalis. I paused beside a striking painting of a woman atop a golden steed, racing across an open plain. Her red hair streamed out like a banner behind her, the war paint on her cheeks highlighting the beautiful savagery of her face. Other riders galloped in the distance, outracing the setting sun as it dipped beneath the horizon and sent ribbons of purple, red, and violet streaking across the sky behind them.

A lump rose in my chest as old memories surfaced. These were the Equinox—one of the three tribes of Ferae, also known as the animagi. Blessed with the power to command animals, each tribe had its own special affinity. My mother and I had spent most of my childhood living amongst the Ferae tribes, and we'd visited the Equinox on several occasions, usually to treat some poor rider who'd suffered a fall from horseback. It was amongst the Ferae that I'd learned the basics of healing and potion making, and those were some of the happiest years of my life.

Jinx meowed insistently, and I tore my gaze from the painting and followed her into a common area. The space was far more expansive than the tiny sitting room in my chambers, scattered with plush seating areas, a fireplace large enough to stand in, and a cabinet that appeared to be filled with a variety of knickknacks and curios. A half-finished game of chess sat at a table beneath a window, and the pillows on one of the couches were askew, telling me that someone had been here recently.

I wanted to investigate the curio cabinet, but Jinx led me to a bookshelf that sat between two armchairs. She leaped onto the fourth shelf and pawed at a slim volume with a red leather cover.

"A book?" I hooked my finger around the top edge of the spine and pulled. But instead of coming off, the book hinged forward, then caught on the edge of the shelf. A soft click fractured the silence, and the shelf slid sideways, revealing a secret stairwell.

The cat jumped down and into the stairwell, her tail curling in a 'come hither' gesture. "How do you always find these places?" I called as I hurried after her. The bookcase slid shut behind me, plunging us into pitch darkness, but a second later, another set of crystals flared to life along the wall.

Shaking my head, I followed Jinx down the spiral staircase. My shadow cat had a knack for finding hidden entrances and secret passages, which had come in handy on numerous occasions during my hunts. We passed several sets of doors before she finally stopped at one that saw less use than the others. I paused to wipe the cobwebs off the doorknob, then grasped the handle and carefully pushed the door open.

Moonlight streamed through tall windows, casting ethereal beams that danced across rows upon rows of bookshelves. It took me a moment to realize that I was standing on the second floor of a library, and a shock of surprised delight hit me as the scents of leather and aged paper teased my nostrils.

Stepping away from the bookshelf I'd just emerged from, I approached the balcony railing and looked up, then down. One more level spanned above me, and another sprawled below me. Wrought metal spiral staircases connected the levels on opposite corners, and I spotted an array of study tables topped with crystal lamps along the far end of the first floor.

"All right," I said down to Jinx, who was staring at me expectantly. "What did you bring me here to find?"

The cat responded by winding her way through my legs with a rumbling purr... and then disappearing in a poof of shadow.

I rolled my eyes. *Typical.* Like most cats, Jinx was as capricious as the ocean's tides, popping in and out as her whims dictated. Trying not to be *too* annoyed, I descended the staircase, then approached the counter by the entrance. No librarian manned the desk, but there was a lengthy row of drawer cabinets, each labeled with its own alphabet sticker, that contained an extensive card catalogue system.

Even though Jinx hadn't left me any instructions—she never did, since she couldn't speak—it didn't take a genius to figure out why she'd sent me here. She had a habit of leading me to people and places whenever I was searching for answers, and what better place to search for answers about what had happened to the world while I'd been gone than in the royal library?

It took me about thirty minutes of rifling through the card catalogue, and another hour or so of traipsing through shelves and climbing up ladders, but eventually I ended up at one of the study tables with a stack of books and an armful of scrolls.

I unrolled the first scroll, a map of Valentaera, and used two of the books—one a treatise on the divisions of territory of the expanded vampire realm, the other a chronicle on the Eternal Night War—to pin down the edges so I could study it. My gaze swept across the detailed cartography, taking in the three realms and searching for any geographical changes. Occupying the western edge of Valentaera was Noxalis, the jagged mountains of House Stellaris's Caelum Crest jutting from its northernmost edge. To the east, on the other side of the valley, was Graviton Heights, a series of craggy highlands that House Invictus called home. I traced the tiny drawing of the Iron Spire with my finger —King Vladimir's seat of power—then followed the mountain pass between the two ranges that led to the Elysium Vale, House Pyschoros's territory. Below that, edging the coast, was the Crimson Cliffs, Sanguis Noctis's territory.

Graviton Heights shared a border with Heliaris—which lay to the east—while Caelum Crest abutted Trivaea's southwestern border. Fierce longing swept through me as I took in the crescent-shaped realm that made up the northern section of Valentaera. Its concave side faced the ocean, with its convex side sharing borders with both Heliaris and Noxalis. I traced the inner edge of the crescent where Crescent Cove had been drawn, the Nocturne Clan banner of a full moon wreathed in ribbons of shadow rendered in painstaking detail above it. Scanning the other clan territories, I let out a small breath of relief as I noted that their banners all remained intact.

The same could not be said for Heliaris. My heart dropped as I slid my finger across Greenwarden—the Verdantia Clan's territory, located in the southeastern part of the Trivaea's crescent—over to the Aetherion kingdom, which bordered both Noxalis and Trivaea. The lush forest kingdom of Ferae stretched beneath it, and to the southeastern coast was Maris, a seafaring kingdom of sprawling coastal regions and archipelagos.

All three kingdoms were riddled with vampire banners. House Invictus's iron sword piercing the center of a blood-red heart appeared the most, but a smattering of banners from the other three houses appeared as well. The astral eye of House Psychoros hovered over Lumina, which was only fifty or so miles from Graviton Heights, but a good two hundred or so from the Trivaean border. Too far for me to travel in a single day.

I scanned the human kingdoms again, and my gaze snagged on one banner, which was different. It featured a wolf's head, and a jolt went through me as I realized it was placed over Wildwood Forest—home of the Wolven Clan of Ferae.

Not under vampire control.

Heart beating faster, I scanned the map again, searching for any other human outposts that existed. I didn't find any others amongst the Ferae, but there was one archipelago along the coastline of Maris marked by a banner featuring a mermaid tail entwined with a black anchor—the Blackwater Isles, aka the Pirate Kingdom.

My mouth curved into a grim smile. Of course, the pirates had found a way to resist Vladimir's rule. The ballsy bastards had made it a point to hire both witches and vampires onto their crews, and had terrorized every port city in Valentaera, even in Trivaea. They wouldn't allow something as pesky as the Eternal Night to interfere with their pillaging.

The sound of heavy boots clomping against the parquet floors of the library echoed off the walls, and I jerked my head up as a curly blonde walked out from behind a row of shelves. "There you are," she said crossly, folding her arms over her unbuttoned coveralls. "I've been looking all over for you."

I winced as I realized it was Eliza—the human thrall I'd put into a sleeper hold the other day. "Hi." I scratched the back of my neck, feeling a little awkward. While I'd felt perfectly justified at the time, knowing that she'd spent nearly a week nursing me back to health made me feel pretty damn guilty about what I'd done. "Uhhh, how are you feeling?"

Eliza snorted. "Great. Had a nice little nap, thanks to you." She glanced over the map and stack of books, her eyebrows rising. "Doing a little homework?"

"I'm trying to get up to speed, yeah." I rolled up the map and set it aside, then reached for a scroll that apparently detailed the allocation of "human provisions" under vampire law. "Seems there's a lot I missed."

"Hmm." Eliza looked me up and down, her eyes narrowed. "You know, you're a lot tinier than I thought you'd be."

I scowled, the scroll rolling out of my hand and back across the table. "What in Hecate's name is that supposed to mean?" I demanded.

Eliza shrugged. "Just, I pictured you taller, is all. After hearing all those stories of you cutting through vampires like melted butter, I thought you were some giant warrior goddess. But instead you're tiny." A small smile curved her lips. "Like me."

The knot of tension in my gut unfurled, and I couldn't help smiling back. Now that she mentioned it, Eliza and I seemed roughly the same height, give or take an inch in her favor. "Your master told me I was pint-sized."

Eliza wrinkled her nose. "Master? Eww. Don't call him that."

I arched an eyebrow. "Isn't that how thralls usually refer to the vampires they're bonded to?" From what I understood, Turned vampires addressed the vampires who had fathered (or mothered) them as 'Sire', regardless of gender, while thralls used the term 'Master' or 'Mistress' instead. Lucius and Nyra had both addressed Maximillian as Sire, so I was surprised to hear that Eliza didn't use the appropriate term for her station.

"Other thralls, maybe." Eliza huffed. "But Max and I don't have that kind of relationship. Now come on. He asked me to give you a tour of the city, and I don't have all day."

Max? I gaped after Eliza as she turned on her heel and began to walk away, then hurried after her. "Wait! I need to put these books somewhere before someone puts them away or takes them."

"Don't worry about them." Eliza waved a hand behind her, not bothering to turn around. "Hardly anyone ever uses the royal library. Your books will be fine."

Resigned, I followed her out of the library. "The building we're in is called the Central Keep," Eliza explained as we walked. "The first floor, which is where we are now, houses the royal library and the armory. The floor above is where the Great Hall and the council chambers are, the third floor has guest chambers and receiving rooms, and the remaining floors are where all the private quarters are located."

"The armory?" I perked up. "Can I see it?"

"On your own time," she said as we strode past the open door. I caught the briefest glimpse of an array of polished swords, battleaxes, and what looked like aetheric shields, before she grabbed my arm and pulled me forward. "If you're anything like Lucius, you'll want to spend hours in there, and we don't have time for that."

Lucius. The hulking, dark-skinned vampire's face flashed through my mind. "He's a warrior?"

Eliza nodded as we passed through the entrance hall. "He's Maximillian's personal bodyguard whenever he travels, and is in charge of all things safety and security. He oversees the training of both the city and the Tower guard."

The double doors of the tower entrance swung open, and Eliza walked out into the courtyard. I paused with my foot on the threshold, skin prickling as I stared up at the sky, unable to shake the feeling that the twinkling stars were watching me.

Eliza turned back, her brow wrinkling. Her face cleared with sudden understanding as she saw me hesitating. "Umm, do you need a minute?" she asked. She looked vaguely uncomfortable, as if she wasn't sure how to deal with my distress. "If you want, we can just stick to the tower for today."

"No." I squared my shoulders. I needed to push past this discomfort, needed to expose myself to the outdoors so I could overcome my fear. I pulled up the hood on my duster, and the sensation of being watched faded a bit. I was definitely playing the 'if I can't see you, you can't see me" game, but I didn't care. Whatever I had to do to get through this. "Let's go."

Eliza nodded, and she turned around again. This time, I followed, keeping my gaze firmly in front of me and away from the sky. Over the next hour, Eliza showed me the rest of the compound—the guard barracks nested along the side of the keep, the training grounds beyond that, the royal forge, and a chapel that had once belonged to Phaeros, but had been torn down and dedicated to Tenebros instead. The gothic structure crafted from blackwood and obsidian and decorated with carvings of ebon roots and ravens—all symbols of the god of the Underworld—seemed obscene as it squatted in the shadows of the Tower. It seemed almost petty to have it here, when this place had so obviously been built to honor the sun god.

But then again, Tenebros had good reason to be petty toward his older brother. After all, if it wasn't for Phaeros, he would still be alive and ruling over the Celestial Heavens. Not trapped in the Underworld and forced to rule over the dead.

I was about to ask if I would be allowed to use the training ground—the idea of taking out some of my frustrations on the dummies was very appealing—when the north gates of the compound opened, and a rider galloped through.

My jaw dropped—not at the sight of Nyra, though she did look very impressive in her riding leathers—but at the beast she sat astride. It bore the majestic form of a horse, with a golden, lustrous coat that reminded me of the painting of the horse I'd seen this morning. Yet its powerful form was intertwined with undeniably mechanical parts. Each step it took was a study in graceful power, and the sound it made was unlike any horse I'd known—the familiar rhythm of hooves against the ground, yet overlaid with a soft, harmonic resonance that seemed to hum from within its mechanical components.

Nyra brought her steed to a halt in front of us, and the—animal? machine?—snorted, tossing its dark brown mane. The vampire smirked as she noticed me gaping, but I couldn't rein in my astonishment. The seamless integration of muscle and metal was both eerie and captivating, delicate metallic filigree tracing along its legs and back to merge into flesh as if the two were born together. A series of metal plates were artfully arranged down the front of the animal's chest, disappearing beneath the underbelly, and in the center glowed an aetheric crystal the size of a large fist.

I lifted my head to meet the beast's gaze. "What are you?" I breathed as it stared intently back at me. There was no doubt that despite its mechanical parts, the animal was very much a living creature. Its eyes were deep and alive, glowing with an inner light beyond the power of an ordinary machine.

"Her name is Zephyra," Nyra said, her smirk softening as the animal nudged her head against my shoulder. Enchanted, I ran my hand along the metallic bridge of her muzzle, then stroked a thumb across her velvet soft nose. "She's an Aethersteed, one Eliza designed for me."

Well, she certainly seems to live up to her name, I thought to myself. She had the long legs and lean, muscular physique of a thoroughbred, with a strong back that would allow her to sprint and gallop at high speeds. "You... invented this?" I asked, glancing sideways at Eliza.

Eliza's lips thinned. "No. That dubious honor belongs to Icarus Stormwelder, Emperor Vladimir's personal inventor. The horses started dying off after the sun disappeared and we couldn't grow enough grain to feed them. Vladimir ordered Icarus to come up with a solution, and he invented a mechanized animal with an aetheric core that doesn't need food to live." She reached out to scratch the underside of the aethersteed's chin, and the animal tilted its head to give her better access. "I just improved upon it, with some input from Nyra."

Nyra snorted. "You did more than improve. Stormwelder's design was barbaric, focused only on power and performance. His aethersteeds were little more than machines with a few organic parts." She dismounted gracefully, then gave the side of her mount's neck an affectionate pat. "Thanks to Eliza, Zephyra has every bit of the grace and intelligence of her ancestors."

My eyes narrowed at the fond look on the vampire's face as she stroked the beast. "You were Ferae before you were Turned, weren't you?" I asked. "From the Equinox tribe." The painting in the hallway belonged to her.

Nyra's gaze shuttered at that. "It's rude to ask a vampire about their human past," she said shortly, taking Zephyra's reins. "Eliza, you ought to get to the factory soon. You need to get that inspection done before the commandant arrives."

"Don't mind her," Eliza said as we watched Nyra lead her aethersteed to the stables. "Nyra's touchy about her past. Her human life didn't end the way she wanted it to."

"Is that how she ended up in Maximillian's service?" I asked.

"That's how all of us did." Eliza's tone turned brisk, and she abruptly changed the subject. "I do need to get to the factory, but let's kill two birds with one stone. You can ride with me, and I'll give you a quick tour of the city along the way."

I wanted to ask Eliza more—specifically about why she seemed so willing to serve Maximillian even though he had conquered her people—but I recognized that the subject was closed for now, so I dropped it. "Does this mean we get to ride on one of the aethersteeds?" I asked, a little more eagerly than I intended.

"Hells no." Eliza shuddered. "Those things might be part machine, but they're still way too alive for me. We'll be taking my bike."

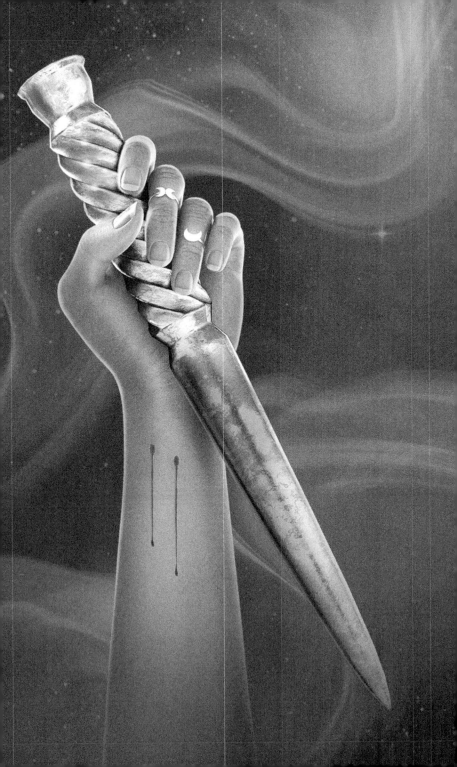

7

"How in all the hells do you find this safer than a horse?" I screeched five minutes later as we blasted through the compound gates.

Eliza laughed over the rush of wind in my ears. "Are you kidding? I'm in full control here." She maneuvered the aether-bike with uncanny precision, its streamlined frame cutting through the city streets. I could feel the pulse of the glowing aetheric core that powered the machine beneath us, and I couldn't help shuddering as the energy buzzed along my skin. "I don't have to worry about the bike deciding it doesn't want to listen to me. It does what I tell it to, when I tell it to."

As if on cue, the bike banked sharply to the left, hugging the curve of the road so closely, it felt like we were one with the pavement. The aetheric core's rhythm quickened, matching our increased speed, and the bike surged forward, responding to Eliza's command with a precision no living creature could match. The sensation was exhilarating and terrifying all at once, a futuristic dance of speed and magic.

We zipped through a busy thoroughfare lined with tall sunsteel buildings, and I noted Eliza wasn't the only biker on the road. Citizens zipped along the paved streets on bikes of varying sizes and styles, and alongside, in specialized lanes, aethersteeds clomped at slower speeds. Walkways lined both sides so that pedestrians could travel safely, and there were flashing aetheric crystals hanging from each intersection to direct the flow of traffic.

"Okay," I shouted as we slowed to a halt in front of one such crystal, which had turned red. The light gilded the side of Eliza's face as she turned to look at me, her brass goggles pulled over her eyes. She'd given me an extra pair to protect my own eyes from the streaming wind. "But how am I supposed to keep track of anything when we're zipping around so fast?"

"By paying attention." She stuck her tongue out at me, then waved a gloved hand to indicate the buildings towering over either side of the broad street. "This is the Lumina's technological hub. The empire's top research and development facilities are located here—or at least what's left of them."

I frowned. "What do you mean by that?"

The cross-traffic began to slow, and I braced myself for Eliza to kick the bike into motion again. "When the sun disappeared, the amount of aether in the atmosphere dropped so drastically, we were forced to shut down all but our most essential labs and factories. We also had to disable large public utilities that took up too much energy, like the railway system we used to have."

The light changed, and we zoomed off, dodging through the flow of traffic once more. I gripped the handles beneath the back of the bike seat and leaned forward, both to keep my balance and to better hear Eliza as she continued to shout points of interest. The massive sleek building to our right was an aetheric weapons development factory with fortified walls and guarded entrances, and a smaller building a little farther out was the crystal refinery where raw aetheric crystals were manufactured. A colossal structure with shiny turbines visible through large windows turned out to be the aetheric power plant. But for every building that pulsed with activity, there were half a dozen others with doors and windows shuttered, walls crumbling and roofs caved in.

"That shop over there is where I bought my first bike," Eliza said a little wistfully, slowing in front of what had once been a mechanic's garage. The building, now abandoned, had a faded sign hanging above the door, reading 'Aetherwheels Emporium'. Its windows were dusty, obscuring the dark, empty interior where rows of sleek aetherbikes must have once stood. Vines crept up the sides, nature slowly attempting to reclaim the structure.

A sense of loss filled me as I gazed at the abandoned building. Even though I'd never set foot in Lumina before, I could sense the grandeur that this city had once possessed, that it still clung to despite the damage Vladimir and the Eternal Night had wrought.

"Why are you helping them?" I asked.

She twisted in her seat to look at me. "Helping who?"

"The vampires." I gestured to the dilapidated garage, outrage rising inside me. "Why are you helping the people who did this to your country? Who destroyed everything you love?" I couldn't imagine standing by as an enemy king swept through Trivaea and destroyed everything, then throwing myself into league with his servants. Eliza might have been a thrall, but she didn't seem to be bound by the same fanatical sense of worship and obedience I'd witnessed in the thralls belonging to vampires I'd hunted down in the past. If I'd been in her situation, I would have taken my own life rather than allow a vampire to use me this way.

Eliza stiffened. "Who says I'm helping them?"

I threw up my hands. "It's obvious you're helping them! That weapons factory—" I jabbed my finger in its general direction, "is overseen by you, isn't it? Along with the rest of this. You're willingly helping Vladimir use your own technology to subjugate you, when you could be—"

"Keep your voice down!" Eliza snapped, her eyes darting across the street to a vampire striding past. He wore a long tailcoat, and a human slave who looked to be an office assistant hurried in his wake, a stack of boxes in his arms. She lowered her own voice as she continued, "I have no choice. If it weren't me, someone else would be forced to do it. At least in Maximillian's service, I have the chance to help my people. To keep the power plants and the crystal factories running so they can continue to heat their homes and feed themselves, and to advocate for them whenever I can." Her eyes flashed. "My entire family was slaughtered fifty years ago, and I could have laid down and died with them. Instead, I sold myself to Maximillian so I could do what I had to in order to protect the survivors."

The fierce conviction in her voice mentally knocked me back a step, and it took me a minute to regroup my thoughts. "I... I didn't think of it like that," I admitted.

"No," she said coolly. "You jumped straight to judgment."

Shame washed through me, but before I could respond, Eliza kicked the bike into gear again. We rode in silence for the next ten minutes, passing through the technological hub into what appeared to be the city's residential section. It seemed to be organized in concentric circles radiating outward from the city center—the upscale, wealthier homes and establishments located closer to the tower, while the outer sections grew progressively more homely. The shops, restaurants and clubs had all been converted to cater to vampiric tastes—as we stopped at another light, I glimpsed one vampire seated at a table by a window, drinking directly from the neck of a kneeling human, and I ground my teeth as the urge to leap off the bike and intervene seized me.

"Don't worry," Eliza said, following my gaze. "The vampire won't kill him. There are strict regulations in place to protect humans, even ones like that slave who are used for feedings."

"Regulations?" I gave her a bewildered glance. "Why would the vampires care about that?"

"They didn't, at first," Eliza said with a shrug. "When the Eternal Night came and Vladimir's armies swept through our kingdom, they were ripping our throats out and gorging themselves until they threw up." A faint ripple of disgust passed across her features. "Max eventually convinced the others to pass laws regulating the treatment and handling of humans under the new empire."

My mind went back to the scroll I'd found in the library, which I hadn't had a chance to read yet. "You're saying that Maximillian is the reason you and I can zip around this city on the back of your bike without being jumped by hungry vampires?"

"That's right," Eliza said as I continued to watch the vampire through the window. He removed his fangs from the human's neck, then delicately dabbed at his crimson mouth with a linen napkin. A vampire server came and took the dazed-looking human by the shoulders, leading him away while the diner picked up his newspaper from the table and began reading.

Despite the horror of it, the scene seemed oddly pedestrian.

I was still trying to digest everything I'd seen when the rows of steel and stone buildings gave way to a massive grid of greenhouses. The aetherbike's headlamp illuminated the misted glass structures sprawling out in front of us—the patchwork of luminescent panels and clear glass a stark contrast to the dense urban environment we'd just left behind.

"This used to be the city's Central Park," Eliza said as we drove through a set of gates. The arched 'Central Park' sign hanging above it was faded, but still legible amidst the glow of the aetheric lampposts set out at intervals along the rows of greenhouses. "All the grass and flowers died, so we repurposed the area. They provide over half the city's produce." She came to a stop outside one of the glass buildings, then glanced over her shoulder at me. "Just to show you that not everything I make takes lives."

The pointed look she gave me made me want to crawl off the bike and disappear beneath one of the park benches. "I'm sorry," I said, and this time, there was no defensiveness in my tone. "You're right, I spoke out of turn." I couldn't imagine what it must have been like for her—judging by her looks, I imagined that she'd been in her teens when she'd taken the blood oath to Maximillian. While the blood bond didn't give humans immortality, it did slow the aging process significantly, allowing them to retain their youthful looks for many decades. Even though it had been fifty years, she looked like she was in her early twenties. "You're a very brave woman, Eliza. Your ancestors must be incredibly proud of you."

Eliza quickly glanced away, but not before I caught the sudden sheen of tears in her eyes. "One of the aetheric cores in the greenhouse is malfunctioning," she said, swinging her leg over her bike. "I figured you could have a look around while I see to it, and then I'll bring you back to the compound."

"Sure."

I tucked my hands into the pockets of my duster as we walked up the paved path to the greenhouse, the sounds of the city fading behind us. The door hissed open, leading us into a world of verdant growth and soft, pulsating light. The air inside was warm and moist, and I sucked in a breath as a sudden rush of magical energy filled me.

"Good morning, Miss Silverstream," a gardener in a brown leather gardening apron greeted us, straightening up from a bed of lettuce he'd been tending to. He was human, tall and spindly, his square spectacles perched on the end of a long nose smudged with dirt at the tip. "I take it you received my report about the malfunctioning core?"

"Yes," Eliza said, but I was barely listening. My eyes roved over the space, taking in the row upon row of leafy greens stretched out before us. This particular greenhouse seemed dedicated to leafy vegetables—lettuce, spinach, kale, as well as magical varieties such as auragreens (for cleansing energy) and velvet chard (for soothing stomach ulcers) grew in abundance here. Their frilly heads basked in the luminescence of the crystal-powered lamps hanging above them, but my gaze narrowed as I noticed another set of crystals dotting the ceiling—pure white and shimmering. A sort of metal grid ran between them and connected them to the lamps below, and I tilted my head, trying to puzzle it all out.

"Are those moonstones?" I asked, interrupting them.

Eliza opened her mouth, but it was the gardener who answered. "Yes," he said, giving me a small smile. As powerful as the aether is, it is not a replacement for sunlight," he explained. "Lunar energy is simply a weaker form of solar energy, so Eliza here rigged a power grid that allows us to gather lunar energy using the moonstones, then amplify it using the aether crystals." He gave Eliza a quizzical smile. "I don't believe you've introduced me to your friend, Miss Silverstream."

"Catherine," Eliza supplied. "Or Cat, for short. She's a new member of the viceroy's household."

I nearly choked on my spit. Nyra had told me I'd be going by Catherine during my stay—Kitana was far too uncommon, and they didn't want to risk anyone connecting the dots—but I hadn't thought about the shortened version.

"You fought well, Kitten." Maximillian's voice echoed in my mind. I had no doubt he'd done this on purpose, just so he

could keep using that stupid nickname. The vampire's audacity knew no bounds.

The aetheric lamps flickered, and I blinked as another surge of energy filled me. *Lunar energy,* I realized. My body was drawing on the lunar reserves in the moonstones, refilling the magical well inside me. Eliza scowled as the flickering intensified, and I gasped as the surrounding shadows began to shift, responding to my magic.

"I need to go."

"Kit—I mean, Cat!" Eliza called as I rushed back down the path. The flickering grew even more erratic, and I burst through the doors, my heart pounding in my ears. Tendrils of shadow curled around my legs, not unlike the way Jinx sometimes did, as if they were welcoming me back, but I shoved them down, away, gritting my teeth to shut down the flow of magic.

"Hey!" Eliza grabbed my arm and yanked me around to face her. "What's happening?"

I tried to pull my arm away, but she held firm to my sleeve. "I can't be in there," I said, my voice tinged with desperation.

"Why not?"

"It's my magical well," I tried to explain. When the look of skepticism on her face didn't abate, I continued, "It's trying to latch onto the lunar energy in the greenhouse. That's why the lights started flickering."

Eliza frowned. "I thought that was the aetheric core malfunctioning."

I shook my head. "I'm sure that's still a problem, but I'm adding to the burden. I'm afraid that if I stay in there, I'll drain the greenhouse dry."

Eliza's face paled, and she glanced back at the building. She pursed her lips at the sight of the lights inside still flickering—a lot less than they'd been before, but still, something was wrong. "Maybe you should get a little farther away," she said, a worried note entering her voice. "There's a café three blocks past the park that caters to humans. Meet me there. And don't go looking for any trouble."

She hurried back inside before I could answer, drawing some handheld mechanical contraption from her tool belt. The hungry entity inside me wanted to follow her back into the greenhouse to devour more magic, but I forced myself to walk in the opposite direction, passing through the gates and back into the urban part of the city.

I made it to the café Eliza had mentioned without incident, only to find that the shop was closed for the day. My empty stomach sank in disappointment, until I remembered the second roll I'd stashed in my pocket. I took a bite out of it as I leaned against the café's corner window, trying to remain unobtrusive as I watched the ebb and flow of traffic. There were a lot more people traveling on foot than by aetherbike—the ones who could afford transportation were vampires, though I still spotted the occasional human thrall.

A few buildings down from the café, a human exited a townhouse, carrying a large trashcan in her arms. I watched as she hurried up the street to the alleyway at the corner, only to trip on a crack in the sidewalk. I winced as she fell forward, spilling the contents of the can all over the front of a well-dressed vampire female.

"My dress!" she shrieked as refuse splattered the front of her pink silk gown. The other pedestrians hurried out of the way while the human servant scrambled to clean up the mess. Rage twisted the vampire's pretty face, and she lifted her skirts so she could deliver a swift kick to the human's ribs. "You wretched little gremlin!" she screamed as the human collapsed to the ground. "Do you have any idea how much this dress cost?"

I pulled a stake from my pocket and advanced on the vampire, my own anger rising to the surface as the passersby did nothing to help. The human tried to fight back, even landing a solid strike on the vampire's face, but the blood-sucking bitch continued to kick the human until she curled into a ball.

I had nearly reached them, was within striking distance, when someone grabbed me by the back of my coat and yanked me into the shadows of an awning.

"I wouldn't interfere," a male voice rasped in my ear. He was a vampire, but his scent was laced with sea moss and a hint of brine, reminding me of the ocean. I tried to stake him, but my muscles locked up, and my arms snapped to my sides. "It won't end well for either you or the human."

Telekinesis.

"Let me go!" I snarled, struggling against the invisible hold. I drew on what little magic I'd gathered from the greenhouse to summon a tendril of shadow, and the vampire hissed as it struck him, temporarily losing his mental hold on me. I surged forward, but stopped at the sight of two city guards pulling the vampire woman off the servant.

"What is the meaning of this?" another vampire demanded, striding up the street. He wore a housecoat over a simple linen shirt and trousers, his feet stuffed into boots that hadn't been properly tied. It was obvious he had left his house in a hurry. "Why is my servant cowering in the street like a beaten dog!"

"Unhand me!" the vampire female demanded. The guards came to a stop—though they did not release the female—allowing her to address the other vampire. "Your insolent wretch of a slave attacked me with a trash can and ruined my dress. I am well within my rights to punish her!"

"You certainly are not," the vampire snapped. He stood protectively over his servant as he faced off against the outraged woman. "It is *my right* to punish her for any infraction as her owner."

"Well, if you'd trained her properly, this wouldn't have

happened!" The female fumed as she shook her stained skirts in the other vampire's direction. "Look at this! I demand you pay for a replacement."

The vampire male pressed his lips together as he looked the woman up and down. I clenched my jaw—her dress was in a sorry state, to be sure, but nothing a good cleaning wouldn't fix. There was no need to replace it, and *definitely* no need to punish the servant so harshly.

"All right," he finally agreed. He pulled a card from his wallet and handed it to the woman. "You may send the bill to my house."

The guards released the vampire woman, who took the card with a sniff. "She also struck me," she said, pointing to the already healed spot on her cheek.

The other vampire looked to the guards, who nodded their confirmation. "Very well," he sighed. "Three lashes."

The human whimpered, and with a flick of her master's wrist, she floated into the air. I gasped as the vampire ripped the back of her dress open, exposing an expanse of olive skin already riddled with scars.

"Please, Master," she sobbed as he undid his belt. "It was an accident!"

"Sorry, pet," the vampire said as he pulled the strip of leather taut between his hands. "But I told you what would happen if you stepped out of line again."

He raised the belt, and I flicked my hand, sending my tendril of shadow magic toward him. The crowd gasped as it wrapped around the belt and ripped it from his hand, then flung it across the street. The four vampires turned as one in my direction, and the male behind me swore.

Then next thing I knew, my arms and legs were bound tight against my body again, and I was flying across the rooftops. It took me a second to realize the vampire who'd tried to stop me had used his telekinetic magic to immobilize me again, then thrown me over his shoulder and took off at a run.

"Put me down!" I shrieked over the roaring wind.

"Not a chance, sweetheart," the vampire said cheerfully. The city blurred around us as he leaped from rooftop to rooftop, clearing the city blocks at a speed that Eliza's aetherbike couldn't hope to match. "While I do have a thing for women who know their way around weapons, your self-control leaves much to be desired. I'm returning you to our benevolent leader so he can decide what to do with you."

"Self-control?" I sputtered. "They were going to beat that poor woman! Someone needs to stop them!"

"No one is going to stop them, and if you try, you'll find your neck on a chopping block," the vampire said darkly. "You'd do well to remember that."

"They can try," I seethed.

"Try?" he mocked as he sailed over the Tower wall in one graceful bound. The guards startled as he landed in the courtyard, but their alarmed expressions settled as they recognized him, and they returned to their posts as if nothing had happened. "It wouldn't be hard. Look how easily I was able to capture you."

I fumed, especially when two of the guards exchanged smug looks, gloating over my predicament. "I am going to pull your guts out of your belly and hang you by them from the battlements," I hissed.

"Mmm, foreplay," he purred. "I do love it when a woman knows how to talk dirty to me."

My cheeks flamed, and I fell silent, refusing to give him any more ammunition. Humiliation burned in my gut as he carried me through the courtyard and into the Tower. Dozens of stares prickled along my skin, and I gritted my teeth, wishing I could fight back. But I'd already used too much of the precious little

I'd siphoned from the greenhouse, and despite the powerless-ness of my position, I wasn't truly in any danger. I needed to conserve what was left.

Especially since it looked like I was about to get into another fight with the vampire lord.

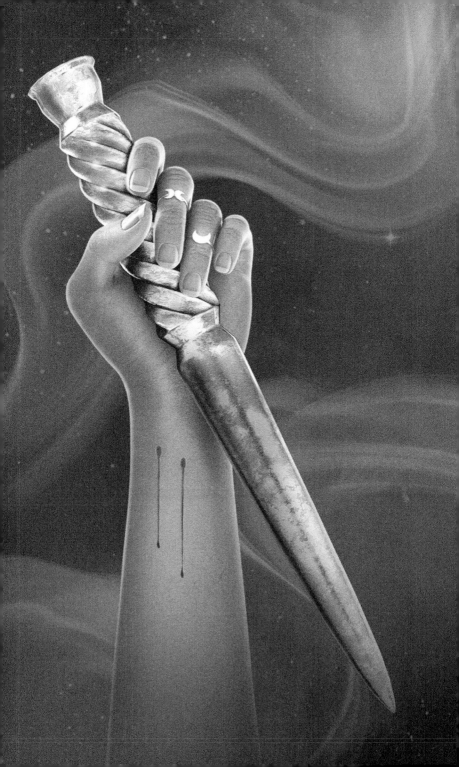

8

"Sorry to interrupt, Sire," the vampire said as he strolled into a room on the Central Keep's third floor. I tried to twist my body around to see where we were, but the vampire hadn't loosened his telekinetic grip, and I was forced to stare down at the carpet instead. "But I found this little menace out on the streets by herself, attempting to murder citizens."

He dumped me to the ground without ceremony, releasing the telekinetic hold on my limbs right before I hit the carpet. Seething, I leaped to my feet and took a swing at him, but he danced out of my reach, his eyes laughing. They were a vivid cerulean, set into a handsome, swarthy face that pointed at human origins, but there was no mistaking his pointed ears and inhumanly beautiful features. His chestnut hair was cropped short, revealing a golden hoop that winked at his left ear, and he wore all black, his button-up shirt open at the collar to reveal the curling edge of a tattoo at his collarbone.

"What do you mean, she was attempting to murder citizens?" Nyra said sharply, drawing my attention away from him. I turned to see her sitting at an oblong table with Maximillian in what appeared to be a meeting room. Papers were scattered across the table's polished surface, along with several leather books that looked like ledgers. "I thought she was with Eliza!"

"She was, but she wandered off, then decided to try to play hero when a human slave was being punished in the middle of the street."

Maximillian arched an eyebrow. "And you just happened to be there to intervene, were you, Sparrow?" he asked, his expression suggesting he wasn't even remotely surprised by this behavior.

The vampire tugged at his golden hoop. "I was on my way back into the city when I saw her. Couldn't help but do a little stalking, especially since you made it my obsession to track her down for the past two years." He winked at me.

"What?" I gaped. This was Sparrow, the vampire who had gathered all the intelligence Maximillian had on me? "What do you mean, for the past two years?"

"Leave us," Maximillian said abruptly. Sparrow shut his mouth, and he and Nyra exited the room in a flash, sending several papers fluttering to the ground on their way out.

"Well?" I demanded once we were alone. "Are you going to explain yourself?"

"Explain what, exactly?"

Where did I even begin? "The gross mistreatment of humans in your city, for starters," I seethed, stalking around the table. I jabbed a finger into his chest, and Maximillian blinked, staring down at it in bemusement. "I just watched a vampire whip his human in the middle of the street, simply because she accidentally tripped and spilled some trash on another vampire. And no one did anything to help, not even the city guards!"

"Is that so?" Maximillian's expression darkened. He grasped my wrist and pulled me down into the chair Nyra had vacated.

"Tell me the whole of it, Kitten. If someone has violated the laws in my city, I want to know about it."

I blinked, so surprised at the sincerity in his voice that it took a second for me to realize he was still holding my hand. I tugged my wrist away and folded it into my lap, then recounted the incident, right up to the point where Sparrow had used his telekinesis to immobilize and spirit me away.

When I'd finished, Maximillian was staring at me over the tips of his fingers, which he'd pressed together, his elbows propped on the surface of the table. My abdomen tensed at the impassive mask that had settled over his face, and a bad feeling spread through my gut. "I don't blame you for wanting to help that woman, Kitana," he said. "It's in your nature. But Sparrow was right to intervene."

"What?" My heart dropped. "How can you say that?"

He sighed. "The vampire female was wrong to mete out physical punishment on a slave that did not belong to her," he said. "Which is why the guards pulled her away. But it is against the law for a human to strike a vampire, even in self-defense. Her master was well within his rights to punish her for it."

"But that's ridiculous!" I shot to my feet and began pacing, unable to reconcile the logic. "That vampire had already kicked the shit out of her!"

"Which in a vampire court would be argued as a separate issue. Not that vampires go to court over human issues," Maximillian added dryly. "They are generally settled with the help of the city guard, as you saw today."

"I can't believe this." I raked a hand through my hair, then whirled around to jab my finger at him again. "Eliza waxed poetic all afternoon about how you're some champion for humanity, yet when I tell you about the atrocities being committed in your own city, you act like you don't even care. You're just as bad—"

"Yes, I am." Maximillian rose from his chair, unfolding to his full height. I swallowed as he towered over me, excruciatingly aware that at any point, he could use his mental prowess to immobilize me and do whatever he wanted to my body. He crowded me until my hips pressed against the edge of the table, and I braced my hands against the glossy wood to keep from falling backward. "Eliza may have tried to paint me as some white knight, here to deliver humanity from the evil clutches of the emperor. But never forget, Kitten, that while I do not share the same proclivity for cruelty as my kin, I am still a vampire, and I am still beholden to the emperor. It is my duty to uphold his laws, no matter what you may think of them."

"And yet you want me to murder him for you," I said bitterly. "Would he still call you his loyal servant if he knew?"

Maximillian's mouth twisted into a sardonic grin. "Ahh, but vampires have been murdering each other for power for centuries. That's simply part of the game." The grin dropped from his face as he skimmed the backs of his knuckles along my cheek. "It's a game I wish you didn't have to play."

His expression shifted to something softer, almost melancholy, and my heartstrings twanged in response. That intoxicating scent of his wrapped around me again, making me want to let my guard down, and I clung tightly to my anger, refusing to let him sway me.

It didn't matter how many hospitals or greenhouses Maximillian built. He was still responsible for the human suffering I'd seen today, still every bit the type of monster I'd dedicated my life to fighting before Sebastian had locked me away. The bastard had just told me as much to my face. And yet he still expected me to help him.

"I don't have to play," I told him. "I don't have to be part of your stupid game, or anyone else's, for that matter. I've had enough of being a pawn, of being kept prisoner. As soon as the full moon comes, I'm gone."

I shoved past him, storming out of the chamber and back to my rooms. And he let me go.

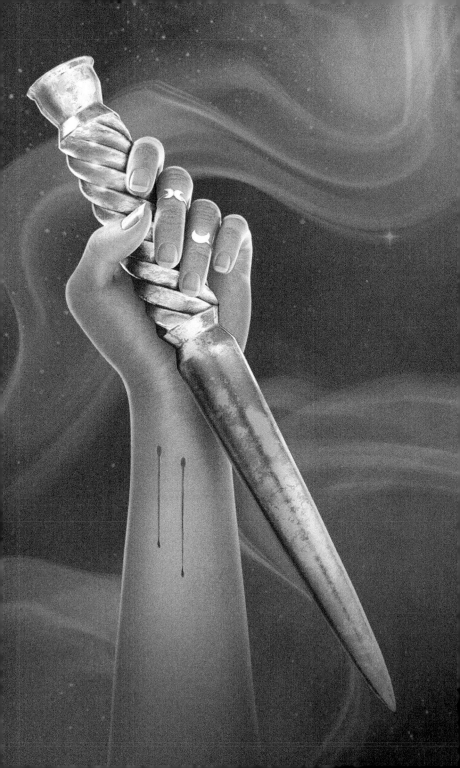

9

I spent the next couple of days holed up in the library, my head buried in books and scrolls. Maximillian didn't seek me out again, and neither did any of his lackeys. They were all busy preparing for some military agent of the emperor, who was coming to Lumina to collect a weapons shipment. That knowledge only cemented my resolve—any help I gave Lord Starclaw and his people would only contribute to more human suffering.

The books and scrolls I read confirmed most of what I'd learned so far—about the Eternal Night, the new territories, the magical witch barrier, and the barbaric laws that humans had to suffer under Vladimir's rule. The more I read, the more murderous I felt toward the vampire ruler. As soon as I killed Sebastian and broke whatever hold he had over the witch clans, I would mobilize them and take down Vladimir. The vampire king would pay for his crimes, but on my terms. Not Maximillian's.

Still, I had to admit that without actually traveling to Trivaea, I had very little information to go on. I needed to find a source of information about the witch realm. But who here could I talk to that would have insider knowledge of the area, when it was cut off from the rest of Valentaera?

A rumbling purr distracted me from my thoughts, and I smiled as Jinx wound her way between my legs in greeting. She'd been my sole companion, curling up into bed so I could reach for her when the nightmares woke me, or keeping me company while I prowled the stacks for books on history and lineages. I scooped the cat up into my arms and set her on the table, and she dropped a quill onto the open book in front of me.

Sparrow, I thought, staring at the brown feather.

I clenched my jaw. Of course. Maximillian's spymaster would have the knowledge, or knew where to get it, at least. I picked up the quill by its tip and spun it between my fingers. But how did I know I could trust his information? He was loyal to his Sire, not me, and would probably tell me whatever he thought would get me to help Maximillian rather than the truth.

Jinx jumped off the table, then pawed at my foot. "Another field trip?" I asked, reaching down to scratch her chin. She tilted her head, allowing the distraction for just a moment, then batted my hand away.

"Fine," I grumbled, leaving the books behind. I expected her to take me to another secret passage, but instead she led me directly outside and to the training compound. As we approached the entrance, she rubbed against my legs again, and her body unraveled into ribbons of shadow that wrapped around me, blending my form seamlessly into the night.

Ahh. We're doing reconnaissance, then.

I slipped inside the training yard, now invisible to any casual observer so long as I stuck to the shadowed areas. The yard was an expanse of well-trodden earth, bordered by tall, weathered wooden fences that seemed to absorb the sounds of the city beyond. Sturdy posts jutted from the ground at intervals, each adorned with various training implements: swords, shields, and more exotic weapons, some of which I couldn't name. Off to one side of the yard, a series of obstacle courses had been constructed. Wooden beams for balance, ropes for climbing, and walls of varying heights designed to test agility and strength. Beyond that, archery targets stood at the ready, their surfaces pockmarked with the constant thud of arrows.

Movement in the center of the yard drew my eye to where two figures sparred in a large, open space designed for hand-to-hand combat training. Lucius and Sparrow, I realized with a jolt, drawing closer to get a better look. I stuck to the edges, weaving my way between the straw dummies that were used for target practice and refinement. Picking a large one dressed in thick, padded armor, I took up a spot in its shadow so I could watch.

The two vampires were shirtless, and both had tattoos, though they moved too quickly for me to make out the designs. Dressed only in cotton trousers and boots, they moved in a deadly dance of rippling muscles and glinting weaponry. Lucius swung a battle-axe with his right hand, following up with slashes of the forearm blade on his left. His movements were devastating, each strike powerful enough to fell a warrior in one blow.

But Sparrow easily evaded Lucius's attacks. His grin was nearly as sharp as the twin swords he wielded with deadly precision, and his movements were fluid, almost serpentine, as he weaved in and out of the larger vampire's reach. Despite his smaller stature, Sparrow met each of Lucius's heavy strikes with the swift, slicing motions of his blades, deflecting the larger vampire's attacks with an ease that belied the danger of each exchange.

"Do you think she's ever going to come out of the library?" Sparrow asked in a conversational tone as he twirled out of Lucius's reach.

Lucius growled, following Sparrow with a series of powerful swings. "You were too heavy-handed with her that day," he said as he smashed the weapon against Sparrow's blades, sending sparks flying between them.

The force of the impact reverberated through the training yard, but Sparrow absorbed it with a dancer's poise, his swords ringing in a high, clear note. "I was exactly the amount of heavy-handed I needed to be with her," he countered, his tone calm despite the intensity with which they sparred. He ducked under another swing, his swords flashing in a counter-attack that Lucius narrowly avoided. "If I hadn't used my power to bind her, she would have killed all four vampires in the square. Even I wouldn't have been able to stop word of that from reaching the emperor."

"Maybe so," Lucius grunted as Sparrow slashed at his ribs. He swung his vambrace blade down to block the blow, then pivoted and brought his axe down for another strike. "But now she's even more convinced we're the enemy. I saw how excited she was when Eliza showed her the armory and the training grounds, yet she hasn't touched them. She's afraid of us."

I blinked. Lucius had been watching me? When? He was a colossal man, nearly seven feet tall and built like a fortress, and I was certain I would have spotted him. But then again, he was a vampire. They had an uncanny ability to blend into the shadows, no matter their size, no magic required. And he knew the compound far better than me, including any number of places to skulk and watch me without being seen.

Lucius lunged with a speed that would have been impossible for an ordinary man of his size, but Sparrow spun away before he could land a blow. "What do you care?" he retorted, his swords a blur as he parried another series of attacks. "You've been opposed to this plan from the start."

"Because I know what it could cost him," Lucius snarled. "It would be better if—"

The wind shifted, and both vampires stilled as the night breeze wafted my scent toward them. Now that they were no longer moving, I could make out their tattoos in the moonlight. I sucked in a sharp breath at the intricate tribal tattoos swirling up Lucius's arms—bold, dark lines that curled and twisted around his muscles, evoking images of wolves in mid-prowl. I knew those tattoos, had seen many markings just like them during my childhood. Lucius was Ferae, but not just any Ferae—he belonged to the Wolven Tribe, the only place marked on the map in Ferae that was still free of vampire control.

The markings on Sparrow's bronzed skin were very different. Swirling waves intertwined with images of marine life covered his arms and torso, and a sparrow with its wings spread wide was inked across the back of his shoulder, a small sun rising behind it. But on his chest was the most damning—a mermaid tail entwined with a black anchor. The emblem of the Blackwater Pirates.

"Looks like we've got an audience," Sparrow sang, lowering his sword. His fangs flashed with a grin as he turned to look in exactly the direction I was standing in. "Why don't you come out and play, Kitty-Cat?"

I scowled, and the shadows cloaking me sluiced off my body as Jinx regained her cat form. The two vampires startled as she sauntered into the center of the ring, her tail swishing as she swiveled her head to look at both of them.

"Who is this?" Lucius asked, his amber eyes wide.

"Her name is Jinx." I followed her into the ring, a little put out that my cover was blown. I'd desperately wanted Lucius to finish that sentence, to explain what he'd meant. "She's my companion."

Sparrow hooted. "You have a cat? That makes Maximillian's

nickname for you even more hilarious." He slapped his thigh, shoulders shaking with laughter.

Lucius frowned as he sank to his haunches. "But you've been gone for fifty years. How could she have survived, especially for so long?"

He extended a hand toward Jinx, his claws glinting in the moonlight. I expected her to turn her nose up at him, but to my surprise, she nudged his hand with her forehead, then rubbed her entire body against him. The giant warrior softened, and he picked up the cat, wonder glimmering in his eyes as he cradled her in his massive arms. The golden beads in his braids clinked as he moved, and I blinked as I realized they'd been sculpted into ornamental wolf heads.

"She's not a normal cat," I explained as he stroked her fur. "I used my shadow magic to create her when I was a kid, because I'd spent a lot of time with the Ferae, and I was jealous of watching all my friends riding around in the forest on their dire-wolf familiars. I wanted one of my own."

Lucius nearly dropped Jinx, and she hissed at him as he fumbled her back into his arms. "You spent time with my—with the Wolven Tribe?" he asked as she jumped out of his arms and returned to my side.

"Now that's something I didn't know about you," Sparrow commented. He had drawn a dagger from his boot and was now using its tip to clean his claws, keeping one eye on Jinx. "As far as I was able to uncover, you were born and raised in the Nocturne Clan. They don't typically allow young witches to leave the clan until they've completed their first Twilight Communion."

I shrugged. "I'm not like most witches," I said, unwilling to divulge more of my past to him. He knew too much as it was.

"Clearly," Nyra drawled, and the three of us turned to see her stride into the training arena. I blinked at the sight of her in a simple cotton tunic and trousers, a markedly different look from the sleek dresses she wore as her professional uniform. Her lips pursed as she studied the cat, and she added, "We don't have meat to feed her."

"She doesn't need food," I said. It appeared that, unlike Lucius, Nyra's love for animals didn't extend to cats.

"Good. Now if you're not going to spar, you should leave." Nyra drew her sword and pointed toward the exit. "This is our training hour, and you're wasting it with all this pointless babble."

Sparrow snorted. "Says the one who walked in fifteen minutes late."

Nyra scowled. "Eliza and I have been running ourselves ragged all day preparing for Vinicius's arrival. That's a perfectly valid excuse."

"Who is Vinicius?" I asked. This was the third time they'd mentioned him, and I was curious to know the identity of the vampire causing so much consternation.

"He's a self-important snake," Lucius growled, his eyes flashing.

"Also known as our esteemed emperor's Master-at-Arms," Sparrow finished. "He's in charge of weapons and procurement for Noxalis's navy, so he visits our factories regularly to check on development and inspect shipments. Our dear Eliza has been working round the clock on a new aether cannon design courtesy of Icarus Stormwelder, and good old Vinicius has come to test the new prototype."

My stomach sank. "What are these cannons used for?" I asked, though I had a sinking suspicion I already knew the answer.

Nyra and Sparrow exchanged loaded glances. "The magical shield that protects the witches from invasion is a land barrier only," Lucius explained when they didn't answer. "They are still open to attacks by sea, and since Vladimir gained control of the Marisian navy when he conquered Heliaris, he has been making full use of those ships to wear down Trivaea's coastal defenses."

My stomach dropped. Crescent Cove was located smack dab in the center of Trivaea's coastline. Our connection to the lunar cycle and the tides made it an ideal location for us to practice our craft, but it also made us more vulnerable to naval attacks than the other clans. The Blackwater Pirates had forced us to develop our own naval defenses a long time ago, but there was a difference between dealing with a handful of pirate ships and an entire fleet. How in all the hells had Sebastian held them off this entire time?

"So you really have been helping him destroy my people," I said, clenching my fists.

"We don't have a choice," Nyra snapped. "We are all blood-bound to the emperor, either directly or through his servants. If we don't make the weapons for him, someone else will."

I shook my head. "I don't believe that. There has to be another way."

"There is," Sparrow said.

My jaw tightened at the meaningful note in his voice. Right. By helping Maximillian kill the vampire king. "And how do I know Maximillian won't continue this reign of terror on his own, especially since he's already got the infrastructure in place for it?" I clenched my fists. He'd been so complacent when I'd told him about that poor slave being whipped in the streets. I couldn't trust him not to turn on me as soon as I helped him take power. No matter how enticing his offer was.

"There's no point in reasoning with her," Nyra said, crossing her arms. "Why did you come here, anyway? Clearly it wasn't to train," she said, raking a scathing look down my body.

I flushed—I was wearing a simple plum day dress, which wasn't exactly suitable for sparring. But how was I supposed to know Jinx was taking me to the training yard? "I came here because I wanted to ask Sparrow if he had any information about Trivaea for me," I said, looking at the spymaster. He cocked his head, drawing my attention to a tattoo of a frothy sea wave splashing up the side of his neck.

It occurred to me then how strange it was that all these vampires bore the marks of their human ancestry so openly. Lucius with his Wolven hair beads, Nyra with her tribal riding leathers and the painting she kept in the Tower, and Sparrow with his visible neck tattoos. None of the vampires I'd fought had ever displayed trinkets associated with the lives they'd lived before they'd been Turned. As I understood it, abandoning all possessions and markings from the past was a requirement all Sires demanded of their Descendency candidates before they could undergo the Turning.

So why didn't Maximillian demand it from his vampire children?

"I see." Sparrow arched his eyebrows. "What information are you looking for, exactly?"

"Any information I can use to successfully plot and execute my revenge."

Nyra, who looked like she was on the verge of an apoplexy, opened her mouth. But Sparrow cut her off before she could try to kick me out again. "I'll tell you what," he said, drawing one of his swords and handing it to me. "If you can draw blood, I'll tell you whatever you want to know."

I caught the sword by its hilt on pure reflex and stared down at the blade. It was forged from starsteel—a nearly unbreakable ore mined in Noxalis's Caelum Crest—and the silvery metal shimmered with a faint, otherworldly glow in the moonlight. It was an excellent weapon, meticulously crafted, and I couldn't help admiring it even knowing where it came from.

"I don't think that's a good idea," I said, hesitating.

"Actually, I think it's a perfect idea." Nyra declared. She smirked at me as she took up a post at the edge of the ring, leaning next to a dummy that looked as though it had been run through with a sword a few dozen times. "Unless you're afraid, huntress."

I stiffened. "Fine," I said, flipping the sword in my hand. Lucius retreated from Sparrow's side to join Nyra, and Jinx rubbed herself against my legs and gave a loud purr of encouragement before she raced after the gargantuan vampire warrior and hopped onto his shoulder. "But none of your telekinetic bullshit, since I can't use my magic."

"Deal." Sparrow grinned, and he drew his own sword as I advanced. He darted forward to meet me, swinging his sword in a wide arc in front of him. I leaped high to avoid it, then brought my borrowed weapon down in an overhand swing. Our blades clashed with a bright ring, and Sparrow smirked as I stumbled back, my footing uneven.

"Rusty, aren't we?" Sparrow crooned, easily parrying my next two strikes. His sword was a blur, a silver streak that seemed to mock my slower reflexes. I gritted my teeth, ignoring his taunts, and focused on countering. Although swords were not my preferred weapon of choice, Sebastian had taught me how to wield almost any kind of blade, and the years of training began to come back to me. My muscle memory kicked in, and my blood surged as the rhythm of battle, the familiar dance of steel and strategy, returned.

Sparrow's expression shifted from amusement to concentration as I picked up speed, forcing him to work harder. I spun and feinted, no longer just defending, but attacking. Our swords rang out in the night, creating a metallic symphony that grew faster and more furious.

"What's the matter, Sparrow?" I taunted as I launched a flurry of defensive strikes. He sidestepped, but only just, narrowly avoiding a slash that would have cut into his arm. "Do you have any more critiques for me, or has this cat finally gotten your tongue?"

Sparrow laughed, and I thought I even heard Lucius chuckle behind me. "You're not terrible," he conceded, even as he aimed a strike at my head. "I didn't expect you to be this fast, either. Didn't know witches could match vampire speed."

I ducked the blow, then spun to the side for a counterattack. But as I raised my sword, my eyes met Maximillian's, who was standing just inside the entrance to the training compound, watching. His gaze burned into me even from across the room, and my breath caught at the unexpected admiration on his face.

And that was when Sparrow struck.

"Kitana!" Nyra cried out as Sparrow's blade bit into me. Fire raced across the left side of my chest, and I turned to see Sparrow stumbling back, a horrified expression on his face. It was clear he'd expected me to block, and had tried to turn the blade aside at the last second when he realized I'd been distracted. I let out a shocked cry as my blood spattered in an arc, dropping my sword so I could clutch at the wound.

A few drops of blood had landed on Sparrow's face, but he hardly seemed to notice as he cast his own weapon aside and rushed toward me. "I'm so sorry," he began, but his tongue swiped against a spot of blood on his mouth, and he stopped speaking. His expression changed in an instant, eyes flaring wide with surprise... and hunger.

A bad feeling ran through me as his irises flashed from cerulean to crimson. "Don't come closer," I said, my voice shaking as I snatched up the sword again. My skin crawled as Sparrow's fangs snapped down, and I raised my weapon, preparing to fight for my life.

But just as Sparrow sprang forward, a blur smashed into his side. A resounding crash echoed through the training field, and

I threw up my arm as a cloud of dust kicked up in my face. When it cleared a few moments later, I saw Maximillian pinning Sparrow against the back wall. Anger radiated from him as he stood firm, his body a solid barrier between me and the blood-crazed vampire who, just moments ago, had been joking and laughing with me.

"You dare to dishonor me like this?" Maximillian spoke into the deathly silence that had descended upon the arena. His voice was soft, yet there was an ominous edge that promised retribution. "Attacking a woman who is under my protection, whom I promised no harm would befall so long as she remained in my city?"

Sparrow panted beneath Maximillian's hold, the bloodlust waning. The eerie red glow faded from his eyes, and he blinked, coming back to his senses. Shock rippled across his features as he stared past Maximillian to where I stood, his eyes going to the wound in my shoulder.

"Oh gods," he gasped as I took a step back, clutching the gash. "Kitana, I'm so—"

He tried to take a step toward me, but Maximillian slammed him back against the wall. "You do not *touch* her," he snarled. Power rolled off him in waves, and the hairs on my arms stood straight up as a golden aura pulsed around his body. I'd never fought a vampire this powerful before, never experienced the intensity of a full-blooded royal before. It was terrifying… and yet, it was oddly thrilling, too. "If you so much as *look* at her right now, I will gut you where you stand. Is that clear?"

"Yes, Sire." Sparrow instantly dropped his gaze to the ground, the picture of obedience. I got the distinct sense that if Sparrow even thought about disobeying, Maximillian would snap his neck with half a thought, then tear his heart out much the same as he'd done to that vampire in the alley.

And this was one of his *own* children.

"Lucius," Maximillian said, his voice ringing through the yard. "Take him."

"Yes, Sire." The hulking vampire warrior appeared along with Nyra. His face was a mask, but the female vampire looked stricken.

"I'm so sorry," she said as she approached, a first-aid kit in her hands. At the sight of the box, my shoulder began to throb in earnest. "He didn't mean—"

"No." Maximillian was suddenly at my side, his hand around Nyra's wrist. He took the box from her and said, "Go with Lucius. I will take care of her."

Nyra looked like she wanted to protest, but Maximillian's tone brooked no argument. She swiftly bowed her head, then hurried to join Lucius and Sparrow on their way out the door. Sparrow glanced back at me over his shoulder one last time before Lucius pulled him away, and to my surprise, pity stirred in my chest at the sight of his guilt-wracked expression. It was obvious he hadn't meant to lose control—in that moment we hadn't been vampire and witch, but simply two warriors, testing their mettle against the other and reveling in the process. Yet I couldn't deny the pain searing my chest, or the fear still quaking through my body.

The moment Sparrow was out of sight, the battle rush left my veins, and it was everything I could do just to stay upright. "I've got you, Kitten," Maximillian murmured, catching me by the underarms as I sagged to the ground. I wanted to tell him to stay away—the last thing I needed was to be in close proximity to a vampire when I was bleeding—but I couldn't seem to find the strength. "You have nothing to fear from me," he soothed, scooping me up in his arms. I sucked in a sharp breath as the movement sent pain radiating through my chest, and my vision grew hazy. "Now hang on."

The world blurred as Maximillian sprang into motion, and

the next thing I knew, he was laying me atop a feather mattress. *His mattress,* I thought fuzzily as the scent of mahogany and leather wrapped around me like a comforting blanket. A tearing sound rent the air as Maximillian used his claw to rip open the front of my gown, and though I knew I should be outraged, I just couldn't summon the energy. He pushed the fabric down my hips, then slid down the shoulder off my chemise to reveal the wound. Curses spilled from his lips, but his hands were gentle as he used a cloth and hot water to clean it. I cried out in pain as he tightly wrapped it using gauze and tape from the first aid kit.

The door banged open, and Eliza flew into the room, her heart-shaped face panic-stricken. "What happened?" she cried as she rushed to the bedside, her green eyes shimmering with worry. "Were you attacked?"

"No," I croaked. "Sparrow and I were sparring, and I got distracted. I didn't block a blow that I should have seen coming, and he wasn't able to pull back in time."

"It's my fault," Maximillian said.

I swiveled my head around to glare at him. "What are you talking about? How could it possible be your fault?"

Despite the situation, the faintest of smiles played across his lips. "The sight of me standing there distracted you. Therefore, this is my fault." He shook his head, the smile fading. "I'm sorry, Kitana. This never should have happened."

"Don't be ridiculous," I snapped as Eliza drew a syringe and a vial full of golden liquid from one of her pouches. I tried not to look at the needle as she plunged it into the vial and filled the syringe. "I'm the idiot who allowed myself to get distracted."

"This will sting," Eliza warned me. She grabbed my arm, used a towel to wipe it clean, then plunged the syringe just below the crook of my elbow. I hissed as pain shot up my arm, followed by an electric sensation as the elixir pumped through my bloodstream. A haze washed over me as Eliza murmured something to Maximillian, and then the door clicked shut behind her, leaving the two of us alone.

Maximillian's face came into view as he leaned over me, his eyes hooded as he brushed a curl of hair from my forehead. "Get some sleep, Kitana," he said, his voice almost hypnotic. "I'll be right outside if you need anything."

He turned away, and my hand shot out to grab him. "Please," I begged, gripped by a desperation I didn't fully understand. "Don't leave me."

He hesitated, and I tightened my grip even as I braced myself for the rejection. I didn't know why I was doing this, why I was reaching out to an enemy for comfort, except that an overwhelming sense of loss hovered just outside my periphery, threatening to crush me. Everyone I'd ever loved had walked away from me, had left me in the dust when I was at my most vulnerable, and I had no one in my life that I could trust.

Pathetic as it was, the wounded little girl inside me needed the illusion of safety he provided. Even if just for a little while.

Maximillian's gaze softened, as if he could read every thought that flitted through my head. He returned to the bed, then gently gathered me into his arms, tucking my back against his chest and curling an arm around my side.

The ache in my chest faded, replaced by a sublime sense of safety and security that defied all reason. I didn't understand how a vampire could possibly make me feel this way, but I was too weakened to do anything but lie there and soak it in.

"I'm not going to abandon you," he murmured into my hair as I drifted off to sleep. "No matter what happens between us, you can count on that."

And for some reason, I believed him.

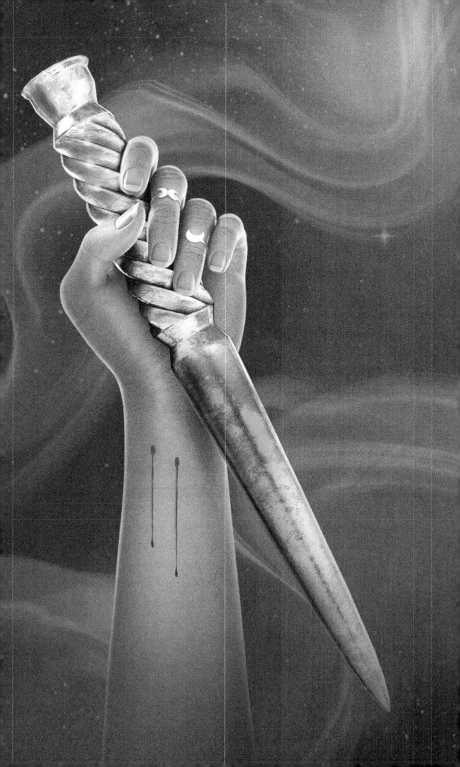

10

W hen I opened my eyes the next morning, Maximillian was gone, and I was back in my own bedchamber.

I blinked, sitting up to find I was still dressed in the same blood-encrusted chemise from the night before. My cheeks heated as I remembered how Maximillian had ripped my gown open to get to the wound—I'd been so delirious with pain and blood loss I hadn't stopped to wonder how much of my body he might have seen.

But then again, modesty wasn't really a factor when you were bleeding out from a blade wound, was it?

Gingerly, I prodded at the bandage wrapping around the front of my chest. When I didn't feel any pain, I slid my chemise down to my waist, then carefully unwrapped the bandage. Blood and adhesive flaked away to reveal fresh skin beneath, unmarred but for the faintest of silvery scars.

I shook my head in amazement. I didn't know if Eliza herself had invented this elixir, but I wanted to kiss her, then demand to show me how she'd made it. This couldn't be the work of aether alone—as I understood it, aether was simply a type of energy; it had no healing or otherwise magical properties. The secret had to be in the ingredients, whatever they were.

My bedroom door banged open without warning, and I jerked upright as Nyra flew through it. "Oh good, you're awake." She hustled over to the bed, a bowl of porridge and a glass of water in her hands. "How are you feeling? Are you all healed?"

"I'm fine." I peered at her as she set the items on my bedside table, noting that she seemed a bit frazzled. "Is everything all right?"

"I came to tell you not to leave the keep today," Nyra said briskly. "In fact, it would be better if you stayed in your rooms altogether."

I scowled. "Why in Hecate's name would I do that?"

"Because the commandant has arrived, and he has a bad habit of flaunting Lord Starclaw's rules when it comes to human slaves and servants," she snapped. "He normally wouldn't dare to touch one of Maximillian's personal servants, but given what happened between you and Sparrow last night, I don't think it's wise to take risks. He's only here for three days, so keep your head down and stay out of sight."

Nyra left the room before I could get in a word of protest, her heels clicking rapidly as she rushed away to deal with gods-knew-what. Huffing, I threw back the covers and crossed over to the balcony to peer out the windows. The compound seemed busier than normal, and I spied a black and red carriage parked just outside the stables, stamped with House Invictus's sword-and-spire crest.

The conversation with Nyra, Lucius, and Sparrow from last night rushed back. *Good old Vinicius has come to test the new proto-type.* A new aether cannon that Vladimir's fleet would use to blast through Trivaea's naval defenses. A cold sort of anger crys-talized inside my veins, freezing out any fuzzy feelings Maximil-lian might have inspired in me from the night before. They were handing this bloodsucking monster the keys to destroy my home, yet they wanted me to help them?

Well, fuck that.

Fuming, I stormed into the bathroom to wash and dress, then emerged from my bedchamber, dressed for battle and armed to the gills. I didn't know how I was going to do it, but I would find a way to sabotage this prototype and kill this warmonger along with anyone else who stood in my way.

A furry form landed on my head with a soft *poof*, then abruptly sank her claws into my scalp. "What the *fuck*, Jinx?" I yelped as she sprang off my head and landed on all fours in front of me. I gaped as my shadow familiar hissed at me, her green eyes narrowed on my face as if I were the enemy.

"What in the hells is wrong with you?" I tried to step past her, and nearly tripped as she tangled herself up in my legs. "Are you serious right now?" I seethed as she put herself between me and the elevator. Her form rapidly expanded until she filled the hallway, baring fangs at me that were long enough to cleave my arm in two. "You're really not going to let me pass?"

The elevator dinged, and I glanced up to see Sparrow step out of the wrought metal cage. He came to a halt at the sight of Jinx in her wildcat form, his dark eyebrows winging up. "Well, that's a neat trick."

I froze at the sight of the spymaster, all-too-aware of the fact that Jinx had drawn blood. Not much, but I could scent it, and I was sure the vampire could too. I took a step back, reaching for the stake in my pocket, and Sparrow's face fell.

"I'm sorry about last night," he said, a chagrined look in his eyes. I braced myself as he reached into his coat pocket, but he only pulled out a small pouch, roughly the size of my palm. "I've heard the stories about witch blood being addictive, but I had no idea I would react that way the first time I smelled it. I promise it won't happen again."

He tossed me the pouch, and I caught it one handed on reflex. "How can you make that promise?" I demanded, not opening it just yet. "And why is it that only you lost control, and not the others?"

Shame flushed Sparrow's cheeks, and he glanced away. "It's not an excuse, but I'm much younger than the rest of them. Maximillian turned me less than a hundred years ago. He trained me to have excellent control over my urges, but I'd never been exposed to someone with your blood type before, and..." he sighed, and met my gaze with a pleading look in his eyes. "Will you just open the pouch?"

I glared at the vampire, not sure if I should trust him, but Jinx shrank back to her normal size and began to groom herself idly, licking her paw and rubbing it across her face. Clearly my shadow familiar didn't see Sparrow as a threat, or she would have clamped his neck between her jaws and shaken him like a rag doll until he broke. Keeping a wary eye on Sparrow, I tugged at the drawstring pouch. A sharp, metallic tang hit my nostrils, and my eyes widened as I pulled out a glossy, dark red leaf the size of my thumb.

"Bloodbane?" I asked in surprise.

"Yes." Sparrow folded his hands behind his back. "It's outlawed here in the empire, but I was able to get my hands on a stash the last time I was in Trivaea. Chewing one leaf every three days should do the trick."

I twirled the stem of the oblong leaf between my fingers as I considered Sparrow's gift. Bloodbane was a magical herb that the Verdantia witch clan cultivated in the aftermath of the Chaos War, when the Nightforged had first been cursed with vampirism. It made a human's blood taste unpalatable, so that if a vampire were to smell it, he wouldn't be tempted to feed from them. When a witch ate it, it masked her magical scent, allowing her to pass as human. I'd used it many times when I'd gone on tracking missions in vampire territory, and vampires had never been able to detect my true nature when it was in my bloodstream.

"Why are you giving this to me?" I finally asked. It had to be worth a small fortune if it was banned in the empire.

"Because I want you to feel safe around me. Around us," he said, gesturing to the general area around him as if Lucius, Nyra, and Maximillian were here as well. "And also because you're going to need it when you go with Maximillian to the Summit."

I glared at him. "You still think I'm going to go? Even though Maximillian is out there right now—" I jabbed a finger in the direction of the administrative building—"schmoozing with Vladimir's Master-at-Arms, and Eliza is setting up a demonstration for him?"

"You make things sound so black and white," Sparrow scoffed. "As if all we have to do is flip a proverbial bird to the emperor, and everything will be just fine and dandy. He has a standing army of over one-hundred thousand, Kitty-Cat. And he controls the most powerful vampires in the realm. If we don't give him what he wants, he will crush us like the ants we are, and put someone else in charge who has little to no regard for human life."

"But there must be something you can do!" I cried, throwing up my hands. "Some way to sabotage the devices, at least, maybe rig the technology to malfunction once it's in Vladimir's hands. You can't just give them these weapons!"

"If Emperor Vladimir finds out that Eliza intentionally sabotaged these weapons," Sparrow said in a low voice, his cerulean eyes darkening with anger. "He will make her his slave and visit every single torture and degradation imaginable upon her. He will spend years killing her slowly, reveling in every agonizing scream and sob he rips from her throat. And then he will strip Maximillian of his viceroy privileges and install another inventor who knows how to keep his head down and do what he's told."

I swallowed back the bile that rose in my throat at the thought of Vladimir breaking Eliza that way. She was a passionate woman who clearly cared about her people. Of course I didn't want that to happen to her.

Sparrow's expression softened at the look on my face, and he sighed. "Come with me," he said. "I want to show you something."

"You're not going to tell me to hide in my room like Nyra did?" I asked.

Sparrow snorted. "That would be like telling the tides to stop turning," he said. "An exercise in futility. At least this way, you'll have proper adult supervision."

I rolled my eyes, but followed him into the common room, popping one of the bloodbane leaves in my mouth as I went. I cringed at the bitter, metallic tang on my tongue, but dutifully chewed it as Sparrow opened the secret bookcase passage. I followed him through it, Jinx on my heels, and we went down, down, down, well past the landing for the library, until I was reasonably sure we were underground.

"Where are we going?" I asked as we entered a sewer tunnel. Jinx yowled and hopped onto my shoulder for a ride, and I pinched my nose closed with my thumb and forefinger to ward off the stench.

"To pray," Sparrow called over his shoulder, picking his way along a narrow path beside the fetid water.

"To *what*?"

But Sparrow only picked up the pace, forcing me to lengthen my own stride. I cursed as I nearly tripped over several rocks, trying not to splash my boots with the sewer water. We walked for what must have been miles, the minutes ticking by into an hour, until Sparrow finally gripped the rungs of a ladder and hauled himself up toward a manhole cover.

My mouth dropped open as we emerged into a vast space filled with the skeletal remains of airships. Some were stripped down to bare frames, others still clinging to their former glory with patches of hull and faded insignias. Tall, ghostly structures of the hangars loomed overhead, their roofs gaping open in places where panels had fallen away, allowing shafts of moonlight to pierce the gloom. The ground was littered with parts and tools, and the silence was punctuated only by the distant echo of our footsteps on the metal flooring.

"What is this place?" I whispered, craning my neck so I could take it all in. I took in my first full breath since we'd entered the sewers, and the air I inhaled was thick with rust and old oil, a testament to the years of neglect.

"This is Lumina's airshipyard," Sparrow said as we moved away from the manhole cover and deeper into the yard. He pointed at one airship that seemed less ravaged by time and scavengers. Its hull was mostly intact, and its design was more elegant than the others, with sweeping lines and ornate decorations that were dulled and tarnished. "I brought you here to visit the temple."

I scowled, but before I could ask Sparrow what in the hells he was talking about, I saw them—figures slipping quietly between the shadows, making their way to this particular airship. They moved with a sense of purpose, glancing around cautiously as they approached. As we moved closer, I noticed a lone guard stationed discreetly near the entry ramp. Each person who approached him lowered their hood as they passed, and he nodded at them—a silent sentinel confirming their right to enter.

Sparrow paused beneath the shadows of one of the stripped-down airships, ducking beneath what was left of the prow.

"Inside that airship is the largest temple to Phaeros in Lumina," he told me. "Human slaves and thralls come here once a week to worship."

"What?" I scoured his face, looking for any sign that he was lying, then back toward the steady stream of people entering. Sure enough, each person who lowered their hood had rounded human ears. "Does Maximillian know about this place?"

"He does," Sparrow confirmed. "As well as all the smaller temples hidden around the city."

I frowned. "And he allows this?"

"He turns a blind eye, as do the majority of vampires in this city." Sparrow gave a small smile at the look of utter confusion on my face. "Emperor Vladimir ordered the main temple to be destroyed, as well as most of the statues of deities and historical figures, but that didn't stop the humans from finding ways to worship. If a temple's location is exposed, Maximillian has no choice but to destroy it, so I use my talents to make sure that any vampire who stumbles upon one and is inclined to report it is incentivized to... look the other way."

I scowled. "How do I know you're telling the truth about it?"

Sparrow shrugged. "Go and see for yourself."

I took a step forward, then hesitated. "You're not going to come?"

Sparrow flicked the tip of one of his ears. "Afraid the sun god wouldn't be too happy to see me, love. But you'll be just fine." He winked at me. "Say hi to Phaeros while you're in there for me."

"You—" I started, but he sped off, blasting me with a gust of wind in his wake. Scowling, I turned in the direction that he'd ran in, but there was little point in trying to catch up with him. He was absurdly fast, and I had no hope of keeping up with his supernatural speed in my current condition.

Sighing, I turned back to see what Jinx thought, only to see she'd left me behind and was more than halfway toward the airship. Exasperated—was absolutely *everyone* going to boss me around today?—I jogged after her, arriving at the base of the gangway just in time for her to jump into the arms of the guard, who looked startled but pleased.

"Sorry about her," I said as she wound her way around his shoulders. "She doesn't really have any concept of personal space."

The guard chuckled. He had salt and pepper hair and a wiry build, his olive face lined with age. Shadows dogged his gray eyes, no doubt from the stress of living under vampire rule, yet there was a cheerful spark in them. "No need to apologize," he said, reaching up to stroke a hand down Jinx's spine. "Cats, especially ones as well-fed as this one, are rare enough in this day and age that seeing one is always a happy occasion."

Jinx purred and rubbed herself against the man's cheek, then jumped down to follow me up the gangplank. Stepping into the interior of the airship, I was struck by the transformation it had undergone. The space, which I imagined had once been meant for passengers and cargo, had been hollowed out to create a humble yet heartfelt sanctuary. The walls were lined with wooden planks, salvaged from who knows where, giving the space a warm, if rustic, feel. Rows of roughly hewn benches lined the makeshift worship hall, with a path down the center leading to a simple altar. The altar itself was a large wooden crate, draped with a faded gold cloth. On it sat a few candles, their flames casting a soft, inviting glow, and hanging behind it was a tapestry of Phaeros.

Though I was a devotee of Hecate, the sight of the sun god, hand-painted with loving care, gripped me with unexpected emotion. The deity was depicted as a majestic figure, draped in robes that seemed to shimmer like the sun's rays, blending vibrant shades of gold, orange, and red. His eyes were painted as two brilliant stars, radiating wisdom and warmth. In one hand, he held a staff topped with a radiant sunburst, symbolizing his dominion over daylight and his role as a bringer of light. Around his feet, a variety of creatures, both mythical and real, basked in his nurturing glow, demonstrating his connection to all life. The borders of the tapestry were adorned with intricate patterns that mimicked the radiance of the sun and the vibrant life it sustains, all coming together to create a sense of divine presence and benevolent power.

"It's almost like looking at the sun, isn't it?" a nearby voice spoke. I glanced to my right to see a young woman gazing at the tapestry in wonder. Her pale brown eyes shone in the light from the aether crystals hanging overhead. She wore a factory worker's uniform; a simple blue jumpsuit with the logo of the aetheric power plant—a sleek, geometric design of an atom with three elliptical rings orbiting around a central, glowing aether crystal—stamped on her breast. Her uniform was open at the collar, and my mouth dropped open at the sight of a vicious-looking bite mark on her neck.

"Are you all right?" I gasped, before remembering that as a human, this might not be such a shocking sight to see amongst fellow slaves.

"Hmm? Oh." Her hand went self-consciously to the mark. "Yes, I'm fine. My overseer... he likes to snack sometimes." She laughed nervously, zipping up her jumpsuit to hide the bite mark. "In return, he lets me go home early so I can spend time with my mother." Some of the light in her eyes dimmed. "She's getting older now, and can't see too well, so she doesn't work at the factory anymore. I don't know how much time she has left, and I want to spend as much of it with her as I can."

"I'm sorry." My heart clenched with pity, and a sense of hopelessness washed over me. Could aetheric medicine not help this woman? I was certain that the elixir Eliza had given me would revitalize her... but she'd said it was in extremely limited supply, so I imagined the healers here weren't giving them out to human slaves. Especially not ones who were essentially dying of old age.

"It's all right." The woman smiled, some of the clouds in her eyes lifting as she gazed at the tapestry. "I'm just grateful I can provide, and also find the time to sneak away for worship." She glanced at me as the priest—an older man in patched yellow robes with sunbursts embroidered upon both breasts—ambled up to the front of the worship hall, an old leather book clutched in his hand. "You're new, aren't you? I've never seen you here before."

I nodded. "My friends told me about this place, but it's very... out of the way. It's the first time I've had an opportunity to attend service here."

The woman looked as if she wanted to say more, but the priest cleared his throat, drawing the attention of the small congregation. We all took our seats as he opened his book, holding it open in his weathered hands.

"Welcome, beloved Children of Phaeros." He smiled, his aged voice carrying a warmth that seemed to ripple through the room. "It gladdens my heart to see each of you here today, despite the dangers that come with making your pilgrimage here every week." His faded blue eyes passed over each of us, lingering on me for just a heartbeat before continuing on. "In these dark times, when our skies remain shadowed and vampires rule our city, it is more crucial than ever to show up for service, to wield the power of prayer in the hopes that our sun god will awaken from his slumber and arise once more to deliver us."

He opened the leather book, his fingers reverently turning the pages. "We may not understand why Phaeros has retreated from our world, but we must trust in his divine wisdom. He has not forsaken us; rather, he challenges us to find strength within ourselves, to kindle the flame of hope and faith in our hearts. It is through this faith, this unyielding devotion, that we will see his glorious light return to our skies."

I frowned, not sure I believed Phaeros's disappearance had anything to do with testing the faith of his followers. But the congregation seemed to take heart in the priest's words, pressing their hands to their hearts and bowing their heads in gratitude.

I sat silently as the priest delivered his sermon, his words echoing around the walls of the airship. He shared a tale from the Book of Dawn about a Marisian prince who found himself lost at sea after the ship he'd been traveling on had sunk during a terrible storm. Isolated and adrift in an endless expanse of water with only a makeshift raft to keep him from drowning, the prince's situation seemed hopeless. Yet despite his fear and uncertainty, the sailor maintained his faith in Phaeros, offering prayers and remaining vigilant as he navigated the lonely waters. His perseverance was rewarded when, three days later a giant sea turtle demigod called Moranga surfaced. He offered the prince a ride and brought him back to his people safely, who threw a massive celebration in Moranga and Phaeros's honor to celebrate the miracle.

"Just as the Marisian prince navigated the treacherous sea, so too must we navigate these times under the Eternal Night," the priest said, his voice rising with conviction. "Our situation, while challenging, is not cause for despair, but a call to maintain our faith and hope. Let this sailor's journey remind us we are not lost in these dark times. Instead, we have the opportunity to find our own guiding light — in our unwavering devotion to Phaeros and in the strength we draw from our community."

The priest then led the congregation in a collective prayer, and finished with a hymn honoring the sun god and his undying light. Afterward, he took up a spot just outside the exit, saying farewell to each congregation member as they passed through the doors. I noted Jinx was nowhere to be found—it seemed sermons weren't her thing—so I lingered at the back of the line, watching the priest as he smiled and shook hands and engaged in short yet personal exchanges with each and every person. It was clear that he cared for each member of his flock, enough to remember individual names and details of their lives. The sight filled me with a wave of homesickness, and I swallowed against a sudden lump in my throat as memories surfaced. My life amongst the Nocturne Clan hadn't been perfect, but I'd still found community amongst my fellow witches, something I was sorely missing.

It had been over fifty years since I performed a Twilight Communion—nearly half a century since I'd sang praises to Hecate, since I'd felt the rush of magic in my veins that came from opening my heart to the goddess and allowing her to fill me with her light. In less than a week, I would be performing it, but on my own, with no priestess to guide me or sisters to dance with.

I forced down the tears that threatened to rise before the priest could see them, and offered him a small smile as I approached. "Thank you for the sermon," I told him, and I meant it. "It's been a very long time since I attended worship, and I'm grateful."

He smiled back, the corners of his eyes crinkling. "It's been a long time since we had a daughter of the moon attend one of our sermons," he told me in a conspiratorial voice as he took my hand.

My mouth dropped open at the knowing twinkle in his eye, and I nearly snatched my hand back. "What do you—"

"Don't worry." He gave me a reassuring smile. "Allies of the rebel movement are always welcome in Phaeros's halls. Your secret is safe with me."

Allies of the rebel movement? It took me a second to realize he was talking about the human stronghold in Ferae, and hope surged in my chest. That had to mean there were witches there —and that those witches sometimes came here, to Lumina.

"I've been traveling for a long time, and I just arrived in Lumina," I confessed, trying to spin a cover story I hoped would sound plausible. "Have any other witches come here recently?"

"Not that I'm aware of," the priest said gravely. "But you may find more news of that nature at the Red Tavern."

"Thank you," I said, even though I had no clue what the Red Tavern was. I left before I could say something that would blow my cover, my mind whirling. Perhaps I could ask Sparrow if he knew about the Red Tavern—but what if it was a rebel hideout, and I inadvertently revealed it to him? Just because Maximillian and his cohort turned a blind eye to human worship of the sun god didn't mean they held the same attitude toward rebels. The last thing I wanted to do was compromise them.

The young woman I'd seen before was standing in the shadow of another airship, talking with two friends. She waved excitedly when she saw me, and I approached, a little nervous, but also excited. Perhaps making friends with the human slaves here would get me answers I wouldn't find in the sterile environment of the Tower compound.

"Friend!" she called, and her two companions turned to meet me. One was a factory worker like her, wearing a similar uniform, and the other appeared to be some kind of clerk, dressed in neat, slightly worn attire: a buttoned-up shirt, a vest that had seen better days, and trousers that were well-pressed but faded. They all smiled, though the clerk seemed wary as he took in my duster and the black outfit I wore beneath. I silently cursed Sparrow for not telling me where we were going—if I'd known I was going to a temple sermon, I would have worn clothes to blend in better with the human slaves.

"The sermon was wonderful, wasn't it?" she said in a rush,

her eyes sparkling. "My name is Hannah, by the way, and this is Simon and Raina. Guys, this is—" she paused, then blushed. "Actually, I didn't get your name, did I?"

"I was just about to ask you for yours." I smiled, charmed by her bubbly enthusiasm. It was a testament to the priest's sermons that she could maintain any kind of sunny disposition, given the dire circumstances she and her fellow humans lived with. "I'm Catherine."

"Nice to meet you, Catherine." Simon stuck out his hand, giving me a critical once over as I shook it. "Whose house do you work in? I've never seen you before."

"Simon!" Raina cried, a scandalized expression on her face. "Don't be so rude."

"What?" He shot back, his moss-green eyes sparking. "It's a fair question, given what she's wearing." He looked me over again, his lips thinning. "You look like the vampire hunters my grandmother used to tell stories about."

"And so what if she is one?" Hannah retorted, smacking Simon on the arm. "Imogen could have used the help of a slayer."

"What are you talking about?" My interest sharpened.

"Nothing," Simon said quickly, but Raina spoke right over him. "Our friend Imogen went missing a few months ago. She lives in the same tenement as I do, and one night she just didn't come home."

"We went to our local barrister," Hannah added, a bitter note in her voice, "but he did nothing. Just said she probably ran off to join the rebels in the east. But that's impossible. She never would have left without telling us!"

"Of course he didn't do anything," Simon scoffed. "All they care about is making sure the power plants and the blood banks and the weapons factory keep running. One human disappearing isn't worth their time."

"But it's not just one human," Raina said hotly. "There was also Mamie's brother—"

"Oi!" a gruff-looking man hissed. His threadbare coat flapped behind him as he stalked our way, looking like he was ready to box some ears. "Will you lot stop gossiping so loudly, and get a move on! If a patrol comes by and finds out we've been congregating here, they'll burn this whole place down!"

"Sorry!" Hannah squeaked. She grabbed me by the sleeve, and the four of us scurried off, heading for an opening in the wire fence. We clambered through it one by one and headed down a steep hill leading to a main road that would take us back into the city proper. I remembered from studying a map of Lumina that the airshipyard was located closer to the outskirts of the city—it was a good six-mile walk back to the Tower from here. No wonder it had taken so long to get here. Sparrow was a real bastard, leaving me here on my own like this. How did he know if I'd be able to get back?

"I'm sorry if I sound ignorant," I said in a low voice as we walked, passing rows of dilapidated homes and businesses that looked as though they'd once been part of thriving communities "But do you know about a place called The Red Tavern? I heard someone mention it as a possible hangout, and I thought it might be fun to check out."

I held my breath, hoping that my hunch about the place was right, and that I didn't just blow my cover. The three human slaves exchanged glances, and then Hannah slowly said, "I've heard of it, but I'm not sure it's the kind of place you want to frequent."

Simon snorted, gesturing to my outfit as we walked. "Are you kidding me? She looks like she'll fit right in." At my quizzical look, he said, "It's a gambling den, frequented by both humans and vampires."

"Humans *and* vampires?" I frowned. "But what do the humans gamble with?"

"Coin, if they're lucky to have it," Raina said with a shrug. "But in lieu of that, blood. A cover charge has to be paid at the door to enter, but you get a free drink, so it's worth it. It's the only place in the city where humans can get alcohol, so it's a popular establishment if you're willing to pay the price."

I bit back a curse. As slaves, humans didn't earn coin. As I understood it, some vampire masters deigned to give their humans an allowance, but that was a rarity, and they certainly didn't get enough to gamble with. Factory workers like Hannah and Raina didn't have an owner—they were property of the city, so there was no master to receive an allowance from.

It made complete sense for humans to use their blood as currency, but there was no way I could engage in that sort of trade. I didn't dare, not when the very scent of my blood would reveal my identity. I didn't think the proprietor would take kindly to me showing up with bloodbane in my veins either—one whiff, and he would probably throw me out on my ass.

But could I really afford to pass up the opportunity to learn more about the rebel movement, especially if it meant I could potentially connect with a fellow witch?

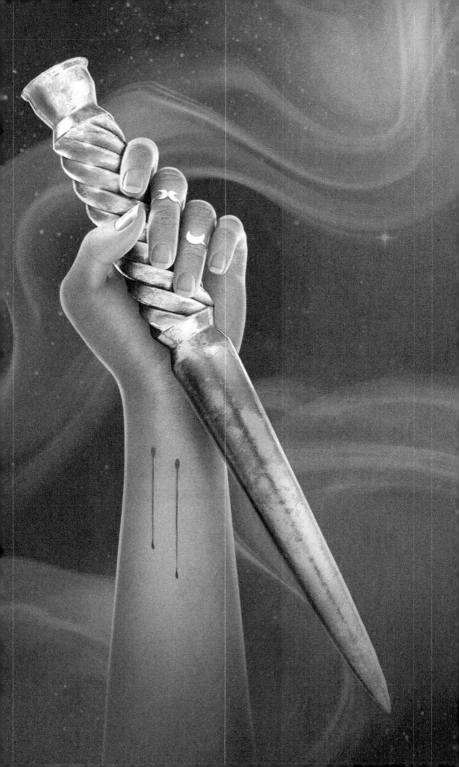

11

I saw the humans home to their tenement building—no way was I letting them walk alone, not after they'd told me one of their friends had gone missing—then returned to the Tower. If Sparrow thought my little outing would soften my attitude toward Maximillian, he was mistaken. I had a bone to pick with the vampire lord, and I wasn't going to let him off the hook just because he was slightly less awful than his compatriots.

The guards outside the administrative building exchanged apprehensive glances, but did nothing to stop me as I strode through the door and marched up to the reception desk. "Is Lord Starclaw here?" I demanded.

The receptionist—a human slave—startled, her glasses nearly slipping off her nose. "I believe so, but he isn't expecting any visitors. Do you have an appointment?"

"It's urgent," I said, ignoring her question. "Where can I find his office?"

"It's on the third floor, at the end of the main corridor, but—"

A clawed hand seized my upper arm, spinning me around before the receptionist could finish speaking. "What in all the hells are you doing here?" Nyra hissed, her hazel eyes spitting fire. "I told you to stay out of sight!"

"Let go of me!" I protested as she dragged me out of the building and back toward the Central Keep. "I'm *not* going to sit quietly in my room just because some scary vampire is in town." Maximillian had promised me his protection—he could find a way to deliver on that promise *without* trapping me inside the tower. If this commandant was here in order to bring a powerful weapon back to the military that could be used against my people with devastating consequences, then I'd be damned if I was going to sit by and do nothing about it.

"Your hotheaded behavior is going to get us all killed," Nyra seethed. "Just because Lord Starclaw gave you free rein doesn't mean you can traipse about doing whatever you like. If the Commandant sees you—"

Nyra choked off her words as Maximillian rode through the front gates on a sleek blue and silver aethersteed. A second vampire rode at his side astride a great black beast, and a shiver crawled across my spine at the sight of him. He was a wiry male with close-cropped black hair, dressed in a dark, tailored military uniform with decorative red epaulets on the shoulders and a cluster of medals and badges on his right breast. His nearly translucent skin and the red glow of his eyes marked him as a member of Sanguis Noctis—the vampire house that wielded blood magic. They were the most savage and bloodthirsty of the four houses, and the ones that I had hunted down most often for violating the Accords by unlawfully preying on humans and witches.

Nyra released me just as both vampires turned our way, folding her hands neatly in front of her. "Welcome back, Sire, Commandant," she said in a sedate voice as they approached, all traces of her frantic anger gone. "I trust your visit to the compound went well?"

"I'd like to think so," Maximillian said as he and the commandant drew their horses to a stop in front of us. He swung a long leg over the side of his aethersteed as he dismounted, then handed off his reins to the stable boy that had rushed over to meet them. "What do you think, Vinicius?"

His tone was mild, but his gaze flickered as he caught my eye, and I could see the tension radiating from his body. Maximillian would never say it, but he was just as displeased as Nyra that I was in the commandant's presence. A sense of unease trickled down my spine— was this military bureaucrat really such a threat?

"It was promising," Vinicus agreed as he turned his horse over to the stable boy as well. "The prototype your inventor presented is clever, and I'm looking forward to seeing it in action tomorrow."

In action? I nearly blurted aloud, before remembering I was supposed to be a submissive little thrall who didn't speak unless her betters spoke to her first. I bit down on my tongue to stop the flood of questions that sprang into my mind—were they going to do a demonstration? Where? And on what?

"Yes, I am very much looking forward to the demonstration as well," Nyra said, giving the commandant a winning smile. "Eliza and I have been working round the clock to prepare everything for you."

"I would expect nothing less." His gaze flicked over to me, and I fought against the urge to reach for a weapon. "And who is this beautiful little morsel?" he asked, his smile growing predatory.

"Her name is Catherine," Maximillian said. He stepped toward me, and the frenetic energy pumping through my veins calmed as he put his body between me and the commandant. "She is my personal thrall."

The possessive note in his voice was clear as the cloudless

dark sky above us, and I could have sworn that Maximillian's scent grew stronger, as if he were trying to mark me with it, to claim me as his property. Another shiver ran down my spine, but this one wasn't wholly unwelcome, and I had to stop myself from inhaling a deep lungful of his scent.

Why in all the hells did I enjoy smelling him so much?

Vinicius arched an eyebrow. "Your personal thrall?" he asked. "I thought you didn't keep food slaves around."

"Oh, she's not just for food," Maximillian purred. He brushed a lock of my hair aside so he could stroke his thumb along the side of my neck, and my knees nearly knocked together as his touch sent a bolt of need straight to my core. Maximillian's eyes flared in response, and unlike the commandant, the predatory hunger in his face didn't frighten me the way it should have. Instead, my own hunger surged in response, filling me with the urge to tilt my head back, to offer my neck willingly.

What in Hecate's name was wrong with me?

"I see." Vinicius smirked. "It's a relief to see you indulge. I was half-worried you were becoming a sympathizer." He ran his tongue over his teeth as he studied me, teasing the point of his incisor. It was clear his interest in me had not waned—if anything, it appeared to have sharpened even more. "Will she be joining us for dinner?"

"Perhaps some other time." Maximillian glanced over at Nyra, who was watching the exchange with pursed lips. "Nyra, would you show Vinicius to my office, please? I will join you both shortly."

"Of course." She bowed her head, then led Vinicius away. The moment the vampire turned his back, Maximillian whisked me inside the Central Keep and into the closest chamber, which happened to be the armory. Sunsteel armor and swords glittered all around us as he shut the door behind us, and I took advantage of the opportunity to back away, putting some much-needed distance between us.

"It would appear that you've caught the commandant's attention, Kitten," Maximillian said, turning to face me. There was an edge to his normally soft voice, and for the first time, there were lines of anger in his sharp face, anger that was directed at *me*. "Was that your intention when you ignored Nyra's order to remain out of sight?"

"It's not my fault!" I protested, heat rising in my cheeks. A hot surge of embarrassment rushed down the back of my neck, and I forced myself to hold Maximillian's gaze even as I wanted to kick myself. Before I'd been imprisoned, I'd never allowed my emotions to lead me around like this, but my constant need to be free, to avoid feeling caged at all costs, was crowding out my common sense. "Sparrow took me to attend worship at a Phaeros temple, and I got so distracted by everything I saw—"

"Sparrow did *what*?" Maximillian hissed. His fangs snapped down, and he began to pace, looking as though he were about to sprint from the room so he could find the spymaster and strangle him. "I told him he was not to go near you again after—"

"Stop that."

Maximillian stilled as I grabbed his arm, forcing him to a halt. "Stop what?" he asked, his eyes flashing.

"Stop acting like an overbearing, protective nanny dog," I snapped. "Contrary to the picture you painted for the commandant, you do *not* own me, and I don't need to be kept in a glass cage. Sparrow brought me bloodbane and an apology for what happened last night, then took me to the temple to try to convince me that human life isn't so terrible here and that I should help you."

"I see." Some of the anger cleared from Maximillian's face, replaced by a thoughtful look. "Did it work?"

I snorted. "Maybe. Until I remembered that you're about to hand a powerful weapon over to that monster I just met in the courtyard so he can use it to kill witches."

Maximillian sighed. "Is that why you were out in the court-yard? You wanted to convince me to destroy the prototype, or perhaps shove it up Vinicius's—"

"No," I said quickly. "Although if you did that, I would defi-nitely help you."

His gaze shuttered. "If you asked for anything else, I would gladly give it to you, Kitten. But I can't."

"Why not?" I dropped his arm and took a step away, feeling the sting of his rejection. "You don't even have to destroy the prototype—just delay it, or something! I don't understand why you have to do this."

"Vladimir has spies everywhere, including the factories," Maximillian said, lines of frustration bracketing his mouth. "I can't risk such an obvious betrayal. Besides, the technology involved has the potential for other uses. I won't ask Eliza to destroy it, not after all the hard work she's put into it."

"Wait," I said as he turned away. "I'll do as you ask and stay out of sight. But I need a favor."

"What is it?" he asked, a wary note in his voice.

I gave him a grim smile. "The case files from a certain barris-ter's office."

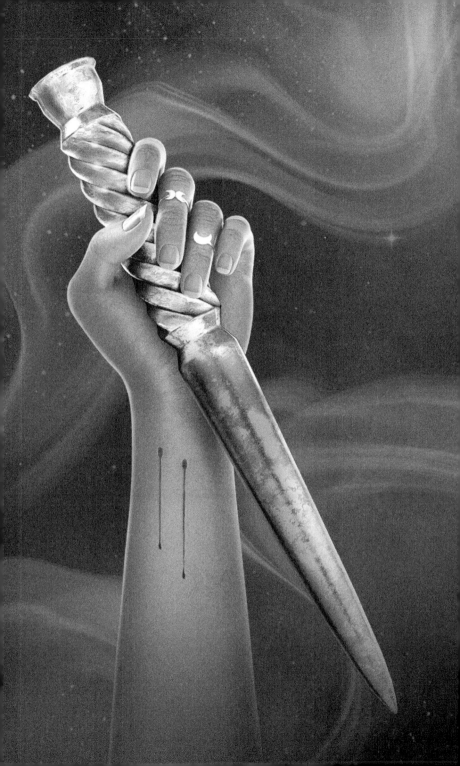

12

"Phaeros's beard," Eliza exclaimed as she walked into the common room. "What in all the hells is this mess?"

I looked up from where I sat on one of the couches, surrounded by stacks of boxes. Case files and notes were spread out on the coffee table before me, along with leftover crumbs from the dinner I'd hastily scarfed while reading.

"Oh, good, you're back." I set down the file in my hand. "I've been waiting for you."

"Have you now?" Eliza snatched a cookie from the plate on the side table as she threw herself into the armchair on my left, and I noticed she looked a little haggard. Purplish shadows dogged her eyes from lack of sleep, an oil smudge marred her right cheekbone, and her short, blonde curls were wild with frizz, as though she'd raked her fingers repeatedly through them. "I'm sorry, but I don't really have time to be your personal tour guide now that the commandant is breathing down my neck. I'm basically his slave for the next few days until this prototype is finalized."

forcing myself not to take up the subject of the prototype cannon. "I just need you to be my date."

"A date?" Eliza's eyes flashed with interest. "Where to?"

"The Red Tavern."

Her eyebrows flew up, disappearing beneath her hairline. "You want me to take you to a *gambling den?*"

"Keep your voice down," I hissed, leaning in. I didn't think Nyra or any of the others were here, but vampires had very sharp ears, and you never knew when one might be listening. "I'm investigating a disappearance, and I've heard that the Red Tavern is a good place to find information on that sort of thing." I decided not to mention that I was also looking for any rebel witches that might be lying low in the city. I liked Eliza, but I wasn't sure if I could trust her with that kind of information.

The aetherion woman's eyes narrowed as she glanced at the files. "Is that what this is about? You're playing detective?"

"I'm not 'playing'." I folded my arms across my chest, mildly offended. "I used to do a lot of investigative work as a vampire hunter."

"Right." Eliza picked up the file I'd been reading, her green eyes flickering as she scanned it. "A missing person's case?"

"About thirty of them." The anger that had simmered inside my chest for the better part of an hour began to bubble again, and I sucked in a deep breath through my nose. "All within the last year. And this is just from one barrister's office." There were six—I'd asked.

Eliza blew out a breath. "I hate to break it to you, Kitana, but people go missing all the time in Lumina. Many are slaves who run east to join the rebel movement."

"That's what the barrister said, too," I told her, "but Hannah believes that if her friend was planning to join the rebels, she would have told them before she left." I scooped a hand through my hair as I considered the spread of files. "The inspector barely even bothered to file incident reports. There's almost no information here to go off—"

"Which means the case files are fairly useless," Eliza finished for me.

We sat in silence for a long minute while I chewed on my frustration. I had so badly wanted to tug on the thread Hannah had presented to me, but in truth it would take far too long to track down all these families and piece together any sort of pattern that would reveal if any of these disappearances had a connection. In all likelihood, Imogen had been preyed upon by a hungry vampire who'd flaunted the rules—an incident that was bound to reoccur no matter how strictly Maximillian tried to enforce his utopian regulations.

I was grasping at straws because I needed something, *anything*, to do that would make me feel like I was making a difference in these humans' lives. And also because when I was doing investigative work like this, I could almost pretend I was still my old self.

"I still want to go to the Red Tavern," I said stubbornly. "You don't even have to come with me—just tell me how to get a few vials of human blood, and where the place is, and I'll go on my own." It was probably better that she didn't come, honestly—if any rebels were there and they recognized her, they'd be a lot less likely to talk to me.

"Don't be stupid," Eliza said. "Of course I'm going with you. The last thing I need is for you to piss off the wrong vampire and start a brawl in one of the most questionable establishments in Lumina." She polished off another cookie, then brushed her pants clean and stood up. "Now, if there isn't anything else, I need to go to sleep. The demonstration is tomorrow, and I need to be up early."

"What time does it start?" I asked, trying to sound as casual as possible.

"Eleven a.m." Her eyes narrowed. "Why? You're not thinking of interfering, are you?"

"I wouldn't dare," I said sweetly. "I just wanted to know."

Eliza rolled her eyes, then left me to my work. But when I opened Imogen's case file, it wasn't the missing human slave I was thinking of.

It was Vinicius.

"Going somewhere?"

Lucius's voice rumbled from behind me as I reached for the fake volume that would trigger the sliding mechanism in the bookcase. Muffling a curse, I grabbed the title right next to it, then spun around to see him standing just a few feet away from me.

"Not at all," I said, even as my heart pounded in my chest. How in Hecate's name had I not noticed him enter the room? I had stayed up nearly the entire night poring over those case files, hoping to find some connection—clearly the long hours had dulled my senses. "I was just looking for something to read, since I'm not allowed to go anywhere."

Jinx—who had been at my heels—darted across the room and took a running leap into Lucius's arms. He caught her deftly and hoisted her onto his shoulder, then folded his arms and regarded me with a stern look. He really was a massive male—taller than Maximillian, and nearly twice as wide. His biceps had to be the size of my head, and his tree-trunk thighs were probably close to the width of my waist span. If that weren't bad enough, he also had telekinetic magic, though I hadn't seen him use it again since he'd put me to sleep and taken me from my prison.

There was absolutely no way I was getting past him, not without my magic.

"The Arcane Dynamics of Aetheric Engineering: Principles and Applications?" he arched an eyebrow, his amber eyes flickering over the title in my hand. "You're a terrible liar, Kitana."

"Well, at least someone around here calls me by my actual name." I huffed in exasperation. "Come on, Lucius. You can't blame me for wanting to get a look at the prototype."

"No, I can't," he agreed. "I would do the same in your position. Which is why I've come to escort you myself."

"You have?"

"Yes." Jinx butted her head against Lucius's jaw, and he reached up with one hand to rub her ears, never taking his eyes off my face. "Lord Starclaw suggested that allowing you to attend under controlled supervision is a better alternative than you potentially crashing the demonstration and trying to sabotage the prototype. And although I have better things to do than be your personal chauffeur, I'm inclined to agree."

"Well, there's no need to sound so snippy," I said, a little put out. I didn't really want a babysitter, but now that Lucius had caught me, I didn't have a choice in the matter. Even if I slipped him, Maximillian's guards had probably been told to remain on high alert in case I did try to sneak in on my own.

"Change out of those clothes and into something nondescript, then meet me in the courtyard." Lucius ordered. "You have five minutes, or I'm locking you in a closet and posting a battalion of guards outside the door."

He strode out of the room without a backward glance, Jinx still perched on his shoulder. *Traitor,* I seethed quietly at her, but did as I was told, stalking back to my room to trade my duster, blouse, and trousers for a simple blue dress and cloak. I kept my armored corset on underneath the dress—no way was I going near the commandant without some kind of protection—and slipped two stakes into my pockets and one into my boot, then hurried down to the courtyard to meet Lucius.

The vampire warrior was waiting for me astride a huge bronze aethersteed that pawed nervously at the cobblestones, eager to be off. My excitement at the thought of finally getting to ride one dimmed when he offered a dinner-plate sized hand to haul me up.

"I don't get to ride my own?"

"I don't trust you not to run off by yourself." He curled his fingers in a come-hither motion. "Now hurry up."

Scowling, I placed my hand in his, and he hoisted me up in front of him in one fluid motion. I hissed as my ass landed hard in the saddle, and I barely had time to get situated before he tightened his thighs against the aethersteed's flanks, urging it forward.

I grabbed the pommel as the destrier launched into a brisk trot, heading for the drawbridge. The guards lowered the gate, and as soon as we cleared the main thoroughfare, Lucius urged his steed into a canter.

My initial displeasure at being forced to share a mount with Lucius faded as the aethersteed surged beneath me. Its mechanized muscles moved with a smoothness that felt alien compared to the warm, heaving flanks of a real horse, and the vibration of its aetheric core was a constant buzz against my inner thighs. Yet I could still feel the spirit of the beast within as it carved a path through the streets, taking less-traveled roads so it could indulge in some of the speed it was capable of.

"Wait a minute," I called over my shoulder as we passed out of the tech district. "Aren't we going to the weapons facility?"

"No." Lucius's deep voice vibrated from his chest and into my back. The scents of wood smoke and fragrant resin overlaid his natural vampire scent, and I had to admit I didn't hate it. "The commandant wanted a full-scale demonstration, and the weapons facility doesn't have the space for that. We're using the airshipyard."

"What?" My stomach dropped, the priest and his congregation flashing through my mind. "But the humans—"

"Will be completely fine," Lucius said gruffly. "I've combed every ship and evacuated anyone who isn't supposed to be there. We've chosen a target that no one will object to destroying."

I let a silent breath of relief. Of course, Maximillian would have asked Lucius to take precautions. He wasn't a cruel person. Still, I found myself gripping the pommel tighter, a sense of urgency coming over me. The aethersteed seemed to sense my emotion—it sped up into a gallop, and Lucius cursed under his breath as it swerved, narrowly missing a cart that someone had left parked in the middle of the street.

We arrived at the airshipyard, and Lucius pulled his steed to a halt just inside the gates, where a pair of guards waited. "Take her," he ordered, handing me down like I was a toddler. "She may watch, but do not let her out of your sight, and do not allow her to come within one hundred yards of the cannon."

"Yes, sir," the guards said. I gritted my teeth as Lucius trotted off without a backward glance, heading toward the middle of the yard where a small group of vampires waited. I could just make out the storm grey shine of Maximillian's hair, and Eliza's curly blonde mop as she fiddled with a large dial.

"Come this way, Miss," one of the guards said. They led me to one of the skeletal aetherships to the left of the gathering, far enough away that I wouldn't be recognized by anyone—especially with the hood of my cloak up—but close enough I had a clear view of the unfolding spectacle.

And what a spectacle it was.

"Order!" Eliza called, her voice magnified by some kind of

aetheric device glowing at her throat. She stood in the center of the airshipyard next to a monstrous amalgamation of sunsteel and glowing aether and moonstone crystals that had to be the cannon. It was twice as big as Lucius, its barrel large enough for an ordinary-sized man to walk through, and it emitted a faint aura I could sense even from this distance. A semi-circle of vampires clustered around it—Maximillian, Vinicius, Lucius, Nyra, and Sparrow, along with a few others who looked to be the commandant's aides.

But the real audience lay outside the airship, just beyond the chain-link fences. Vampire citizens pressed up along one end of the fence, humans on another, the two races segregated by the pole placed at the corner of the perimeter. The vampires were clearly excited, almost restless, while the humans looked on with faces drawn with apprehension. My stomach tightened as I noticed more than a few faces fixed on the hidden temple, and I wondered if Hannah and her friends were in the crowd. I sent a silent prayer to Hecate that the three of them were safe.

Eliza waited until the crowd fell silent before speaking again. "Ladies and gentlemen," she called, addressing the crowd with a professional demeanor that showed nothing of her spunky personality, "Today we are demonstrating a significant advancement in our defense capabilities," she stated, indicating the aether cannon beside her. "This new iteration of the aether cannon that we have been working on for the past year harnesses both lunar and aetheric energy, a combination that yields greater efficiency and a more powerful output than earlier models."

Vinicius seemed pleased as he listened to Eliza's speech, and the vampires crowded against the fence to get a better look at the cannon. But though Eliza remained coolly professional, I could have sworn there was an undercurrent of apprehension in her voice as she pointed toward a rickety airship roughly four hundred yards away. "The target for today's test," she said, then stepped aside.

A sense of expectation hung in the air as all eyes focused on the cannon and its target. Maximillian turned to Vinicius, extending an arm in invitation. "Would you like to do the honors, Commandant?" he asked politely.

"I would," the commandant said. The relish in his tone was unmistakable, and I gripped the deck railing as I watched him approach the cannon. Stepping onto the platform, he adjusted the control panel with a deftness that told me he was already familiar with the device's workings. The air thickened with anticipation as his hand hovered over the glowing launch button, and we all waited for him to discharge the cannon.

Without warning, the vampire gripped the steering handles of the platform and swung it around, aiming it directly at the hidden temple. Lucius and Maximillian startled, but before they could do anything to stop him, the commandant slapped his hand against the button.

A blinding beam of violet light erupted from the cannon, hurtling across the yard and striking the airship. The impact was immediate and explosive, the structure erupting into flames that sent a wave of shock and disbelief through the crowd. The vampires hissed, recoiling from the surge of heat and light, and the humans screamed in anguish.

I vaulted over the railing, my vision hazed red with rage as I zeroed in on the commandant. I didn't care who he was—I was going to end him for what he had done. Memories of the inside of the temple tore at me—the mismatched furnishings, the lovingly hand-painted art and tapestries, all gathered painstakingly by humans who had nothing other than the faith burning in their hearts. But the guards caught up to me halfway, and they grabbed me by both arms, hauling me into the shadows behind a stack of crates.

"Miss, stop!" one of them said as I struggled to free myself. I slashed out at him with one of my stakes, and he knocked the weapon out of my hands. "It's too late! There's nothing you can do."

The earnestness in the guard's voice reached me through my fury, and I went still as I realized he was right. Acrid smoke billowed in the surrounding air, and the sound of the human slaves sobbing was muffled by the crackle of flames as they devoured what had once been a sacred place for them.

"You can let me go," I muttered, my shoulders slumping. "I won't fight."

The guards reluctantly released me, and I peered around the crates to see Vinicius facing Maximillian, offering the vampire lord a bemused smile. "It seems my actions have caused some consternation amongst the slaves," he said, speaking over the wails from the human crowd. "Was there something special about that airship?"

"Not at all." Maximillian's face was a cool, expressionless mask, but there was a dangerous glint in his eyes. "Though I would like to know why you chose to recklessly endanger everyone by changing the trajectory of the cannon at the last minute. We chose that airship because we knew there were no components inside that would react with the cannon's energy discharge. The one you fired was not inspected."

"My apologies," Vinicius said, though he didn't sound in the least bit sorry. There was a smug, almost triumphant look on his face as he swept his red gaze across the humans. "Sometimes I forget how frail humans can be. It won't happen again."

A cry of rage rent the air, and the vampires turned to see a small group of humans charge through a hole in the fence. The firelight from the burning airship flickered across their tear-streaked faces, and horror rose in my chest as I saw the gruff, middle-aged man who'd scolded us outside the temple yesterday leading the charge, along with several others from the congregation.

"Phaeros smite you, vampire scum!" he screamed, raising a short sword high over his head. The others had various weapons as well, and I realized that they'd come armed, prepared for a confrontation. Had they known this was going to happen? Or was there some other reason they'd shown up armed? My heart surged in my throat, and I leaped over the crates before my guards could stop me, unable to stop myself from rushing to the humans' aid.

The commandant let out a sinister chuckle, drawing a clawed finger across the center of his left palm. "Your sun god is dead, human," he said, a ribbon of blood rippling from the center of his hand to form a crimson blade that acted an extension of his arm. "And so are you."

He surged forward to meet the humans, and I let a stake fly from my hand—or at least, I tried to. A ripple of power cut through the air, and my stake flew sideways, then clattered to the ground. In the next second, I was frozen in mid-air—and so was everyone else.

"Stand down, Commandant," Maximillian ordered, his voice vibrating with command. Like me, Vinicius was frozen in midair, his pose almost comical—legs stretched out at odd angles off the ground, his sword arm flung wide in mid-swing. The humans were also caught in various action poses, their eyes bulging out of their skulls as they struggled against the invisible spider's web they'd been caught in.

I gaped at Maximillian, too astonished to be angry. It was one thing to immobilize me, even at a distance like this. But to be able to hold a dozen or so people with only a thought... just how powerful *was* this vampire lord?

Vinicius snarled, and the blood sword in his hand transformed into a long, snaking whip. "You dare come between me and my rightful prey?" he accused, his eyes blazing.

"This is *my territory*," Maximillian said, his voice icier than I'd ever heard it. "You do *not* get to decide which humans are prey and which aren't. Not here."

"They were about to attack me!"

"And they will be punished by *me*, the viceroy of this city, according to law," Maximillian said sharply. "Not by you. Now put the whip away, Commandant, or I will report this to the emperor."

The commandant let out a scathing laugh even as the whip dissipated into a blood red mist between his fingers. "You're going to report this incident?" he sneered. "Perhaps it's you who should be worrying about whether *I* report this to the emperor."

"And what will you tell him, exactly?" Maximillian asked, arching his eyebrow. "That you allowed the base, savage nature of your house to get the better of you, and lost control of yourself in front of thousands of witnesses?"

"No." Vinicius took a step forward as Maximillian released his hold on the vampire soldier—but only him. The rest of us were still trapped in the stranglehold of the vampire lord's magic. "But I will tell him how lenient you are with these humans, how you allow them to worship enemy gods and protect them at the expense of your own." He flung a hand toward the smoldering ruin of the airship. "Do you really think I believe you don't know what was inside there?"

"What I believe," Maximillian said softly, moving closer until he and the other vampire were nearly nose to nose. "Is that your cushy bureaucratic position has filled your ego with a false sense of confidence, Commandant. Despite your rank and title, you are still a soldier, while I am the son of a high lord. Do not believe for one second that if you test me, I will not separate your head from your shoulders, consequences be damned."

"I'd like to see you try." The commandant smirked, then spun on his heel, his cloak billowing out behind him. Maximillian watched, stone-faced, as the vampire officer stalked toward the exit, his aides hurrying after him. The commandant never noticed me hovering just a few yards away, jaw clenched, my entire body quivering with pent-up rage.

Maximillian finally released me from his hold, and I stumbled, trying to get my bearings. The blood lust surging in my veins was so intense, my teeth ached.

I had half a mind to go after Vinicius, but Eliza, who had watched the entire exchange unfold with a shell-shocked expression on her face, collapsed to her knees. No one seemed to have noticed—Lucius, Sparrow, and the guards were busy rounding up the insurgents and doing crowd control, Maximillian was coordinating with the fire brigade that had arrived to put out the flames, and Nyra was off to the side with the other administrators and engineers, snapping rapid-fire orders at them.

"Eliza!" I rushed over to where she knelt and dropped to my knees next to her. "Are you hurt?"

"N-No. I... he..." Her chest heaved as she stuttered, unable to tear her eyes away from the burning airship. "This is my fault," she said, her horrified whisper barely audible over the chaotic din.

"No, it's not," I said fiercely. I gripped her shaking shoulders, trying to get her to face me. "You are not responsible for what that monster did."

"B-but I created the weapon." She turned her tear-streaked face toward me, and my heart ached at the stricken look on her face. "You were r-right, Kitana. I'm just as bad as the emperor. It should be m-me being thrown in those cells tonight, not t-them."

I glanced over the top of Eliza's head at the insurgents, who were being loaded into a prison wagon in chains. Their heads were bowed, but I could see the anger and resentment on their faces as they were herded together, and the defiance in their tight shoulders. What was going to happen to them? Would Maximillian put them to death, simply for lashing out against their oppressors?

As if summoned by my very thoughts, the vampire lord appeared, his tall form casting a shadow across us. I glanced at Maximillian as he knelt in front of her, blocking her view of the airship while he wrapped a cloak around her shoulders. Some of the icy anger in his face was still evident, but his expression had softened at the sight of his thrall in such obvious distress. She leaned into him immediately, like a distraught child seeking comfort, and he scooped her into his arms, tucking her face against his chest.

The sight of him cradling her melted some of my ire, and I swallowed against a swell of emotion in my throat.

"Come," Maximillian said as he rose. He didn't seem to care what the onlookers thought as he strode across the airshipyard with Eliza in his arms. I glanced back at the prison wagon one last time, then hurried after Maximillian, questions burning on my tongue.

A carriage painted in House Psychoros's colors was waiting just outside the gates, the door held open by a human driver. Maximillian climbed in and settled Eliza onto one end of the velvet-upholstered bench, then sat down next to her. I took the seat across from him as the footman shut the door, and a few moments later, the carriage was in motion.

"You don't need to fuss over me," Eliza grumbled as Maximillian tucked the cloak a little tighter around her. "I'm not a child anymore."

"Maybe so," Maximillian agreed, "but to me you'll always be the brave orphan girl who tried to sneak into the Tower to kill me when she was only fifteen years old. So forgive me for indulging in my fatherly affection for just a moment."

I tilted my head, surprised at this bit of information. "You took her in after she tried to kill you?"

Eliza nodded, sniffing. "It was a year after the vampires took the city. My parents were killed during the war, and I wanted to make him pay. But the guards caught me before I could make it inside the Central Keep."

I waited for her to say more, but she fell silent, a faraway look in her eyes as her gaze turned to the window. "I should have found someplace else to do the demonstration," she said woodenly, clenching her hands in her lap. "Should have known the commandant might try to pull something like that."

"No," Maximillian said. "It was I who should have anticipated it." A muscle ticked in his jaw. "I'm well-aware of Vinicius's penchant for both brutality and fanfare. I just never thought he would dare to challenge me so openly."

"What are you going to do about him?" I demanded. "He clearly knew about the temple, and that you turn a blind eye to illegal human activities. He's a threat to you."

"There is nothing I can do about him," Maximillian said baldly. "The commandant may have crossed a line, but he knows that if I were to retaliate, it would call my loyalty to the emperor into question. And that is not something I can afford."

Frustration ballooned inside me at his words, even though I knew he was right. "Well, what about the humans?" I demanded. "Are you really going to punish them in accordance with the law?" I'd read up on the laws after watching that poor human servant get whipped in the street—such a fate would be a blessing for this bunch. Insurrection and attempted murder against a vampire was punishable by death, not a whipping. The more heinous the infraction, the more horrific the execution method.

Maximillian's gaze hardened, but Eliza lunged across the seat and clutched at his wrist. "Please, Max," she said, a desperate look in her eyes. "You can't."

He hesitated. "They've left me little choice. Not after such a public violation."

"Give them another sentence," she begged. "Hard labor, or prison time. But don't kill them. Please."

He met my gaze over the top of her head, and the troubled look in his eyes stirred something within me. For the first time, I began to feel for Maximillian's predicament—struggling to protect the humans under his purview while enforcing the laws he was bound by.

"I'll consider it," he finally said, but the bleak look in his eyes didn't give me much hope.

Those humans were as good as dead.

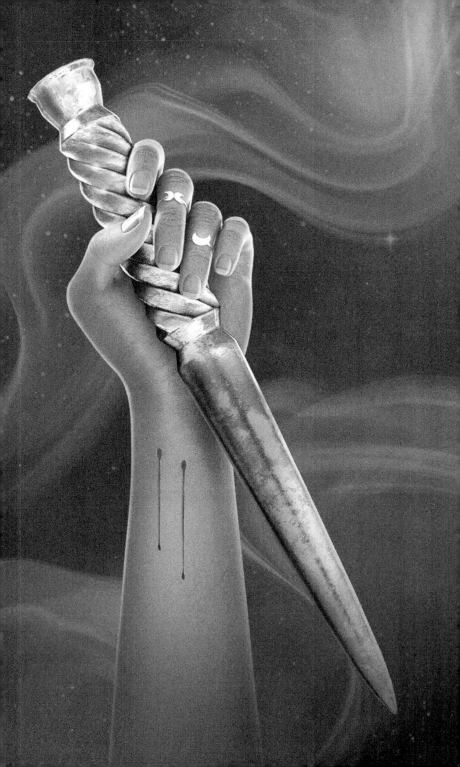

13

"Are you ready for this, Jinx?"

My shadow familiar meowed softly in answer as the two of us stood in the shadow of an alleyway, staring at the building across the street. Aged brick, darkened with time and soot, made up the exterior, with heavy wooden beams criss-crossing at intervals. Large, wrought-metal lanterns flanked the entrance, their glow casting ominous shadows across the tavern's front. A hand-painted red sign hung above it, swinging slightly in the breeze, the words "The Red Tavern" painted across it in flowing script.

"You're sure?" I asked as I rolled a vial of blood between my fingers. "I need you to be my eyes and ears in there tonight. You're the only one I trust."

Jinx purred and butted her head against my calf, assuring me she wasn't going to up and vanish. Satisfied, I scooped her up in my arms, where she promptly dissolved into a puff of shadow that disappeared into one of my pockets. I could feel the weight of her diaphanous presence, soft and smoky and reassuring, as I stepped out of the alleyway and approached the tavern.

Eliza was so distraught after the events at the shipyard

yesterday that I hadn't asked her to accompany me. I didn't think she even remembered agreeing to go. Besides, all I'd needed was the tavern's location, which she had given me, and the human blood, which had been easy enough to procure from the Tower's stores. Maximillian and his cohort always had a supply on hand, provided by the human servants in lieu of drinking directly from the vein. "It's more humane, and more convenient," Nyra had said when I'd asked her about it.

I approached the brutish-looking vampire bouncer standing by the heavy wooden door, who was large enough to give Lucius a run for his money. He wore an ill-fitting suit that strained against his broad shoulders, and looked like he swallowed humans whole for breakfast.

"Good evening," I said in what I hoped was a pleasant tone.

"Payment," he grunted in a deep voice, not bothering to return my greeting. I placed the vial of blood—one of five I'd brought with me—into his meaty palm, and he deftly popped the cork, then took a deep whiff. The scent must have satisfied him, because he replaced the stopper, then opened the door and waved me inside.

I stepped through the doorway and found myself in what could only be described as a den of iniquity. A haze of pipe smoke hung in the air along with the scents of sweat, blood, and alcohol, and the main room was packed to bursting, the round tables filled with vampires and humans alike as they engaged in intense card games or games of chance. Women wearing low-cut dresses that exposed their necks and cleavage wove between the tables, bringing glasses of blood and alcohol to the waiting patrons, or in some cases, draping themselves in a vampire's lap and offering their own necks. I glimpsed one of them leading a particularly amorous vampire up the staircase along the back wall of the room, who kept pawing at her skirts, and figured there were upstairs rooms for rent by the hour for customers who wanted more than just a swallow of blood.

"Yes!" a scrawny human crowed, leaping up from his chair and punching a fist in the air. He slapped his cards down on the table to reveal a winning hand, then reached for the pile of coins and blood vials in the center. The other players at the table grumbled good-naturedly, but one of the vampires snarled, baring his fangs as the human attempted to scrape his winnings over to his side of the table.

A bouncer was at the vampire's side in an instant, one hand coming down hard on his shoulder. "Is there a problem?" he asked, a sinister threat in his tone.

The vampire froze, then turned his head to look up at the bouncer. Like the one outside, he was a massive male who looked fully capable of crushing the smaller vampire's head between his hands. He probably didn't even need both hands—one was more than enough.

"No," he said. There was a hint of resentment in his tone, but his fear was stronger. "No problem at all."

"Good." The bouncer released his shoulder. "I'll be watching."

His warning hung in the air as he returned to his post against one of the walls. Hannah had mentioned that humans and vampires were equal here at The Red Tavern, but I hadn't realized how strictly that was enforced here. It almost gave me hope, until I remembered that once the human left, there was nothing stopping that vampire from tracking him down, murdering him, and taking those winnings for himself.

I hope it's worth it, I thought, shaking my head as I moved toward the bar on the far-left side of the room. Round stools upholstered in red leather stood in a row along the length of a dark walnut bar counter, and behind it were two bartenders—one human, one vampire. The human served up regular cocktails made with hard liquors and herbs, while the vampire mixed up blood-laced concoctions. I watched the vampire sitting in front of him sip at a glass that smelled of vodka, blood, and pickle juice, and swallowed hard as he licked the bloody drink from his lips.

The vampire arched his black eyebrows as he caught me staring, then grinned and held the glass out to me. "Want to try?"

I shuddered. "No, thank you," I said, taking a seat two spaces away from him.

He rolled his eyes. "You humans are so prudish," he complained, tipping back his head so he could drain the contents of his glass. "Oh well, more for me."

The human bartender saved me from having to come up with a response to that by leaning against the counter in front of me and offering a lopsided smile. "You look like you could use a drink," he said, his blue eyes twinkling. He was boyishly handsome, with tanned skin and blonde hair typical of the aetherion race. The black sleeves of his button-up shirt were rolled up to reveal well-muscled forearms, and I caught a glimpse of scrolling ink peeking out from beneath his open collar.

"I definitely could," I said, making a show of glancing around at the room before leaning in to whisper to him. "I think I'm going to need some liquid courage in me before I approach one of those tables."

He chuckled. "Is this your first time here?"

"Is it that obvious?" I asked, giving him an embarrassed smile.

"Well, I think I'd remember if I saw someone as enchanting as you walk through the doors." He gave me a flirtatious grin. "Now, what can I get you?"

"Something without blood *or* pickle juice," I said, wrinkling my nose in disgust.

The bartender laughed. "I think I can accommodate you," he said. As he moved down the counter to make my drink, I felt Jinx slip out of my pocket, slinking down my leg in shadow form. She would investigate for me while I chatted up the bartender, then come back and alert me if there was anyone—or anything—in this place that was worth looking into.

"Crazy what happened at the airshipyard yesterday, isn't it?" I asked casually while he poured ingredients into a shaker.

A shadow passed over the bartender's face, and his smile dimmed. "Horrific is more like it," he said quietly as he worked. "Those poor people, rotting in jail cells, all because of one power-drunk vampire who wanted to put them in their place."

"I know." I swallowed back a rising wave of anger. "Were you there? I've only heard rumors about what happened—I didn't get to see the aethercannon in action."

Something glimmered in the bartender's eyes as he shook the shaker, but it disappeared too quickly for me to decipher it. "I was," he said, pitching his voice low. "The sound of the blast, the heat of the explosion... I haven't seen anything like it since the war. And that smug look on the commandant's face..." He trailed off, a muscle working in his jaw. "I don't blame those people for attacking. I only wish I'd been brave enough to join them."

"What they did was stupid," a human to my left said a little too loudly. He clutched a tankard in his hands, his face ruddy from drink. "There was nothing to be gained by attacking that bloodsucker, and now their wives and children are never going to see them again."

"Is it wise to refer to vampires as 'bloodsuckers' when you're in a room full of them?" I asked, feeling a little uneasy.

The bartender chuckled as he slid my drink across the table. "You'll find that within these walls, vampires and humans don't bother with masks and pleasantries. Anything goes, so long as you don't try to steal or cheat or harm anyone."

I took a casual sip of my drink, completely forgetting that it had been over fifty years since I'd last touched a drop of alcohol. The sharp, crisp taste of the vodka was a jolt to my senses, burning down my throat and filling me with a familiar warmth.

The bartender frowned at the look on my face. "Is the drink all right?"

"It's more than all right." I set it down, the warmth already melting into the beginnings of a buzz. Which was a little embarrassing, considering that I'd only had one sip. "It's wonderful. I just... haven't had alcohol for a long time, and the sensation took me by surprise."

The bartender smiled softly. "Well, I'm glad I could offer you a bit of joy in these dark times, Miss...?" his eyebrows rose along with the unspoken question.

"Catherine." I smiled back. "And yours?"

"Trystan." He leaned a little closer, his voice dropping into a conspiratorial murmur. "I must confess, Catherine, you don't really strike me as the gambling type. What is it you've come here for?"

I made a show of glancing around before I leaned in close and lowered my voice. "The truth is... a friend of mine has gone missing, and I've been losing my mind trying to find out what happened to her. I'm told that this is a place where one might find answers to such questions."

"I see." His expression turned serious. "How long has she been missing for?"

"A few months." I bit my lip, affecting the appearance of a damsel in distress. It wasn't too difficult to slip into the role—I was feeling very relaxed, almost floaty. "She didn't come home from work one evening, and I haven't seen her since. Some think she ran off to join the rebels, but..."

"But you don't think so."

"I don't know." I grasped his hand atop the counter. "It's driving me crazy, not knowing. Surely you understand."

"More than you know," he agreed, his gaze darkening. He said something else then, but the words came out funny, as if he were talking into a pillow. I shook my head and leaned closer, trying to make out what he was saying, but the room tilted, and I found myself sliding sideways. Strong hands caught me under the arms before my head could hit the floor.

"Got you," Trystan grunted, hauling me up. "Gods, you're heavy for such a wee thing."

I pawed at the heavy arm that banded around my waist, but my limbs were leaden, as if I were moving through water. The tavern faded around me, and before I could process what had happened, I was out.

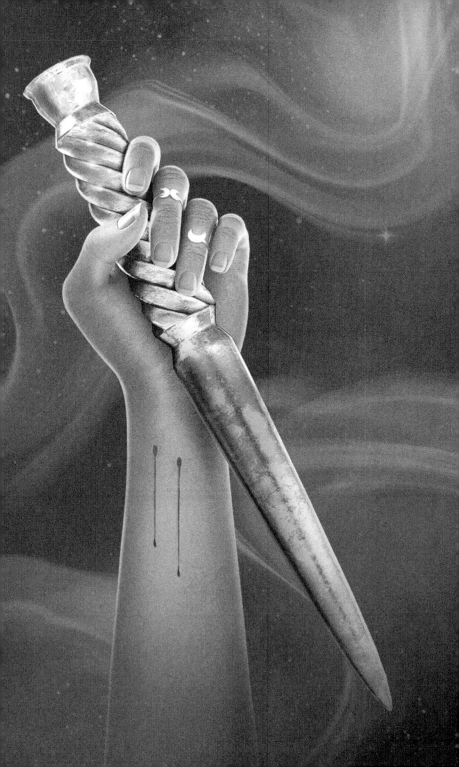

14

When I came to, I found myself tied to a chair in a dimly lit room filled with crates, while two people stood before me.

"Well, that didn't last long," Trystan muttered, his arms folded across his chest. The flirtatious smile on his handsome face was long gone, replaced by a puzzled frown. "The drugs should have kept her out for at least thirty minutes."

"She must have fed her master recently," the woman said. She perched atop a small crate, her emerald green hair curling around her diamond-shaped face. Her matching green eyes narrowed as she looked me up and down. "Got a fresh boost from that good ol' blood exchange."

"I know how being a thrall works," the bartender said irritably. "I was one myself for many years."

I shook my head, trying to clear it, then immediately regretted the action when a bolt of pain lanced through my skull. "What in the hells are you two talking about?" I barked.

"You, darling." The bartender smiled at me again, but this smile was sharp and filled with the promise of pain. "We're trying to figure out what it is you *really* came here for."

"I told you already!" I protested, my heart slamming in my chest. I strained at the bindings fastening my arms and legs to the chair, but they seemed to wind tighter around me the more I struggled. Glancing down, my mouth parted in a surprised 'o' as I realized my restraints were not made of rope, but of thick, rubbery vines.

"Wait a minute." I jerked my head back up to look at the woman. "You're a witch?"

"I sure am," she purred, and the vines snaked up higher on my calves. "And if you don't tell me what you're doing in our tavern, I'll be more than happy to show you *exactly* what my powers can do."

"Thank Hecate." Excitement rushed through my veins despite the very real danger I was in. I'd been hoping to encounter a witch, and here one was, standing right before me. "The priest said I might find you here. You're working with the rebels, then?"

Confusion washed over the witch's face, and Trystan scowled. "See! I told you. The viceroy sent her here to sniff out our cell."

"What?" I asked, taken aback.

"Don't play dumb. I was at the demonstration, and I saw you there with Lord Starclaw and his little inventor. That's how I know you're lying."

I bit back a curse. Telling Trystan I hadn't been at the demonstration when I'd been in plain sight of the crowd had been a mistake. "You don't understand," I said, desperately trying to think of a way to make them see reason without revealing my identity. Why hadn't I prepared myself for the possibility of this conversation? "Maximillian didn't send me. I came here of my own volition."

"Maximillian," the witch mocked. The vines around my wrists sprouted thorns, and I cried out as they bit into my skin, drawing blood. "You're on a first name basis with the viceroy, and expect us to believe you aren't working with him?" She rotated a hand, and the vines began to twist.

"Fuck!" I screamed as the thorns shredded my flesh. The harder I struggled, the deeper they cut, until blood trickled down my fingers and dripped onto the floor. "Godsdammit, let me go! I'm not your ene—"

An earth-shattering roar cut off the rest of my plea, and I jerked in my chair as Jinx manifested right in front of me in her wildcat form. Trystan and the witch shrieked in surprise, and in the blink of an eye, my shadow familiar had the human pinned to the ground, her jaws fastened around his throat. Trystan panted as he stared up at her with terror in his blue eyes, and when he tried to go for the knife at his side, she rumbled a warning he probably felt down to his bones.

"That's Jinx," I said, as calmly as I could through the pain. "My familiar. She won't hurt your friend as long as you release me."

The witch let out a string of curses, her eyes darting between me and Trystan lying on the floor. It was clear she didn't want to let me go, but there was no way she would be able to save her friend before my shadow familiar severed his jugular with her inch-long fangs.

"Fine," she hissed, slashing her through the air with her hand. The vines around my wrists and ankles went limp, and I staggered to my feet, still feeling woozy.

"What in the hells did you spike my drink with?" I asked, glaring at Trystan. Jinx removed her teeth from around his neck, but held her position, placing one paw just beneath the base of his throat in case he decided to get any ideas.

"Soporoot," the witch said sweetly. "An undetectable variety I cultivated myself."

Of course. Soporoot contained narcoleptic properties—a few shredded pieces brewed in tea made for an excellent sleep remedy. Strained into oil form, it was a lot more potent, and could knock a target out within a few minutes depending on the dosage. "Clever work," I muttered, rubbing at my bleeding wrists. "You don't have any bandages, do you?"

She scoffed. "You're seriously asking me to patch you up while your beast is pinning my partner to the ground?"

"You're the one who did this to me! With no provocation!"

She pursed her lips. "You're obviously a witch," she said, glancing toward Jinx, "but you're not like any witch I've ever met. I didn't detect any magic on you, and I've yet to meet any witch who's able to summon a wild animal out of nowhere like you just did."

I eyed her, then motioned for Jinx to let Trystan up. In true cat fashion, she followed my order with her own interpretation by shrinking down to her normal, cat-sized form, and sitting on his chest. Trystan gave her a wary look as she began to groom herself, then cautiously attempted to prop himself up on an elbow. She let out a feline growl, and I suppressed a snicker when he immediately returned to his supine position.

"If you want me to tell you the truth about who I am," I said to the witch, "then you're going to have to tell me who *you* are, first."

The witch sat back down on her crate with a sigh. "I'm Belladonna Greenspan," she said, "And this is Trystan Balour. We're the unofficial owners of the Red Tavern, and we gather intelligence and coordinate rescue and relief efforts for the rebellion."

Greenspan. One of the three most influential witch families of the Verdantia Clan. "The unofficial owners?" I asked.

"Trystan's master is the official proprietor... but we arranged for him to go on a very long trip, and he's yet to return."

Belladonna gave me a wolfish smile. "As far as the viceroy and his staff are concerned, Trystan merely runs it in his absence."

"Donna," Trystan said sharply. "You're telling her too much."

I sighed, then walked over and scooped Jinx into my arms so the rebel bartender could finally get up. "If I told you my name was Kitana Nightshade, would that mean anything to you?" I asked them both.

Trystan shook his head, but the Verdantia witch's eyes widened. "Kitana Nightshade as in the vampire hunter from the Nocturne Clan?" She crossed her arms over her nearly flat chest. "You must think I'm stupid. Kitana was slain in battle fifty years ago, and she was an extraordinarily powerful witch. She would never have allowed herself to be incapacitated as easily as you were tonight."

Ouch. Clearly, I was not living up to my reputation. "*Was* she killed?" I asked lightly as I stroked Jinx's fur. My shadow familiar unraveled into a coil of thick, smoky shadow, wrapping around my arms like a diaphanous shawl. "Or did someone fake her death so she wouldn't be able to interfere with their nefarious plans?"

That last bit was a guess—I still didn't know the exact why behind Sebastian's decision to imprison me. But I did have my theories, and I looked forward to prying the truth out of him once I got my hands around his slimy neck.

"It would have had to be an incredible fake," Belladonna argued. "There was a massive funeral attended by all the clan heads, and the body was presented and displayed before they put it on the pyre."

An incredible fake. My knees began to wobble, and I sat down heavily in the chair. All these years, I'd thought that my clan had abandoned me, that no one had bothered to come look for me. But Sebastian had presented them with a body double so convincing, not one of the Grand Matrons or Patrons had questioned whether it was really me.

"I dunno, Donna," Trystan said. "She seems pretty shocked. I don't think she's faking."

"The Whisperweave witch," I said woodenly, staring off into space. I had guessed that Sebastian had used one to cast the illusion that had hidden my prison from the outside world, but Donna had confirmed it. The Whisperweave witches were powerful illusionists, and Sebastian would have needed one to successfully pass off another dead body as my own without alerting the clan heads that any magical trickery was afoot. He would have also had to commission a powerful Stoneheart witch to craft the sarcophagus he'd sealed me in.

Who else had been in on my imprisonment? Had Sebastian found witches from all five clans to aid him? The thought was disheartening, and only reinforced the warning Maximillian had given me.

"If you really are Kitana Nightshade," Donna said, and the healthy dose of skepticism in her voice told me she still didn't believe me, "then what are you doing, allying yourself with the son of a vampire high lord? The Kitana I heard stories of would never debase herself like that."

"You're right," I agreed. "But that Kitana was from a different time, when the sun was still shining and humans could walk free through their own lands." I puffed out a breath. "I can't tell you why I'm working with Maximillian, not without compromising my mission. But I can tell you that my dedication to bringing the vampire king to justice has not wavered."

The words I spoke rang true, taking even me by surprise. It had been days since I'd thought about my revenge plan for Sebastian, days since I'd stopped trying to figure out how to get out of this place and started thinking about how to help the people who lived here.

"I hope you'll stay, Kitana." Maximillian's words from that first dinner so long ago echoed in my ears. *"I have grand plans for us. And you may even find them fun."*

Jinx rematerialized in my lap and butted her forehead against my chest, asking for head scratches. "Well, I can't deny that the cat is pure shadow magic," Donna said wryly. "I'd heard stories of you riding a giant panther into battle, but I thought those were made up."

I snorted. "Jinx would never deign to let anyone ride her, not even me. But she's definitely ripped off the heads of a few bloodsuckers," I said, giving my cat an affectionate smile as I scratched beneath her chin. "Haven't you?" I cooed, and she purred, leaning into my hand.

"So, you really did come here to ask about the disappearance of a friend?" Trystan demanded.

"Yes. Well, a friend of a friend," I amended. I explained to them how I'd met Hannah, and what she'd told me about her friend Imogen. "I figured if there really was a rebel cell here at the Red Tavern, you guys could tell me if an Imogen came to you for help."

Trystan sighed. "The name doesn't ring a bell, but I can check our records. Sometimes people give assumed names, too," he warned. "So, if your friend's friend has any aliases or nicknames, that would be helpful."

"I'll ask her." I got to my feet again, and Jinx promptly jumped down, vanishing before she hit the ground. Apparently, she'd decided her services were no longer needed for the night. "Thanks for your help. And for not killing me."

"Anytime." The Verdantia witch smirked, but the expression faded as her eyes dropped to the gouges on my wrist. "Let me get those taken care of for you before you go. The last thing you need is to be walking around these streets smelling of fresh blood."

Belladonna fixed me up with a poultice and bandages, then sent me on my way. I walked back to the Tower in a daze, lost in my thoughts about what I'd learned.

There really was a rebel base here in Lumina, helping humans escape to the Wildwood Forest in the east. And there really were witches helping them.

I desperately wanted to ask Belladonna more about that—about how many witches were working with the rebels, about whether Sebastian or the other clan heads were offering any aid, about the stronghold itself. But I knew I was lucky to have escaped that first encounter with my life. Trystan and Donna would chew on what I'd told them, put out feelers to see if they could verify any of what I'd said, and draw their own conclusions. In the meantime, I would visit Hannah tomorrow to get more information about her friend, then return to the Tavern and see if we could put this mystery to rest.

I was so lost in thought that I failed to notice the carriage rumbling down the street until it was coming up on my heels. Startled, I moved aside to let it pass, but before I could fully get out of the way, the door flew open, and a meaty hand yanked me inside by my upper arm.

"Hey—mmph!" I cried as a bag was shoved over my head. The door slammed shut as my assailant yanked my arms behind my back and secured my sore wrists with a tie. I slammed the back of my head into his face, and he swore loudly as his nose crunched. But my victory was short-lived when a fist crashed into my jaw, making stars swim in my obscured vision.

Which gods had I pissed off to deserve being captured not once, but *twice* in one evening?

As the carriage creaked and groaned around us, I became aware of the sound of muffled sobbing. Concentrating, I took in a deep breath through my nose, trying to get a sense of my surroundings through scent. There were two vampires—the one holding me in his lap, and the one who had punched me—and three humans. The scents of blood, tears, and piss tainted the air, and the wave of terror rolling off the humans was a sharp, icy thing that made my skin prickle.

I held perfectly still as I waited for the ride to end, listening carefully for any opportunity to escape. But the vampires didn't give me one. The moment the door creaked open, the vampire holding me in his lap threw me over his shoulder. The situation was far too reminiscent of the time Sparrow had snatched me off the street and dragged me back to the Tower—except that this time, I had no idea who had taken me, or where we were going.

A few minutes later, the vampire dumped me onto the ground. I yelped as my ass hit the hard stone floor, and the thuds and sobs around me told me I wasn't the only one here.

"Be quiet," the vampire hissed, ripping the bag off my face. I could barely make out his features—the room was pitch-dark aside from a small, narrow window set high into the opposite wall, allowing a scant amount of moonlight to stream through. "The master will be along in a little while to inspect you all, and he has a tendency to pick whoever screams the loudest for dinner."

The woman sobbing next to me immediately clamped her lips together, and the others around me followed suit. Satisfied, the vampire and his lackey friend went around the room, checking that all our bindings were tight, then closed and locked the door behind us.

I blinked a few times to let my eyes adjust to the darkness, then looked around the room. There were five humans here—all lower-ranked slaves, judging by their simple garments and the lack of a vampire family crest that would usually be stitched onto their clothing to signify private ownership.

"How long have you all been here?" I asked in a whisper.

The humans who had arrived with me stayed silent, but a young man sitting in the corner lifted his head. "Fancy seeing you here," he rasped, a pair of broken spectacles askew on his bruised face.

"Simon?" I gasped, recognizing him at once. "By the gods! Are you all right?"

"Am I all right?" He barked out a laugh as he shook his head. "I've been sitting here since yesterday without any food or water, along with these two." He jerked his chin to the man and woman huddling a few feet away from him. "That vampire wasn't joking, by the way. There was another girl who arrived with us who wouldn't stop crying, and the commandant ripped her throat out right in front of us, then made us watch as he drained her."

Fuck. An icy shiver crawled down my spine. "What do you mean, the commandant? As in Commandant Vinicius?"

"The guy who blew up the temple, yeah," he said bitterly.

My mind raced. The commandant was kidnapping human slaves? But why? Was he responsible for Imogen's disappearance? "Any idea where he's planning to take us?"

"He didn't say," Simon muttered. "Probably wherever Imogen disappeared off to." His shoulders slumped. "Hannah was right to be concerned. I shouldn't have dismissed her like that."

"There's no time to think about that now." Urgency pumped in my veins, and I scooted across the floor until I was seated next to him. "Turn your back toward my hip, and reach into my pocket," I ordered.

"Why?"

"Just do it."

The human obeyed, awkwardly wiggling and leaning until he was able to wedge his fingers into the pocket of my skirt. "What in the hells is this?" he asked as he pulled the vampire stake I had hidden there out of my pocket.

"Our ticket to freedom." The last two inches of the stake had sharpened edges, although a knife would have been better suited to this task. I shimmied my body until my bound wrists pressed against his. "Now use this thing to cut the rope, and I'll free the rest of you."

"What's the point?" the human girl who had been sobbing her heart out whined. "It's not like we can get out of this room."

"Shut up," Simon snapped. "Just because you're willing to lie down and die doesn't mean the rest of us have to."

That's the spirit.

I felt Simon fumble with the stake, then swore when burning pain slashed across the heel of my hand. "Be careful!" I snarled as the scent of my blood permeated the air. "Are you trying to get us killed? The last thing we need is for my blood to draw them back here!"

"Sorry, sorry!"

It took nearly thirty agonizing minutes, but eventually, the human managed to cut through the ropes binding my hands. Sweet relief flooded me, and I grabbed the stake from him, used it to free my bound ankles, then went around the room and cut the bindings off everyone else.

"Is there anyone here who knows how to use a weapon?" I demanded in a hushed whisper.

Simon raised his hand along with a mousy brown girl, and I handed them both two stakes—leaving me with two for myself. "I knew there was something weird about you," he said as he stared at the silver weapon in his hand.

"You could try showing a little gratitude," I suggested.

His face flushed. "What do we do with these? Stab them in the heart?"

"That's the plan." I lied back down and curled myself into a ball. "But for now, we pretend that we're still tied up. All of you, sit back down and be quiet. Simon and—what's your name?" I asked the girl.

"Lucy," she said with a sniff.

"Lucy. You two snivel a little when they walk in the room, but not too loud. I'll be the one who fusses and makes a scene, so hopefully he goes for me first. When they get close enough to expose their breastbone, you strike. Not a second before. If you go for it too soon—"

I clamped my lips shut at the sound of footsteps, and we all went silent. My heart raced, and I took steady breaths, trying to calm the frenetic energy pulsing through me. I wish I knew where Jinx had gotten off to. It was a total crapshoot as to whether she would come—I wished I could summon her, but the shadow feline very much marched to the beat of her own drum. I couldn't help but feel a little hurt by her absence, but I swallowed back the emotion and tried to focus on the situation at hand.

The door flew open, and my entire body tensed as the commandant's silhouette filled the entryway. His white teeth flashed in a sinister grin as his glowing red eyes found mine, and dread coiled in my stomach at the recognition on his face.

"Well, look at what we have here," he purred, stepping inside. "Lord Starclaw's little pet, caught in my rat trap." His nostrils flared as he scented my blood, and his expression glazed over with bloodlust. "You smell delicious. I'm not sure if I should have you for dinner, or if I should keep you alive as a trophy."

I leaped to my feet, the first stake already flying from my hand. It had been nearly three days since I'd taken the bloodbane, and if Vinicius got his fangs in me, there was a good chance he'd figure out what I was. I was lucky he hadn't smelled it on me already. But the vampire was ready—he snatched the weapon out of the air as four of his lackeys rushed in behind him, then flung it back at me. It zipped by my ear, and the human behind me let out a death scream as the stake plunged into her body.

"No!" I raised my other stake, but the commandant lifted his hand. Ribbons of blood wrapped around my wrist and yanked my arm down, and I realized he was using the blood of the human he'd just killed to bind me. Simon and Lucy tried to fight the other vampires, but they were quickly disarmed and restrained, clawed hands wrapped around their necks by their assailants, fangs poised to strike.

"Silver stakes?" The vampire used another ribbon of blood to take the weapon from my hand and lift it in front of his face. "Did the viceroy arm you with these?"

"Fuck you." I spat in his face. "I'm not going to let you use me as a pawn in whatever game you're playing with Maximillian. Just kill me and get it over with."

"I'm sure you'd prefer that, since death would be far kinder than what I have in store for you." The commandant yanked me to my knees with his blood ribbons, then pulled my head back by my hair until I felt like my neck was about to break. "But you're not going to die, and so long as you cooperate, neither will anyone else in this room. Killing humans in cold blood isn't profitable for me, you see. Not when your bodies have so many delicious uses."

My skin crawled at the perverse delight in his voice. "What in all the hells does that mean? What are you doing with all these people?"

"I own and operate a few underground clubs in the human portions of the empire," Vinicius said, his eyes roving over my face. "They are staffed with humans, much like yourselves, who provide a number of illicit thrills that, thanks to your viceroy, are considered illegal under vampire law." His lip curled. "Maximillian may have convinced some of us to pamper their humans, but the rest of us recognize you as what you are—slaves to be used for our pleasure. And it will give me *great* pleasure to knock you down from whatever false pedestal Lord Starclaw has placed you upon."

Terror threatened to choke off my airway as the vampire knelt down, fisting his hand in my hair. Desperation drove me hard as he dipped his face toward my neck, and I reached for the tiny kernel of power still left inside me, yanking it from the depths of my magical well as I struck with my free hand.

The vampire howled as shadow magic exploded out from my palm, smashing into his face so hard that his neck snapped sideways. He collapsed to the ground, his neck twisted nearly one-hundred and eighty degrees, and I sprang back as the blood magic holding me loosened.

The vampire lifted his hands to his face, then grabbed his head and yanked his neck back into place. The crack of his spine realigning echoed ominously through the room as he got to his feet, and everyone shrank back. My pulse thundered in my ears as I snatched up my stake again, bracing myself for his next attack. I wish I'd used my shadow magic to pin him against the wall instead, but I'd reacted on instinct, and now I had nothing left to defend myself with.

"I see," he said, a crazed look entering his eye as he advanced on me. "You're not human at all, are you? You—"

The rest of his words were cut off by a loud explosion that vibrated through the floor. Vinicius stopped, confusion twisting his features as dust trickled from the ceiling. It sounded as if someone had blown a *very* heavy door off its hinges. "What in the name of—"

The rest of his words sputtered out, and his hands flew to his throat, clawing at an invisible hold. The other vampires in the room choked as well, releasing Simon and Lucy, and a wave of relief flooded me as the ribbons of blood unwound their grip from my limbs, slithering back to the human body they'd been stolen from.

"Wh-wha—" Vinicius said in a garbled voice.

"It's really too bad for you that vampires can't die of asphyxiation," Maximillian said as he strolled into the room with Jinx at his heels. The little minx scampered directly to my side, looking far too pleased with herself for bringing the rescue brigade. "Because that would be a far kinder death than the one I'm about to give you."

He released his hold on Vinicius's windpipe as Sparrow and Nyra entered the room behind him. Vinicius's eyes bulged at the sight of them, but he could do nothing as Sparrow used his magic to drag the vampires unceremoniously forward, then threw them out of the chamber and into the hall, where I could hear a loud commotion unfolding. Hopefully that was Lucius with his guards.

"Catherine." Nyra rushed to my side. Her features were pinched with worry, none of her usual scorn or annoyance present, but I waved her off.

"I'm fine. Go help the humans," I told her. "They've been trapped here for almost two days."

"My death?" Vinicius snarled, trembling with rage. I could tell he wanted to leap at Maximillian, but his feet were rooted to the ground by the vampire lord's magic. "You can't seriously mean to kill me, Starclaw. I am the emperor's Master at Arms!"

"And I am the heir of House Psychoros," Maximillian reminded him. His voice was deadly soft, but his eyes blazed with fury, and sparks of magic snapped in the air around him. Nyra hastily herded the humans out of the room while her sire advanced on the vampire soldier, clearly wanting to get them out of harm's way before the bloodbath started. "I warned you what would happen if you tested me again, Vinicius."

He lifted a finger, and the commandant shrieked as his leg bone snapped like a twig. My mouth dropped open—could telekinetics really snap bones like that, with a mere thought? I'd never seen anything like it. The leg buckled beneath him, forcing Vinicius to one knee, and Maximillian wrenched his other leg out of his hip socket next. The vampire groaned as he toppled over—he would heal in a matter of minutes, but the wounds still had to hurt—and Maximillian stepped over his body and stalked over to where I still knelt.

I struggled to my feet, and the vampire lord caught my hands, pulling me upright. "Are you all right, Kitten?" he asked quietly, searching my face. He glanced down at the bandages on my wrists and the slice on my hand, and his expression turned downright arctic. "Did he do this to you?"

"No, but he did kidnap me, and all those other humans, too." I swallowed and looked to where the commandant still lay on the ground under Sparrow's watchful eye. The spymaster had both swords out and aimed toward the vampire officer, just in case he somehow broke free of Maximillian's hold. "He was bragging about how he takes them to some underground club, then rents them out to vampires searching for illegal thrills. He..." I swallowed. "He was debating whether he wanted to take me there too, or keep me for himself to spite you."

Maximillian closed his eyes. "I'm so sorry, Kitten." He pressed his forehead against mine, as if needing to reassure himself with the physical contact. "This is my fault."

I was about to argue that this was most definitely *not* his fault when Vinicius let out a barking laugh. "Look at you, fawning over that human," he sneered. "Or should I say witch, Maximillian? Does the emperor know you keep one handy?"

Maximillian's eyes opened, a chillingly blank expression on his face. Another loud crack echoed off the walls, and Vinicius screamed as his spine bent at an unnatural angle.

"Take her, Sparrow," Maximillian ordered, turning away from me. "I'll be along once I've finished with him."

"Wait," I said as Sparrow came forward. I grabbed Maximillian's arm, and he whipped his head around to face me, his eyes burning.

"You would beg clemency for this monster?"

His icy voice was like death itself whispering in my ear, and goosebumps raced across my skin in response. "No," I said. "I just want to make sure that you find out where this club is located. He says he has one here in Lumina, and a few in other cities, too." Maybe Hannah's friend was there, maybe not. But either way, there was a building full of brutalized humans somewhere in this city, and I meant to help them.

"Consider it done," the vampire lord said. "Now go. Please," he added, his voice softening just a fraction.

I nodded, and he turned away, his predatory focus on Vinicius once more. I allowed Sparrow to lead me out of the room, the commandant's screams echoing down the hallway with every step we took. The sound was music to my ears, and I sincerely hoped Maximillian wrung every drop of pain he could from that monster before he ended him.

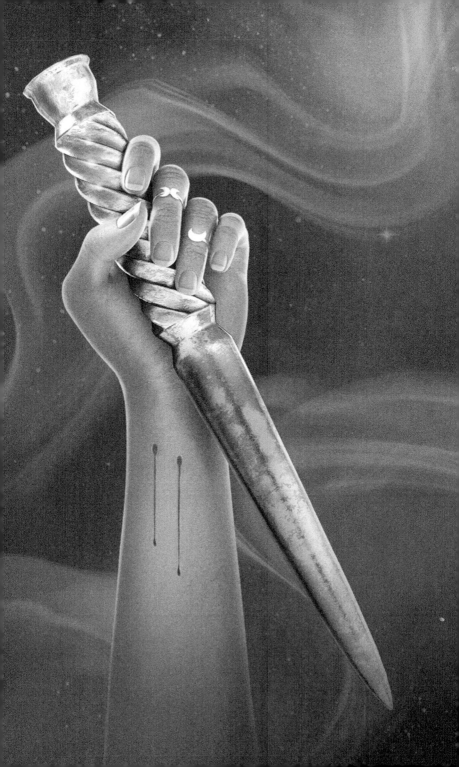

15

Many hours later, I found myself back in my bed, staring up at the canopied ceiling without seeing it as an unending stream of horrors playing out in my mind's eye.

It had taken four hours for Maximillian to break Vinicius, then another six for Lucius, Sparrow, Eliza, and me to find and evacuate the dilapidated warehouse in one of the rundown, mostly abandoned districts. Vinicius had transformed it into a sadistic pleasure den where, for a price, vampires could rape, maim, abuse, and even drain dry the humans they rented— depending on how much they were willing to pay. The slaves were heavily drugged to keep them compliant, and many of them had actually fought back when we'd attempted to remove them. I wasn't sure if watching a fourteen-year-old girl cling to the leg of her vampire pimp as we removed him was the worst thing I'd seen, or the incinerator in the back of the warehouse that the vampires used to get rid of the humans that their clients had gone 'a little too far' with.

Simon had bravely agreed to come along to see if Imogen had been amongst them, but he hadn't recognized any of the slaves we'd rescued. Despite all the good we'd done, my heart still sat heavy in my chest at the failure. It was very likely that the girl was dead, if Vinicius had taken her, her life callously used and thrown away by a vicious bloodsucker who had forgotten what it was to have a heart.

A knock at my door tore me from the vicious memories, and I sat up to see Eliza come into my room. Her olive skin looked unusually wan in the firelight, and there was a haunted look in her green eyes.

"Mind if I come in there with you?" she asked, giving me a shaky smile. "I... I don't think I can be alone after what we saw tonight."

"Of course." I scooted over to make room for her, then lifted the bedcovers so Eliza could crawl underneath. She grasped the edge of the coverlet and pulled it tight beneath her chin, and Jinx, who had been curled up by my feet, nuzzled up to her with a soft meow.

"You couldn't sleep either, huh?" she whispered, stroking the cat as she looked at me.

I shook my head. "I thought I would." Eliza and I had stayed up until nearly six in the morning helping Lucius and Nyra search the entire place from top to bottom for slaves, dead bodies, and contraband, and I'd also worked with the healers to help triage and give first aid to the humans we'd rescued. I would have stayed longer, but Maximillian had spotted me swaying on my feet, and Eliza slurring her words, so he'd ordered the guards to take us both home to rest. "I guess I just feel too guilty about lying here doing nothing to fall asleep."

Eliza shook her head. "I'm the one who should be feeling guilty, not you." She bit her lip, an anguished note entering her voice. "If I hadn't ignored your concerns about your human friend, if I'd gone with you to the Red Tavern like I said I would—"

"Don't." I grabbed Eliza's slim shoulder, refusing to allow her to spiral into what-ifs. "There's no point in beating yourself up about this. If you'd come with me, you might have been seriously hurt, or worse."

Eliza snorted. "Please. I know I look like a glorified grease monkey, but I can be handy in a fight." She lifted her fingers from the sheets, and a small current of aetheric energy crackled at her fingertips. "Vampires don't much like being incinerated. That's why they enthralled those of us left who can still manipulate aetheric energy."

I tried to smile at that, but I knew it didn't reach my eyes. I hadn't told Eliza about my close-call with Trystan and Donna. I'd been lucky Jinx had intervened, but I wasn't sure they would have stayed their hand if Eliza had been there with me. She could have very well gotten us both killed if she'd come, which was why I hadn't brought her.

"Look at it this way," I told her. "If you had come with me, Vinicius's goons might not have snatched me off the street, and we might never have found out about his slave trafficking operation. I know what we saw tonight was nightmare-inducing, Eliza, but look what we accomplished. We saved all those people."

"She's right, Eliza," Nyra said, her voice floating through the door. I scowled as she walked into the room, still wearing the same blue and silver-striped dress from yesterday. Her expression was a tad drawn, but despite being awake for over twenty-four hours, she didn't have a hair out of place. One benefit of being an immortal who didn't need much sleep. "But don't think that just because the commandant is dead that this is over, huntress. You've forced Maximillian to open up a can of worms that may very well put us all in danger."

"What do you mean by that?" I asked, sitting upright.

Nyra crossed the room and perched on the edge of the bed, a troubled look on her normally no-nonsense face. "While Maximillian is well-within his rights to kill a lower-ranking vampire for stealing personal property—" I clenched my jaw at the pointed look she gave me, "—and engaging in a number of illegal activities in his territory, the fact that Vinicius was one, a member of another vampire house and two, a high-ranking military officer who has influence with the emperor, complicates things. Trial and imprisonment would have been customary in this situation."

"Then why didn't Maximillian do that?" I asked. "I didn't tell him he had to kill Vinicius." Though I was glad he did.

"Because you used *magic* on him," Nyra said, her tone so forceful that I clenched my fists in the sheets to keep from rearing back. "You exposed your true nature, and if Lord Starclaw had allowed Vinicius to make it to trial, he would have told everyone who you were."

"And what was she supposed to do?" Eliza demanded. "Just stand there and let him kill her?"

"No, of course not." Nyra pinched the bridge of her nose and closed her eyes, as if staving off a headache. "I'm not saying Kitana shouldn't have defended herself. What she did was admirable." She opened her eyes and looked at me again. "But there's no denying that you've made things complicated for Maximillian, regardless of whether you choose to go to the Summit with him."

My stomach squirmed with guilt at the look of genuine frustration in her eyes, and I dropped my stare to my lap, feeling suddenly ashamed. "I haven't really been thinking of anyone but myself, have I," I said.

"How can you say that?" Eliza demanded. "You helped save fifty humans from slavery tonight!"

"Yes, but I've behaved recklessly these last few weeks, and have judged you all harshly even though all of you have been nothing but patient with me. Sometimes even kind," I said, giving Nyra a wry smile. "I refused to acknowledge any of your kindnesses because you're vampires, but witches are just as capable of kindness and cruelty as you all are." Sebastian's face flashed in my mind, and my stomach clenched. "I don't regret what I've done, not when the outcome resulted in so many lives saved, but I could have been a lot more thoughtful about it."

To my surprise, Nyra let out a soft chuckle. "I was once a young, brash warrior myself," she told me, "and I wasn't the most thoughtful person either when I was convinced I was in the right."

"You were?" I blinked, taking in Nyra's sleek, professional outfit and perfectly coiffed hair. "You don't strike me as the type."

She laughed. "Oh, I'm still more than capable of mowing down a company of soldiers on horseback," she said. "But I left those days long behind me after Lord Starclaw Turned me and brought me into his service."

"Will you tell me how it happened?" I asked. "Why you allowed Maximillian to Turn you and take you from your people?"

Nyra turned to look out the window, and the moonlight poured over her features, casting her high cheekbones and pointed chin in sharp relief. I held my breath as I waited, not wanting to push her too hard given how she'd reacted the last time I'd asked her about her past.

"I was the daughter of an Equinox chief," she finally said, her voice almost trance-like as she stared off into the middle distance. "The pride of my family, and set to become the next chieftess. But when I was twenty-two years old, a terrible illness struck me. It ate away at my muscles until I could barely walk, never mind ride a horse. The healers told me I would never ride again, and that it would be a miracle if I survived at all. But even worse was watching my mare, Lliona, waste away alongside me, our life-forces tied together. I couldn't stand to see her like that, so I begged my mother to send for someone who could cure me so we both might live.

"She came home with Lord Starclaw in tow, and I cursed them both so soundly, I swore Maja herself boxed my ears." Nyra shook her head ruefully. "I didn't want to be Turned, didn't want to spend the rest of my life without the sun on my face, or the bond of my familiar flowing through my veins. But Lord Starclaw seemed to understand my fears, and he assured me that although I would have to say goodbye to the sun, I would not have to say goodbye to my familiar, or my family. He said that if Lliona wished it, I could bring her to Noxalis, and that even though I was in his service, I could visit my homeland as often as I wanted." She swallowed. "It was hard, holding my mother's hand as she died, watching my sisters and their children grow old and die, too. But I was grateful for the privilege of being able to watch them live, and to provide for and protect them, too. Until now, at least."

A lump formed in my throat as she turned to look at me, tears glimmering in her eyes. "What happened to them?" I asked, afraid to hear the answer. "Your tribe?"

"Gone," she whispered. "Our horses could not survive without sunlight, and therefore neither could we. Ferae who lose their familiars become a shadow of themselves, losing their will to eat and sleep. They wander the world aimlessly until they either die of exhaustion or someone kills them. The only ones who did not meet this fate were those of us too young to bond to familiars, and those people are now slaves, scattered throughout the vampire realm. There are a few thralls who work in service to the empire, breeding the aethersteeds alongside the engineers. But for all intents and purposes, my people were genocided. The Equinox tribe is a footnote in history now."

"Yet you still support Maximillian?" I pressed "Even though he fought for your emperor?"

"We all fought for him," Nyra said woodenly. "There was no choice. The hold he has over us—" she shook her head. "You cannot comprehend it, the power he wields. I am only glad that I wasn't forced to slaughter any of my own people. I don't think I could have lived with myself."

I looked down at my hands, shaken by Nyra's story. "And what about the others?" I asked. "Lucius and Sparrow? Do they have stories like this?"

"You'll have to ask them." Nyra said. "Though good luck getting Lucius to tell you anything. He's more private than I am."

Jinx climbed into my lap as silence fell across the room, and I rubbed her ears idly as I weighed Nyra's story in my mind. I suspected that if I were to ask Lucius and Sparrow about their pasts, they would have similar stories about how their lives had been crumbling when Maximillian had reached out to them and offered them a way out of whatever purgatory they were trapped in. He seemed to have a knack for finding troubled souls who were down on their luck and convincing them to pledge themselves to him.

That was certainly what he'd done for me—except that he hadn't made my freedom a condition of his bargain. He could have forced me to agree to the bargain before he freed me, could have used his magic and resources to keep me under lock and key until I accepted his offer. But he'd done none of those things. Instead, he'd given me a safe place to stay and the time and space to recover, adjust, and draw my own conclusions.

The sense of confusion that had been rattling around in my brain since my arrival settled, and I took a full breath as the tightness in my chest eased. I lifted my head to meet Nyra's gaze as a sense of determination solidified inside me.

"Can I ask you for something?"

Nyra's brows creased. "What is it?"

"The full moon is tonight, and I need to perform the

Twilight Communion." I swallowed hard, feeling strangely vulnerable. "I need someone to stand in for my sister witches. Both of you, if possible," I added, turning to Eliza.

Eliza reached out and gripped my hand. "Of course we will," she said. "I've been waiting for this moment for weeks—I wouldn't miss it for the world."

"Agreed," Nyra said. "We'd be delighted to help."

I exhaled a breath I didn't realize I'd been holding. "Thank you," I said, gratitude swelling within me. I'd been so afraid they would say no—if Nyra had asked me to participate in a death god ceremony, I probably would have rejected it on the spot, and yet they hadn't hesitated. "You don't know what this means to me."

"We know exactly what it means," Eliza said. "Now tell us what else you need from us, and we'll get it done."

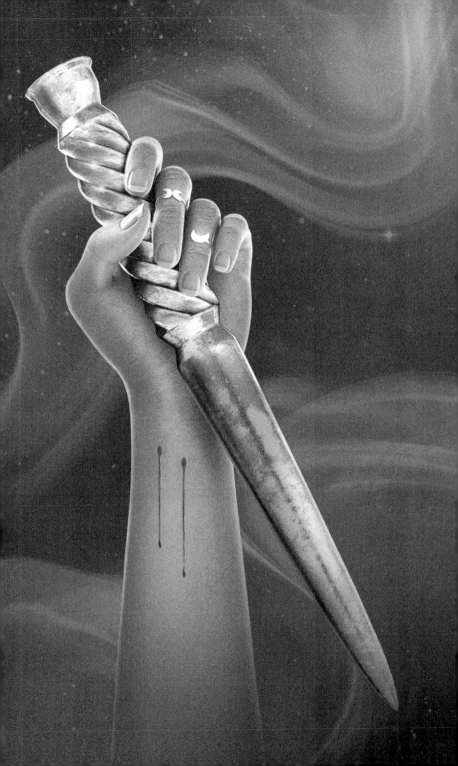

16

A few hours later, I stood outside the chapel of Tenebros, my hand hovering over the door handle. I'd never entered one of the death god's temples before, and a shiver of apprehension crawled up my spine at the thought of doing so for the first time. But I'd been told that Maximillian was in here, and I needed to speak to him. I could still feel the tingle of his forehead pressed against mine every time I thought of him, still see the incandescent rage glowing in his eyes on my behalf. There was still so much unsaid between us, and I couldn't ignore it any longer.

Gathering my courage, I curled my hand around the raven-shaped handle and pulled. The heavy door creaked open, revealing the intimate sanctuary beyond, and I paused on the threshold, taking it in.

I'd expected the chapel to feel sinister and forbidding, but while it certainly was dark, there was a sacredness to the space that couldn't be denied, its vaulted ceilings and intricate stonework lending it a sense of grandeur despite its small size. Dozens of candles flickered, lending an intimate glow to the space, and moonlight seeped through stained glass windows casting muted patterns of deep purples, blues, and blacks onto the dark stone floor.

A simple black altar sat at the far end of the temple, an intricately carved obsidian statue of Tenebros towering behind it. The artist depicted him as a tall, imposing figure, with elongated limbs and chiseled features. His feathered wings were folded behind him, his broad-shouldered frame cloaked in a flowing robe, and he held the symbol of his sacred office in one clawed hand—a scepter crowned by a closed eye, with a raven perched atop it and a serpent snaking up the rod.

Maximillian knelt before the altar and statue, hands clasped before him in silent prayer. The weight of the world seemed to press in on him as he bowed his head, his shoulders slumped ever so slightly. The moonlight rippled over his storm-cloud colored hair and down the back of his crisp white shirt, and I thought he resembled a glowing star, tucked away in some far corner of the celestial heavens his god had once ruled over.

I lingered by the temple entrance, feeling suddenly awkward. I could only imagine the thoughts going through Maximillian's head—the rage he felt toward Vinicius, the sense of shame at failing to safeguard the humans snatched off the streets right under his nose, and the betrayal he felt at seeing his own citizens violate his principles in such a flagrant manner. It felt too personal, and I took a step back, prepared to slip out the door again.

"Stay." The gentle rumble of his voice stopped me in my tracks, and I halted. He rose, the motion lacking some of his usual grace, as if that invisible weight dragged at his limbs. There was a troubled look in his eyes as he turned to face me, dressed simply in a white shirt and dark grey trousers with none of his usual finery present. Despite everything—that he was a vampire and I was a witch, that we stood in a temple dedicated to a god whose children were responsible for everything wrong in this cruel, terrible world—something caught in my chest at this vulnerable side of him, a side I was sure very few people had ever, or would ever, see.

"Sorry to intrude," I said as casually as I could. I clasped my hands behind my back as he approached, mostly to keep from fidgeting. Gods, why was I so *nervous*? "But Lucius said I could find you here."

"And here I am." The shadows in his eyes lightened a bit, but his face remained uncharacteristically serious, his usual smirks and teasing expressions nowhere to be found. "Come and sit with me."

He slid into one of the pews toward the back of the chapel, and I followed suit. Silence passed between us as he looked up at the set of stained glass windows to our left. Each depicted a different arc of Tenebros's story—his original birth as Astellion, the God of Night, his untimely death at the hands of Phaeros, his brother, and his resurrection as the God of Death and the Father of Vampires.

"We weren't always like this, you know," Maximillian said as he stared at a panel depicting Athanasia kneeling before Astellion's corpse, silver tears pouring down her dark face to pool atop his broken body.

I blinked. "Like what?"

"Cruel. Avaricious. Consumed by lust for blood and power." His gaze shifted to the panel of Astellion floating in the night sky, a crown of stars haloing his head as his midnight wings spread out behind him. "Vampires have co-existed with humans far longer than we've been enemies."

I frowned. According to history and legend, vampires hadn't always been blood-sucking servants of the God of Death. Once, they had been known as the Nightforged, a peaceful race of celestial beings who dwelled in Noxalis, ruling over their subjects with compassion and using their starborn magic to make the world a better place. When Astellion had died, Athanasia, his mother, had used her dark powers to bring him back as an undead god. But in doing so, she had inadvertently cursed the Nightforged, transforming them into the undead creatures they were now.

"That was thousands of years ago," I said. "Long before even you were born." I'd looked up the Starclaw family tree on my third day here—Maximillian was close to six hundred years old. Not ancient by vampire standards, but no spring chicken, either.

"Yes, but even after the Chaos War, we found ways to co-exist with humans. Formed mutually beneficial arrangements despite the oppressive terms of the Midnight Accords. It's true that some of us, like the Sanguis Noctis, engaged in less than savory practices, but we Psychoros vampires have always conducted ourselves with honor. Our ancestors understood that while not all beings are created with equal skill or ability, that we are connected, all part of the great weft and warp of the universe. It is something that we have done our best to hold on to, even after we were cursed, and yet, ever since Vladimir took control..."

"You can't tell me that Vladimir is responsible for all the actions of vampires," I argued. "Your kind has behaved badly long before he ever became Highlord of House Invictus, never mind the emperor. And from what I've read, you happily slaughtered humans alongside him during the war."

Maximillian was silent for a long moment before he reached into his pocket and pulled out a pocket watch. Wordlessly, he passed it over to me, and I opened it to find a miniature portrait of a woman inside the cover. She had long, silver-white hair, kind blue eyes, and a timeless, elegant beauty about her. And she also has the pointed ears of a vampire.

"Who is this?" I asked.

"Odessa Starclaw," Maximillian said. "My mother."

My mouth dropped open, and I stared at the portrait. I could see it now—her full mouth and the down-tilted corners of her eyes were the same as Maximillian's. "Your mother is a vampire? But I thought—"

"That only *amorte* can give birth to original vampires," Maximillian confirmed. "Which is true. My mother is one of the rare few who survived the birth long enough for my father to turn her into a vampire."

"So you were essentially raised by a human mother and a vampire father," I said. No wonder Maximillian hadn't tried to stamp out the humanity from his vampire children. Unlike the rest of his kind, he didn't see it as a flaw to be eliminated.

The vampire lord nodded. "She retained her humanity long after she was born, which is why I think I have such a different outlook on humans compared to my brethren. She was Marisian, so she'd tell me tales of the Maris's most revered nautical heroes, who navigated treacherous waters filled with sea monsters to discover new lands. And on stormy nights, she'd recount the legends of the sea sirens who controlled the tides with their voices, and could also lure a man to his death."

He smiled, and the nostalgia in his voice made my heart ache with longing for my own mother. She'd told me stories when I'd been a child too—of Hecate's three daughters of fate, the Moirae, and of their male counterparts, Mischos and Skotos, twin chaos gods who relished in upsetting the natural order of things as much as possible just to spite their older sisters. Their antics across the ages had left a tapestry of myths and legends behind in their wake, and I'd often found myself relating to them far more than their older sisters.

"What happened to your mother?" I asked. "Is she still alive?"

"My father killed her."

The grief and rage underscoring those four short words were like a punch to the gut. I said nothing as Maximillian stared straight ahead, his jaw flexing as he fought to control the emotion radiating from him.

"My mother was strongly against the Eternal Night War," he finally said, his gaze fixed on Tenebros's statue. "She hated all the death and destruction we brought to the humans, hated that my father and I were a crucial part of it. She begged us to listen, but we were too far gone, too..." he raked a hand through his hair, a tortured look on his face. "We didn't realize she was secretly helping the humans until one of Vladimir's children caught her red-handed. She was dragged before the emperor in chains and sentenced to die at her husband's hand."

His expression turned wooden as he gripped the back of the pew in front of him, his claws digging into the dark walnut. "I'll never forget the blank look on my father's face as he beheaded her in front of the entire vampire court with our family sword. Will never forget how it felt as though it were my heart being cleaved in two instead of her." He turned his face to look at me, and the intensity of his gaze rooted me to the spot, leaving me no choice but to stare right back. "My father loved my mother more than anything else in this world. There is nothing he would not have done for her—no storm he would not have braved, no mountain he would not have moved for the privilege of her smile. When I watched him not only callously end her life, but move on as if nothing had happened, I knew then that something was very, very wrong."

"What do you mean?" I asked.

Maximillian gently took the pocket watch back from me. "When Vladimir declared war on Heliaris, it was as though a tidal wave of bloodlust had swept over the vampire kingdom. We were all caught up in it—the need to conquer, to expand, to prove our dominance over the daywalkers. It was an insatiable thirst for power that went far beyond survival or tradition." Shame colored his voice, heavy with the weight of untold regrets. "Psychoros vampires pride ourselves on our mental control—we spend hours meditating every day from the time we are young in order to cultivate our abilities and protect our minds from the strain. Yet I didn't realize an unnatural haze had descended upon me until the news of my mother's arrest jarred me awake."

His gaze hardened, and he gripped my hand, hard enough that the bones in my knuckles ground together. But I was too captivated by the moment to care. "The emperor has some kind of magical hold on us, Kitana. He is using some dark sorcery to force us to do his bidding. That is the only explanation for how he was able to get my father—the most powerful mentalist in our house—to kill my mother without an ounce of hesitation or regret. It also explains how he was able to unite all four houses for the first time in history, when no vampire high lord has ever managed such a feat before. No one can gainsay him, and once my inner eye was opened to the truth, I saw the signs of mind-control everywhere."

"Are you saying you believe the emperor has somehow managed to enthrall every vampire in Noxalis?" I asked, my voice pitched high with disbelief. "That's impossible. No single person has that much power. And besides, vampires can't enthrall each other." As far as I understood it, sires could compel their children to obey them, but that invasive level of control ended there. They couldn't directly control their offspring's offspring, and they definitely couldn't compel vampires from other houses.

"I don't understand exactly how he does it," Maximillian growled. "And I'm uncertain about how far his magical influence extends. But I do know that regardless of which house or family line you come from, it is physically impossible to resist an order from the emperor. That's why no one has tried to depose him."

"That's why you want *me* to kill him," I said, realization dawning.

"Precisely." Maximillian gave me a grim smile. "It is impossible for vampires to enthrall witches. You're the only one who can circumvent his influence long enough to drive a stake through his heart and bring an end to his reign of terror."

I stared at Maximillian as the full weight of his words crashed into me. King Vladimir had been crowned centuries before I was born, so I'd never thought much about the unification of Noxalis, or how strange it was that the houses had come together so suddenly. If it was true, that King Vladimir was using dark magic to seize power and bend everyone to his will, then Maximillian wasn't merely making a power play by asking me to kill Vladimir. He was doing it to end centuries of corruption and tyranny.

"How do you know I won't be affected?" I demanded. "That his power doesn't work on witches, too?"

"I've seen him attempt to compel one once." Maximillian let out a mirthless chuckle. "She spat in his face and told him exactly what he could do with his commands. He executed her, of course, but it gave me a sliver of hope that whatever mysterious power he has does not work on everyone."

I glanced at the statue of Tenebros, nervous again. "How do we know your god isn't the one who gave him those powers, and that he's not listening to us right now?"

Maximillian snorted. "Our dark father is not limited to altars and temples when it comes to eavesdropping. If he wanted to stop me from enacting my plan, he would have found a way to thwart me long ago."

He loosened his grip on my hand, and my pulse skittered as he turned my palm up so he could trace slow circles across the inside of my wrist. I turned back to see him watching me with that intensity again, and an electric current ran between us that pulled my body taut like a bowstring. I found myself unconsciously leaning toward him, wanting... I wasn't sure.

More. More of whatever this was.

"So this is it, is it?" he asked, his voice whisper-soft. "You're going to climb up to the top of my tower, perform your ritual, and then walk out of my life without a backward glance?"

"I..." my words caught in my throat, and it took me a minute to dislodge them. "How did you know I wanted to go to the top of the tower?"

He gave me a knowing smile. "I did a little research. You want a place that's high up, removed from the worldly hustle and bustle of the city, with unfettered access to the moon and the heavens." His smile shifted into one of those infernal smirks. "What a long way you've come since you first arrived, Kitten. No longer cowering in fear of the sky... or anything else, for that matter."

"I... you're right." I blinked, wracking my mind to recall exactly when the phobia had disappeared. I genuinely couldn't remember; the change had been that gradual. "But you're also wrong."

"Oh?" He arched an eyebrow.

I pulled my hand out of his—not because I didn't want his touch, but because I wanted it too much, and it was driving me to distraction. I didn't know how this enigmatic vampire lord had managed to breach my walls, but he had turned both his presence and his touch into something I desired.

Maybe it was the way he protected me without making me feel caged or belittled. Maybe it was his unwavering support as I'd struggled to regain myself, despite my lack of faith and trust in him.

Or maybe it was simply the fact that, despite having never led a mortal life, Maximillian Starclaw possessed a surprisingly human heart.

"I'm not going to leave, not after everything that's happened between us," I said firmly. "It would be a poor way to repay you after all the times you've saved my life, especially since I've brought so much trouble to your door."

"Trouble?"

I sighed. "Nyra told me why you had to kill Vinicius that night. Because I used my witch magic, and he would have threatened to expose me if you'd allowed him to go to trial. She said that because of the way you handled things, you might wind up in trouble with the emperor."

"Is that what she told you?" Maximillian laughed. "Nyra knows me better than almost anyone else, but she's wrong."

"She is?"

"Oh yes." A dangerous note edged his voice as he slipped his forefinger beneath my chin, and my pulse tripped as he tilted my head up to meet his. "It's true that Vinicius would have complicated things should I have allowed him to live, but that isn't why I killed him. I could have found another way to ensure his silence."

"Then why did you do it?" I asked, breathless.

"Because." He leaned in close enough for his next words to caress my lips as he spoke. "I told you on your first night here that as long as you remain in this city, you are mine. And anyone who touches what's mine, dies. I meant every word of that, Kitana."

He purred my name as he spoke it, and the vibrato in his tone traveled from his mouth to mine and straight into my core. The molten need he ignited in me was far different from the scathing, defensive response those words had inspired a mere few weeks ago. His mahogany and leather scent filled my lungs, stoking that fire even higher, and it took every ounce of willpower I had not to close that final inch separating us.

Maximillian's nostrils flared as the scent of my desire thickened in the air between us, and his mercurial eyes deepened, becoming almost liquid so that I felt like I was drowning in them. The hand beneath my chin slid to the back of my neck, his elegant fingers slipping into the strands at the base of my skull.

"Is there something you want, Kitten?" he asked, his voice low and rough in my ear.

I opened my mouth, but whatever words my lust-addled brain had been about to say vanished as the temple door creaked open. I sprang away from Maximillian, my heart pounding so hard I could barely hear myself think over the roaring in my ears, and whipped my head around to see Sparrow standing in the doorway, his frame backlit by the moonlight.

"Well, if it isn't two lovebirds necking on sacred ground," he teased, the golden hoop in his ear glinting as he tilted his head. "Not exactly what I was expecting to find in here, but I'll take it."

My entire face flamed, and if I wasn't in the death god's temple, I would have wished for the ground to open up and swallow me whole. But with my luck, and Tenebros standing just behind us, I'd probably end up falling straight into the underworld. "We weren't necking—" I began hotly.

"What is it, Sparrow?" Maximillian asked, cutting me off before I could devolve into a mess of defensive blathering. There was no mistaking the displeasure in his voice at being interrupted, and the foolish, needy part of me wondered what would have happened if Sparrow hadn't chosen that exact moment to walk in.

Sparrow sobered instantly, straightening up. "Nyra asked me to find you," he said, his gaze meeting mine. "She and Eliza have gathered everything you asked for. They're waiting for you at the sundial."

"Oh!" A rush of anticipation filled me, taking the edge off the lust that had nearly driven me into the vampire's arms. "That's excellent." I turned back to Maximillian. "Will you come?"

He arched an eyebrow. "You want me there?"

"Eliza and Nyra volunteered to assist me, but I need a third." I bit my lip, feeling self-conscious. "I was hoping it would be you."

"I would be honored."

We rushed out of the chapel and into the central keep, Maximillian keeping pace with me. My heart raced with nerves and excitement as we entered the elevator, the metal box creaking and clattering around us. A part of me wondered if the ritual would still work, or if the moon goddess would refuse to answer if vampires were in attendance. But I had no choice—it wasn't as if there was a coven of witches around that I could ask. Besides, if the goddess refused me after all I'd been through simply because the vampires who'd helped me were present, did she even deserve my devotion?

Blasphemy, the voice of Grand Matron Seraphina, the head of the Nocturne Clan, snapped in my ear. It was a voice I hadn't heard in decades, and I nearly hunched my shoulders before remembering she wasn't here. None of my clan were.

The elevator doors opened, and I shoved the grand matron's voice, along with all thoughts about my fellow witches, out of my mind. I would reclaim my power on my own terms, and if anyone tried to get in my way, not even Hecate could save them from my wrath.

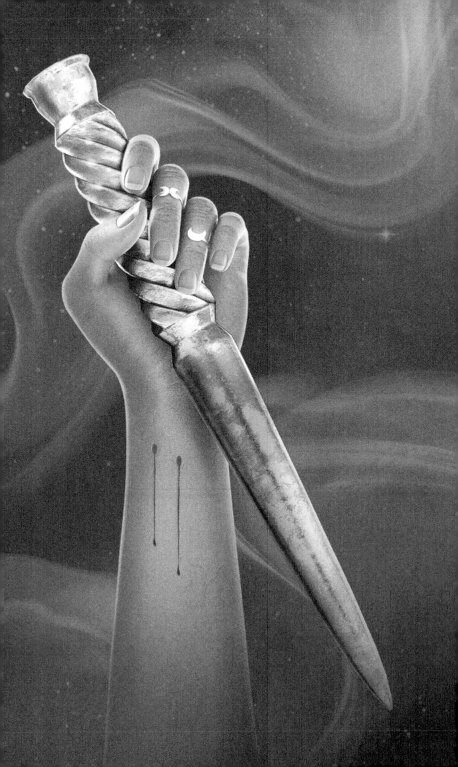

17

I stepped onto the sundial at the top of the tower, a sense of awe washing over me as I took it in for the first time. It was an enormous disk that occupied the entire rooftop, its face exposed to the night sky. The sunsteel surface shimmered beneath my feet, reflecting a warm, amber glow that contrasted beautifully against the cool silver of the moonbeams streaming down from above.

The edges of the sundial were intricately inlaid with twelve aetheric crystals that marked the hours, each glowing softly with an inner light. Their colors shifted with the passing seconds, dancing between breathtaking shades of azure, emerald, and amethyst. A long, ornate railing, wrought from the same metal as the sundial, ran along the outer circumference, and in between the posts were twelve statues that corresponded to the runes, each one meticulously sculpted. Their heads had all been removed, but judging by the scepters they carried and the robes of state they wore, I gathered these were previous rulers of Aetherion. The one at the twelve o'clock mark had been replaced with an imposing statue of Emperor Vladimir glaring down his nose at us, and I had to resist the urge to glare back.

Eliza and Nyra waited at the base of the gnomon in the center, while Lucius and Sparrow leaned nonchalantly against one of the balustrades. I drew up short at the sight of them, and Lucius raised an eyebrow at my reaction.

"We can go if you want us to," he asked, his eyes shifting to Maximillian standing by my side.

"No, it's all right," I said. "I just... I didn't think you'd want to come."

Sparrow snorted. "Are you kidding? We've been waiting for this moment forever." He pushed off the railing and eyed the altar Nyra and Eliza had set up for me a few feet away from the gnomon. "Max had the crystals and everything ordered months ago."

I turned to face Maximillian, my eyebrows flying up to meet my hairline. "Months ago?"

He scratched the back of his neck, looking uncharacteristically self-conscious. "I knew sourcing the materials you would need would require time, especially given that witchcraft is banned in the vampire kingdom," he said. "I did some research, then sent Sparrow to get what you needed."

Unexpected tears burned at the corners of my eyes, and I was struck by a nearly overwhelming urge to throw my arms around him. Instead, I shoved my hands into my pockets and cleared my throat. "Umm. Well, thank you."

An expectant silence descended upon the sundial, and I realized everyone was waiting for me. Crossing to the altar, I knelt before it and picked up the items sitting atop it to inspect them. Candles, incense sticks and burners, matchsticks, a sage bundle, and six crystal chunks—five of which represented the elements, and one large, pure white moonstone to represent the goddess.

I gathered five of the candles, then handed them to Eliza, who dutifully placed them in a circle around the altar, lighting each one as she went. While she did that, I lit the sage bundle and used it to purify both the circle and the crystals, murmuring a cleansing incantation under my breath. The wind shifted around me, catching the smoke and fettering it away into the night, and I took in a clear, crisp breath that filled me with energy.

Finished, I put out the smudge stick, lit the incense sticks, then picked up the crystals. I rolled each one between my fingers—Maximillian hadn't charged them, but the stones didn't need to be charged since I had so many helpers tonight. "Since you two are here," I said, turning to Lucius and Sparrow, "you might as well participate."

Lucius started, while Sparrow bounced on the balls of his feet like a giddy toddler. "Are you sure?" Lucius asked, his gravely voice deepening with concern. "You don't need to include us just because we're standing here."

"Speak for yourself." Sparrow elbowed Lucius in the ribs, earning him a death glare. "I want to help."

"Then come here," I said, a smile twitching at my lips. Normally, I wouldn't have needed any of them here—the Twilight Communion could be performed alone with the right modifications. My mother did it all the time when we'd lived in the human lands. But my connection to Hecate had withered away to nothing after my confinement, and I was so depleted, I needed another presence to ground me.

Besides, these types of ceremonies worked better when performed with others who could lend you their energy. And I needed all the energy I could get right now.

The four vampires and their aetherion inventor all stepped forward, each one coming to stand next to one of the five candles. I moved around the circle, handing each one of them the crystal I felt best responded to their energies. To Lucius, I gave moss agate, representing the earth. For Sparrow, aquamarine, which represented water. Nyra got clear quartz for air, Eliza carnelian for fire, and to Maximillian, I handed a deep, purple crystal with veins of white running through it.

"Amethyst?" he inquired, rolling the stone between his long fingers.

"Yes." I smiled. Amethyst was a very spiritual stone, known for enhancing intuition and connecting to higher planes of consciousness. As a telekinetic, he was the perfect fit for it. "I can't think of anyone better to represent the element of spirit."

A flicker of emotion passed across his face as he closed his hand around the crystal and brought it to his chest. Tearing my gaze from his glittering eyes, I turned to the others, then explained what their stones represented. "I want you to close your eyes and visualize your individual element as I perform the ritual," I told them. "This will help form an energy field which will hopefully allow me to access the higher realm, where the gods live." And with any luck, the goddess would hear me.

The five of them nodded, then closed their eyes as I sat down in the middle of the circle. Taking the moonstone in my palms, I closed my own eyes, then simply sat for a few minutes, focusing on my breath. I waited until my nerves were calm, until my pulse had smoothed out, until the chaotic thoughts cleared from my head and the sounds of the world faded away, leaving only me and the darkness.

And then I began to chant.

The ancient prayer came slowly at first, the words rusty on my lips from decades of disuse. I'd tried whispering the prayer from inside my coffin a few times, but the sarcophagus greedily drained any energy the goddess sent my way, so I'd eventually stopped trying. But with each passing second, my voice strengthened, and I could feel my head lifting, tilting my face up to receive the kiss of moonlight from above.

"Mother, maiden, and crone," I chanted as the moonstone in

my palms began to warm. "I offer you my life, my loyalty, my faith, and my heart. I offer you my body as a vessel for your light, so that I may fulfill my sacred purpose. To create. To nurture. To protect. To serve. I ask that you hear my prayer, and give me the guidance and strength I need, so that I may execute your divine will."

The wind, which had been oddly still, picked up around me as I spoke, lifting the hair from my shoulders and raising goosebumps along my flesh. The insides of my eyelids lit up as light exploded from the moonstone, and a shocked cry tore from my lips as a field of white spread across my vision, searing my retinas even though my eyes were closed.

"There you are, child," a feminine voice that was somehow light and dark all at once whispered in my ear. "I've been waiting for you."

I blinked my eyes open to see Hecate walking toward me, a gentle smile on her face. She moved with an ethereal grace, her form a mesmerizing blend of shadow and radiance, as if she'd been woven from the very fabric of the night sky. Her hair, long and flowing, shimmered like the surface of a moonlit lake, cascading in waves of silver and ebony. It framed a face of timeless beauty, where eyes as deep and fathomless as the night sky regarded me with an intensity that was both comforting and awe-inspiring. Her tall, curvaceous figure was cloaked in a gown that seemed to shift in color and texture—appearing in one moment to be made of the darkest velvet of the night sky, and in the next, sparkling with the brilliance of starlight. Around her neck hung a pendant that pulsed with a soft, otherworldly glow, its light ebbing and flowing like the phases of the moon. Trailing ribbons of mist and shadows swirled around her bare feet, and the air around her hummed with the power of ancient magic.

"Great Mother," I breathed, rising to my feet without

thought. Pure awe rolled through me as I watched her approach, and as she came to stand before me, I felt incredibly humbled.

The goddess occasionally whispered in our ears during rituals, or even sent us dream visions when we prayed for guidance. But for her to appear to me in all her divine glory, even if it was only in my mind's eye, was an honor few witches ever received.

Her dark eyes twinkled as she came to a stop in front of me, and I dipped my head, unsure if it was proper to look directly into the eyes of a deity. Swallowing hard, I fixed my gaze on the black beauty mark nestled in the divot between her upper lip and her nose. This close, I could see it was shaped like a four-pointed star, and my fingers unconsciously flew to the mark on my left cheekbone, which was nearly identical.

Hecate's smile broadened, revealing blindingly white teeth. "I am happy you have finally found your star," she said.

I started, my eyes flying up to meet her gaze. There were flecks of silver swirling in her black irises, like tiny stars in a pocket-sized galaxy. "My star?" I asked.

She smiled and gestured toward Maximillian, who was still standing with his eyes closed, the amethyst clasped in his palms. I instinctively knew from the unnatural stillness that had settled over the world that this was a moment suspended in time—that neither of the others could sense or hear the goddess speaking.

"He will be your guiding light on this journey," she told me. "The one you will return to when the world grows dark and all seems lost."

I glanced around at the city spread out below us, a sense of irony filling me. "Seems like things are pretty dark already," I said with a shrug.

The goddess chuckled. "I always did enjoy your flippant tongue," she said. "But heed my words, Kitana. Although I answered your call today, I will not always come, and nor should you always turn to me. You may be a daughter of the moon, but you are also a daughter of multiple realms, multiple gods. There are many forces you may call upon in Valentaera, should you only find the courage to."

A sense of dread coiled at the base of my spine, and I shook my head. "I don't know what you mean."

"Don't you, though?" A slight edge entered the goddess's tone as she stepped closer, and I shivered as her magnetic energy crackled over my skin. "There is a reason you were born with the power to command only shadows, child. A reason that the Grand Matron shunned you, that your lover feared you, that you were locked away. And if you do not embrace the dark side of your nature, you will find yourself trapped in a prison of your own making. One that no one can free you from, not even your vampire lord."

A sick fear began to churn in my stomach, and I swallowed back the hint of bile that surged into my throat. "I don't think I can do what you ask," I told her, my voice shaking.

Hecate's expression softened, and she reached out with a moon-pale hand to brush a lock of hair from my shoulder. The gesture was gentle, motherly even, and the fear eased just a little. "I know," she said, a tender smile curving her dark lips. "You aren't ready yet. But you will be. And when you are, he will be there to guide you."

She leaned in and brushed her lips against my forehead, and I gasped as pure power rushed through me at the contact. Shadows exploded around my feet, rippling out like dark ribbons in the wind, and my spine arched as a pillar of moonlight engulfed my body. Shocked cries echoed around me, and I knew that the others could see what was happening as the storm of shadow and light surged around me.

I knew I should have been concerned, but the magic storming my blood wiped away every thought, every feeling, filling me with an exhilaration the likes of which I hadn't experienced in a long time. Every cell in my body seemed to crackle with power, and I lifted my hands to the sky, watching as the lunar energy rippled along my fingers.

No longer was I the weak, terrified girl that had been dragged out of prison only a few weeks ago. No longer was I trapped in a frail body, cut off from my birthright, dependent upon the mercy of others.

I was Kitana Nightshade. Witch. Vampire Slayer. Daughter of all worlds, according to the Great Mother. And I would fear nothing and no one.

Opening my eyes, I aimed my right hand toward the sneering statue of Vladimir Invictus. A blast of lunar energy erupted from my palm, screaming through the air, and the statue exploded, the blast echoing like cannon-fire. The tendrils of shadow around me swarmed, deflecting the shrapnel, and a triumphant grin tugged at my lips until my cheeks ached from the force of it.

I wouldn't be able to do that again—the lunar energy had been a temporary gift, one that always faded back into shadow energy after the ritual was complete. But it felt really damn good to be able to wield it, even if just for a moment.

"Well, that was terrifying," Sparrow remarked, and I turned to see the others staring at me, a comical array of expressions varying from impressed to annoyed to intimidated etched onto their faces. "Is that what you'll be doing to Emperor Vlad in a few weeks?"

"Gods, I hope so," Eliza said with relish.

Lucius grunted as the intense glow around me began to fade. "It's a good thing your shadows were there to protect us," he said as the ribbons of darkness retreated across the ground to curl up around my feet. "Without them, we would have all been incinerated by that blast."

I blanched, my gaze flying to Maximillian's face. "Was it really that bad?" I asked.

"It was... intense," he acknowledged with a slight dip of his chin. "But it was also everything I hoped it would be. You were magnificent, Kitana."

His eyes glowed with pride, and a warm flush spread through my body at his praise. But the sensation of a furry body brushing up against my ankle distracted me from him, and I glanced down to see Jinx crouching between my legs, pawing at the tendrils of shadow.

I laughed, then reached down and scooped her into my arms. "Are you happy to see your little friends again?" I crooned, nuzzling my face into hers.

"That cat is so strange," Nyra remarked, shaking her head.

"I still don't understand why you hate that cat and Lucius adores her," Sparrow said, crossing his legs at the ankle as he leaned against one of the statues. "You're both Ferae—aren't you all animal lovers?"

"I don't *hate* her," Nyra said stiffly, her eyes narrowing on Sparrow. "I'm just not much of a cat person. And I don't like how she just pops in and out of nowhere, like some apparition. One time I was in my office, doing paperwork, and she materialized right on top of the finance report I was writing. Spilled a bottle of ink and ruined a full day's worth of work."

She glared at Jinx, who simply flicked her tail, then jumped out of my arms and sauntered over to Lucius. "Cats are chaotic creatures," I said as Lucius bent slightly so she could climb onto his massive shoulders. "They respond better to people with stabilizing presences."

Nyra crossed her arms. "Are you saying that I'm a destabilizing person?" she demanded.

"Don't be silly," Eliza cut in before I could respond. "You bring a lot of order to this place. But you're also pretty rigid sometimes, Ny. Lucius might be a grumpy old fuck, but he's a solid, grounding presence, and even though he's built like a mountain, he knows how to give when it matters." She grinned at me as Lucius lifted a surprised eyebrow at Eliza's impromptu analysis. "That's why you gave him the earth element stone."

"Speaking of which," Sparrow said, tossing his piece of aquamarine into the air and catching it. "Are we allowed to keep these? I confess that in the short time we've been together, I've gotten a little attached."

"Of course you can," I said. The stones were all charged now —they would provide a bit of good luck and protection, and maybe even enhance their intuitive abilities a little. "In fact, you should all keep yours. Consider them my gift to you."

"Sweet," Eliza said. She held her carnelian stone up to the moonlight, turning it this way and that. "I think it'll make a pretty awesome bracelet."

"You're going to make it into jewelry?" Nyra asked, sounding intrigued. She studied the clear quartz she'd been given, a thoughtful look in her eyes. "Do you think you could make a necklace for this?"

"Sure." Eliza waggled her eyebrows at Lucius and Sparrow. "Do you boys want jewelry too?"

Lucius rolled his eyes as Sparrow laughed, but I noticed him tuck the moss agate into his pocket. I turned to see Maximillian smiling faintly as he watched them, and I realized I was witnessing a rare moment of the five of them together, relaxed and with their guard down, laughing and teasing each other the way I always imagined a real family did.

The sight opened a yawning ache deep in the pit of my chest, a wound that had torn into my heart the day my mother had walked out of my life and had never fully healed. The desire to belong, to have a family of my own someday.

I'd had glimmers of such things in the past—cautious

friendships formed over the years, and a dark passion I'd once mistaken for love. But I knew that true friendship and lasting bonds required the opening of one's heart, the baring of one's soul, the sharing of secrets clutched deep to one's chest.

And the last time I had dared to be that vulnerable, that open, the person I'd foolishly trusted had nearly destroyed me.

As if sensing my inner turmoil, Maximillian's gaze snapped to mine. His smile faded, and he came to me, stepping through the circle of candles that had guttered out.

"Are you all right?" he asked, his eyes roving over my face.

I blinked away the sting of tears, not wanting him to see them. "I'm fine," I told him. "I'm just... taking it all in. Tonight has been... a lot."

"The past few days have been a lot," he agreed, taking my hand in his. He stroked his thumb across the back of my hand, and some of the ache in my chest eased. "And there is much that needs to be done to prepare you for what's ahead. Are you ready to begin?"

He will be your guiding light on this journey. Hecate's voice echoed in my ears, and I wondered if this was what she meant. That Maximillian would be the one to bring me back to myself, to hone me into the weapon I needed to be.

"Yes." I curled my fingers around his, my resolve strengthening, and gave him a grim smile. "Let's go end an empire."

PART II

THE RECKONING

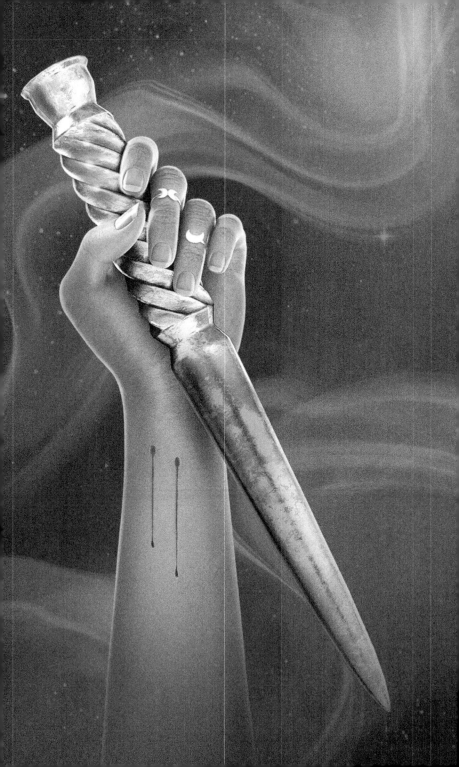

18

Casimir

Casimir Invictus didn't consider himself particularly prone to vices.

But even he could see the appeal of the Midnight Menagerie.

The Crown Prince of Noxalis lounged in a wing-backed velvet chair, his head tipped back as the thrall in his lap fed him sips of bloodwine from a crystal goblet. His citrine eyes roved over the scene splayed out beyond him—a sensory feast that was a decadent blend of high society luxury and untamed wilderness. High ceilings adorned with intricate moldings loomed above, while lavish chandeliers cast a dim, sultry glow over the patrons. The walls, draped in dark, sumptuous fabrics, were juxtaposed with the verdant lushness of faux vines and exotic plants that crept along the edges, lending an almost jungle-like feel to the opulence.

Interspersed between groupings of couches and chairs were gilded cages elevated on platforms, each one housing an exotic offering for the clientele to feast their eyes on. In one, a majestic snow leopard, its coat a tapestry of black on white, paced with restless energy. In another cage suspended from the ceiling, a golden eagle perched, his keen eyes scanning the room. And in yet another lay a silver stag, its antlered head bowed as it rested on folded legs that were meant to stretch long and roam through fields and forests.

All of these animals had once been plentiful, commonplace even, throughout Valentaera. But that was before the Eternal Night had descended upon the world, plunging the continent into darkness. Many of the animals that had once roamed the wilds had gone extinct. The only ones left were those who had been saved by collectors like the proprietor of this establishment, who bred them exclusively for those who could afford the extravagant luxury of keeping and feeding an animal that had no practical purpose.

Casimir personally considered this to be wasteful behavior. With such a shortage of food supplies, keeping such animals for vanity was foolish. Yet there was a small part of him that was grateful that the bloodlines of these great beasts, captive though they might be, continued to live on.

Perhaps when technology and science improved, they would be able to find a way to create sustainable habitats for them. So they could exist outside of cages, and bring some semblance of balance to the continent's necrotic ecosystem.

"Cas," the vampire seated next to him groaned, a long-suffering note in his voice. "Can you look like you are at least *pretending* to have fun? You're spoiling the ambiance."

Casimir turned his head to look at Caelum Stellaris, who was sprawled out on the chaise next to him. The heir to House Stellaris's black-and-white streaked head rested in the lap of a thrall who was massaging his scalp, while a second perched on his thighs, hand-feeding him grapes. His midnight eyes were half-lidded with lust, but there was a spark of annoyance in them as he looked back at Casimir.

"You hardly seem to be suffering," Casimir said, arching an eyebrow. "In fact, I'd say you're well attended."

"As are you," Caelum said, giving a pointed look to the thrall in Casimir's lap. Casimir belatedly realized that the woman had been running her hands up and down his chest, and had even opened the top two buttons of his collar. He caught her delicate fingers between his before she could unbutton a third, and she pouted up at him from beneath her lashes.

"Is there nothing else I can offer you, Your Highness?" the thrall asked in a breathy voice, presenting her swan-like neck to him. "Nothing you want to... take?"

Casimir glanced away from Caelum's expectant look to survey her properly. She was a pretty little thing, with long golden hair that flowed past her hips and a lush figure barely concealed by the sheer silk robe draping her body. As she leaned in closer, one of her breasts slipped free, the nipple brushing against his chest. It was a calculated move, one Casimir was certain she'd executed many times

"Sorry, darling," the crown prince drawled, deftly grasping the edge of her robe to cover her. "I'm not really into blondes."

The thrall's face flushed with embarrassment, and she quickly slid off his lap. Holding her head high, she flounced across the room to a table, where two male vampires were engrossed in a card game. She nestled into the lap of the larger male, who wrapped an arm around her without hesitation, then turned his face into her neck and buried his fangs in her soft flesh.

Casimir could hear her moan from across the room.

Caelum scoffed in disgust. "'I don't like blondes'?" he mocked, sitting up. The thrall in his lap squealed as he dislodged her, but Caelum caught the woman before she could tumble off. "Since when?"

"Her hair is the same shade as my father's," Casimir

muttered, running a hand through his own black-brown tresses. He'd reportedly inherited the dark strands from his mother—a human woman whom, like most women who were unfortunate enough to be *amorte*, had died immediately upon birthing him. "He's the last person I want to think of when I have my fangs or my cock buried in someone else."

"Well, there's a plethora of other women here for you to choose from," Caelum said, waving his hand about the room. Indeed, there were many—some dressed in sheer silk like the thrall he'd offended, carrying goblets of bloodwine or blood cocktails to vampires from the bar, others dancing on tables and clad in animal pelts belonging to creatures that *had* gone extinct. "Gods, if I knew you were going to be such a stick in the mud, I would have brought Lazarus instead."

Casimir scoffed. "You hate Lazarus." The Sanguis Noctis heir, with his capricious nature and volatile moods, was an acquired taste at best. He was like a bloodhound when it came to sniffing out the weaknesses and hot buttons of others, and Caelum was particularly susceptible to his taunts. The two usually came to blows at least once every Summit, much to the consternation of their respective fathers.

"Yes, but at least he knows how to have a good time," Caelum said. "Lazarus is a bastard, but he'd be drinking and reveling right along with me if I'd brought him, not sitting there looking like someone had just squatted down and took a massive shit right in front of him."

Casimir rolled his eyes, but kept his mouth shut. He knew Caelum was right. There were plenty of human thralls here who would suit his preferences—the raven-haired woman dressed in a gown like liquid silver who draped herself across a male lounging on a settee was exactly his type. But unlike many of his peers, Casimir preferred his women fully aware and consenting, and he knew for a fact that the owner of the Midnight

Menagerie laced the food he fed his thralls with a light aphrodisiac to keep them pliant and willing.

Truthfully, Casimir would have never chosen this place on his own, or any of the establishments like it here in Umbral, Noxalis's capital city and the heart of the empire. He would have much preferred to spend the evening with his brother, Taius, but the general was unusually late. Casimir wasn't sure why Taius was delayed, but Caelum had cajoled him into coming out with him despite the mild concern he felt at his brother's absence. As the commander of the empire's naval fleet, Caelum spent much of his time at sea, so it had only been natural for him to want a night out on the town before the Summit began. And while Casimir technically outranked Caelum, refusing the invitation would have cast suspicion upon him. He might have responsibilities as the crown prince, might be expected to embody the "Iron Fist, Iron Heart, Iron Rule," motto of his house, but even the staunchest members of House Invictus indulged in the pleasures of human flesh.

After all, what was the point of conquering the human race if one wasn't allowed to reap the benefits?

"Ahh, did someone finally catch your eye?" Caelum said with a grin. He turned to follow Casimir's line of sight, and the lascivious look on his face vanished. "Tala's tits! Is that my sister?"

Casimir started, looking back at the woman he'd been staring at earlier. Her waterfall of black hair shifted as she slid up the male's chest, revealing a pointed ear pierced with diamond hoops, and high-boned, elegant features he knew like the back of his hand. The prince realized then that it wasn't a vampire she was lying on top of, but a human thrall—there were both male and female servants on offer at the menagerie, after all. He watched with rapt attention as she licked up the side of the man's neck, her fangs snapping down, and the human gripped her waist, preparing for the intrusion.

"She's not supposed to be here," Caelum fumed, leaping to his feet. He ignored the thrall this time as she crashed to the ground and took three steps forward, his attention glued to the dark-haired female, who appeared not to have noticed them. "If our father finds out—"

"Don't." Casimir grabbed Caelum's arm, pulling him to a stop. Already, heads were turning toward them, drawing far more attention than he wanted. "Let me handle this."

"Are you sure?" Caelum asked, his brow furrowing. "She's my responsibility, not yours."

"Of course I am," Casimir said, a little impatiently. "I need to get back to the castle to prepare for tomorrow, anyway. I might as well take her with me, and she's far more likely to listen to me than you." He loosened his grip on Caelum's arm and clapped him on the shoulder. "Don't get your drawers in a twist, Commander Stellaris. Enjoy what's left of your night. Your sister is safe with me."

"Fine," Caelum grumbled. "But only because it's you." His eyes seared into mine. "Crown prince or not, if anything happens to her, I'll have your head, Casimir. Take care of her."

With that threat hanging in the air between them, Caelum returned to the couch, which was now empty. A new pair of thralls approached as soon as he sat down, happily offering to pick up where the last two had left off. But Casimir could feel Caelum's eyes on him as he crossed the room to where his sister was now drinking from the thrall, her long, black lashes sweeping against her high cheekbones, a look of pure bliss on her features.

"Viviana," Casimir said quietly, standing over her. "It's time to go."

Caelum's twin sister pulled away from the human's neck, then slowly lifted her head to look up at him. Her eyes were heavy-lidded, her pupils blown with lust, and her pouty lips glistened with blood. This close, he could see the flecks of silver in her midnight irises, like tiny stars lit up against the blackness of her soul.

"Your Highness," she said in a low, throaty voice. "How convenient that you are here to spoil my fun."

"Convenient is not the word I'd use," Casimir said, his voice drier than tombstone dust. "You should know better than to flaunt your father's rules the night before the Summit. He'll be harsher with his punishments than usual if he finds out."

"Ahh, but that's what makes the thrill so much more intense." Viviana grinned at him, her fangs glinting in the low light. "We all have to live a little, Prince. Even those of us who are kept in cages."

The irony that they were standing in the center of a sex club, surrounded by caged animals, wasn't lost on Casimir. Wordlessly, he offered her his hand, and she took it with a sigh.

"Caelum is right," she said as she allowed him to pull her to her feet. "You really are a stick in the mud."

Casimir's brows arched. "You were listening, were you?" he said as he led her to the exit, weaving through the cages and couches and fake plants all around them. "That means you knew we were here, and you chose a spot in plain view of us anyway."

"Perhaps I wanted you to watch."

Viviana licked the blood off her lips, and the sight of her tongue darting against her mouth made Casimir clench his jaw. Tearing his gaze away from her, he marched them through the doors, then signaled for the bouncer outside to call them a cab.

"A vehicle?" she asked, a little surprised. "Where's your mount?"

"We took Caelum's carriage, so I left him at home." His destrier-style aethersteed with its distinctive red and gold metal design drew too much attention, and he'd wanted to maintain a low profile.

A black hansom cab pulled up to the curb, and Casimir handed Viviana into it before joining her inside. He gritted his teeth as his knees knocked into hers, but the lady of House Stellaris didn't seem to notice. She hooked a lock of white hair behind her ear and turned her face to stare out the window as the cab began to navigate Umbral's winding streets.

Viviana and Caelum both shared a distinctive white streak that cut across one wing of their otherwise black hair—hers on the right, his on the left. Star-touched, some called them—the twin heirs of House Stellaris that should have never been.

Technically, only one of them was the heir, as female vampires could not have children. Since the curse of vampirism had struck them over two thousand years ago, only male Night-forged were able to procreate, making Noxalis's surviving bloodlines patriarchal by default.

Still, the fact that Viviana wasn't the heir of her house didn't make her any less special. While Caelum was born with the typical abilities of House Stellaris—shadowfire, and a natural affinity for astronomy—Viviana was a seer, gifted with the power of prophecy and foresight. Her ability was wildly unpredictable, her visions as likely to strike during a meditation session as they were during a simple conversation over tea. Yet she was still considered precious not just by their fathers, but by all of vampire nobility. A seer hadn't been born to House Stellaris since the death of Astellion, Tenebros's previous incarnation as the God of Night and the Celestial Heavens. She was rarer than a falling star, and fiercely guarded.

Unfortunately for her guards, she was an expert at evading them.

Viviana frowned as she noticed Casimir's gaze on her face and turned her attention from the window to look at him. "You don't have to treat me like a child, you know," she said, her dulcet voice full of reproach. "I know I don't look it, but I'm two hundred years your senior."

Casimir rolled his eyes. "Everyone at this court is centuries older than me." At only seventy-four years of age, Casimir was a baby by vampire standards, especially when compared to his father. Emperor Vladimir was over twelve-hundred years old, and *his* father before him had been alive during Astellion's Descent—the chaotic period of transition when the Nightforged had transformed into vampires, followed by the Chaos War that had erupted between the three realms. It was honestly a wonder that one of the other Invictus families hadn't assassinated him after ruling for so many centuries without producing an heir. Casimir supposed he was his father's saving grace, though the emperor certainly didn't treat him as such.

"Besides," he continued, fixing Viviana with a stern look, "I wouldn't have to treat you like a child if you behaved like an adult. There is a perfectly valid reason your father commanded you to stay at the castle, even if you don't want to admit it."

Viviana folded her arms, saying nothing. It was a well-known fact that Lady Stellaris's prophetic ability had also left her with a touch of madness. She had blackout episodes where she was prone to speak in tongues, tear at her clothing, and even dance naked in the streets. These episodes weren't frequent, but like her visions, they could happen anywhere, at anytime, which was why she was not permitted to roam the streets of Umbral, or go anywhere without an escort.

Her brother, Caelum, was extremely protective of her, but Viviana found him overbearing. Had she refused to go with him out of spite, he would have tossed her over his shoulder and stormed back to the castle with her, and their father would have punished them both—her for leaving, and Caelum for leaving her unattended in the first place. By taking her back, Casimir could avoid all that mess, and if Highlord Ingatius saw them together... well, he couldn't very well object to the Crown Prince himself taking his daughter out on the town, could he?

The hansom cab came to a stop outside the gates to the Iron Spire, and Casimir stepped out so he could hand Viviana down and pay the driver for his trouble. The guards at the gate leaped into action as soon as they saw the prince's face, opening a small door built into the gate so they could enter discreetly.

"Your Highness," the guard murmured they passed. "Lady Stellaris."

As soon as they cleared the gate, Casimir grabbed Viviana's hand and stalked toward one of the castle's side entrances. There was enough commotion from servants and slaves running around to carry out last minute preparations that no one paid them a second glance, and he sent a silent prayer of thanks down to Tenebros.

They'd nearly made it to the entrance when Casimir heard the main gates of the castle groan open.

Despite his better judgment, Casimir found himself turning toward the sound. "Oooh," Viviana cooed as they watched a midnight blue carriage pulled by two aethersteeds roll into the courtyard. "Maximillian has finally arrived. I've been dying to meet his little pet."

"Oh?" Casimir lifted a brow. What was so special about a single human to merit the seer's attention?

"I heard he's presenting her as a candidate for the Descendency," Viviana said as the carriage came to a stop outside the stables. "It's been over fifty years since Desdemona passed, so I'm excited to see who he's finally chosen as her replacement."

Casimir narrowed his eyes as a footman rushed to open the door for the arriving vampires. Lord Starclaw emerged first, the moonlight glinting against the top of his distinctive blue-grey hair. Of the four house heirs, Casimir had always found

Maximillian the most tolerable—he was level-headed and practical, and tended to lend more reasoned viewpoints to debates and discussions regarding statecraft. The crown prince didn't always agree with Maximillian's recommendations, but he respected the vampire male for his consistent efforts to put the welfare of his subjects—vampire and human alike—over his personal needs and desires.

There was a strange sort of natural order when it came to vampire procreation, and Casimir wasn't certain whether Tenebros himself had implemented it, or if it was enforced by the universe itself. Natural born vampires such as Maximillian and Casimir could only produce four vampire children at one time —any attempts beyond that number resulted in the death of the human every time, with no known exceptions.

Maximillian's youngest vampire childe, Desdemona, had been killed during the War of Eternal Night, and he had loved her deeply enough that he had elected not to replace her, much to the consternation of his father. It was generally encouraged for vampires to replace their children as soon as possible, because each successive generation could produce more vampires than the one before. A child of a natural vampire could produce seven more children, and those offspring could produce ten more, and the number continued to increase exponentially all the way down to the sixth generation, which could produce unlimited numbers, though the Turning success rate was far lower. Those vampires tended to be the weakest, with no magic to speak of, but they made excellent fodder for the emperor's military.

It was a surprise indeed to see that Maximillian had finally made the decision to replace Desdemona. And Casimir found himself curious to see who the Psychoros heir had chosen.

Lucius, Maximillian's oldest childe, exited the carriage after Maximillian, his sharp amber eyes sweeping the surrounding area for threats. They found Casimir's at once, and he inclined his head fractionally before continuing his assessment. Casimir nodded back, appreciative that the vampire had respected his unspoken need for anonymity by not drawing attention to him. He watched as Lucius strode over to the footmen unloading the carriage trunk to bark orders to them, while Maximillian returned to the carriage door, offering his hand to the woman still inside.

Casimir wasn't sure why, but he held his breath as she emerged. Her hair, black with brown highlights and wavy, cascaded around her shoulders, a stark contrast against her pale, moonlit skin. The bodice of the midnight blue velvet gown she wore clung to her figure, accentuating her curves before flaring out into a flowing skirt that swirled around her ankles. The gown, combined with her hair, seemed to absorb the surrounding light, making her appear as if she had stepped out of the night itself. As she raised her head, Casimir noticed a beauty mark just beneath the corner of her left eye, enhancing the striking features of her square-shaped face. Most arresting were her violet eyes—a shade Casimir had never seen before.

As the crown prince stared at the woman, he became aware of a tug in the center of his chest. It was as though someone had hooked a finger into his torso and was trying to pull him forward. Frowning, he placed a hand against his solar plexus, wondering if perhaps he had a cramp. But the strange sensation persisted.

Before he could decide whether to act on the impulse to move closer, Viviana seized his arm. Her claws shredded the sleeve of his jacket, and he whirled just in time to see her eyes roll back into her head, her spine wrenching as though she'd been speared by a bolt of lightning.

"She is the one who will awaken you," she rasped in a voice much higher and breathier than her usual dulcet tones. *"The one*

who will open your eyes to the deadly truth your mother buried within you."

Her mouth snapped shut, and she collapsed like a stone as whatever entity that seized control of her body vanished. "Viviana!" Casimir caught her by the shoulders before her knees could hit the ground and hauled her upright, shock and confusion whirling inside him. "Lady Stellaris, are you all right?"

Viviana's eyelashes fluttered as she came back to herself, and Casimir exhaled in relief as her inky eyes found his in the darkness. "Well, that was interesting," she muttered, shaking her head as if trying to clear it. "I haven't had one of those in a while. What did I say this time?"

"Something about a deadly truth I'm about to discover," Casimir said darkly as he set her back on her feet. He wasn't about to tell Viviana the details—there was no explanation as to why she remembered some of her prophecies and not others, but in this case, it was a blessing.

"Well, that's annoyingly vague." She yawned, swaying on her feet the way she always did after an episode—the visions always exhausted her regardless of their scope or importance. "Would you escort me back to my room, Your Highness? I think I ought to turn in early."

"Of course." Casimir offered her his arm.

She frowned at the claw marks that had torn through his sleeve and into his skin. "I'll ask my father to have this replaced for you," she said as she looped her arm around his.

"No need. I've been meaning to throw this out, anyway." A lie —this was one of his favorite coats, and he'd only had it made a year ago. But if Viviana told her father about this, he would inquire about the vision. It was clearly about Casimir's future, and he had no desire for anyone else to know about it until he figured out what it meant.

Casimir looked over Viviana's head toward the mystery

woman to see if there was something about her that would shed some light on this odd bit of prophecy. He didn't see anything out of the ordinary about her aside from her eyes, but he did note the possessive hand Maximillian placed at the small of her back as he led her to the front steps of the castle. She clearly wasn't just a servant to him—there was some attachment there, strong enough to compel Maximillian to gift her with immortality and make her a permanent member of his house.

But what was it?

And how was she connected to *him*?

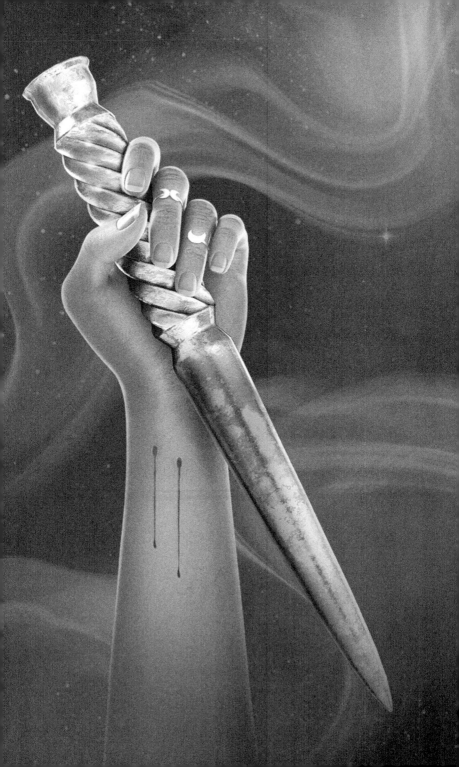

19

Kitana

"Are you ready for this, Kitana?"

Maximillian's low voice penetrated through the fog of my thoughts as we sat in the carriage, and I turned away from the view outside to see him watching me. The intensity in his gaze sent nervous energy skittering across my skin, and I fisted my skirts in my hands, resisting the urge to shiver.

"Of course I'm ready," I said, a slight edge in my tone. "The five of you have been preparing me for this for the last three weeks." Lessons on etiquette, on vampire politics and history, on vampire bloodlines and house rivalries, on ritual and ceremony, and even dancing. So. Much. Fucking. Dancing. My feet were still sore from all the ballroom lessons Sparrow and Nyra had put me through, which in my opinion were even worse than the brutal training and conditioning drills Lucius had tortured me with every evening. Those at least had a purpose I could appreciate. Even if dancing *was* good footwork training.

"Three weeks isn't nearly enough," Lucius growled from his seat next to me. I wish I was sitting next to Maximillian instead

—the massive warrior took up three quarters of the seat and crowded me against the wall—but for some reason Maximillian insisted upon keeping as much distance between us as possible. He had put up a wall between us after the near kiss we'd shared in the chapel, one I didn't fully understand, but was grateful for. The last thing I needed was to be distracted by whatever feelings I'd sprouted for him. "Most Descendency candidates have months, sometimes even years, to prepare."

"You've only said that to me half a dozen times, and it isn't any more helpful now than it was the second time you mentioned it," I retorted.

Lucius glowered, but Maximillian smiled faintly. "I'm glad you're not frightened," he said, leaning back in his seat. "But I want to make sure you remember the part you are here to play. That the world you are about to enter is not like the one we left, and that no matter what you might see or hear, you must not let your mask slip. If you do, even for one second, you could doom us all."

"I know," I said quietly. I understood more than he realized what was at stake if I exposed my true nature.

The carriage came to a stop, and I pressed my face to the window, looking at the spiked gates looming just ahead while the driver spoke to the guards. A few seconds later, they opened, and my pulse drummed faster as we drove through the gates and into the courtyard of House Invictus's stronghold.

The Iron Spire.

A wave of surrealism rippled through me as I realized I was truly here. At the heart of the vampire kingdom, where Vladimir Invictus sat on his accursed throne. At long last, the vampire king would be within staking range, and he would finally answer for the crimes he'd committed not just against witches, but all of Valentaera.

"Easy now," Maximillian said as bloodlust surged in my

veins. He placed a hand on my knee, and the contact send a current of awareness up my thigh, distracting me from my train of thought. "Remember. Until the time comes to strike, you are not Kitana the Vampire Slayer. You are Catherine the Vampire Thrall, my adoring, devoted servant. As long as you play that part, there is nothing to fear."

I lifted my head to meet his starfire gaze. "I'm not afraid," I told him, my resolve stronger than ever, and I meant it. With my magical well alive and humming inside me once more, and weeks of training and conditioning under my belt, I felt stronger than ever.

But Maximillian was right. I needed to be careful. I might have my magic and my combat skills, but if I used them before the time was right—if I killed a vampire before I took out the vampire king, the jig would be up. My advantage lied in the vampires assuming I was a harmless little thing, a demure human servant who was utterly loyal to her master and wouldn't dare dream of laying a hand on her vampire overlords.

The carriage rolled to a stop, and a few seconds later, a footman opened the door. Maximillian disembarked first, followed by Lucius, and then he waited for me, offering his palm so he could help me down.

I accepted his offered hand, then used my other to lift my heavy velvet skirts so I wouldn't trip as I descended the short platform the footman had placed in front of the carriage door. As my slippered feet alighted on the cobblestones, I craned my neck so I could take in the Iron Spire for the first time.

I used to imagine the Iron Spire as a single tower jutting out of the craggy highlands of Graviton Heights, but the name was a bit of a misnomer. It wasn't one spire, but seven that jutted out of a sprawling castle, each designed to resemble iron spikes. They rose from the ground like colossal daggers, their tips reaching for the star-studded sky of the eternal night. Arranged in a triangular formation, they created an illusion that made the central spire appear the tallest, dominating the heart of the city with its imposing presence. Their metallic surfaces reflected the ghostly light of the moon, lending the entire structure an ethereal glow.

"It's impressive, isn't it?" Maximillian said from beside me.

"It is," I agreed, trying not to sound begrudging. After all, we were surrounded by Vladimir's servants. I couldn't afford to sound anything less than impressed. "Beautiful, even."

An icy wind whipped my skirts around my ankles, and I dropped my gaze to adjust my outfit. As I did, I felt a set of eyes on me, and I scanned the courtyard, looking for the watchful presence. But there were too many vampires here, some milling about and chatting while others hurried about doing chores. Any of them could have been looking at me.

"Let's get inside," Maximillian said. He placed a hand at the small of my back, leading me toward the front steps that led to the castle entrance. The doors had been thrown wide open, and as we ascended the steps, a male figure stepped out from behind a pillar.

Maximillian paused at the top of the stairs, taking in the newcomer. He was a few inches shorter than Maximillian, and stockier, but still of formidable height. His long, blood-red hair was pulled back at the nape, highlighting his diamond-shaped face with pronounced cheekbones, a sharp nose, and a cleft chin. He wore a high-collared, black leather tunic, fur-trimmed and open at the throat, revealing a necklace of what looked very much like human incisors resting just above his collar bones. His legs were clad in crimson, rough-textured trousers tucked into black leather boots, and his rolled-up sleeves displayed rugged leather bracelets adorned with bloodstone beads.

"Lazarus Bloodmare," Maximillian said, inclining his head.

"What a surprise. I was expecting the castle steward to greet us. Are you standing in for him?"

"Please." Lazarus sneered, exposing his fangs. His glowing red gaze snapped to mine, and something icy skated through my veins as his nostrils dilated. "I came to get a look at the human slave I hear you're so infatuated with."

"Infatuated?" Maximillian raised a brow. "That's a touch dramatic. But then again, you always had a flare for theatrics."

"Is that so?" The Sanguis Noctis heir scoffed. "If you aren't obsessed with her, then why do I hear you murdered Vinicius to save her? That you risked provoking war with Sanguis Noctis by attacking a member of *my house*?"

"It would be impossible for Pyschoros to provoke a war with Sanguis Noctis," a cold voice said from behind Lazarus. "Not when we are both part of the same kingdom, and serve the same monarch."

Maximillian, who had been perfectly calm, stiffened as Lazarus turned to face the vampire who approached us. He was tall and lithe, with long silver hair that fell nearly to his waist, dressed in swirling blue robes embroidered in a web-like pattern. His eyes, the color of hoarfrost, glittered out of his rawboned face, and his lips thinned as he pinned Lazarus with a thousand-yard stare.

"Of course, Highlord Starclaw," Lazarus replied, a cold mask sliding over his face to wipe away all traces of volatility. He inclined his head toward the older vampire. "I agree that we are not at war. Which is why I don't understand why your son killed a decorated member of not only my house, but Noxalis's military."

"If you have a problem with Maximillian, you may file a formal complaint with my house, or with the emperor," Callix Starclaw said. "And I would take care about making threats you don't plan on following through, Lord Bloodmare. Now come," he said, turning his frosted gaze on Maximillian. "The hour is late, and there is much to discuss."

He turned with an imperious sweep of his robes, leaving us to follow in his wake. Maximillian, Lucius, and I entered the castle, and as we passed Lazarus, the vampire lord took in a deep whiff of my scent, as though he were marking it. Like a fucking bloodhound.

I flexed my fingers, resisting the urge to clench my hands, and turned my attention to the castle itself. Inside, the Great Hall stretched out before us, its high ceilings adorned with intricate carvings that told the history of Noxalis. Tapestries depicting scenes of vampiric glory and conquest adorned the walls, and the dim light from the chandeliers overhead bathed the hall in a golden glow.

The Highlord said nothing as we moved swiftly through the hall, our footsteps echoing on the marble floors. The tension between Maximillian and his father was so thick, you could cut it with a knife, and a sense of both apprehension and anticipation filled me as he led us out of the Great Hall and through a series of ornate corridors that eventually brought us to an enclosed bridge.

Lucius had given me a map of the Iron Spire before we'd left Lumina, and I had spent hours studying it, so I knew where we were going. The structure we were exiting now was the Central Hub, and the enclosed bridge would take us to the westernmost of the seven spires, where House Psychoros resided during the Summit.

The celestial motifs became more pronounced as we approached the covered bridge, with murals of the night sky and constellations gracing the walls. The bridge itself was a gorgeous piece of architecture, its glass walls offering a breathtaking view of the spires as they pierced the eternal night sky. I wished I could pause and look out at the view, but Callix Starclaw did not slow his brisk stride, and I didn't think it would be wise to ask.

As we entered the Psychoros Spire, the ambiance became more tranquil. The hallways here were quieter, the light softer. Plush carpets muffled each step we took, and the air held a hint of incense that took the edge off my nerves as I breathed it in.

The Psychoros Highlord led us into a large, elegantly appointed sitting room three times the size of the common area I'd shared with Maximillian's cohort. The colors here were muted, a palette of serene blues, soft grays, and gentle whites, and the furniture was understated yet luxurious, with comfortable chairs and sofas that invited relaxation. Soft throw pillows added a touch of warmth, and strategically placed aether lamps cast a gentle glow that complemented the peaceful atmosphere. I was a bit surprised to see aetheric technology here in Noxalis, but I supposed it made sense that Vladimir would make use of it here, especially since he had an inventor on staff.

A vampire reading a book on the sofa closest to the fireplace looked up as we entered, then immediately rose to his feet. "Sire," he said, acknowledging his high lord, but his eyes were on Maximillian as he strode across the chamber, his leather book forgotten on the cushions. "Brother," he said warmly, his blue eyes sparkling as he opened his arms.

"Stesha," Maximillian returned, smiling. The tension in the room lessened as the two vampires embraced, and behind me, I could have sworn Lucius let out a small sigh of relief. This was Stesha Starclaw—Callix Starclaw's second eldest childe. Of the four vampires Turned by the Pyschoros high lord, Stesha was reportedly the one Maximillian was closest to—or so Sparrow had explained when we were going over the family trees and the relationships both within and without the four houses.

"It's good to see you," Stesha said, pulling away. Like Lucius, he was built like a warrior, though not nearly as massive. He wore a simple blue-grey tunic and leggings, which I imagined was casual wear given the hour. He had platinum hair, a broad-boned face, and a square jawline highlighted with stubble. He greeted Lucius, then settled his blue gaze on me. "So this is her, eh? Your candidate?"

"Yes," Maximillian said, addressing both him and his father. "May I present Catherine Seabream, Highlord Starclaw?"

Stesha looked expectantly at his Sire, and the high lord crossed the room to the sideboard, where he poured himself a glass of bloodwine. The coppery-sweet scent filled the air, and my stomach rumbled, reminding me that I hadn't eaten in many hours. But I didn't dare think about food as the vampire fixed his cold gaze on me, staring unblinkingly at my face for a long minute.

"She's pretty," Callix eventually said, "but I don't see anything about her that's particularly remarkable."

"Sire," Stesha protested, but Callix steamrolled right over him, his eyes flashing to Maximillian's. "You said in your letter that you expect her to be an asset to our house, but you never explained *why* you believe that to be the case. You also did not bring her to Lake Intuous to present her to me for my approval, which would have been the proper thing to do instead of blindsiding me by bringing her directly to the emperor's court."

The vampire's face was stony as he spoke, but there was no mistaking the rage crackling in his tone. "It is almost," Callix continued in a tone frigid enough to freeze the very bowels of the underworld, "as though you no longer value your father's opinion."

A suffocating silence descended upon the room, making me feel antsy. The beginnings of outrage stirred inside me at the way Callix spoke to Maximillian, but Lucius, who was standing on Maximillian's far side and out of the highlord's line of sight, shot me a warning look. *Do not interfere,* his amber eyes seemed to say. *It will not end well for any of us.*

Maximillian took the opportunity to pick at his nails, affecting a bored expression. "I'm not sure I understand why you are upset," he said, his tone deceptively light. "After all, you've been harrying me to produce another childe for the past fifty years. I assumed you would be pleased now that I've found one, not caught up over such a petty grievance. In case you haven't heard, I've been quite busy. It isn't as if I've had time to come visit."

"Yes," Callix growled, his eyes crackling with ire. "Busy slaughtering your fellow vampires and bringing conflict to my doorstep."

Maximillian blinked. "Are you certain you read the letter I sent? Because I very clearly explained—"

"I did read the letter," his father interrupted. "And while I agree that the commandant deserved death, you should have allowed him to be convicted and executed via the proper channels instead of meting out vigilante justice."

"Vigilante justice?" Maximillian's eyes flashed in a rare show of temper. "Lumina is my city, I have full authority—"

"Over *your people!*" The highlord roared, spittle flying from his mouth. "Not over Nightforged who answer directly to the emperor!"

His chest heaved, and I was convinced Maximillian would back down, or at least show some kind of submission to his highlord. Instead, he merely leaned against the wall and surveyed his father, allowing a hint of disdain to enter his tone.

"Only five minutes in and you're already shouting," he said. "I think you're growing feeble-minded in your old age, Father."

"Catherine." Stesha's hand closed around my upper arm, his voice an urgent whisper in my ear. "I think now would be a good time for me to show you to your room."

I hesitated, but Lucius gave me a swift nod, and I relented. There was a part of me that wanted to stay and watch this confrontation, but there was a good chance Maximillian's father would take his rage out on me, and I wasn't allowed to defend myself. Better to leave the father-son duo to their family spat than to risk blowing my cover so early on.

Stesha led me out of the room and up a winding staircase. "Forgive my Sire for his abrasive welcome," he said as we climbed the stairs. "As you may have surmised, the Highlord and his son do not have an easy relationship."

"I know," I told him. "Lord Starclaw told me about what happened to his mother."

Stesha's broad shoulders slumped a little. "Odessa is very much loved and missed by everyone in our house," he said as he opened the door to the fourth level. There was a small antechamber with a table placed against the far wall, and a painting of Callix and his late wife hung directly above it. "And no one loved her more than our high lord."

We paused in the antechamber, and I took a moment to study the painting. It was a formal portrait, with Callix seated and Odessa standing behind him, her dainty hand resting on his broad shoulder. I was struck by how different the vampire in the painting was from the one I had met downstairs. His features were kinder, a soft smile playing around the harsh line of his mouth, and his eyes, while still pale as ice, held a touch of warmth to them.

"I can see that," I said, feeling a touch of sadness for the couple who had obviously once been happy together. Regardless of what Maximillian believed, his father clearly hadn't discarded his wife from his heart, at least not completely. After all, why would he still have a portrait of the two of them hanging in the spire, if he no longer cared for her?

"Maximillian informed me you do not have a maid, and that

you may require some additional help since you will be expected to act and dress like vampire nobility," Stesha said as he led me down a corridor lined with doors. "I will lend one of my thralls, Marisse, to attend you for the duration of the Summit."

"Oh," I said, a little taken aback by this kindness. Were all Psychoros vampires this nice, Stesha's sire notwithstanding? "Well, thank you. I appreciate it."

Stesha showed me to my room, then bade me good night and shut the door. I let out a small sigh of relief at finally having some privacy, and leaned against the door, taking in the chamber. It was smaller than the one Maximillian had given me in the Tower, but still luxurious, with an elegant four-poster bed dominating much of the space. The walls were painted in the same soft blue as the sitting room, while the carpet underfoot was a deeper shade of the same hue, creating a soothing, cohesive look. A fireplace occupied one wall, and a large bay window took up most of another, offering a breathtaking view of the castle complex and the city beyond. A comfortable chaise lounge sat in front of it, an ideal spot for reading or simply taking in the view. All in all, it was cozy.

A servant had left my luggage at the foot of the bed, and I knelt in front of it, wanting to unpack my things. There were two trunks—one filled with the wardrobe Maximillian had ordered for me to wear during the Summit, and another filled with personal, practical items. I spent the next hour hanging up gowns and tunics, putting away underclothes and nightgowns, finding places for toiletries and jewelry, and so on.

There were also a few books—one on the legends and myths of Valentaera's pantheon, and another on House Invictus's lineage and history—that I hadn't finished before we'd left. And there was also my armor, stakes, and the pouch of bloodbane Sparrow had given me. These items were hidden in a false compartment at the base of the trunk, just in case anyone came in here to snoop through my things.

Aside from Lucius and Maximillian, no one from House Psychoros knew my true purpose for being here. And we wanted to keep it that way.

After I finished putting everything away, I changed into a knee-length nightgown, then stood in front of the mirror, taking a minute to study myself. Between Eliza's mysterious elixir, Nyra consistently shoving meals down my throat, and Lucius's brutal training, I had undergone a complete transformation. My face was fuller, the curves at my breasts and hips more pronounced, the muscles in my arms, legs, and shoulders defined and graceful.

Maximillian's cohort had rebuilt me into the lethal weapon I was born to be. And in just five days, the vampire king would be dead at my hand.

A firm knock at the door interrupted me from my musings. "Who is it?" I called, hoping that I wasn't about to be summoned to go somewhere or meet someone. I was dead on my feet and wanted nothing more than to curl up in that plush-looking bed and get some much needed rest.

"It's me," Maximillian called back. There was a short pause before he added, "I wanted to check on you."

"Oh." A tiny blossom of warmth unfurled in my chest, and I opened the door to find him standing in the hallway. He'd stripped off his coat and waistcoat, leaving only the trousers and white linen shirt, the top three buttons open to reveal an expanse of marble-white skin. A long black box was tucked under his right arm, and he smiled as I raised a quizzical brow.

"May I come in? I've brought you a gift."

"A gift?" Curious, I stepped back, allowing him to enter. His powerful presence filled the small room, and a shiver of awareness rushed over me as I realized that this was the first time we'd been alone together since our conversation in the chapel.

Maximillian set the box on the bench by the foot of the bed, then crossed over to the fireplace to lean one broad shoulder against the mantle. He looked tired, his usually flawless hair mussed, the starfire glow in his eyes dimmed. "I'm sorry about my father," he told me. "I know I warned you what to expect, but hearing him deride you like that couldn't have been easy."

I shrugged. "I was a lot more bothered by the way he treated *you*." I pursed my lips as I studied him. "Though to be fair, if I didn't know better, I'd say you were riling him up on purpose."

A shadow of a smirk appeared on his full mouth. "I was."

"But why?"

A glimmer of pain flickered in his eyes, and for a moment, I thought he would tell me. But then he shrugged, the emotion vanishing like mist in the morning sun. "Father-son things," he said, pointing toward the box he'd left on the bed. "You should open that."

"Oh. Right." I'd completely forgotten. Crossing over to the bed, I flipped up the metal clasps holding the box shut, then opened it. A gasp flew from my lips at the treasure trove that lay inside—a small arsenal of silver blades, masterfully forged, with amethysts winking up at me from the filigreed handles. There were a dozen, ranging from tiny throwing knives to razor thin stilettos to a dagger that was nearly the length of my forearm.

"These are beautiful." I picked one up and gently pressed the pad of my forefinger to the edge. Blood welled up along the cut far sooner than I expected—fuck, these things were *sharp*—and I snatched my finger back and stuck it into my mouth. "Deadly, too," I said around the digit.

"Yes. Much like the woman they were made for."

I looked up to see Maximillian's gaze fixed on my mouth, and for a second, I wondered if he was thinking about what it would be like if I allowed him to lick the blood off my skin instead.

Warmth pooled in my lower belly at the thought, and I hastily removed my finger from my mouth. "I meant to give these to you before we left, but the blacksmith delivered them only hours before we set off for the Summit," he told me. "I know they aren't your preferred weapon, but if anyone catches you with a silver stake on your person, our ruse will be exposed. The daggers will at least allow you to defend yourself if you find yourself in a precarious position." He gave me a wry look.

"I love them," I told him, and I meant it. The knives were a beautiful gift, but also very thoughtful. They weren't ideal for vampire slaying—the blades weren't large enough for a beheading, and it was more difficult to drive them through the breastbone and into the heart than a stake was. But wounds inflicted on vampires with silver blades were slow to heal, and would buy me time if a hungry attendee decided to ignore the rules and take a bite out of me. "Do they come with any sheaths or holsters? If I try to put these in my pocket, they're going to cut right through my skirts."

Maximillian smiled. "The throwing knives are retractable, but the larger blades come with sheaths. They're at the bottom of the box."

I removed the daggers and the padding beneath them, unearthing the leather straps and sheaths. I grinned when I noticed that two of them were thigh sheaths, and planted my foot on the bench so I could slip one of them up my leg. I fumbled with the buckles as I tried to adjust the leather band, but it was too wide, and it kept slipping down.

"Here." Maximillian said as I bit my lip in frustration. "Let me help."

He got down on one knee beside the bench, and my heart stuttered as he took my foot in his hand. His touch was gentle as he slid his hand up the side of my leg, carefully pushing up the white lace of my nightgown to expose my thigh. Transfixed, I watched as he deftly grasped the strap, his long fingers working the leather and metal until the sheath was snugly fixed to my thigh.

"Is that comfortable?" he asked.

I nodded, not trusting myself to speak. The warmth in my lower belly had spread to my core, turning into a molten, pulsing sensation that sent a tremor running through my legs. His wickedly handsome face was far too close to the source of my need, to the nexus of nerves that had awoken, and a sudden urge to fist my hand in his storm cloud hair and use his mouth to soothe that ache seized me.

Before I could act on that insane impulse, he pulled back, then removed a silk handkerchief from his pocket and used it to pick up one of the daggers. My mouth went dry as he tested the balance of the blade with his forefinger, then slowly, carefully slid it into place. I shivered as the cold metal of the handle bit into my heated flesh, but instead of dousing my desire, the contrasting sensation only stoked the flames higher.

Maximillian sucked in a sharp breath, his nostrils flaring as he scented my desire. He lifted his head, and as our eyes met, I saw those same flames reflected in his burning gaze. I knew in that moment that if he pulled me down and pinned me to the ground with his big, hard body, that I would allow him to do just about anything he wanted.

And while I wanted that, part of me was terrified by the thought.

But with a blink of his sooty lashes, the lust in Maximillian's eyes vanished as though it had never been. In the next second, he was on his feet again, placing my foot on the bench and allowing my nightgown to fall back into place. Something cold rushed through my veins as he put space between us, and my heart dropped at the chagrined look that flashed through his eyes before a mask slipped over his features, cutting off all emotion.

"Sleep well," he said, inclining his head. "I'll see you in the morning."

And with that, he left me standing there, heart racing, hands fisted at my sides, torn between the desire to run after him and the need to bury myself in the bedcovers and never come out again.

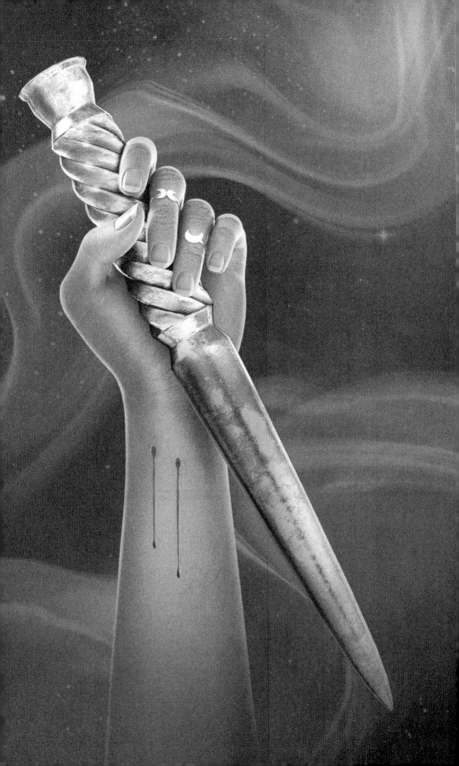

20

Kitana

It was really late when I tiptoed into the mortuary, wrapped up in my shadows like a secret cloak. They made my steps quiet and kept me hidden from the guards who watched the night.

All the Nocturne Clan, even my foster mother, was asleep. But I couldn't understand how they could sleep after such awful news.

I walked up to the metal table where my mama lay. She looked so peaceful, wearing a simple white dress. I didn't want to look at the hurts still on her.

My throat hurt as I held her hand. It was really cold and felt different. The Grand Matron tried to make her look better, but there were still tiny marks where she got hurt.

It's been just a month since Mama went away. A month since my foster mama brought me to her house, a month since Mama left and promised to come back. But she came back in a way we didn't want.

Tears came down my face, and I pressed my lips together, trying to stay quiet. The shadow watch found Mama this morning. Someone had sucked all the blood out of her body, then chopped her into little pieces and stuck her in a horrible box. The birds found her first, and that's how the shadow watch knew something was wrong.

My little cat, Jinx, came and rubbed against my legs, meowing. But I couldn't pick her up, because I didn't want to let go of Mama's hand. I didn't want to stop looking at her, not when I knew they were going to burn her up tomorrow, and I would never get to look at her again.

The door made a noise, and my foster mama, Astrid, came in. Her hair was all over, and she wore her robe. "Kitana?" she said. "Oh, dear, you should've woken me if you couldn't sleep."

"I didn't want you," I told her. "I wanted my Mama."

Astrid stopped, and I looked back at Mama. I knew what I said sounded mean, but it was true. I didn't want to live with Astrid, or go to that school where they make me try magic stuff that I can't do. I don't like when the other kids stare or whisper about me.

I just wanted my Mama.

But she's not here now. It's just her body, and that's not the same.

"I don't understand," I whispered, my voice shaky. "Why did Papa do this to her?"

"We don't know who did it, dear," Astrid said, wrapping her arm around me. "The shadow watch is still looking."

I shook my head. Astrid was trying to be nice, but I knew the truth. My papa was the one who did this. And someday, when I found out who he was, I was going to make him regret it.

A wave of sudden nausea jerked me from the dream, and I blinked my eyes open to find myself tangled in the bedsheets. Groaning, I sat up so I could extricate myself, then glanced at the clock at the wall. Three in the morning. Way too early to be up.

I flopped back onto the mattress, hoping to fall back asleep. But the grief from the memory-dream sat heavy in my chest, and as I touched a hand to my cheek, I realized the tears I'd cried were real. I squeezed my eyes shut, trying to recall the details, but they were already hazy, slipping back into the recesses of my mind.

And to make matters worse, my stomach let out an angry rumble.

Sighing, I threw back the sheets and got up, giving up on the idea of sleep. I'd been so keyed-up by our arrival last night I'd completely forgotten to eat, and now my body was throwing a tantrum. That's probably why I'd woken up in the first place. There was no way I was going to fall asleep now, not until I got some food.

Rummaging through my closet, I found the dressing gown I'd packed and tied it over my nightgown. I had fallen asleep with the thigh sheath still fastened to my leg, so I slid the dagger into it, then shoved my feet into a pair of slippers.

If my mental map of the Iron Spire served me correctly, the castle kitchens were on the ground floor of the central hub. Silent as a shadow, I slipped out of my room, the halls eerily quiet at this hour. I crept down the spiral staircase to the common level, then crossed the covered bridge, leaving the safety of the Psychoros Spire.

To my annoyance, it took far longer than I expected to navigate the series of corridors leading back to the main hall. By the time I arrived, I was disoriented, my hunger pangs wreaking havoc on my sense of direction. Frustrated, I stopped in the middle of the hall and looked around, trying to reorient my mental map. The kitchens weren't far from here, that much I knew. But which direction to go in?

A movement to my right caught my attention, and I turned to see a tall figure step into the hall from a shadowed archway. He was nearly a hundred yards away, yet he spotted me right away, his citrine eyes flaring with recognition.

But how did he know me, when I had never set eyes on him before?

The vampire began to walk toward me, his long-legged stride closing the distance far faster than I was comfortable with. As he drew closer, his features became more clear—square face, strong, stubbled jaw, patrician nose, and a hard, unsmiling mouth. His wavy, jaw-length hair was slightly disheveled, and he was shirtless, dressed only in a pair of cotton trousers and combat-style boots. The sweat glistening off his broad chest and shoulders suggested he'd just come from some exercise or training session. A member of the palace guard, maybe? But was it normal for them to have training sessions at such an early hour?

I was so busy studying his features that it took a second for me to realize that a peculiar sensation had started up in the center of my chest. It felt like someone had hooked a finger into my ribcage and was trying to pull me forward, and I didn't like it one bit. Digging in my heels, I forced myself to stand still even as all kinds of conflicting instincts flared to life inside me. Part of me wanted to run, part of me wanted to fight, and another part of me...

Well. Another part of me felt like I had been waiting my whole life for this moment.

The vampire stopped a few feet away from me, his eyes narrowing as they scanned me from head to toe. "Has your master not informed you of the dangers of wandering the Iron Spire alone at night?" he asked in a low, ominous tone. "That when you are not by his side, you are fair game for any other vampire who may be lurking about, looking for a midnight snack?"

His voice was deep and resonant, and there was something so familiar about it, even though I was certain I'd never heard it before. Seconds of silence stretched between us, and as he arched a dark eyebrow, I remembered I was supposed to answer.

"Umm. I'm very sorry, Sir." I ducked my head as a flush came over my cheeks, not finding it difficult to play the part of a contrite and submissive human in that moment. "But I haven't eaten in almost twenty-four hours, and I woke up hungry. I didn't want to trouble my master by waking him, so I thought I'd sneak down to the kitchens on my own. Only, I can't quite figure out how to get there."

I expected the vampire to scold me, but he didn't speak. After a few more seconds, I risked glancing up at him through my eyelashes. He was still staring at me, his muscular arms crossed over his broad chest, a scowl darkening his face.

"You don't know who I am?" he demanded.

Oh shit. I straightened up, wracking my brain for any clue that would reveal his identity. "Am I supposed to?" I blurted out.

The vampire chuckled, a sinister sound that sent a chill racing down my spine. "Oh, Lord Starclaw is playing a dangerous game, bringing you as a candidate for the Descendency even though this is only your first Summit. If you continue to display your ignorance like this, the others are going to eat you alive."

I bristled at the taunting note in his voice, unable to stop the instinctive reaction. "Are you going to tell me who you are, or are you going to stand there and watch me continue to embarrass myself?"

I regretted the words the moment I spoke them, and nearly clapped a hand over my mouth in horror. What in all the hells was I doing? I was supposed to be acting like a submissive human, not sassing high-ranking vampire nobles. If Lucius was here, he would be throttling me right now. And I would deserve it.

I needed to get my shit together before I got myself killed.

"Oh no," the vampire noble said, an amused smirk slashing across his handsome face. "I think not. It will make the opening ceremony far more entertaining for me to watch the look of horror on your face when you see me tomorrow and put the pieces together yourself."

Fuck. Fuck, fuck, fuckity, *fuck*.

The vampire turned away, heading toward one of the arched doorways at the back of the hall. "The corridor leading to the kitchens is on that side of the hall," he said without turning around, flinging an arm out to indicate the direction. "I heard Cook stashed a few tarts in the larder left over from today's baking, but don't let her catch you taking them, or she'll gut you and serve your entrails at dinner."

He disappeared into the shadows of the hall, leaving me with that wonderful parting shot. And none the wiser as to who he was.

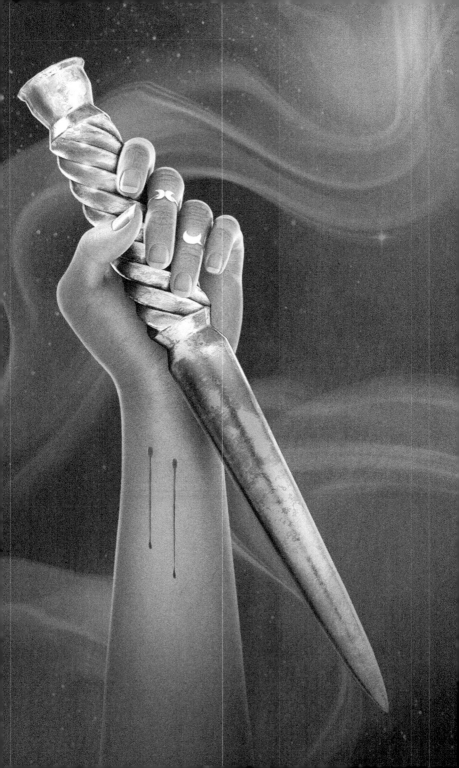

21

Maximillian

As all three-hundred and twenty-two vampires gathered in the summit hall for the Sanguine Summit's opening ceremony, Maximillian knew he should pay attention to what his father was saying.

But from the moment Maximillian and the rest of the Psychoros delegation had walked in, the Crown Prince of Noxalis had fixed a predatory gaze on Kitana. And he hadn't looked away from her since.

Kitana, for her part, was deep in conversation with Marisse, Stesha's thrall. She was one of four blood slaves that his house had brought for the express purpose of feeding their delegation, and had been in Stesha's service for over one hundred and seventy years. She was the perfect person to ease Kitana in and show her the ropes, and Maximillian was grateful for his brother's assistance.

Even so, he noticed the tension in Kitana's shoulders, and the occasional glances she sent the crown prince's way. She was just as aware of his attention on her as he was, and didn't seem any happier about it.

"Maximillian," his father said, his cold voice jarring Max from his thoughts. "Is there a reason you are staring at Casimir Invictus so intently? Admiring his haircut, perhaps? Or his impeccable fashion sense? Or his unshakable loyalty to his father, something you sorely lack?"

The sarcasm in his father's tone was sharp enough to sever flesh from bone, but Maximillian didn't allow it to affect him. "That particular shade of crimson is rather fetching on him," he said mildly. "Perhaps I should ask him for his tailor's name before I leave the city."

Callix Starclaw let out a low hiss that would have made most vampires soil their pants. "If I knew your mother's death would have turned you into an insolent brat, I would have thought twice about killing her, if only to spare myself your insufferable attitude."

Maximillian turned his head so fast, he nearly gave himself whiplash. "*That* is what would have made you think twice?" he snarled, and several vampires turned to watch the heated exchange.

Callix bared his fangs in response, his eyes glowing red as bloodlust surged to the forefront. Maximillian knew he should back down. Such a public spat between high lord and heir would make their house look weak, and invite challenges from the other Psychoros families who were looking for any excuse to depose their high lord and take the mantle for themselves.

But though Maximillian prided himself on keeping a cool head in even the most dire situations, there was nothing that riled him so much as the callous way his father refused to take responsibility for murdering his mother in cold blood.

That's not true, a silken voice in his head whispered. *There is one other.*

Yes. Kitana Nightshade, the vixen vampire slayer who had consumed his thoughts for longer than she would ever know. Maximillian resisted the urge to glance over at her, knowing it would infuriate his father even more. Lazarus was correct—he *was* obsessed with the little witch. She was a chaotic little spitfire with a passionate heart that ignited his own burning spirit, and even though he knew she was more than capable of standing on her own two feet, he was still gripped by the unshakable need to protect her.

The sight of Kitana standing over him in that too-short nightgown, one leg propped on the bench, her lacy skirt rucked up nearly to her hips while he'd cradled her dainty foot in his hands, had nearly undone him last night. He could see the desire in her eyes, smell the delicious need dripping from her core, and he had come so close to pushing her nightgown all the way up so he could kiss his way up her inner thigh and show her what pleasure could feel like under the skilled hands and tongue of an immortal.

But he couldn't afford to give into that temptation. Not when it was imperative for them to stay focused on their mission. Sometimes he hated that he was so attuned to the emotions of others—it was usually a blessing, one that allowed him to intuit the motives and desires of others so he could leverage that knowledge to turn them into allies. Or, at the very least, get them to cooperate.

But when he sensed an acute need in someone he cared about, a need that he was unable to fulfill, it often tortured him to the point of distraction.

One of Callix's advisors stepped up to whisper something in his ear, and Maximillian's father reluctantly broke their staring contest. Relieved, Maximillian turned his attention to Kitana, only to find that Casimir was *still* watching her.

The rage that filled him at the sight was ugly and vicious, but not unreasonable. It was worrisome that Kitana had caught the crown prince's attention so early, before he'd even presented her to the court. She was here to kill his father, after all, and if Casimir caught even a whiff of that, he would crush her with his iron fist. He was the dutiful son, fiercely loyal to the crown, and wouldn't tolerate even the slightest threat toward his father.

If Maximillian wanted to keep Kitana safe, he needed to find out the reasoning behind the prince's fascination with her. And nip it in the bud before it grew into something more.

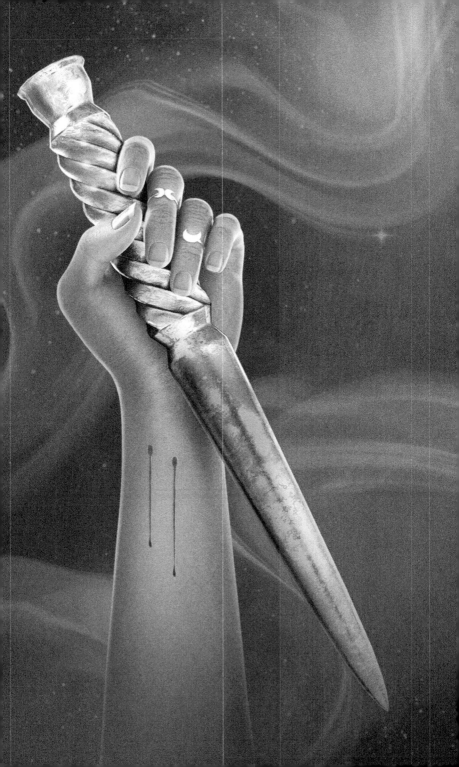

22

Kitana

"…And that's Soren Ironheart, the head of the second most powerful family in House Invictus," Marisse told me, pointing toward a mountain of a vampire seated in the front row of House Invictus's section, located on the far-left edge of the summit hall. The matronly thrall, with her silver-streaked blonde hair and kind, faintly-lined features, had been chattering in my ear with the enthusiasm of a gossipy teenager the moment we'd arrived in the summit hall, pointing out all the different vampire nobles and giving me a brief overview of each. "He serves as a general in the emperor's army, mainly in charge of the recruit training program."

"I see," I said, only half-listening. I knew I should be paying closer attention—after all, these were the people responsible for enslaving the human race and forcing my people behind a magical barrier that cut them off from the rest of the world, and there was a good chance they would continue to be threats even after I killed the emperor. But my mind was fuzzy and distracted, and it had nothing to do with the fact that I'd only gotten five hours of sleep last night, and everything to do with the vampire watching me.

I'd spotted the crown prince the moment I'd walked into the Summit Hall, had figured out who he was by the iron crown he wore before Marisse had told me who he was. And yes, he was absolutely right—I *was* horrified. But I'd done everything in my power to lock down my expression and glance away as our eyes met, refusing to give him the satisfaction of a reaction.

I wondered if anyone else in the hall noticed that the insufferable bastard had refused to take his eyes off me since. Maximillian didn't seem to care—he was sitting a few feet away from me, in conversation with his father. He'd been cordial to me when I'd come downstairs to the common area for breakfast, introducing me to the other Psychoros delegates and explaining who I was. Gone was the male who had put a possessive hand on my lower back when he'd led me into the castle, who had slaughtered an important vampire from a rival house for daring to take me, who had gifted me with an exquisite set of blades last night, then knelt at my feet and looked into my face with the kind of ravenous hunger that would have had me burying a stake in his heart if he'd been any other vampire.

But he wasn't any other vampire. He was Maximillian Starclaw, the enigmatic heir of House Psychoros who led a double-life, playing devoted servant of the empire in one breath, while plotting its downfall in the next.

My gaze shifted to the Sanguis Noctis delegation, where Lazarus sat next to his father, Highlord Lysander Bloodmare. They were nearly identical with their blood-red locks, glowing red eyes, and savagely carved faces, but the older vampire had a stoic air about him compared to the slightly chaotic nature of his son. Lysander was scanning the crowd, taking in the arriving attendees as they filled the seats of the amphitheater, but

Lazarus's gaze was fixed on Maximillian, their bloody depths glittering with the promise of retribution.

I was about to ask Marisse if there was any previous bad blood between Maximillian and Lazarus when a herald marched onto the stage and called for order. "All rise for his Imperial Highness, Vladimir Invictus, Emperor of Valentaera!"

A wave rippled through the hall as everyone got to their feet. My entire world narrowed on Vladimir as he glided into the room, dressed in his gold and crimson robes of state, his long, golden hair hanging loose around his shoulders. The citrine eyes he shared with his son had an almost reptilian look about them, the pupils narrow, and his oblong face with its narrow nose and thin, unsmiling lips leant him a severe look. He wore little adornment aside from the spiked iron crown tipped with black diamonds that rested atop his head and a dark red metal torque around his neck, and he carried a golden staff topped with an egg-sized ruby fashioned into a blood drop.

Pure, unadulterated hatred bubbled up inside me, but I remained perfectly still, aware that any sign of enmity toward the emperor, especially given my position as a candidate, would doom me. We all waited until the vampire monarch settled himself on his throne before retaking our seats. Silence settled over the cavernous space as he sat back, his eyes roving over the assembled crowd. While the planes of his face were smooth and ageless, there was something about it that was harsh and unforgiving, like the sheer, rocky face of a mountain watching impassively as you foolishly attempted to scale it.

It had been over fifty years since I'd started down the warpath to bring Vladimir to justice for his multiple violations of the Accords. And as I finally looked upon his wicked face for the first time in my life, I felt like I was standing on a precipice, and that my destiny was a single leap away.

A ghostly hand slid down my spine, and I straightened, startled away from my murderous thoughts. Blinking, I turned my head to see Maximillian watching me. *Settle,* his eyes seemed to say even though his expression revealed nothing. *Your time will come soon enough.*

I tore my gaze from Maximillian and back to the dais as another vampire climbed the steps to the stage, taking up a place to the emperor's right. He was a wizened male with white hair, a hawk nose, and blue veins running through his translucent flesh. Pure black robes with crimson vestments embroidered with ebon roots, serpents, and ravens, hung off his skeletal frame, and his eyes, though pure white and devoid of pupils, seemed to see everything as he looked out at the crowd.

A cold, slimy sensation slithered over my flesh as those otherworldly eyes landed on me, lingering for several seconds before moving on.

"That's Alaric Grimcrest, the High Nexon of The Order of Tenebros," Marisse whispered to me. "He'll be leading the Dark Mass on the third night of the Summit."

I shuddered. I was going to have to listen to this ancient, creepy vampire preach for over an hour? "Sounds like a good time," I muttered.

Marisse shook her head. "It's a night you'll never forget," she said softly, a haunted look entering her eyes.

Before I could ask what she meant by that, Vladimir Invictus began to speak. "Welcome to the Sanguine Summit," he said, his deep voice echoing through the amphitheater. His diamond-hard gaze swept over the crowd, and stillness swept over the room, as if the mere sound of his voice had ensnared every person within. "We gather here every year with the blessing of our dark god to celebrate not only our six centuries of unity as one kingdom, but our unquestionable dominion over the human race and our ascension as the rightful rulers and custodians of Valentaera."

Enthusiastic agreement rippled through the crowd, and Vladimir continued, his voice rising. "For two thousand years we suffered under the oppressive restrictions of the Midnight Accords, cut off from the world that is our birthright. And all because of a curse inflicted upon us for a crime committed not by us, but by the sun god!"

The crowd's emotions swelled in response to the righteous anger in the emperor's voice, and the hairs on my arms rose along with their enmity. "The witches sent their vampire hunters to stalk and punish us for the slightest infractions," he continued, "and the humans reneged on even the slightest of agreements between our kingdoms, leaving us with no recourse!"

My jaw slackened, and I had to clench my teeth to keep my mouth from falling open. Seriously? The vampires thought *they* were the victims in this story? Despite bathing in rivers of human and witch blood during the Chaos War, and then, in the decades leading up to the Eternal Night, engaging in numerous illegal enterprises, not the least of which included the drugging, trafficking, and experimentation on humans *and* witches?

But as I looked around the summit hall, I could see that the other vampires were eating up Vladimir's impassioned speech. Their eyes were alight with a sick sort of zeal, their expressions ranging anywhere from smug satisfaction, to starry-eyed awe, to a savage hunger that made me want to reach for the dagger strapped to my thigh. The sight of their unified determination and collective thirst was truly unsettling, and my heart sank as I wondered if killing the vampire king would really do anything to stop this war.

"They called us monsters," Vladimir went on, his voice rumbling through the hall like dark thunder, "and so we became monsters, shedding all former ties to the other realms and turning to the one thing that has always kept us alive—our faith.

And our dark god answered by presenting us with the glorious gift of Eternal Night."

"A gift that we did not waste!" Lysander Bloodmare roared, and the crowd's voice rose with him in collective triumph.

But I noticed that not everyone in the room shared the high lord's fervent approval. Casimir's face was a stoic mask, his arms hanging loose by his sides, and Viviana, the twin sister of House Stellaris's heir, had an oddly blank expression on her face that was almost comical next to the pride shining in her brother Caelum's eyes. Lazarus's expression, of course, was the picture of delight, just like his fellow house brethren. But while Maximillian perfectly mirrored the savage ardor of his fellow vampires, I caught a glimpse of something that looked very much like sadness glimmering in the depths of his starfire gaze.

"Indeed," Vladimir agreed once the noise had died down. "The long years my court and I have spent plotting and scheming finally came to fruition, and the human kingdoms crumbled like the fragile dominoes they always were. No longer shall we be hunted and scorned by those who are beneath us. Our vengeance is just, our conquest righteous, and once Trivaea is laid bare before us, we will claim our rightful place as the supreme rulers of this continent. *In Tenebris, Regnamus!*" he boomed, standing and punching his staff into the air in one motion.

In darkness, we reign, I translated numbly as the attendees roared it back.

I couldn't think of a more appropriate motto if I tried.

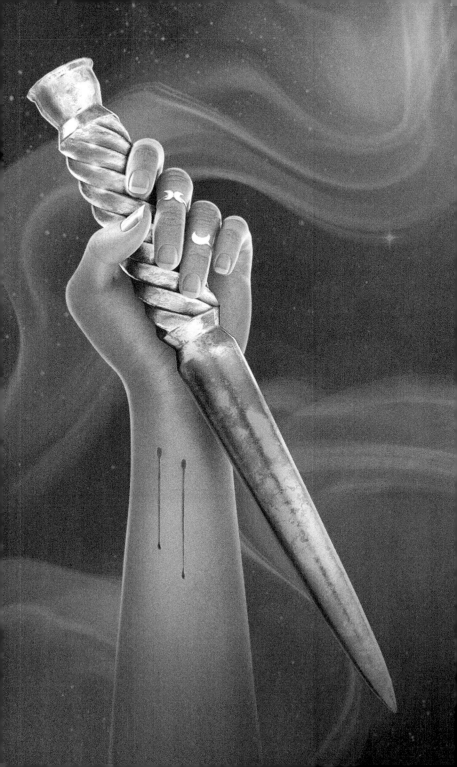

23

Casimir

"Now," the herald intoned, stepping forward as everyone in the summit hall took their seats again. "Let any petitioners come forward with announcements or concerns they wish to bring before the crown and assembly before the official sessions begin."

As Casimir expected, Maximillian Starclaw rose from his chair. But so did Lazarus, and he moved swiftly, stalking toward the dais with predatory focus before the Psychoros heir could beat him to it.

The emperor's brow furrowed as the Sanguis Noctis heir executed a deep bow before him. "Your Imperial Highness," he said, his voice echoing through the chamber, "I stand before you and this assembly to bring forth a grave matter. It concerns the death of an esteemed member of my house, at the hands of a vampire outside of my purview to punish."

Vladimir's gilded eyebrows rose, and Casimir found himself leaning in a little, which surprised him. Unlike his peers, he

rarely found court politics or drama especially interesting—
though he was the youngest, he had been raised here at the Iron
Spire, and there wasn't much he hadn't seen at this point.

"Who is the victim, and who is the accused?" his father
asked.

Lazarus straightened. "The victim is Vinicius Clemante,
commandant in the imperial army, and a member of Sanguis
Noctis. And the accused..." he turned, jabbing a clawed finger-
nail toward the Psychoros delegation, "is Lord Maximillian
Starclaw."

A murmur rippled through the crowd as the two vampire
heirs locked gazes, staring each other down in a silent battle of
wills. But a faint expression of annoyance flickered across the
emperor's face, and Casimir could already tell this conversation
would not go the way Lazarus wanted. "This matter has already
been brought to my attention," Vladimir said, flicking his hand
in dismissal. "I see no reason to rehash it."

"With all due respect," Lazarus said before the spire guards
could rush him away, "I do not believe you are aware of all the
facts."

"Is that right?" Vladimir asked, a bite of cold steel entering
his voice. The look in his eyes was one Casimir recognized well
—Lazarus was treading on dangerous ground. "And what, pray
tell, do you suppose has escaped my notice? The disgraceful
incident at the airshipyard, the abduction of Lord Starclaw's
thrall, or the audacious theft from the empire's coffers in the
delightful form of tax evasion?"

The whispers in the crowd erupted into gleeful chatter,
hundreds of gazes sharpening on Lazarus's back. Casimir hid an
amused smile—the Sanguis Noctis heir had not thought his
plan through before he'd dared to broach this subject. "This
'esteemed member' of your house took advantage of his position

—a position *I* granted him—to abduct slaves all across the empire instead of legally purchasing and registering them, all so he could avoid having to pay the yearly tax on them. And yet you have the audacity to come before me and demand justice for him?" Vladimir bared his fangs. "Have you forgotten who it is you speak to?"

A lesser male would have cowered before the emperor, but though the tips of Lazarus's pointed ears reddened with humiliation, he stood his ground. Casimir had to give him points for that—the Sanguis Noctis heir was without a doubt the ballsiest of the four of them.

"I am more than aware of the disgrace Vinicius has brought upon our house," Lazarus said, his voice grating as if every word was an effort to get out. "And I agree he should have been punished to the fullest extent of the law. But that is the grievance I bring before you—one violation of the law does not excuse the other. Vinicius had the right to stand trial before the crown, with a representative from his house, for the alleged crimes he committed. But instead of arresting him and delivering him into the crown's custody, Maximillian took justice into his own hands. There was no reason I can think of for Lord Starclaw to kill Vinicius so swiftly. Unless," and here Lazarus turned his glittering gaze on Maximillian, "Maximillian Starclaw has secrets of his own, and allowing Vinicius to speak, to defend himself, would have exposed them."

The emperor's eyes shifted to Maximillian, who had remained standing, his hands clasped behind him. Unlike Lazarus, who was practically salivating at the mouth, the Psychoros heir appeared unruffled, as if the vampire accusing him of treason was simply commenting on the weather.

"I do not know what secrets Lazarus is referring to," Maximillian said. "We vampires have many of them, after all.

For all I know, he could be referring to my penchant for wearing lacy undergarments. Or the collection of life-sized dolls I keep in the Tower for the express purpose of hosting tea parties and playing dress up."

Snickers arose from the crowd at this, and Casimir suppressed a snort. He watched as the Stellaris twins exchanged amused looks, and even his father's lips twitched. The only two people who did not seem to find Maximillian's remarks amusing aside from Lazarus was Lysander Bloodmare—who had sprouted a pulsing vein in his temple—and Callix Starclaw, who looked to be grinding his teeth so hard, Casimir could almost hear the sound from across the room.

"Do you think this is funny?" Lazarus hissed, his eyes crackling with pent-up rage. "You may have everyone else fooled, Maximillian, but—"

"Enough." The emperor's voice cracked through the air like a whip, pulling Lazarus up short. "Everyone at this court knows you consider Lord Starclaw's policies to be soft-hearted, but there is no denying he has saved the empire countless time, energy, and resources. And there is little more that House Invictus values above efficiency. So, unless you have specific accusations to levy against Lord Starclaw, cease hogging the floor and get out of my sight."

But Casimir was enjoying this too much to let it end so soon, and he rose from his chair, drawing the attention of everyone in the room. "Your Eminence," he said, and the hall quieted. "I would like to propose a solution."

Vladimir's eyes flared in surprise as he turned to face his son. "I was not aware this required a solution," he said coldly.

But Casimir stepped forward, undaunted. "Regardless of your judgment on the matter, it is clear Lazarus means to achieve satisfaction against Maximillian one way or another, whether that is here at court or on a potential battlefield in the distant future. Rather than allowing nature to take its course, why don't we allow them to settle things the old-fashioned way, with a bit of bloodsport?"

For a heartbeat, Casimir thought his father would eviscerate him. It wouldn't be the first time—the emperor rarely approved of anything Casimir did or said, no matter how hard he tried to please him. The dynamic between them was complicated—on the one hand, his father's harsh standards had pushed him to excel in every aspect of his life, to exceed the expectations of his role as crown prince and prove he was worthy of the mantle that would one day be passed to him.

But as Casimir had grown older, he'd watched the emperor acknowledge and praise his vampire siblings, while only occasionally tossing him crumbs of approval. So while he was loyal to the crown and to the empire, that blind devotion did not extend toward the male who owned them. There was only so much cold-shouldering he could take.

That was why he'd recently begun to push the envelope. Like he was doing now.

But the emperor noticed the subtle shift in the room's energy —from anger and resentment to anticipation and glee. He knew the value of playing to the emotions of his subjects just like any good ruler, so he leaned back in his throne, a thoughtful expression easing the severity of his face. "Very well," he said, propping his sharp chin on his fist. "What do you suggest, my son?"

Casimir's smile widened as he spread his hands, one in Lazarus's direction, the other in Maximillian's. Neither seemed particularly pleased with his intervention, but they remained silent, waiting for him to speak. "Tournament Day is coming up in two days. I propose we set aside a portion of the festivities for a match between the two heirs. Fisticuffs only—no magic or weaponry. And they fight either until the death, or until one yields."

"Now see here!" Callix Starclaw protested, jumping up from his seat. "I am all for allowing my son to pay for his mistakes, but a fight to the death—"

"It won't be to the death," Maximillian Starclaw said, his soft voice cutting across his father's. "Lazarus wouldn't be so foolish. He'll yield."

Lazarus bared his fangs. "Don't be so sure of that, Starclaw. I'd sooner tear my own throat out than admit defea—"

"You will do no such thing." Lysander's voice rang through the hall, and everyone fell silent. "For once, I agree with High-lord Starclaw. With the emperor's approval, the two of you will settle this with bloodsport, but only until one of you is rendered unconscious, or yields. There will *be* no killing."

"Agreed," Vladimir said. He thumped his staff, a clear signal that the matter was closed. "Now sit down, all of you, or I will have you thrown out."

Lazarus snapped his mouth shut, but he returned to his seat, and Casimir did the same. But Maximillian remained standing, and he gestured to Catherine to join him as he approached the dais.

"Imperial Highness," he said, bowing low. His thrall executed a perfect curtsey, her blue damask skirts rustling like falling leaves around her. Casimir met her eyes for a second, and his breathing hitched in his throat at the expression blazing in her violet depths before she looked away.

She was *furious*. With *him*.

"Before the official events of the summit begin," Maximillian continued as he and his thrall straightened to face the emperor, "I would like to introduce to you Catherine Seabream, one of my devoted thralls. As a reward for her bravery and loyal service, I would like to present her to the crown and the assembly as a candidate for the Descendency."

"I see," Vladimir said softly. There was a cunning glint in his eyes as he surveyed Catherine, who lowered her head, awaiting his judgment. She really was a stunning woman, Casimir thought idly, tracing the contours of her petite form with his gaze. Far more poised than the lost little human he'd found stumbling about the Spire in the middle of the night looking for snacks. She wore a silvery blue gown that made the most of her small-yet-curvy frame, the heart-shaped bodice drawing the eyes to the contour of her large, well-formed breasts and tiny waist before her skirts flared out around her legs. But most interesting to Casimir were the defined muscles he could see shifting beneath her pale skin. This was not a body that belonged to a simple blood-slave that lounged around her master's house, waiting for him to come home and feed on her. Those muscles had been honed by hard work, possibly even training.

But what would Maximillian be training her for?

"I'm pleased to see you have finally chosen a replacement for Desdemona," Vladimir finally said, returning his attention to Maximillian. "I shall grant your request." He lifted his head to address the delegations, his voice rising. "Let it be known that Catherine Seabream, thrall of Lord Maximillian Starclaw, has been formally entered as a candidate for the Descendency. During this period of consideration, any natural-born vampire may fraternize with her, but no vampire aside from her master may feed from her or cause her irreparable harm for the duration of the summit."

He slammed his staff to the ground, and Casimir's eyes widened as a ripple of crimson energy emanated from his father's body. He watched as it spread throughout the entire chamber, and the hairs on his arms rose as the energy sizzled across his skin. But although nothing happened to him, a blank look passed over every single attendee in the room, and they nodded simultaneously, like puppets being jerked on a string.

Yet in the next second, their expression flickered back to normal. It all happened so fast, Casimir almost wondered if he'd imagined it.

That is, until his gaze found Catherine's again, and he beheld the same shock reflected in her own eyes.

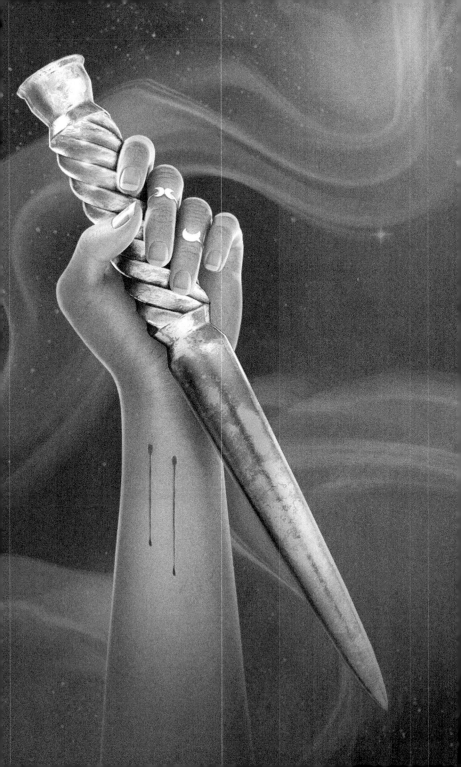

24

Kitana

"And you're absolutely positive you didn't see anything?" I demanded several hours later as I paced the confines of my bedchamber.

Lucius shook his head, his massive frame perched on the settee in front of my bay window. "None of us saw what you did, Kitana," he said, his gravelly voice grating against my frazzled nerves. "There was no dark energy."

"That's not possible." I raked a hand through my hair, dislodging several of the pins Marisse had placed in it this morning. "Someone else had to have seen it. I'm not imagining things."

I knew I wasn't imagining things, knew that the sizzle of energy against my skin had been real, because after it had happened, I'd looked over to see Casimir staring at me, my shock mirrored in his eyes. I was positive he'd witnessed the same event, and judging by his reaction, I didn't think this was a normal occurrence for him.

"I'm not saying you didn't see anything, Kitana," Lucius said levering himself to his feet. His head nearly brushed the ceiling, and he had to swerve his head to the side to avoid tangling his braids in the chandelier. "I'm only saying that the rest of us didn't. It could be a phenomenon that's only observable through witch eyes. Which means Maximillian's hunch about you was correct, and you are the right person for this mission." He clapped a hand on my shoulder. "Now try to get some rest and calm your nerves before tonight. You'll need your wits about you for the soiree."

Lucius left me, and I collapsed onto the settee he'd vacated with a frustrated sigh. Leaning my forehead against the window, I allowed the cool glass to bite into my skin, hoping the sensation would clear my head.

I'd wanted to speak to Maximillian about this—not just the strange magical phenomenon I'd witnessed, but the false narrative that Vladimir has so expertly spun, and whether Maximillian bought into it like everyone else seemed to. But Highlord Starclaw had whisked Maximillian off to a meeting almost immediately after the summit session had ended, leaving me with no choice but to seek out Lucius instead.

Perhaps you can ask Casimir about it at the soiree tonight.

I scowled as soon as the idiotic thought popped into my head. There was absolutely no way I was going to be broaching this subject with the crown prince. I'd already attracted far too much attention from him, which, given that I was here to kill his father, didn't seem like the wisest move. Why had I felt the need to talk back to him when I'd run into him last night? Why couldn't I be a good little mouse and keep my head down?

Sighing, I glanced over at my bed, which looked far too empty. I wished Jinx was here so that I could have someone to vent aloud to, or at the very least, snuggle her and let her take the edge off my nerves. But she couldn't manifest within the walls of the Iron Spire, just as I couldn't shadow travel into it. It was no accident that Vladimir had encased the entire structure in iron despite the extraordinary cost involved—the thick coating of metal made it impervious to magical attacks or tampering from the outside, which meant that no witch or human could use their powers to breach it from the outside. It was why neither I nor the Moonlight Conclave—the governing council of Valentaera comprised of the five witches who ran the clans—had ever been able to confront him in person. The coward had simply holed up in his iron fortress and refused to show his face.

Luckily, the iron didn't prevent me from using magic *within* the castle walls. I could still use my other powers inside, which was a good thing because I didn't think I'd be able to kill the king with fighting prowess alone. But that didn't change the fact that I was stuck here without my faithful companion to guide or soothe me, and even though Maximillian and Lucius were here, they were occupied with summit business, and I couldn't help feeling a little lonely. I wished the others had come—during the many hours that the cohort had spent training me, I'd grown closer to them, to the point that I'd begun to fool myself into thinking I was part of their little family. But Sparrow had been sent off on some clandestine mission, and Nyra and Eliza had to stay back in Lumina to keep things running.

I wasn't sure how long I lay on the bed, chasing my thoughts in circles, but eventually my exhaustion got the better of me, and I dozed off. A sharp knock at the door jerked me from a sound sleep, and I shot upright, my eyes going to the clock on the wall. Seven-thirty. Only thirty minutes before the soiree began.

"Catherine?" Marisse called through the door. "Are you almost ready?"

Shit. I glanced down at myself to find that my dress was rumpled from sleeping in it, and I suspected that if I glanced in the mirror, my hair would be in similar condition. "Umm... I might need a little help."

Marisse marched into the room, her eyes widening with panic as she beheld me. "Stars! You're not even dressed! Quick, get up!"

I leaped out of bed, and between the two of us, I managed to get out of the dress from this morning and into a violet gown with aquamarine crystals scattered throughout the fabric. It took some skillful maneuvering to keep her from glimpsing the knife and sheath still strapped to my thigh, but somehow I managed it. The thrall attacked my hair with a brush, then gathered it into a high bun atop my head, leaving a few strands to coil around my face. She grabbed the cosmetics bag sitting atop my vanity, and used it to apply light make up to my eyes, cheeks, and lips.

"Good," she said briskly. "Now let's get downstairs. The rest of the delegation is already there."

Well, shit. "Did Lord Starclaw send you to find me?" I asked as I followed her outside.

"He did," she confirmed. "He mentioned that you seemed a little drained after the session, and asked me to go check on you."

My cheeks turned pink at that. Had I really looked so awful? I thought I'd done a good job of hiding my exhaustion, but then again, Maximillian had always been able to read me. I wondered if that had anything to do with his mental abilities as a Psychoros vampire—before the Nightforged had lost their connection to the celestial heavens, they'd possessed an array of magical abilities, or so I'd been told. That was thousands of years ago, and much of the knowledge we had on the vampires pre-Chaos War had been lost to time and memory.

I followed Marisse across the bridge, through the maze of corridors, and up a winding set of staircases that led to the rooftop. I knew from the map that there was a greenhouse garden up here, but the rough sketch Lucius had provided paled in comparison to the verdant wonder that awaited me as we ascended the final stair and stepped onto the roof.

The greenhouse was a stunning piece of architecture, its wrought metal frame intricately designed, its glass panels shimmering under the moonlight. Unlike the ones in Lumina, which were designed strictly for function, this one was a perfect fusion of elegance and utility, the crystal technology integrated seamlessly into the roof to cast a soft, otherworldly glow over the garden below. But it was the plants themselves that were the real stars of the show—a dazzling blend of flora native to Noxalis, most of which I'd never seen in the flesh. Trees with metallic trunks stood like pillars scattered throughout the greenhouse, their silvery branches laden with leaves so dark red, they almost appeared black. Bushes sporting delicate, star-shaped flowers nestled alongside rows of serene blue orchids, their scents blending into a heady perfume, while vines with tiny luminescent blooms reminiscent of fireflies climbed ornate trellises. Throughout it all, high-top tables and elegant garden benches were arranged, all occupied by vampires dressed in evening finery, laughing and socializing. Human servants moved through it all with practiced grace, offering guests glasses filled with bloodwine, and in some cases, their own necks.

I was so transfixed by the sight that it took a moment for me to realize that a man had come to stand by my side. "Impressive, isn't it?" he rasped, his voice tinged with a strange, metallic echo. "One of the first projects I undertook here at the Spire after the Eternal Night descended upon us."

I turned to see who had approached, then startled so badly, I nearly jumped into a passing servant. The man standing before me was some horrific amalgamation of human and machine, as if someone had plucked out parts of him they considered defective, then replaced them with synthetic counterparts. He was a thin, wiry man, about six feet tall, with a mop of wild, unkempt hair streaked in grey and white, dressed in a long chartreuse tailcoat, orange trousers, and a pink waistcoat over a white shirt and silver cravat. The clashing outfit was bizarre enough, but even stranger was the metallic box built into the base of his throat, and the large, slightly off-center left eye with a gold pupil and purple sclera that was completely different from the mundane green one in his right socket.

The man chuckled at my reaction, revealing white, even teeth that were at odds with the rest of his chaotic appearance. "My voice box," he rasped, tapping at the metallic thing in his neck. His fingers—no, the entire hand—were also made of metal, each digit tipped with a different mechanical implement. "I was afflicted with a terrible illness when I was nine years old that forced the doctors to remove it, so I replaced it myself."

"You must be Icarus Stormwelder," I said, finally finding my voice. Emperor Vladimir's personal inventor, who Eliza hated. A chill ran down my spine as a snippet of memory floated to the surface—something that had come up in the investigation I'd launched into the missing witches—but it winnowed away before I could grab hold of it.

"At your service." He bowed, his hair flopping into his eyes with the motion. The inventor pushed it back from his face with his normal hand, a crafty gleam entering his regular eye while the golden pupil in his purple one began to pulse. "You look like you have interesting insides," he hissed, leaning in. "I'd love to get a better look at them sometime."

Every single warning bell in my head went off, and I locked my instincts down to keep my shadows from surging forward to defend me. How in the hells was I supposed to respond to that? Marisse would have known how to handle this situation, I was certain, but she had disappeared, probably to go feed some vampire. "That's flattering, but—"

"Kitten." Maximillian appeared out of nowhere, looking devastatingly handsome in his evening attire. His stormcloud hair and alabaster skin glowed faintly in the soft light of the aetheric crystals, the dim glow highlighting the angular planes of his face. He extended his arm to me as he nodded a greeting to the inventor. "Excuse us."

"Of course, Lord Starclaw," the inventor rasped as I curled my arm around Maximillian's. The moment I made contact with him, his scent surrounded me like a cloak swirled around my shoulders, and my nerves began to settle. "Enjoy your little morsel."

Maximillian led me away, tucking me protectively against his side. "Sorry to interrupt," he said, his voice a low murmur in my ear. "But it looked to me as though you required assistance."

I hid a smile as he echoed the exact words he'd spoken to me after rescuing me from that vampire grunt on my first night in Lumina. "You have a thing for rescuing damsels in distress, don't you?" I asked.

"Only when they are as exquisite as you are," Maximillian responded with a low purr. The teasing note in his voice sent a current of warmth through me, and I blinked as I realized I was flirting with a vampire, in the middle of a vampire soiree, and actually enjoying it. It was a situation the old me couldn't fathom, and that the new me was still wrapping my head around.

Who was I becoming, exactly?

"Don't allow yourself to be alone with Icarus Stormwelder if you can help it," Maximillian continued as he led me through the garden, his expression growing serious. "He may be mad, but he is also highly intelligent and has a penchant for experimenting on live subjects. It is the worst of combinations, which is precisely why the emperor keeps him around."

A shudder went through me, and I resisted the urge to look back at the aetherion inventor, whose eyes I could still feel on my back. "No wonder Eliza hates him," I muttered.

"Indeed." Maximillian squeezed my arm, then straightened as we arrived at a high-top table, where the Stellaris twins were holding court along with a gaggle of other vampire nobles. The female twin, Viviana, lit up at our approach, the silver flecks in her midnight eyes lighting up as they landed on me.

"Oooh, you've found her!" she squealed, clapping her hands like a child that had been given an unexpected gift. Her long nails were painted silver, with black tips, and they seemed to mirror her hair, which had been swept off her neck in an updo, leaving only the long white streak to hang down by her face. "I have been dying to get a taste of you since Maximillian presented you at court this morning."

Her words caused my insides to coil with dread, and I glanced up at Maximillian, uncertain. "But I thought—"

"Ignore my sister," Caelum said with a drawl, picking up his cocktail glass so he could take a sip. I tried not to focus on the way he licked the blood off his teeth before he spoke. "She's simply trying to get a rise out of you. No one but Maximillian is allowed to drink from you—the emperor proclaimed it, and so it shall be."

"I've always found that to be a silly rule," Viviana said with a pout. Her lips were painted a vivid shade of red that contrasted beautifully with her ivory skin. "After all, it's not as if one bite alone is enough to complete the Descendancy. If that was the case, we would have run out of humans a long time ago."

"Yes, but that's not the point," Caelum said, his words edged with annoyance. "The rule is in effect so that no Nightforged can claim that they merely got 'carried away in the heat of the moment', or some other nonsense."

"Have people really used that defense in the past?" I asked, genuinely curious.

"Oh yes." Caelum gave me a sharp smile. "Feuding house members will often steal a descendant out from under the nose of another, simply to assert dominance, or as revenge for some petty slight. It can happen within houses, too. But the emperor wants us all to act as if we are one big, happy family, so he does as much as he can to ensure minimal scrapping between the houses."

"Are we not one big, happy family?" Soren Ironheart interrupted as he stepped out from the shadows. Like Caelum, he wore a military dress uniform, this one in dark red to indicate his status as army commander as opposed to Caelum's dark blue navy attire.

"Sure we are," Caelum said, his voice rife with sarcasm. "The Psychoros gunners on my ship get along wonderfully with my Sanguis Noctis deck officers."

"Perhaps you should restructure your crew assignments if you are having issues with inter-house conflict," Soren suggested coolly. His grey eyes found Maximillian, barely acknowledging my presence by his side. "Lord Starclaw, may I have a word? It concerns the cannon prototype."

"Of course. Please excuse me," he said to the others, then stepped past me, his hand brushing the small of my back before he disappeared into the foliage with the army commander, leaving me alone with the Stellaris twins. Caelum's words hung in the air in their wake, reminding me he was on the forefront of the battle between Noxalis and Trivaea. It was his ships relentlessly attacking our coastline, and the Crescent Cove—my clan's home—was right in the middle of it.

"Is the new cannon really going to make such a difference?" I asked Caelum, trying to sound like I was only casually interested, as if the lives of my people didn't depend on the answer. "I thought your ships already had guns."

Caelum snorted. "The guns that we have are little more than sparklers. The crystals take forever to charge, the blasts are not very powerful, and they can only hit at around three hundred yards on a good day. This new prototype is supposed to be able to hit targets from up to fifteen hundred yards, and from what I heard, a single blast from one was enough to reduce an entire airship to kindling."

"Ahh, that's right." Viviana leaned in, a conspiratorial smile on her face. "You were there for the demonstration, weren't you? Was the cannon as impressive as Caelum describes?"

"Yes," I admitted.

"Good," Caelum said with a grunt. "We'll be able to actually launch strikes on the coastline. And maybe even rip those sea monsters apart."

"Sea monsters?" I asked, raising my eyebrows. "Didn't those all die off after the Eternal Night?" From what I'd read, the lack of sunlight had severely disrupted the ocean's ecosystem. I didn't see how creatures who required large amounts of food, such as sea monsters, could have survived.

"They did," Caelum said darkly. "But the Necrospire Clan used their dark magic to resurrect them, and that crafty bastard, Sebastian Nocturne, has bribed the Blackwater Pirates to lend Trivaea a portion of their fleet. Now every one of their accursed ships has a necromancer witch on it, and they send all manner of horrific creatures to attack our ships—Shadow Krakens that rip our masts off with their tentacles, Wraith Whales that blow holes into our hulls with sonic blasts, and even Necrotic Sirens who use their dark forces to sing my sailors into madness until they turn on each other."

Caelum's grip tightened on his glass as he spoke and it shattered in his hand on the last word. The naval commander swore as one shard cut deeply into his palm, and Viviana tsked, reaching for a cloth napkin folded on the table.

"You really need to learn how to leave your work at home, brother," she scolded, scooping up his hand so she could mop up the blood. I figured it was more about the mess than anything else—the wound was already healing before my eyes. "This is a party. You're supposed to be relaxing."

"Yes, well, she asked about it," Caelum said, jabbing the finger of his other hand in my direction. "And we'd probably have those prototypes already, if not for you."

"Me?" I recoiled, surprised at the sudden vehemence aimed in my direction. "I have nothing to do with the prototype's delay," I protested, which was true. The blame for that rested with Vinicius. His cruel display of power by choosing to use the aether cannon to blow up the hidden temple had forced Eliza to reconsider the wisdom of putting such a powerful weapon in vampire hands, and she'd fudged reasons to delay it, citing mechanical flaws that needed to be shored up.

"Oh, leave the poor girl alone, Caelum," Viviana said. "It's not her fault her master is smitten with her. If anyone is to blame, it's Maximillian." She crooked a finger at a servant standing a few yards away beckoning him to come closer. "Now let's get you another drink. You need to relax."

"And you shouldn't drink so much," Caelum snapped as Viviana plucked two glasses of bloodwine from the servant's tray. "The last thing we need is for you to have an episode in the middle of the summit."

Viviana stiffened, all traces of amusement vanishing from her face. "My 'episodes', as you call them, have nothing to do with what I do or do not consume," she said. "Besides, they're the reason the emperor values me more highly than you, anyway."

Caelum laughed. "You, more valuable than me? Please. When the emperor gives you command of fifty thousand men and sends you off to battle an army of witches and pirates, you can come back and tell me you're the more valuable one. Now put that down," he scolded, trying to take Viviana's glass from her.

The female Stellaris twin scowled, holding the drink out of reach, but her expression shifted to something feline. "Well, if I'm not allowed to drink this, then what about our new friend?" she purred, locking eyes with me. "After all, I'd hate for this to go to waste."

Caelum's eyebrows rose as Viviana held the glass out to me, and my breath stuttered in my throat. "N-no thank you," I said, fighting against the urge to physically lean away. "Blood isn't really my thing."

"Is that so?" Viviana pushed the wine glass in my face, until the rim was directly beneath my nose, nearly touching my lips. The scent of the sanguine beverage teased my senses—a complex, rich aroma with a metallic tang that spoke of dark fruits and a hint of smoke. My mouth began to water, and I locked down every one of my muscles—this time to keep from leaning in, rather than leaning away.

"You're about to become one of us," Viviana said, her black eyes gleaming. "No longer Catherine Seabream, but Catherine Starclaw, a mistress of the dark. Don't you think blood is a taste you ought to acquire?"

I opened my mouth to answer, and Viviana tipped the glass forward, closing that millimeter of distance. The bloodwine flowed across my tongue, and I gasped at the burst of flavors—a copper tang overlaid by the fruity richness of the wine, interlaced with a hint of oak. Before I could stop myself, I snatched the glass from Viviana and drained it, my greedy tongue swiping along the rim.

I lowered the glass to see Caelum and Viviana staring at me with a mix of shock and fascination. Horror curdled in my gut when I realized what I'd done, followed by a sudden shift deep within my being. Something dark began to stir in my veins, my gums and fingernails aching, my skin suddenly too tight across my bones.

"How unexpected," Caelum remarked. "If I didn't know better, I'd say she enjoyed that."

"She most certainly did." Viviana's eyes were glued to the empty glass in my hand, and I thought I glimpsed a look of satisfaction on her face. "Do you feel—"

I clapped a hand over my mouth as that darkness surged inside me, and the twins stopped talking. "Please excuse me," I said around my hand as sweat broke out across my forehead. "I think I'm going to be sick."

And without another word, I bolted.

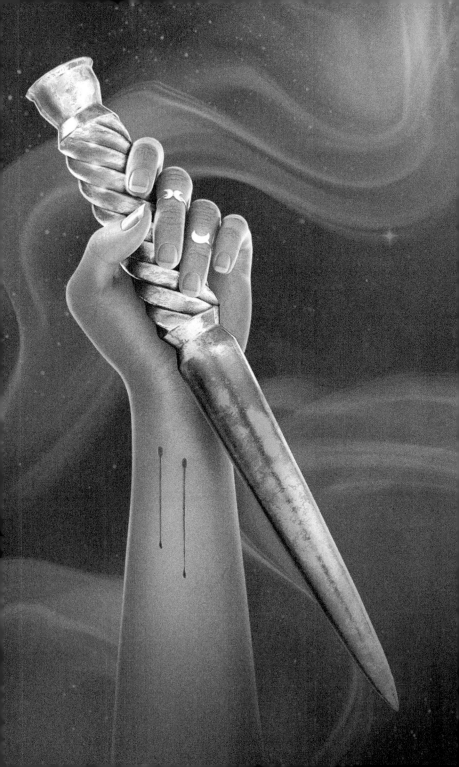

25

Casimir

C asimir watched from beneath the boughs of an ironbark tree as Catherine sprinted away from the Stellaris twins. He'd been listening to her exchange with Caelum and Viviana, more interested in the human thrall's reactions to the twins' antics than he was in what the siblings themselves had to say. He'd known them both for decades, and nothing much they did or said surprised him anymore, including when Viviana had offered Catherine the bloodwine.

But what did interest him was the way the human thrall had downed the entire glass with the gusto of a vampire fledgling, then bolted from the table as though she was going to be sick. As she disappeared into the foliage, he felt that tug in his chest —the one that always appeared whenever he saw her—intensify, and he took a step forward without thinking.

"Your Highness?" the simpering courtier who had been talking his ear off asked.

"Later." He waved off the noble—a lower scion from his own house who undoubtedly wanted a favor, and followed Catherine away from center of the greenhouse and into the western section, which was peppered with tall, potted fronds and thickets, designed for guests looking for a little privacy.

It wouldn't do for Maximillian's pet to run into a trysting pair. Proclamation or not, she could still end up getting hurt, and then his father would have to punish someone, which could cause yet more inter-house conflict. Casimir was nothing if not a pragmatist—these situations were best avoided if one wanted to keep the precarious balance between the four houses from collapsing.

To be honest, Casimir wasn't sure how his father had kept the houses together for this long, never mind unite them in the first place. The feuds between some of them were long and bloody—especially Sanguis Noctis and Psychoros. During the Chaos War, the Psychoros vampires were the first to come to their senses, rising out of the collective fog of bloodlust that had descended upon the Nightforged to see their former alliances in shambles around them. They had been the first to reach out to the other two realms and offer an alliance, in exchange for help from the humans in the form of voluntary blood donations in order to keep the bloodlust at bay, and from the witches in terms of magical interventions. House Stellaris had followed suit shortly after, and with half of the vampire realm turned against them, Houses Invictus and Sanguis Noctis had been forced to surrender. When the witches had drawn up the Midnight Accords, Psychoros and Stellaris had been exempted from many of the sanctions, while Sanguis Noctis had been given the harshest. And the blood mage vampires had never forgiven them for it.

Casimir could see both sides—on the one hand, the sanctions had been extremely unfair, and had practically beggared their realm. But he was not too proud to admit the Nightforged had been unhinged and out of control, and that their bloodlust would have probably been their own downfall if left unchecked. This new regime his father oversaw, where the use of human blood and slaves was regulated, was far better. It ensured there was a proper allocation of resources, and that the Nightforged could continue to sustain their supply of humans even without the sun.

It took a minute for Casimir to catch up with Catherine—she moved far faster than any human, even a thrall, had the right to—but he found her on her hands and knees in a cluster of bushes, throwing up. Her petite form shook as she wretched and heaved, and Casimir found himself annoyed at her foolishness. She had probably downed that glass in one go to show Viviana up, and it had been too much for her tiny body to handle.

Her entire body suddenly grew still, and Casimir knew she had sensed him. "What do you want?" she said in a thick voice, not turning around.

Casimir frowned. Was she really going to continue to give him her back like that? "I told you not to wander around alone," he said, taking a step forward.

"I'm not wandering," she snapped, shifting away from him. Casimir could see the pool of blood on the ground, mixed with bits of food from her midday meal. "I just needed to be sick somewhere in private. Now leave me alone."

The vehemence in her tone, which Casimir was unused to having directed at him by anyone other than his father, riled something inside him, and he closed the distance between before he could think better of it. "You impudent little wench," he snarled, grasping her underarm and hauling her around. "Maximillian clearly never taught you—"

He caught the briefest glimpse of what he could have sworn were fangs before something bright and hot flared in his chest, searing him from the inside out. Gasping, he clutched at his heart, fear lancing him, and he wondered if he was suffering a heart attack, even though that was a human malady.

"Your Highness!" Catherine's eyes were huge with concern, and she reached for him, her anger forgotten. There was no trace of fangs or anything else amiss on her face aside from a streak of blood at the corner of her mouth. "Are you all right?"

Casimir flinched away from her outstretched hand, but before he could say anything, footsteps sounded along with the rustling of bushes. "Catherine?" Maximillian called, appearing from around a tall trellis crawling with vines. His eyes widened at the sight of his thrall alone with Casimir in the bushes, and then narrowed on the prince. "Have you been feeding on her?"

Casimir barked out a laugh. "You should get those eyes of yours checked, Starclaw," he said, backing away from the thrall. "She's the one with blood on her mouth, not me."

He stalked away, leaving the Pyschoros vampire to deal with his thrall. He didn't know what the fuck had just happened, but he needed to get away, now, before whatever this *thing* between them was cleaved him in two. He could already feel it happening, the core of his being split wide open from a single *touch*.

Whoever this woman was, she was bad fucking news. And he needed to stay away from her.

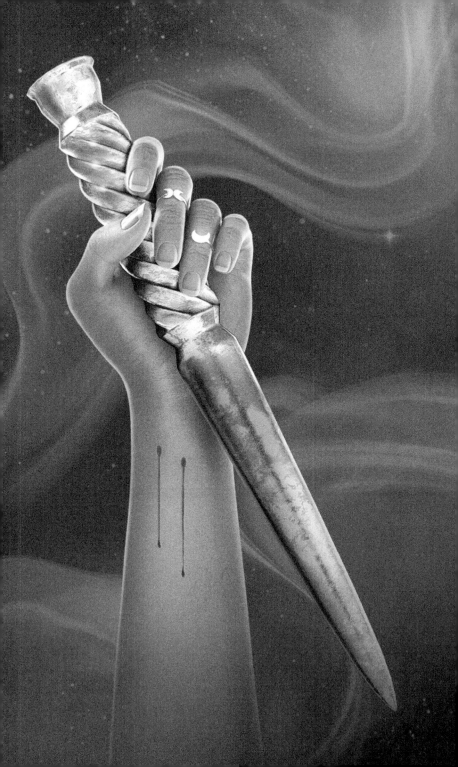

26

Kitana

"And you're certain you didn't use your magic on him?" Maximillian asked for what felt like the hundredth time after he'd brought me back to my bedchamber.

"Yes," I groaned, clutching at my head. My tongue felt thick and fuzzy, and I had a splitting headache, as if I'd just woken up with a hangover. "I swear on all the gods, Maximillian, I didn't use my magic on him. I didn't do anything at all! *He's* the one who touched *me*."

"Then why did he look as if you'd struck him?" Maximillian demanded, his eyes burning. I'd never seen him so agitated before, pacing in front of the window like a caged animal. "I saw his face—he was trying to hide it, but he was in physical agony, Kitana. How is that possible, if you didn't do anything?"

"I don't know!" I cried, throwing up my hands. And that much was true—I had no idea why Casimir had reacted so violently after putting his hands on me. The tug in my chest had intensified when he'd grabbed me... was it possible that he felt the same pull? But how could that be? After all, while the sensation had been intense, it wasn't painful for me. And Maximillian was right—Casimir had looked as though someone had buried an axe in the center of his chest, his eyes glassy, his features contorted with pain.

And even though he was the son of my hated enemy, I'd taken no pleasure in seeing him that way.

"I swear to you, Maximillian," I said, my voice brimming with pain and frustration. "I didn't use my magic on him, or attack him physically." Although I would have used the knife if I'd sensed he was going to hurt me. "I was just in the bushes, throwing up the bloodwine Viviana forced me to drink, when he came up and grabbed me. I have no idea why he reacted that way, or even what he wanted. And I feel terrible about it, and now I don't know what to do, because—"

I broke off on a sob, and Maximillian cursed. "Come here," he said roughly, striding forward and pulling me into his arms. I tried to fight him at first, terrified of what he might see or sense, but my treacherous, touch-starved body rebelled, throwing my arms around his waist and pressing my cheek into his abdomen.

"I'm going to eviscerate Viviana when I see her," he swore, the violence in his tone a stark contrast to the gentle way he stroked his hand over my hair and down my back. "I should have never left you alone with them, Kitana."

Against my better judgment, I clung to him, allowing Maximillian to soothe me with gentle touches and murmured reassurances. It seemed that all my time trapped in that coffin had eroded my impulse control—I had been unable to resist the bloodwine, unable to control my temper around Casimir, and was now unable to pull away from Maximillian even though I was exposed and vulnerable, and he was far, far, *far* too close.

"I'm sorry I'm such a mess," I croaked out.

"There's nothing for you to apologize about, Kitten," Maximillian said, sliding his fingers through my hair at the roots. I swallowed a moan as his nails scraped against my scalp, releasing the tension built up there. "And if you're a mess, you're the most magnificent one I've ever seen."

His words sent a thrill through me, but the wounded animal in me recoiled from them. He didn't know the truth about me, the secret that lurked so close to the surface, that Casimir had nearly stumbled upon tonight. That Sebastian had condemned me for, then attempted to bury me with, all those decades ago. Shame coiled within me as those dark memories threatened to surface, and my skin suddenly felt as if a layer of grime had settled on it, one I would never be able to scrub off.

"Kitana?" Maximillian grasped my shoulders as I started to pull away. "What is it?"

I shook my head, turning away from the concern shining in his eyes. Something about this vampire made me want to open my heart and spill all my secrets, and I knew that if I looked into his face now, I might very well give into that impulse.

"I just... I need to be alone for a little while, okay?" I whispered. "Tonight was rough. There were a lot of vampires in that room, and I didn't handle it as well as I could have. I need to pull myself back together."

Maximillian's mouth tightened, and for a second, I thought he would refuse. But then he pulled away, disappointment glimmering in his eyes even as he nodded. "All right," he said gently, getting to his feet. "But let me know if you need anything, Kitana. You're not alone."

He closed the door behind him with a soft click, and I fisted my skirts in my hands as I stared into the fire, watching the flames dance in the grate. As soon as his footsteps faded, I stripped my gown off, using tendrils of shadow magic to undo the buttons in the back. As I moved to the closet, I caught a glimpse of myself in the mirror, then did a double take at the sight of the flower tattoo on my abdomen.

"They will never see you as you truly are," my mother said, her faraway voice echoing in my ears. *"You will be safe and protected, no matter how high or low he searches for you. So long as this remains."*

My heart hammered in my chest as I leaned closer, tracing my fingers over the edge of one flower. The color had dwindled to almost nothing, leaving only the faintest of outlines on my flesh where a full flower had once bloomed.

This had never happened before. And I had no idea what it meant that it was starting to happen now.

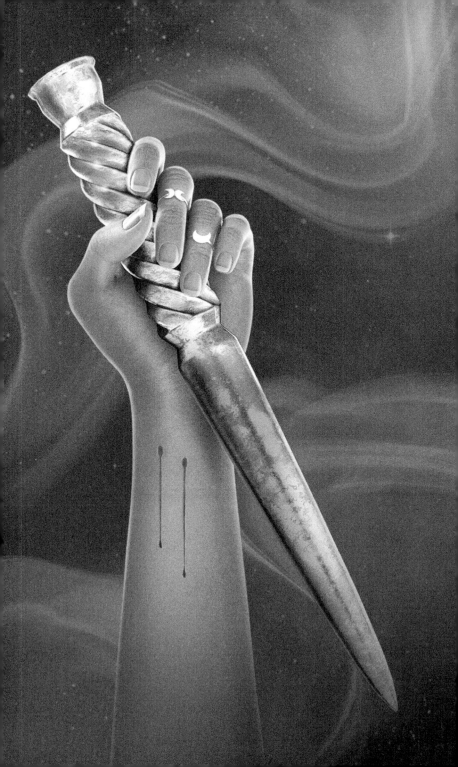

27

Kitana

I'd expected the second day of the Summit to be just as filled with political tension, drama, and rivalry as the first.

Instead, I was so bored I could barely stay awake in my chair.

"...it is therefore essential to increase the standard levy on all imports passing through the Crimson Cliffs," a vampire noble said, his nasally voice buzzing through the hall as he stood just before the dais, facing the emperor even though his address was also meant for the crowd at his back. "This measure will help regulate the influx of foreign fabrics, ensuring our local producers remain competitive."

In all fairness, I might have found some of this interesting if I'd gotten any sleep last night. But I'd spent yet another night tossing and turning, replaying the encounter with Casimir over and over in my mind, trying to dig up some tidbit that would explain his violent reaction to touching me.

The vampire in question was sitting on the opposite side of the hall from me, his chin propped in his hand as he watched the vampire lord continue to drone on in a voice that would have put even the most energetic toddler into a coma. Unlike yesterday, he hadn't looked at me at all, his fascination supposedly put to an end by whatever had happened between us last night.

But there was another explanation for the look on his face when he'd spun me around, and my hand unconsciously drifted to the center of my torso, fingers skimming across the missing flower.

He saw you.

No. That couldn't have been it. I'd thrown up all the blood, had purged it from my system before it could take root inside me. If Casimir had truly seen me, he wouldn't have kept silent, nor would he have run off the way he had. He would have gone straight to his father, and I would be chained up in an interrogation room somewhere—

My train of thought cut off as someone pinched my side, and I jerked, looking around for the perpetrator. It couldn't have been Marisse, who was seated next to me, nor the vampire on my other side—neither of them had moved, and unlike me, they seemed to have no trouble paying attention to the speaker. But as my gaze moved down the row, I noticed Maximillian watching me. His expression was placid, but there was a gleam in his eyes as he stared back, as if they were silently saying, *"Pay attention. I saw you drifting off."*

Annoyed, I tore my gaze from him and focused on what the vampire noble was saying. "This tariff will support our naval defenses against pirate activities in the region, stabilizing the trade routes..."

I tried to pay attention, I really did, but my gaze drifted back to Casimir, almost of its own accord. A jolt went through me as his citrine eyes met mine, and that tugging sensation increased, until I had to grip the edge of my seat to keep from coming out of my chair. It was as if there was a lodestone in my chest, incessantly trying to drag me toward him, and I didn't understand it.

Casimir Invictus was the *last* person in this castle I should be getting close to.

Another pinch came, sharper this time, and I whipped my head around to glare at Maximillian. The glint in his eyes had turned dangerous, and I hissed when he pinched me a third time, the sensation sharper, almost punishing. This time, lines of displeasure bracketed his mouth, and I watched as he turned to look at Casimir, his right hand flexing as if he would have very much liked to drive it into the vampire prince's face.

Wait a minute. Was Maximillian... jealous?

That's absurd, I told myself. But when I turned my attention back to the speaker, I couldn't help noticing Maximillian relax. Curious, I waited a few minutes, then allowed myself to look at Casimir, who this time was thankfully engaged in whispered conversation with the noble sitting to his left.

This time, the pinch was not on my side, but the place where my neck and shoulder met. And I could have sworn that I felt the scrape of phantom fangs against my skin.

Furious, I looked down the row at Maximillian, only to see his lips twitching with amusement. That bastard. Was he actually angry with me for staring at Casimir, or was he just toying with me because he found the current topic being discussed as mind-numbing as I did?

Well. Two could play at that game.

Dropping my gaze to his feet, I focused my attention on the shadows pooling beneath his chair. They responded at once, and I directed them with my mind, sliding a thin ribbon up his trouser leg, subtle enough that no one else would notice.

I expected Maximillian to start squirming, but either he had no nerve endings in his flesh, or he had extraordinary control, because he remained perfectly still. An almost bored expression settled on his face as he watched another noble stand up to argue against the proposed tariff. Several others joined in, and a lively debate ensued, but I hardly paid any attention, my annoyance with Maximillian peaking.

Determined to get a reaction, I urged my shadow ribbon to climb higher, watching in my mind's eye as it snaked its way up his calf and around his thigh. I pinched the sensitive skin on his inner thigh, and his gaze flickered, but he showed no visible sign of distress.

So I went a little higher.

Maximillian's eyes widened as my shadow tendril slipped between his thighs and wrapped around an even *more* sensitive part of him. I swallowed a grin as I squeezed lightly, intending for it to be a subtle threat. But when his hands gripped the arms of his chair, his eyelids sliding to half-mast, an unexpected heat began to gather in my lower abdomen.

A phantom hand wrapped around my throat, and my heart hammered in my chest as I felt an invisible caress trail down my front, between my breasts, over my belly. The control Maximillian had over his telekinetic ability was beyond anything I'd ever seen. Most Psychoros vampires could use their power to hit targets with telekinetic blasts, immobilize them, or move their bodies about—smashing them into walls, forcing them to bury a blade in their own gut, or even kill their friends.

But to know that he could use that power with such finesse —to break bones and snap tendons, as he'd done with Vinicius, or to tease and seduce, as he was doing with me—was incredibly terrifying and arousing at the same time.

But before that phantom hand could drift any lower, the main doors to the Summit Hall opened with a bang that slammed me straight back into full awareness of my surroundings. "Your Imperial Highness!" a messenger cried, sprinting into the hall as though he were being chased by hellhounds. He skidded to a stop in front of the dais and bowed hastily. "Apologies for the interruption, but Taius has been found."

I saw Casimir straighten in his chair out of the corner of my eye, his full attention on the messenger. "Well?" the emperor demanded. "Where is he, then? He should have arrived days ago."

"His head was found on the gates of the Iron Spire just a few moments ago, impaled on one of the spikes," the messenger said. A gasp rippled through the hall as he extended a bloodied scrap of paper to the emperor. "We don't know who left it, or where the rest of his body is, but they pinned this note to his scalp."

The emperor unfolded the paper, his eyes narrowing, and when he read the words aloud, my entire world tilted on its axis.

"I know you're awake, darkling girl."

Each word hit like a punch to the gut, and I felt my vision tunneling, gaze fixed on the paper in Vladimir's hands as if I could read the words myself if I just stared hard enough. "Darkling girl?" the emperor repeated, his harsh features twisting with rage. "What kind of nonsense is this?"

"Maybe he's referring to Viviana," Lysander said, pointing to the female Stellaris twin. "With her black eyes and hair."

"That's preposterous," Caelum argued. "Why would the rebels send a message to *her*?"

"Excuse me?" Viviana tossed a skein of hair over her shoulder, looking affronted. "I'm plenty important for men to send dead bodies with messages written on them for me."

"This isn't just any dead body," Vladimir thundered, and everyone in the room froze as his eyes seared into them. "This is a member of my house, one of my children!" He leaped off his throne and grabbed the messenger by his collar, shaking him hard enough to rattle his skull. "Send out a search party to scour the city and surroundings! I want these rebels rounded up and executed!"

He flung the messenger across the room, and my mouth

opened in shock as the vampire slammed into the opposite wall with crushing force. The echoing boom shook the air, dust raining down from the ceiling as the marble cratered from the impact. Shocked cries rippled through the hall as the messenger's pulverized body slid bonelessly down the wall, landing in a bloody heap on the floor.

The emperor's chest heaved, his eyes blazing red as he fought to control his anger. The others watched him with a mix of shock, dismay, and fear—all except for Casimir, who remained stoic as ever.

Eventually, the emperor regained enough of his sanity to point to a servant and growl, "Get that cleaned up, and deliver my orders to the captain of the guard. This session is closed for today," he added, his voice booming across the hall.

As the servant sprang into action and the hall erupted into chaos, Maximillian caught my eye again. I could tell by the grim look on his face that, just as I did, he knew exactly who had sent the message, and who it was for.

It was Sebastian Nocturne, the unofficial Witch King of Trivaea. And the message was for me.

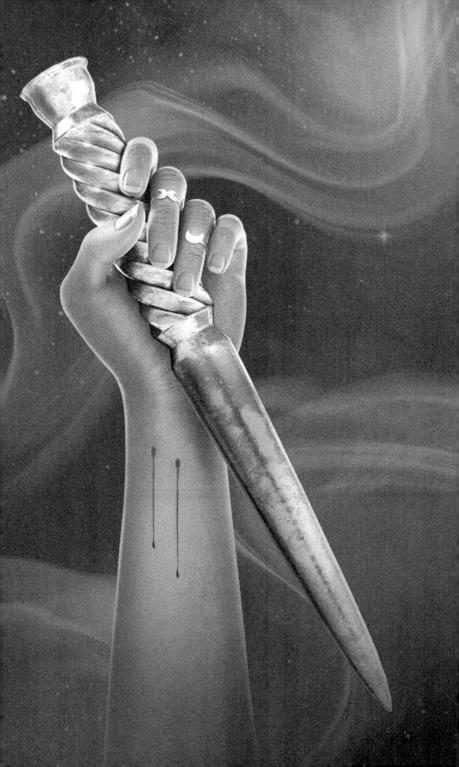

28

Kitana

There was so much chaos as everyone left the summit hall, no one noticed when Maximillian, Lucius, and I slipped away to one of the private meeting rooms upstairs.

"Darkling girl?" Lucius asked as he locked the door behind us. "Is that some kind of nickname?"

"Hang on." I held up a hand, and shadows poured from my fingers, curling through the air like tendrils of smoke. With a flick of my wrist, I scattered them, sending them into all the crevices, cracks, and corners to search for any peepholes or eavesdropping devices that might be lurking. Once they'd wedged themselves into all possible openings, I let my guard down a little, crossing over to the sideboard so I could pour myself a stiff drink.

"Impressive," Lucius muttered, staring at the shadow I wedged into the crack beneath the door.

I poured two fingers of whiskey into a glass, thanking the gods that there was no blood mixed into the beverage. "Darkling girl was Sebastian's pet name for me," I told them as I lifted the glass to my lips. "It was a reference to my strange powers—how I could do things with shadow magic that most others couldn't, but I also couldn't use any lunar magic."

"Which is unusual among your clan, isn't it?" Maximillian asked, seating himself in one of the chairs by the unlit fireplace. He leaned forward, elbows on his thighs, fingertips pressed together, a pensive expression on his face. It was insane to think that just a few minutes ago, we'd been practically eye-fucking each other in the middle of a hall full of people, and had been seconds from doing a lot more than that.

What kind of madness had taken over me?

"Very unusual," I said as the whiskey carved a burning trail down my throat. I clutched the glass as memories both sweet and bitter surfaced, coating my tongue like ashes. "Almost every Nocturne witch is born with the power of shadow and light. Lunar and shadow magic. It's why we're considered the bringers of balance between the five clans, and also why the witches were appointed as the custodians of the Midnight Accords. We exist in the twilight, belonging neither to the day or the night, yet siblings of both."

"A pretty speech," Maximillian acknowledged. "Yet perhaps not so pretty in practice."

My eyes narrowed on him. "Are you saying that you believe in the emperor's spiel?" I asked, thinking back to the impassioned speech Vladimir had given yesterday. "That the terms of the Accords were unfair, and that vampires were unjustly punished and victimized by witches?"

"The terms of the Midnight Accords were harsh," Maximillian said in a voice sharp enough to cut glass, "Harsher than necessary, considering that we'd been cursed, but understandable given the horrors my ancestors visited upon our neighbors. But there is no denying that witches have abused their power as custodians of the Accords in the past. That is partly how we ended up in this situation in the first place."

"We are getting off-track," Lucius growled, holding up a hand as I started to argue. "We didn't come here to discuss the Accords. We came here to talk about your ex-lover, how he knows you're here, and why he sent you such a public message."

Anger bloomed in the pit of my stomach as Sebastian's words ran through my head again. How dare he try to fuck with me like this, to get inside my head and attempt to intimidate me, without having the balls to show his face?

"Perhaps someone alerted him that the coffin was empty," Maximillian said. "He could have had some spell in place set to trigger an alarm in the event of a breach."

"If that's the case, then why wait until now to send a message?" Lucius demanded. "It's been almost eight weeks since we freed Kitana from that hellhole. If the witch king wanted to get to her, Lumina would have been a far easier place to strike."

"Fair point." Maximillian tapped his chin thoughtfully. "Any thoughts, Kitana?"

There was no judgment in his gaze, only curiosity and concern. Yet I swallowed hard, not sure how he would react to what I was about to tell him. "The night after Vinicius blew up the secret temple, I paid a visit to The Red Tavern. And ended up running into some rebels."

I told Maximillian and Lucius about the witch and the human I'd met at The Red Tavern, leaving out that they not only worked there, but unofficially owned the damned place. "I didn't want to reveal my identity to them, but it seemed like the only way to get out of there without bloodshed," I told them, ignoring the scowl on Lucius's face. "The last thing I wanted to do was murder people who are trying to help the humans, especially a witch."

"One of them must have told their superiors you were in

Lumina, and word got back to Sebastian," Lucius growled. "We didn't want him to know you were free, Kitana. Not until after—"

"Hush," Maximillian said. "There are some things that shouldn't be spoken aloud here, even if we do have a magical sound barrier." He sighed, raking a hand through his hair and messing up the sleek, stormy strands. "My guess is that Sebastian merely wants you to know he's watching, Kitana, and that he's ready and waiting for you. I doubt he'll try to interfere with our plans, not when he stands to benefit. But this does take away the element of surprise I was hoping for," he said, standing. "We'll need to rethink our strategy once we're through here."

"Wait," I said, getting to my own feet. "Where are you going?"

"I have another meeting I must attend," he said, moving to the door. But as I drew close, he hooked his arm around my waist and pulled me into him. "Try not to have any more run-ins with the prince, Kitten," he murmured, his lips grazing the shell of my ear. "Whatever he did or did not see, it's clear he knows too much."

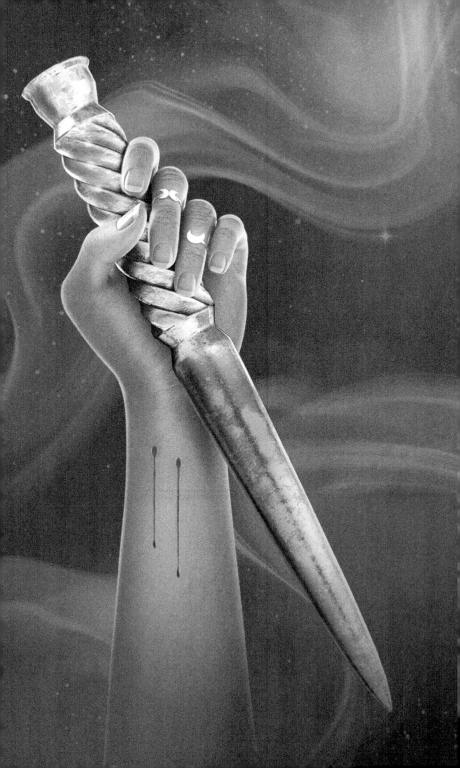

29

Casimir

C asimir half-expected his father to cancel the dark mass in the wake of his brother's death. The emperor had been beside himself when he'd beheld Taius's severed head in the mortuary—a chamber seldom used in the Iron Spire, since Nightforged rarely left corpses behind when they died. Their bodies disintegrated when they were stabbed or staked through the heart, but not when beheaded. That was why whoever had murdered Taius had opted to sever his head—so they could use his corpse to send a message.

Casimir had hoped that perhaps the guards had it wrong, that the head had not belonged to his brother. But there was no mistaking the silver scar bisecting Taius's left eye, nor his distinctive, russet-colored eyes. The vampire who had taught Casimir to wield a sword, who had drilled him in the art of battle and warfare, and who had encouraged him to excel despite his father's criticisms, was well and truly gone.

But the High Nexon would hear nothing of the sort, and as the head of their realm's religious order, he was one of the few people who could gainsay Casimir's father. The very idea of canceling the dark mass during the one time of the year when the majority of Noxalis's nobility were present would be an affront to the dark god, the old bastard had warned. He would honor Taius's life and commend his undead soul to Tenebros during the ceremony, but the dark mass would proceed as scheduled.

"I still don't understand how someone could have stuck his head on the gates without anyone noticing," Caelum said under his breath as he and Casimir entered the Sanctum of Tenebros. The two of them had joined the search party, scouring the city for any sign of the culprit, but the assassin had left no trace, not even so much as a scent for them to track him with. The city guard had flushed out a few rebels operating on the outskirts of the city, but though they had been thoroughly interrogated, they did not know who had killed Taius or the identity of the person who had impaled his head on the gates.

Such a feat could have only been accomplished with witchcraft. Which pointed to either the rebels... or Trivaea itself.

"What are the chances that the witch-king himself is behind this?" Casimir asked as they entered an antechamber off to the side of the main hall so they could wash, as was their custom.

"Anything is possible," Caelum admitted as he scrubbed his hands using the small sink and bar of soap in the corner of the room. "But given that Taius was nowhere near the Trivaean border, it seems unlikely that the witch-king could have intercepted him. Sebastian doesn't send his witches through the border passes unless it's absolutely necessary."

True. The border passes were extremely treacherous to navigate—magic surges erupting from the barrier often killed any who attempted it, and even if they managed to survive the trek, they would then have to deal with the guards waiting on the other side.

"Still, someone thought it necessary to not only murder Taius, but travel all the way to the capital to leave his head on a spike with a message for someone we do not even know," Casimir growled as Caelum stepped aside so he could use the sink next. "Who is this 'darkling girl' this murderer is so desperately seeking the attention of?"

Almost as soon as he spoke the words, an image of Catherine rose in his mind's eye. Wavy, brown-black hair, violet eyes, a star-shaped beauty mark on her cheekbone, and secrets that clung to her like some dark perfume.

But no. That made little sense. She was just a human woman. No one of consequence.

No one of consequence? a voice in his mind asked, sounding faintly amused. *Even though you gravitate to her like a moth drawn to flame?*

Casimir clenched his jaw as he stepped into the main worship hall of the temple. Towering ceilings arched above them, adorned with intricate carvings too high up to be viewed clearly. The hall was dimly lit not just by the moonlight filtering in through the stained-glass windows, but from the thousands of black candles scattered throughout the grand space. Clusters of them were placed in front of statues of minor deities and religious figures that stood watch along the perimeters, and still more flickered in massive candelabras arranged on the worship stage. The pews were already filled near to bursting, but as Casimir scanned the crowded hall, he saw no sign of the woman plaguing his thoughts.

"I'll see you later," Caelum muttered, splitting off to join his father and sister, who were already seated in their pew box directly in front of the stage. The pews, arranged into four sections with three aisles between and two on the outer edges, reflected the order of the vampire clans. Nobles occupied the ground floor, their seating closest to the High Nexon indicating their status, while commoners filled the upper galleries, observing from above.

Casimir made his way down the center aisle to where his father and his siblings sat. His brother and sister stood upon his arrival so he could edge past them and take his place next to his father. But the emperor barely acknowledged his arrival, his diamond-hard gaze fixed on the altar.

"Did you find anything?" his father asked, even though he'd likely already received the report from the city guard.

Casimir shook his head. "They left nothing behind for us to track or trace them with."

"Witches," his sister, Sarai, hissed to his left. She ran her tongue over her canines, her dark blue eyes glittering with suppressed rage. "Bold for one of them to sneak right up to the spire gates. Whoever this 'darkling girl' is, she must be important."

Casimir looked over Sarai's shoulder to the Psychoros pew, where Maximillian sat with Callix Starclaw. The rest of the Psychoros delegation was present, save for Catherine. Why wasn't she with them? Thralls usually weren't permitted to attend the dark mass—it was meant to be a communion between the Nightforged and their god alone. But as a Descendant, Catherine was expected to attend. In fact, by not doing so, she risked rejection from the dark god himself.

As if Sarai could hear his thoughts, she leaned in and whispered, "I heard Lord Starclaw telling Alaric that he excused her from the dark mass due to indigestion. Evidently she had a bad reaction to the bloodwine from last night."

"A reaction to the bloodwine?" Soren Ironheart scoffed from his seat behind Sarai's. "How can he expect us to accept her as a candidate if she can't handle a few sips of blood?"

"Perhaps it's not the blood she had a reaction to," Ruslan,

who sat on the emperor's right, said, twisting in his seat to address Soren. "She could have a low tolerance for alcohol."

"Silence," Casimir's father said, his tone as cold as the catacombs that ran beneath their feet. "We are about to begin."

The four of them faced front as the High Nexon ascended the stage, two attendants at his side. All three of them were anointed with blood, the dark streaks painted in swirling runes over their powder-pale faces. The attendants remained a few feet behind the ancient vampire as he approached the pulpit, a heavy black book of sermons clutched in his gnarled hand. He took a moment to set the book on the wooden surface before lifting his head to address the gathered masses.

"Children of the Night," he began, "we assemble under the watchful gaze of Tenebros, to whom we owe our eternal allegiance. As the shadows gather, so do we, united in sacred darkness. We come together to reaffirm our dominion over the night, to draw strength from the abyss, and to renew the covenant with our dark father."

He paused, allowing his milky gaze to sweep over the audience as if to assure himself that he had everyone's attention before speaking again. "Yet tonight, our hearts are heavy, for we also gather in the shadow of a great loss. General Taius, beloved childe of our emperor, a titan amongst us, has been taken by the very darkness he so fervently defended. His life, a testament to the power and resilience of our kind, now becomes legend whispered in the corridors of the night. As we commend his valorous spirit to the eternal embrace of Tenebros, we vow to uphold the legacy he leaves behind." His raspy voice softened as he added, "Let us now observe a moment of silence to honor his indomitable spirit."

Movement rippled through the hall as everyone bowed their heads in honor of Taius. Casimir clenched his jaw as his brother's face filled his mind's eye. He had wanted to follow Taius into war, but his father had forbidden it—as the emperor's only heir, Casimir was not allowed to engage in anything that could be considered a threat to his life. His father was ridiculously over-protective for a male who didn't particularly seem to like his only natural born son—for every word of praise, his father had visited a thousand criticisms upon him, criticisms Taius had defended him from whenever he'd had the opportunity.

And now Taius was gone.

The general wasn't the only sibling Casimir had—there were three others, including Sarai, who was next to him, Ruslan, who sat on his father's right, and Darius, who was away on a mission. As the royal spymaster, Darius turned up whenever and wherever he liked, so unlike Taius, his absence was not a red flag.

The one thing Casimir didn't understand was why his father had not been aware of Taius's death. While the crown prince himself was not old enough to have sired children, from everything he had heard, the bonds between sire and child were incredibly strong. Shouldn't the emperor have felt something, even if just a slight twinge, when Taius died? Or was the sensitivity of the bond dulled by distance, to the point that Vladimir had been unable to sense the change?

The High Nexon's sandpaper voice filled the hall again, rising from the silence like an eerie specter. "Now, let us call upon the dark majesty of Tenebros," he intoned. The congregation began a low, resonant chant that vibrated through the stone beneath their feet, and Casimir joined his voice to theirs, allowing himself to fall into the familiar embrace of worship.

His connection to the dark god had always been a tenuous thing. Other Nightforged, natural born and Turned alike, had told him they'd been visited by Tenebros at least once in their lifetime, through dreams, visions, and even the occasional whispered word of advice. But though Casimir had never experienced such a thing in the countless hours he had spent praying in this hall, something about tonight felt different. The air in the sanctum hummed with the presence of something otherworldly, as if the god of night stalked in the shadows just outside of his periphery, watching his assembled children as they prayed for his dark blessing.

The chant came to a close, and a hush fell over the crowd as the High Nexon raised his arms. "And now, to thank our dark father for all that he has provided, and will provide, we offer him this sacrifice."

He turned to his left, drawing the congregation's eye to an attendant leading a human slave up the steps and to the black slab altar in the middle of the stage. The male did not resist— the glassy look in his eyes and the way his arms and legs dragged told Casimir he was in full thrall, unable to resist even the simplest of commands. But while Casimir had expected this —the High Nexon made it a point to sacrifice at least one human to Tenebros per month, usually picking from the lowest of the slave ranks—he did not expect three more humans to follow after him, their chains clanking ominously around their wrists and ankles. His eyebrows winged up, and he turned to see his father staring avidly at the sacrifices, a vengeful look in his eyes.

"You will notice tonight's sacrifice is more bountiful than usual," the High Nexon said, and Casimir looked back to see all four humans kneeling before the altar. "These humans were part of a rebel cell the city guard discovered operating on the outskirts of Umbral. We offer them to our divine father as penance for allowing these agents of the enemy to go unchecked, and pray he will grant us forgiveness in his infinite wisdom and offer us guidance so that we may better execute his dark will."

One of the attendants stepped forward, offering the High Nexon a shining starsteel axe. Anticipation filled the hall as the rebels were told to kneel, and Casimir found himself on the edge of his seat as he watched the High Nexon lift the axe, preparing to sever the first head. He wasn't sure what about this situation had him on tenterhooks—it was unusual to offer so many sacrifices, but he'd seen dozens upon dozens of humans beheaded on that black altar. Nothing about this should have been especially interesting.

But Casimir felt something stirring inside him, something bright and hot that felt very much like the thing that had awoken inside him when he'd grabbed Catherine last night. He'd almost convinced himself it had been a bad case of indigestion, but it had been many hours since he'd last eaten—there was no reason he should be feeling this now. Gritting his teeth, he did his best to ignore it, focusing his attention on the axe as it came down with an echoing thunk, severing the first head in a bright spray of blood.

One head. Two. Three. Four. The heads tumbled off to the side, and rivers of jewel-bright blood sloughed across the flat surface of the altar and into the trough carved into the floor just beneath. The entire congregation watched eagerly, their collective hunger rising at the sight of so much fresh blood flowing freely across the stage, and acolytes walked up and down the aisles, offering each member of the congregation a small glass of bloodwine.

"As our dark father drinks, so shall we partake in this communion," the High Nexon proclaimed, taking a goblet from one of his own attendants. "Let us drink deeply, so the divine power that flows through our god may in turn flow through us, and give us the strength and courage to prevail!"

The old priest punctuated his cry by raising his goblet, and the rest of the congregation mirrored the movement, then tipped their glasses to their lips. Casimir closed his eyes as the bloodwine flowed across his tongue, smooth and thick and slightly smoky, waiting for the familiar rush that always followed.

Instead, the hot, bright thing inside him flared so intensely, Casimir doubled over, clutching his chest.

"Cas!" Sarai cried, grabbing his shoulder, but whatever else she was about to say was cut off as an avalanche of darkness crashed over him.

Suddenly, Casimir found himself on hands and knees, staring into a vast pit of darkness that had opened in the middle of the floor. The ground beneath his palms pulsed with a blinding light, but his gaze was riveted on the abyss that stared back at him out of eyes forged of the coldest starlight. A thrill of awe and terror raced through him as a face took shape, contours emerging from the void like a sculpture carved from night itself. Raven hair that appeared to be made of feathers framed the fearsome and majestic visage, and the silhouettes of serpents writhed in the shadows surrounding it.

They said that sometimes when you stared into the abyss, the abyss stared back.

Bit this was no ordinary pit. Or even a hallucination. This was Tenebros, God of the Underworld, Father of Vampires.

The dark god reached for him from the pit, and Casimir cried out as his clawed hands dug into his shoulders. The light seared him, as if trying to repel the deity, but those claws only dug in farther, sending stabs of pain through the crown prince's body. Inky shadows spilled from the claws, sluicing down Casimir's arms and spreading across the ground until every inch of white was blanketed in darkness. The only light came from Tenebros's eyes, which burned into Casimir with divine rage.

"You may be her son," the dark god hissed in a voice like a thousand serpent tongues, "but you are also *mine*. Mine to command, mine to mold, mine to use. Remember whom you serve."

He shoved Casimir, sending him reeling back into reality. Another set of hands grabbed his shoulders, shaking him, and he blinked his eyes open to see the emperor kneeling over him, his eyes wide with panic. The entire service had come to a halt, nobility from all four houses gathered around to gawk as the crown prince lay on the pew floor. For the first time in Casimir's memory, his father was staring at him not with anger, or disappointment, or even mild disgust, but with honest-to-gods concern.

Yet in the wake of what he'd just seen, Casimir couldn't bring himself to care.

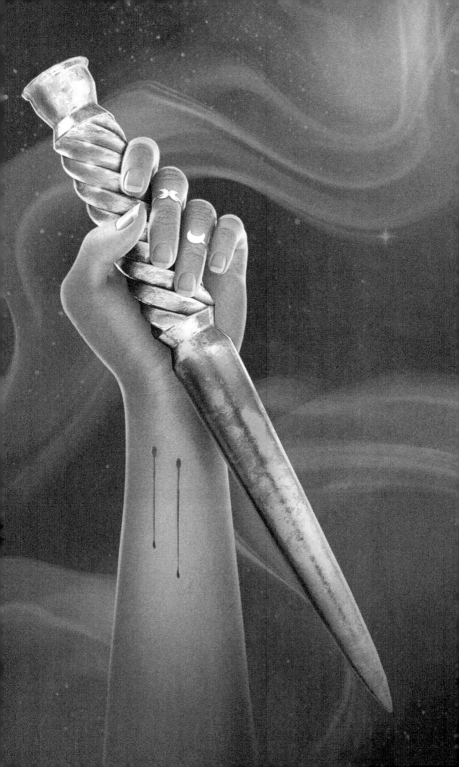

30

Casimir

After a good thirty minutes of poking and prodding, the royal physician stepped back with a click of his tongue. "Aside from mild dehydration, I see nothing wrong with the crown prince, Your Imperial Highness," he said, addressing the emperor who stood a few feet away, his hands and hips braced on the table behind him. As soon as the dark mass finished, his father had dragged him back to his personal sitting room in Spire Invictus, then called the royal physician to examine him. "A few glasses of blood and a night of rest and he should be back to normal tomorrow."

"Good," his father said, not even bothering to glance at the physician. His eyes bored into Casimir's, as if they could penetrate the depths of his skull and ferret out the thoughts lurking in the dark corners of his mind. "Leave us."

The physician bowed swiftly, then made himself scarce. A heavy silence descended upon the room, and Casimir allowed it to thicken as he stared back at his father, waiting for him to speak.

"Well?" the emperor finally demanded. "Are you going to tell me what happened in there, or do I have to beat it out of you?"

Casimir suppressed a snort. *There* was the doting father he knew and loved. "I had a vision," he said, seeing no point in beating around the bush. "From our dark father."

Vladimir pushed off the table, his eyebrows flying up as genuine surprise flashed across his face. "Tenebros gave you a divine message?" he asked sharply. "What was it?"

"He told me..." Casimir grappled for a moment, still not sure how to interpret what the god had said. He eventually settled on repeating it verbatim. "He said, 'You may be her son, but you are also *mine*. Mine to command, mine to mold, mine to use. Remember whom you serve.'"

His father's expression shuttered, like a curtain being drawn over a window. "I see," he said. "How disappointing."

An old, familiar anger ignited within Casimir, and he pushed himself to his feet before he could think better of it. "Disappointing?" he repeated, trying not to sound as incensed as he felt. "I didn't realize your ego had grown big enough to eclipse a message from the gods themselves. Besides, I thought I was the only one who disappointed you."

Vladimir's fist crashed into Casimir's jaw so hard, the bones shattered on impact. The crown prince went sprawling to the floor, agony exploding through his skull as his father towered over him. The air around the emperor crackled with power, shimmering over his skin and lifting long, golden strands of hair from his broad shoulders to float around his face like gilded snakes.

"I thought I'd beaten that flippant tongue out of you a long time ago," Vladimir growled, his eyes glowing red. "Perhaps the lessons from your childhood ought to be repeated."

The fear that had been stamped into Casimir's bones from a young age tried to rise, but he beat it back, clamping down on his emotions with the iron will he had forged over decades of discipline. He pushed himself to his feet, his jaw bones already knitting back together, and clasped his hands behind his back as he waited for his ability to speak to return.

"My apologies, Your Imperial Highness," he said once he could move his jaw again. "I did not mean to speak out of turn. The vision appears to have addled my senses."

It wasn't so much that he wanted to grovel before his father as he realized the futility of talking back to him. Casimir needed answers, answers the emperor might provide should he play his cards right, but that would never happen if he allowed his temper to get the better of him. He needed to stroke his father's ego, not tear it down.

"Clearly." Vladimir said. His eyes glittered like the edges of a broken mirror as he raked his gaze over Casimir, but some of the anger seemed to dissipate. "You should heed our divine father's words, Casimir, and remember who you serve."

"I have always and will forever be loyal to the crown," Casimir said, and every word was true. He waited a beat, then asked the question he should have started with in the first place. "When the dark god said I was "her son", he must have been referring to my mother. But why would he mention her? What is so important he felt the need to assert his superiority over her?"

"I have no idea." Vladimir's lips thinned. "Your mother was a useless scrap of meat, barely fit to push you out from between her legs before she expired. Merely thinking about her fills me with disgust."

Disgust filled Casimir, too, but not at the thought of his mother. No, it was at the notion that anyone would ever say anything like that about the person who had brought their child into the world. It didn't matter that his mother had belonged to an inferior race—she had given her life for him, and without her, Casimir would not exist. Yet his father refused to honor that sacrifice, and barely acknowledged she'd ever existed in the first place.

"There must be something about her," Casimir pushed, knowing he was walking a fine line. "Perhaps something in her lineage—"

"Have you noticed any changes recently?" his father interrupted. "Any fluctuations in your powers, or strange physical symptoms?"

The emperor's eyes bore into Casimir's as he stared back, prompting him to answer. Casimir opened his mouth to tell him about the burning sensation he'd felt during the dark mass, when a feminine voice whispered into his ear.

"Don't tell him. He will use it against you."

The words died on his tongue as a surge of astonishment swept through him. First, a vision from Tenebros, and now a message from another deity, all in the same night? What was happening to him? "No," he said out loud, the words coming almost involuntarily. "I haven't noticed anything."

His father narrowed his gaze. "Perhaps I should have Icarus keep you overnight for observation," he said. "He can run some tests on you."

"No." The words burst from Casimir's lips with a vehemence, and he nearly took a step back as glimpses of horrible childhood memories flashed through his head. Glass tubes hooked up to his veins, his screams echoing off the walls as mysterious serums pumped through his body, searing his insides and turning his brain to mush. These were memories pushed so far to the back of his mind, Casimir forgot they existed. And when they did surface, he questioned whether they had actually happened, or if they were figments of an overactive childhood imagination.

Even so, the icy fear that coursed through him at the suggestion of spending a night in the lab was all too real, and every instinct Casimir possessed screamed for him to avoid it at all costs.

"No?" His father thundered, advancing on him. For a heart-stopping moment, Casimir thought the emperor would strike him again, but instead he fisted Casimir's shirt by the collar and yanked him forward until they were nearly nose to nose. "You do not have a choice in this matter, son. You will go to Icarus Stormwelder's lab, and you will allow him to run the tests."

This time, there was no mistaking the ripples of red energy that emanated from Vladimir's body along with the command. Casimir gasped as he felt the electric zaps bite into his skin, but other than the pain, he felt nothing. And he knew from the look in his father's eyes he was very much supposed to.

"I have no problem with submitting myself to whatever tests the inventor wants to run," Casimir said, his tone remarkably calm considering the circumstances. "I am merely considering how it will look if the crown prince disappears for the rest of the summit after having a vision in full view of the delegations." He waited a beat for the implications to sink in. "Such a thing may cause others to question the integrity and viability of the crown."

Vladimir's lip curled, and he shoved Casimir away. "Pretty words," he sneered as the prince caught himself before he stumbled. "You've learned to play the game. Now get out of my sight."

Casimir was only too happy to obey.

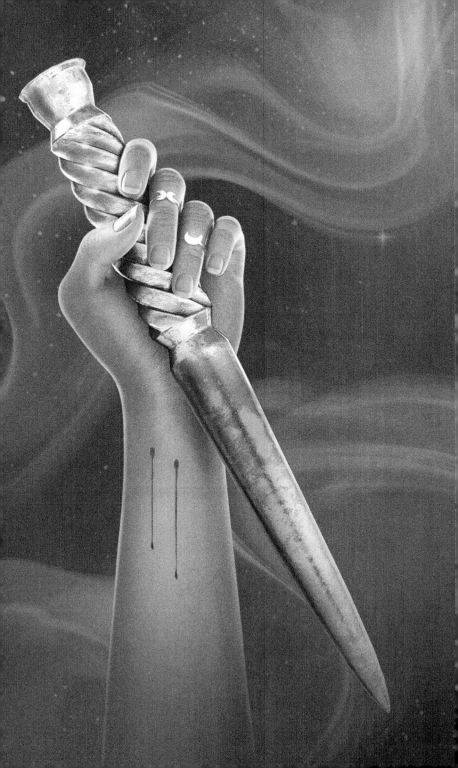

31

Maximillian

Maximillian thanked the stars Kitana had remained in the Spire instead of attending the Dark Mass tonight.

He'd suggested she stay behind because he didn't know how Kitana would react to watching innocent humans sacrificed on stage to a dark god they didn't worship. While he had prepared her as best he could for the horrors she might encounter at the Iron Spire, he knew his little witch. She had a very strong sense of justice, and even if she could stomach watching the human sacrifices, he knew it would kill her on the inside to stand by and do nothing as they were killed in cold blood in front of thousands of people.

There was also the matter of the mandatory bloodwine communion, which Kitana would not have been exempted from even if she was still 'human'. Maximillian didn't know why Kitana had such a violent aversion to blood—he'd seen her flinch on more than one occasion when she'd watched him or his children consume it—but he didn't need her vomiting in the aisle and drawing even more attention to herself.

Especially not from the crown prince.

But then again, it was Casimir who'd made a spectacle of himself tonight, not Kitana. And what a spectacle it had been, watching him collapse to the floor, his limbs flailing like a puppet being jerked around on strings. Everyone thought the bloodwine had poisoned him at first, but the prince had come back to himself only a few seconds later, claiming that the dark god had granted him a vision.

Maximillian wasn't entirely sure he believed that. But he remembered feeling Casimir's eyes on him before the service started, and knew the crown prince had been searching for Kitana. He could sense there was something between them—an invisible tether that pulled them toward one another, and for the life of him, Maximillian couldn't understand what it was about, or why the gods would do this to him.

Could she be an amorte? He wondered as he leaned against the wall, watching Kitana sleep soundly. She was curled on her side in the fetal position, her dark lashes fanning against her cheekbones, her lips slightly parted.

Maximillian was utterly obsessed with those lips. They were rosebud pink, the lower one fuller than the upper, and he was consistently tempted by the urge to lean in and tug it with his teeth.

He'd fantasized about kissing her a thousand times, wondering how her lips would feel, how they would taste.

Wondering how they would look wrapped around his cock.

He shook his head to clear the vision from his mind even as he grew hard. It wouldn't do for him to torture himself with lustful thoughts about her, especially since he had no intention of waking her. At least not anymore. He had come in here wanting to question her, to see if he could get to the bottom of this connection she had with the crown prince, but she was sleeping so peacefully, he was loath to disturb her.

She can't be an amorte, Maximillian told himself, running a hand through his hair. Kitana was a witch—a child of Hecate, not Phaeros. It was impossible for witches to bear vampire children.

And if it *was* possible, and she *was* fated to be the mother of Casimir's children, then the gods had well and truly cursed Maximillian. For he was utterly besotted with the little witch, and he would gladly murder anyone who so much as looked at her with desire. Even if that someone happened to be the son of the most powerful vampire in Valentaera.

But that was a problem for another day, Maximillian told himself as he pushed off the wall. Tomorrow came with a more immediate problem—defeating Lazarus in single-armed combat *without* killing him in the process.

So, he brushed a lock of hair away from Kitana's face, kissed her forehead, then disappeared into the night to prepare for battle.

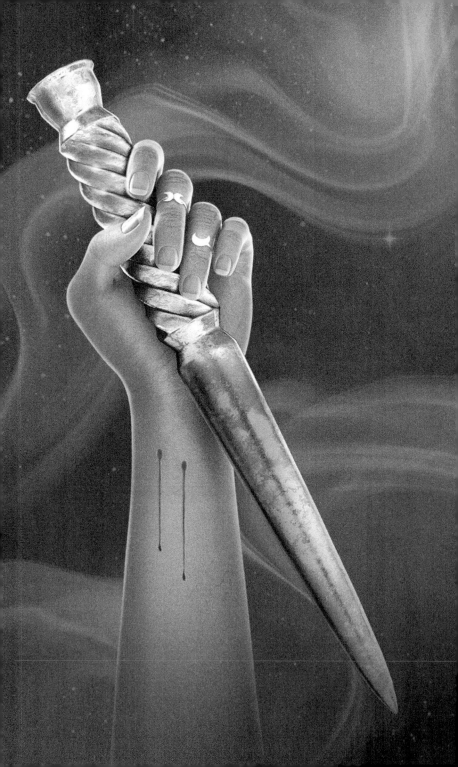

32

Kitana

"I must admit, this is the most exciting part of the Summit for me," Marisse gushed as we walked through the fair-grounds. "We get to eat and drink to our heart's content and spend the entire day watching all these performances of strength and skill!"

I nodded around a mouthful of grilled mushrooms as we stopped outside an arena to watch a Stellaris female and a Psychoros male go head to head in some kind of dart board game. The targets were set at insane distances, much too far away for a human, but both vampires hit them with incredible accuracy, the Psychoros vampire using his telekinesis to guide the darts, while the Stellaris woman used controlled burst of shadowfire to subtly manipulate her darts, giving them an extra boost to propel them forward every time she threw one. The two of them threw the darts faster than the eye could follow, the audience cheering them on as the game operator called out increasingly difficult targets.

"It would be a lot more fun if we could participate," I said as we moved on.

"Participate?" Marisse laughed. "What would be the point? There's no way we could win against even the weakest of these vampires."

We stopped by a food stall so Marisse could purchase a grilled fish for lunch. The human running the stall seemed well-cared for enough, though a little ragged, his vampire master nowhere to be found. "What do you think?" I asked him, just for the hell of it. "Do you think humans should be allowed to participate in the games?"

The slave blinked, as if surprised to be addressed directly, even by other humans. "I don't really see what the point would be unless the human in question had magic," he said with a shrug. "I don't have any, but I had a friend who could create little breezes if she thought hard enough. That might be useful for some of these games."

We continued on, biding our time until the main events began. I'd woken up this morning feeling more rested than I had in weeks—and with Maximillian's scent clinging to my skin, as though he'd embraced me recently. But that made no sense. I hadn't seen him since the previous morning after the summit session had been cut short, and I'd bathed before bed. I'd wondered if he'd come to visit me last night, and had gone to search for him so I could ask him myself, only to be told by the house guards he was off doing some last-minute training with Lucius in preparation for his combat match.

Part of me had wanted to watch them work, but I remembered how distracted I'd been when I noticed him watching me spar with Sparrow, and the disastrous consequences that had followed. I didn't think the same thing would happen with Maximillian if I walked in on him, but it was better not to take chances. It was important for him to stay focused, especially with the ugly looks Lazarus had been giving him all week. I wouldn't be surprised if the Sanguis Noctis heir tried to maim Maximillian during the match. Vampires could heal from a lot of things, but some injuries, such as the severing of a limb, took much longer to heal than others. If Maximillian was temporarily crippled, he would become an easy target once the summit ended and everyone began the return journey to their homes.

Marisse stopped to watch a trio of Stellaris performers juggle balls of shadowfire, but my attention was drawn to the shot put field a few feet away. This was no ordinary shot put; rather than using standard-sized shots, the vampires were heaving man-sized boulders across the field.

"No magic," the operator warned as a Psychoros vampire approached, rubbing his hands together with glee. "This is a strength game only."

The telekinetic slumped off, obviously disappointed, and I moved closer to watch the competition. The vampires were mostly from House Invictus, though a few Sanguis Noctis and Stellaris vampires had joined in with a valiant effort. Their throws would have been impressive in any other setting, but their performances paled in comparison to the Invictus vampires as they launched their shots with the terrifying strength their house was known for. The boulders flew through the air, landing hundreds of yards away with ground-shaking impacts that left craters in the barren field.

"Amateurs," a deep voice said from behind me.

I spun around to see Casimir Invictus standing behind me, arms folded across his broad chest in what I was coming to recognize as his default stance. His muscles strained against his white shirt and red waistcoat as he stared over my head at the competitors, and if he hadn't spoken aloud, I would have thought he was ignoring my presence.

"Your Highness," I said, curtsying respectfully even as my

heart pounded. I'd been so focused on the event that I hadn't even noticed the tugging in my chest. "I'm surprised to see you up and about. I heard rumors you were unwell last night."

Casimir's mouth tightened with irritation. "I heard that *you* were unwell," he said pointedly, his citrine eyes flicking down to meet mine. "So unwell that Lord Starclaw asked the High Nexon to excuse your absence at the Dark Mass last night, despite knowing it would count against you for the Descendency. Yet here you stand, looking fresh as a daisy."

"Getting a full night of sleep will do that to a person," I said sweetly, even as I silently kicked myself for my behavior. Why in all the hells could I not seem to keep my snarky mouth shut around the crown prince? "Interesting how we both happened to fall ill on the same night."

I hadn't meant to speak those words out loud, but when Casimir's eyes darkened, I knew he'd been thinking the same thing. "It certainly is," he said softly, his gaze roving over my face. He looked as if he wanted to crack open my skull and examine the insides piece by piece, and a shiver of apprehension raced through me. I wanted to step away from him, but the strange thing tugging me toward him rooted me to the ground.

Casimir leaned in, close enough to brush his mouth against my skin if he wanted, but he refrained from touching me. "I want you to tell me what it is you saw during the opening ceremony," he said, pitching his voice low so as not to be overheard.

I jerked back in surprise, and this time, I did step away. "During the opening ceremony? What are you talking about?"

The crown prince scowled. "Come with me," he said, then turned on his heel and strode away.

Alarm bells went off inside my head, but I knew that without Maximillian around to gainsay him, I couldn't refuse a command from the crown prince. Reluctantly, I hurried after Casimir, following him behind a shed that had been erected to hold extra tent poles and supplies. I braced myself for an attack, but while the crown prince did use his big body to cage me against the wall of the shed, he didn't touch me.

"When my father ratified Lord Starclaw's request to enter you as a candidate for the Descendency, something happened," Casimir said, his rough voice agitating my nerves. "Something that shocked you enough to make you look like you'd seen a ghost even though nothing out of the ordinary happened." He slapped his palm against the wall by my head, and I flinched. "I want you to tell me what you saw."

Oh. The memory came back to me—of Vladimir slamming his staff against the ground, of that current of crimson energy that rippled through the assembly. I must not have controlled my expression well enough if Casimir had noticed my reaction. But why *had* he been looking at me in that moment, when everyone else's attention had been glued to the emperor?

"Why don't you tell me what you saw first," I said in an even tone that bellied my flip-flopping stomach, "and I'll tell you if I saw it, too."

Casimir snarled, his eyes flashing red. "You push me too far," he hissed, shoving his face into mine. The sight of his long fangs glinting inches from my neck should have filled me with a healthy dose of fear, but then, this vampire had never inspired a rational response in me. "We are not equals—I am the crown prince, and you are a lowly human slave who thinks she can get away with flapping her lips simply because her master gave her a few fancy dresses and whisked her off to a grand castle. But I am not him, and I have no qualms about putting you in your place. You *will* answer me."

A muscle twitched in his jaw, and the air around us thickened with power, threatening to suffocate me. But the huntress inside me picked up on a scent, one that told me to stand my ground and push back.

"Why do you care so much?" I demanded, my hand drifting to the dagger at my thigh in case I needed to use it. "Why are you always watching me and finding excuses to be near me, when I'm a *lowly human slave*, as you put it, who's clearly beneath your attention?"

I spoke the words in a tone that was low but vicious, unsure where the anger inside me was coming from. After all, it wasn't as if I knew the crown prince. We'd only met a few days ago. Why did his presence inspire such reckless violence inside me? It wasn't the same murderous rage I felt when I looked at the emperor, the kind that pushed me to visualize his death at my hands over and over. No, my anger toward Casimir was different. It wanted to throw him to the ground and pummel him, the way angry children scrapped with each other when they were hurt or frustrated.

A taut silence stretched between us as Casimir held my gaze, and I let it go on, refusing to be the one to break. Finally, the crown prince stepped away with a curse, giving me space to breathe. "I don't understand what it is about you," he said, shaking his head in disgust. "Why I can't seem to stay away from you, why this thing in my chest—"

He cut himself off, but I pounced on that tidbit of information. "What thing in your chest?" I asked sharply. "There's a thing in your chest?" Could it be he felt the same tugging sensation I did?

Casimir's jaw worked for several seconds, as though he were chewing his way through several possible responses. Finally, he scraped a hand through his dark hair and said, "I saw a wave of dark energy spread from my father's body and throughout the chamber after he declared your candidacy," he said in a voice almost too quiet to hear. "I thought I was imagining things, except that the exact phenomenon repeated itself last night."

A triumphant surge filled me as Casimir vindicated my

hunch. "What was he doing?" I asked, unable to keep the eagerness from my voice. Was there some kind of pattern to this?

"He ordered me to—" Casimir started, then pressed his lips together. He glowered at me, and I glared right back, refusing to be intimidated even though the prince was fully capable of crushing my skull with a mere flick of his wrist. "Why are you so interested?" he asked, his tone heavy with suspicion.

I laughed. "Are you serious? Anyone would be interested if the emperor suddenly started using dark magic."

"My father is not using dark magic," Casimir growled, closing the distance between us. I reached for the dagger again, but the prince stopped short once more, and I realized he was deliberately refusing to touch me. Something pulsed in the air between us, our chests heaving simultaneously, and I fisted my hands at my sides as I grappled with my seething emotions.

"I don't know what this is between us," Casimir growled, "or what you think you saw that day. But stay the fuck away from me, Catherine. Be a good little thrall, sit at your master's feet, and stop sticking your nose where it doesn't belong."

He spun on his heel and stalked away, and I slid my back down the wall of the shed until my butt hit the dirt. The tug in my chest wrenched at me, commanding me to follow, and I fisted my hands at my sides, refusing to heed the impulse.

I didn't care if the gods themselves were behind this insane urge. I wouldn't go near Casimir again. Not until I'd reduced his father to ash.

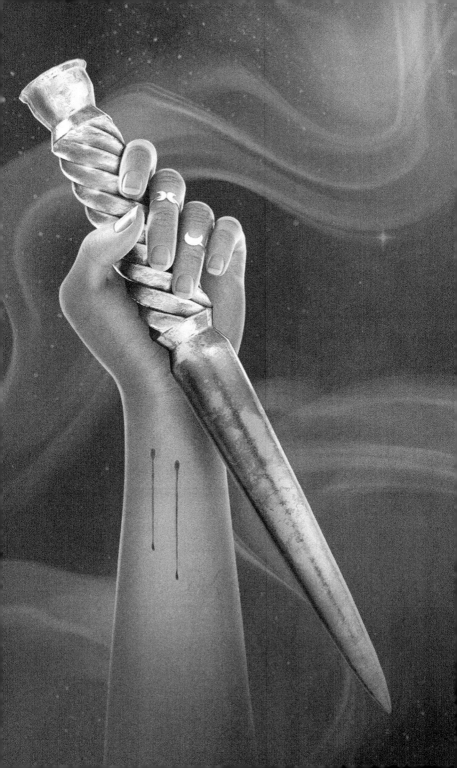

33

Kitana

Three hours later, I sat in the fairground arena stands, transfixed by the performance below. I knew I should be nervous about Maximillian's upcoming fight, and I had been when I'd first walked in here. But I was so mesmerized by the Stellaris delegation's meticulously planned performance, I couldn't focus on anything other than the burning strokes of ghostly blue-black flame they painted the night sky with.

I was well-acquainted with the brutal nature of shadowfire—unlike normal fire, it couldn't be extinguished unless the welder either perished, or commanded it to stop. It could eat through flesh, bone, steel, stone, and anything else in between. Yet the Stellaris delegation did not use their terrifying power to melt or char targets, but instead wove the shimmering flames into vivid, fiery images depicting mythical creatures, celestial bodies, and various scenes of historical significance to their house.

"Spectacular, isn't it?" A dulcet voice purred from my right, and I startled as Viviana Stellaris took the open seat next to me.

"They practiced for months, you know. I watched every second of it."

Lucius, who was seated on my other side, stiffened. "Lady Stellaris," he greeted her, his tone stiff. "Shouldn't you be seated with your family?"

"Pfft," she said, tossing her hair over her shoulder. "Why should I, when the company over here is so much more interesting? Besides, there's no rule against it. In fact, the emperor encourages us to intermingle."

Lucius glowered, but he didn't object further. "What do you mean, only watched?" I asked, curiosity getting the better of me. "Why not participate as well?"

Viviana let out a tinkling laugh. "The heirs are usually forbidden from participating in these events," she said, the slightest edge of resentment in her voice. "We are considered too valuable to risk for mere entertainment, even something as harmless as this." She flicked an elegant hand toward the performers, and a plume of shadowfire danced along her fingertips before snuffing out. "Which is a pity, really. I think I would be quite an asset."

"I don't understand," I said, confusion wrinkling my brow. "Isn't Caelum the heir of your house? You can't inherit the mantle since you're not capable of bearing children." I also didn't understand why Caelum was allowed on the front lines, if his status as heir was so precious.

Something bright and sharp flared in Viviana's eyes as she tore her gaze from the arena to look at me. "Too right, you are," she hissed, her midnight eyes glowing. "It is only the males of our line who are granted that privilege. But my gift of foresight makes me equally valuable. My visions are fruitful, even if my womb is not."

She gave me a bitter smile, and despite the trouble she'd caused during the soiree, I couldn't help feeling a little sorry for the female vampire. It was clear she wished for children of her own, something that was impossible due to the nature of the vampire curse.

"I'm sorry," I said, and I meant it. "I know how it feels when people only want you for what you can do, instead of who you are."

Viviana's blinked, and she titled her head at me in surprise. "You are an insightful little creature," she said. "I can see why both Maximillian and Casimir are taken with you."

"The Crown Prince?" I asked, resisting the urge to scoff. After the way Casimir had threatened me earlier, 'taken' wasn't the word I'd use. "He has no interest in me."

Viviana smirked. "Humans really are the worst liars." She reached out to flick a speck of dust off the sleeve of my dress. "Casimir and I were sneaking back into the castle after a night of debauchery when you and Lord Starclaw arrived. He noticed you right away, and couldn't stop staring. 'Smitten' might be a better word to describe his feelings for you."

My stomach lurched, and I automatically swept my gaze across the perimeter of the arena, seeking out the crown prince. He sat next to his father in the royal box, the nearly full moon limning the top of his dark head with silver. He wore his usual stoic mask, and I shook my head, amused at the idea that a male like Casimir could be *smitten* with anyone, least of all me.

"I can't presume to know the prince or his feelings," I said, choosing my words carefully, "but I find it difficult to imagine him engaging in any kind of debauchery."

"Oh, it wasn't his choice," Viviana said with a laugh. "My brother coerced him into it, and when Casimir found me at the club, he used my presence as an excuse to escort me back to the Iron Spire so he could escape. He was very eager to get inside until you showed up."

I had no idea what to say to that, so I decided to change the subject. "Why is this event called 'Tournament Day' if there is no actual tournament?" I asked her.

"Because the emperor does not want to waste vampire lives when they are sorely needed during the war," Viviana said. "That's why the combat match between Maximillian and Lazarus is so highly anticipated. Watching two heirs fight each other is a rare treat."

The atmospheric drumbeat faded as the Stellaris performance came to an end, replaced by enthusiastic applause from the audience. The stands were packed not only with the delegates attending the summit, but also Umbral's citizens, who had turned out in full force for the festivities. Even the humans were permitted to watch from the nosebleed seats, though I wondered how they felt about these displays of power from the monsters who had conquered and enslaved them.

As the shadowfire guttered, Ruslan, the master of ceremonies and one of Vladimir's three remaining sired children, rose from his seat in the royal box. "And now," he cried, his voice booming across the arena as a hush settled over the crowd. "The moment you've all been waiting for: the showdown between Lords Maximillian Starclaw and Lazarus Bloodmare!"

The crowd erupted into a frenzy as Maximillian and Lazarus emerged from opposite sides of the arena, dressed for battle. Both were stripped to the waist and dressed in simple boots and trousers—Maximillian in blue, Lazarus in red. The Psychoros heir was a storm barely contained as he stalked across the arena, his features set with a determined calm that masked the tempest brewing beneath. His broad chest was painted with intricate strokes of blue and gold that swirled together to form the astral eye—a hallowed symbol of his house. The war paint was also streaked across his high cheekbones, and it made him look fierce and primal in a way I'd never seen before. The knots of anxiety in my stomach melted away at the sight of him like this, replaced by a fluttering sensation low in my belly.

"Delicious, isn't he?" Viviana said in a knowing voice, glancing sidelong at me. "It's rare that Lord Starclaw lets his inner warrior out to play. And to think that he's doing this all for you, a mere human."

I ignored that comment, my attention fixed on the arena as the two vampires met in the middle where Soren Ironheart stood, ready to referee. Lazarus was also adorned with body paint, his thicker torso covered in swirling red and black geometric patterns that seemed to pulse with life. Unlike Maximillian, he made no attempt to disguise the savage glee etched on his face, and a taunting grin lifted his mouth. Maximillian, for his part, appeared utterly bored, but my knuckles ached at the smarmy look on Lazarus's face. For a heartbeat, I wished that I was in that arena, if only so I could drive my own fist into the bastard's face.

But this wasn't my battle to fight. It was Maximillian's. And I was looking forward to watching him trounce that insufferable prick.

"It has been over fifty years since combat matches were allowed during Tournament Day, making this the most anticipated event of the evening!" Ruslan roared over the crowd. "But in keeping with the emperor's infinite wisdom, the rules for this bout are different from those of times past. No weapons or magic shall be allowed!" he declared, and the audience booed. "Only the raw prowess and skill of our combatants will decide the victor! The match ends either when one of the combatants yields, or is knocked out. And if one of the fighters should take the life of the other..." Ruslan's voice deepened into an ominous rumble, "their life shall be forfeit."

Murmurs rustled through the arena, and Maximillian and Lazarus stood in stony silence as Soren Ironheart reiterated the rules. When both vampires nodded that they understood, the Invictus general stepped back, then raised his hand, signaling his permission for the fight to commence.

"Let the match begin!" Ruslan cried, and Maximillian and Lazarus wasted no time. The two clashed like titans, Lazarus opening with a powerful jab that Maximillian expertly dodged before following up with a swift upper cut. The strike connected, and Lazarus's head snapped back, but the Sanguis Noctis vampire swiftly recovered, avoiding Maximillian's next blow and countering with a flurry of kicks.

I was on the edge of my seat for the next fifteen minutes as the two vampires fought, reducing Sparrow and Lucius's sparring match to mere child's play in comparison. The vampires didn't adhere to the strict rules of a boxing match—the two slashed at each other with their claws every chance they got, and on one occasion, Maximillian lifted Lazarus over his shoulder, then flung him bodily across the arena. The Sanguis Noctis heir snarled as he skidded across the dirt, but he volleyed to his feet as Maximillian sprinted after him, blocking a downward strike with his forearm before launching yet another counterattack.

"He's winning," Viviana said, sounding a little surprised. "I'm impressed by how many more hits he's gotten in compared to Lazarus. I thought he would be the weaker fighter since he relies on his telekinesis so much."

"I'm going to pretend you didn't say that," Lucius growled as Maximillian weaved through Lazarus's relentless onslaught. His strategy seemed to be focused on agility and speed, allowing the larger vampire to exhaust himself, then taking advantage of openings to land powerful hits. "Just because we Psychoros are masters of the mind doesn't mean we don't spend considerable time mastering our bodies as well. Even *your* father made sure that you had adequate training, Viviana."

"True," she said with a sniff, "but that was hundreds of years ago, and I have not kept up with it. I have no illusions of how I would perform if I was in the ring instead of your sire. You should be proud of him."

I tuned them both out as I gripped the railing, watching Maximillian deftly avoid another of Lazarus's flying kicks. Despite the fact that he was clearly overexerting himself, I had to admire the Sanguis Noctis heir's fighting style. There was a fluidity to his movements, a disciplined elegance born of rigorous training and a warrior's pride. Each kick and punch was executed with precision and an artist's flair, as if each motion was a brushstroke in a blood-red war painting. It was a stark contrast to Maximillian's controlled and efficient movements, each strike and parry delivered by the Psychoros vampire with surgical precision.

Which was why everyone in the arena was blindsided when the Psychoros vampire, in the midst of launching a punch at Lazarus's exposed side, suddenly froze, his fist inches away from connecting.

It was a split-second pause, but I knew from experience that even a fraction of a second could be an eternity when it came to fighting creatures with superior speed and strength. Lazarus took advantage at once, squaring up with Maximillian and smashing his fist into the side of his opponent's head. Cries of shock echoed from the crowd, and I felt more than heard a scream tear from my throat as Maximillian staggered sideways, a dazed look in his eyes.

Lazarus pressed his advantage, raining blow after blow down on Maximillian. I leaned over the railing, my heart in my throat as I watched Maximillian rally, his arms coming up in a tight defense, each muscle coiled to absorb the impact. Blood streamed from the side of his head where Lazarus had struck him, but his expression was focused and determined as he bobbed and weaved, his feet shifting with practiced agility as he once again danced around Lazarus's offense. Hope rose in my chest as Lazarus's movements grew frustrated, and the Sanguis Noctis vampire unwittingly exposed his kidneys—an excellent weak point. It took vampires longer to heal their internal organs than it did broken bones, and the more hits Maximillian could land in those areas, the more he could slow Lazarus down.

But once again, just as Maximillian was about to land the blow, he froze. And this time, as Lazarus squared off with him, I felt the unmistakable prickle of magic against my skin.

I turned in my seat, searching for the source, only to see Callix Starclaw focusing intently on Maximillian, his skin glowing faintly. I stared in horror at the trance-like expression on his face. Was he using his powers to interfere with the match?

Before I could think better of it, I reached out with my own magic and seized the shadows around Lazarus's feet just as he reared back for another kick. I was nearly at the height of my full power again, so I had no trouble connecting with the inky darkness despite the distance, and I expertly tangled the vampire's own shadow around his ankle, forcing his kick to fly wide. Breaking free from the psychic hold, Maximillian swept Lazarus's feet out from under him, then pounced on the other vampire and rained punishing blows onto his face.

Lazarus raised his arms in a desperate attempt to shield himself, but Maximillian smashed through his defense with a vengeance. His fist crashed into Lazarus's jaw with devastating force, and the crowd gasped as the other vampire's head whipped to the side in an unnatural angle, his body going limp.

Soren Ironheart was there in an instant, hauling Maximillian away as the crowd went wild. "Lord Starclaw wins the bout with a decisive knockout!" Ruslan roared, but I could hardly hear him. Everyone surged to their feet, but I couldn't bring myself to join in the cheering as I looked at Callix Starclaw again. The blank expression was still on his face, no hint of joy or pride or any other emotion.

Suddenly, he turned to look at me, and I sucked in a sharp breath as our gazes collided. His frosted irises seemed to see right through me, and fear squeezed my heart as I wondered if he'd witnessed my interference—if he'd seen the shadow magic, and had somehow traced it back to me.

"Kitana!" Lucius shook my shoulders, drawing my attention from the high lord. A wide grin split his dark face, his eyes alight with exhilaration I'd never seen in him before. "Didn't you see? He won! Maximillian won!"

"I did see," I told him... but I didn't. I didn't see how Maximillian's father could stare so nonchalantly as his son stood bloody and triumphant in the arena. Especially after he'd just tried to sabotage him.

Or maybe even kill him.

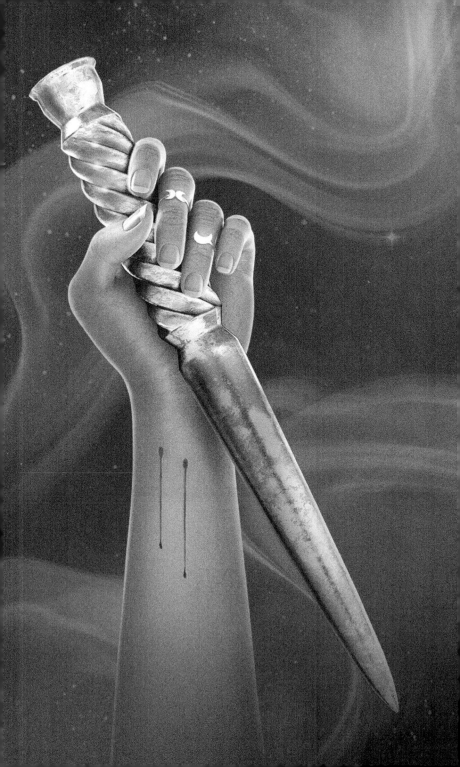

34

Kitana

After Tournament Day came to a close, the four delegations gathered in the Great Hall to celebrate with a grand feast.

I could feel the weight of Maximillian's gaze on me as we sat at a long dining table with the other heirs and highlords, the emperor at the head with Casimir, while Lysander occupied the foot. Lazarus was nowhere to be found. Once he'd gotten his head on straight—literally—he'd erupted into a howling fit of rage, accusing Maximillian of using his powers to cheat. It had taken twenty guards to drag him away, and I doubted the Sanguis Noctis heir had recovered from the humiliation. Which was probably why he hadn't shown his face tonight.

I stared into my cup of wine, the weight of unspoken words heavy on my tongue. I hadn't had a chance to speak to Maximillian after his victory—the entire Psychoros delegation had flooded the arena so they could pick him up and carry him away on their shoulders, making it impossible to get close. And once we'd gotten back, Lucius had asked Lucian to clean him up for the feast. But to be honest, I wasn't sure what to say. Was Maximillian aware that someone had used magic to sabotage him? Did he know I had used my magic to intervene? And how was I supposed to tell him I suspected his father, when the news would devastate him, especially on the heels of such a victory?

I couldn't ask him any of this now, not while the emperor was sitting so close. But the questions were burning me up from the inside, making it impossible for me to get into the otherwise festive atmosphere that filled the hall.

"That was an impressive match, Lord Starclaw," Ignatius Stellaris spoke from across the table. His black hair was tied back at his nape, leaving his long face unframed so he could eat freely. "You and Lazarus had the entire arena on tenterhooks with your performance."

"It was riveting," Casimir agreed as he cut into his fillet. "You acquitted yourself far better than I expected."

"I suppose I'll take that as a compliment," Maximillian said dryly. "We Psychoros vampires are more than just brains, you know."

"You must be," the emperor said, his citrine eyes glittering. Unlike the others, he had forgone food entirely, instead taking sips from a thrall female seated to the right and slightly behind him. The woman was pale and glassy-eyed, and a flash of anger filled me as I wondered how long the emperor would continue to feed from her in one sitting instead of allowing her to rest. "From my vantage point, it appeared you were losing right until the end, when you made that miraculous comeback. So miraculous, I almost wonder if you had help."

Dread pooled in my stomach at the sharp edge in the emperor's tone. But no one at the table even bothered to glance my way—all eyes were on Maximillian. Thankfully, the Psychoros vampire didn't allow the scrutiny to ruffle him. He merely lifted his goblet of wine, then said, "If I did have help, it could have only come from our dark father, who blessed me with the strength and fortitude to see this match to the end."

He raised his goblet to the statue of Tenebros that stood in the center of the Great Hall's entrance, and everyone else at the table followed suit, then drank. The emperor's eyes narrowed as he licked blood from his lower lip, but there was nothing he could say, not while Alaric Grimcrest sat right next to him, nodding his wizened head in approval.

"Have you had any fresh blood since your fight, Maximillian?" Callix asked. "To replenish your strength?"

Maximillian paused, his fork halfway to his mouth. "My strength is perfectly adequate, Father."

He spoke lightly, but I could almost see the line of tension his words drew between the two vampires, taut as a bowstring. I held my breath, waiting for Callix to retaliate, but the emperor interrupted.

"Your father is right," Vladimir said. "You should feed. Besides, the Summit is drawing to a close, and it is customary for a potential sire to feed from his candidate one final time. A symbolic gesture to close this chapter of your lives and move onto the next."

The emperor's gaze fixed on me, and I stilled. Everyone at the table settled their attention on me, their expressions ranging from mild interest to outright bloodlust. The only exception was Casimir—he fixed his expression on something across the room, his feature schooled into indifference.

And for some reason, that really pissed me off.

It was Casimir's fault we were in this situation. He was the one who opened his big fat mouth and suggested Maximillian and Lazarus settle things in a public duel. If he'd minded his own business, if he'd stayed out of their conflict, and if he hadn't made his own obsession with me so obvious, perhaps the emperor wouldn't be having this conversation with Maximillian right now. The urge to leap across the table and strangle him was so strong, I had to bury my hands in my skirts to keep from acting on it.

Maximillian slipped his hand beneath the table to find mine, even as he addressed the emperor. "I have no intention of circumventing tradition," he said as he rubbed slow circles along the inside of my wrist. The gentle touch distracted me, my anger fading as a different emotion stirred my blood. "But this is one tradition I would prefer to conduct in private."

"I didn't ask for your preference, Lord Starclaw. You will feed. Now."

True panic seized me then, and it took everything I had in me, all those meditation and breathing exercises Lucius had put me through during training, to keep from fleeing the room. Melting down would send up a giant red flag to the others—after all, I was supposed to be a thrall, someone who had fed her master countless times over the years.

But that fiction had no basis in reality. I had never allowed a vampire to sink his fangs into my flesh before, and the idea of doing so now was terrifying. Even with the bloodbane tainting my veins, there was every chance that the taste of my blood could turn him into the same feral monster I'd glimpsed in Sparrow.

Or even worse, he might figure out what I *actually* was.

"Of course," Maximillian said, pushing his chair back to make room for me. I struggled against the urge to fight as he circled his hands around my waist, then lifted me into his lap and settled my legs around his hips. The position was horribly intimate, especially considering how many eyes were on us, and it took everything I had not to squirm.

But when Maximillian cradled my face in his elegant hands, something shifted between us. His touch was gentle, tender even, as he stroked his thumb across my cheekbone, and the way he stared into my eyes made me feel like I was precious to him. Something to be cherished, not used or owned like the slave everyone at this table saw me as.

"Do you trust me, Kitten?" Maximillian asked. The words were a breath of a whisper, meant for my ears alone.

And despite my terror, despite knowing what was about to happen and that I had no power to stop it, I nodded.

Because I did trust Maximillian. With my life, and maybe, just maybe, with my heart.

"Good girl," he murmured, and the velvet caress of his voice stroked some hidden need inside me. My head tilted back of its own accord when he slid his hand into the hair at the base of my skill, and I felt his other hand brace the small of my back, cradling me as he prepared my body for the intrusion. I shivered as he pressed a soft kiss against a spot just above my collarbone, and a breath trembled out of me as his fangs scraped against my skin.

Maximillian struck swiftly, a punch of bright pain through soft flesh, and I cried out, digging my hands into his broad shoulder for support. But the moment he began to suck on the wound, the pain turned into a warm rush of liquid pleasure. My eyes slid shut as the sensation spread through my entire body, a pulsing beat of desire that drove all rational thought from my brain. An unabashed moan slipped from my throat, drawing chuckles from our audience.

But I wasn't the only one affected. Maximillian's grip tightened on my hair, and his hand slid down to grab a handful of my ass. He pulled me flush against his body as he continued to drink, and I gasped as his hardness pressed directly against my needy flesh. Unable to stop myself, I ground my core against him, and was rewarded with a burst of pleasure that radiated from my center and sent tingles all the way into my fingers and toes.

Maximillian groaned against my skin, then slowly pulled away. I whimpered at the sensation of his fangs leaving my flesh, and clutched at him as another wave of lust crashed over me. I looked down to see him watching me with heavy-lidded eyes, and the sight of him running his tongue over his bloodied fangs was nearly enough to make me come right then and there.

I wanted him back inside me, wanted it so much I was ready to beg for it right here in front of everyone. And not just his fangs, but whatever else he was willing to give. His fingers, his tongue, his c—

Maximillian's starfire eyes flared, and he shot to his feet, his chair crashing to the floor as he hauled me up with him. "Please excuse us," he growled, and our surroundings blurred as he whisked me out of the great hall using his vampire speed.

Mindless with need, I clawed at the lapel of his jacket, trying to remove the garment. But it refused to cooperate—he was in motion, and my body was in the way. Frustrated, I nipped at his earlobe, then, feeling contrite, licked it to soothe the hurt.

"Fuck," Maximillian growled, the sound vibrating through my chest and straight into my core. "You're going to be the death of me, Kitten."

He shoved into a room I didn't recognize—some kind of salon on the public meeting area floor, I think—then slammed the door shut. A second later, my back was pressed against it, and he was kissing the breath out of me, his fingers digging into the backs of my thighs as he held me up. I shoved my hands into his hair as I kissed him back, reveling in the decadent taste of him—the coppery tang of blood, the sweetness of black licorice, and a lush note of something dark and sinful that I couldn't quite identify, but drove me absolutely wild.

"Kitana," Maximillian rasped against my mouth, pulling away slightly. His pupils were blown, his cheeks flushed from both lust and his recent feed. "I... we shouldn't do this."

What? I tried to focus past the lust, to the look of concern on his face. "Why not?"

"Because," Maximillian groaned, leaning his forehead against mine, "this reaction... it isn't you. It's a chemical response to the bite. You're not in your right mind."

I could hear the words Maximillian was speaking, but their meaning didn't penetrate. "Are you saying you don't want me?" I asked, shrinking back against the door. Could I have been misreading him this entire time?

"Don't want you?" Maximillian let out an incredulous laugh. "Kitana, I've been dreaming about this moment for longer than you'll ever know. I've spent hours fantasizing about what it would be like to have you. The taste of your mouth. The softness of your skin. The sound of your moans. The way your pussy would feel as it clenches around my cock, and the look on your face when you come so hard, you forget all about that bastard who locked you away because he was too weak to love you. Want is an understatement. I *crave* you."

I opened my mouth to respond, but tears blurred my vision and blocked my throat, rendering me speechless. No one had ever said anything like this to me before, and the wounded animal inside me didn't want to accept it. But I couldn't deny the way my heart ached with the need to receive what he was offering. It had been decades since I'd received affection from anyone other than Jinx, and this time, it was being offered to me with no strings attached.

A tear slipped from the corner of my eye, and Maximillian's gaze softened. He brushed the liquid from my cheek, then kissed the spot where it had been. "I don't want you to regret this tomorrow," he whispered. "I don't want you to wake up with shame in your eyes, not when I've waited so long for this."

Regret? *Shame?* Is that what he was worried about?

Narrowing my eyes, I slid one hand between us and slipped

it under the waistband of his trousers. "The only thing I'm going to regret," I told him as I wrapped my hand around him, "is if I have to dismember you because you left me standing here, unsatisfied, out of some mistaken sense of honor."

Maximillian's laugh choked off as I squeezed his cock, and the moan he rewarded me with sent a heady rush straight to my head. But in the next second, he regained control, and he ripped my hand from his cock with a growl that would have been terrifying if I didn't want him so gods-damned much.

He hauled me around, switching our positions so that my back was pressed against his chest. The next thing I knew, we were standing in front of an ornate mirror hanging on one of the walls. My breath caught as I stared, transfixed at the sight of us framed like this, looking so wanton and undone. Maximillian's hair was a tousled mess, his cravat askew, his eyes blazing with lust. And I was no better with my crumpled skirts, my falling hair, and the strap of my dress that had slipped off one shoulder to expose the bloody bite mark he'd left. It was already half-healed, and the sight of it filled me with another rush of longing. I wanted him to bite me again, wanted the same rush of pleasure I'd felt, but this time with his cock inside me.

"Please," I begged, arching against him.

Maximillian swore, and he turned his face into the side of my neck. I moaned as he licked the wound, using his saliva to speed up the healing process. Watching his tongue lapping against my flesh through the mirror sent another flood of heat between my legs, and I clenched my thighs, trying to relieve the ache.

I had never felt so out of control in my life, and there was a small part of me, in the back of my mind, that knew Maximillian was right. This was not me, at least not entirely. I had acknowledged my desire for Maximillian privately, but I wasn't at the point where I was ready to shamelessly throw myself at him. At least not under normal circumstances.

Yet I couldn't deny the need pulsing inside me, making my core ache and my nipples tighten almost to the point of pain. I needed some kind of release, or I was going to lose my mind.

"Kitana," Maximillian said roughly in my ear. He slid one hand up my throat to grip the underside of my jaw, and the second one down the front of my abdomen until he grasped a fistful of my skirts. I moaned as the cool air of the chamber caressed my overly heated flesh through my underwear, but when I pushed my hips forward, begging him with my body to touch, he remained still.

"I'm not going to do anything to you, not while you're in this state," he growled. "But I know how much you need this, and I'm not such a bastard that I'd leave you hanging." His voice dropped to a seductive rumble, and his lips feathered over my jaw as he said, "Touch yourself while I hold you like this, Kitten. Let us watch together as you come undone by your own hand."

"I..." the words caught in my throat, and absurdly, I found myself blushing. Maximillian wanted me to finger myself while he stood behind me and watched? The idea was somehow embarrassing and arousing at the same time. I wasn't a virgin, not by any means, but my couplings with Sebastian were all done under the cover of darkness. Certainly not in front of a mirror, and definitely not in a public space where anyone could walk in and find us.

A tingle swept down my arm and into my fingertips, and my hand moved across my mound of its own accord. I stiffened as I realized Maximillian had used his magic to position my hand, but as soon as my hand touched my aching flesh, a pulse of pleasure rippled through my center. The tingle of Maximillian's telekinetic power faded, and he simply waited, his gaze fixed on my hand in the mirror.

Slowly, I began to stroke myself through the fabric of my underwear. My juices had soaked through the lacy white fabric, making the outline of my pussy visible, and Maximillian's eyes glowed as he followed the motion. Emboldened, I slipped my hand into my underwear, and my head fell back against his shoulder as my fingers made direct contact with my aching flesh.

"Tell me how it feels," he said, his voice a velvet whisper in my ear.

"I'm so wet," I whimpered, my finger slipping through my folds to find my clit. My hips bucked involuntarily against my hand, and the hand on my throat tightened in response. "I need more, Max. Please."

"Dip a finger inside yourself," he ordered. "Two, if you can."

I did as he said, pushing the first two fingers of my left hand inside myself. My inner walls clenched hard around my fingers, and I groaned as a sensation I hadn't felt in decades filled me. But it wasn't enough.

I didn't want my fingers. I wanted *him*.

But how could I get him to give me what I wanted?

A wicked idea struck me, and I pulled my hand from my underwear, then reached up and pressed my slick fingers against Maximillian's lips. He automatically sucked them into his mouth, and his groan vibrated along the length of my arm as he tasted me. I grinned when his eyes flew open, realizing his mistake, but I pushed my fingers in farther, refusing to let him retreat. To my delight, he gave in, licking the juices off my hand with slow, deliberate strokes of his tongue that made my core clench.

"You're a wicked little witch," he growled, pulling my hand away.

I smirked. "You're not the only one who knows how to incentivize people into giving you what they want. Now, is that tongue of yours only good for talking, or does it do other things?"

Maximillian chuckled darkly in my ear. "Oh, no you don't, Kitten," he said, snagging my damp hand and pressing it back between my thighs. "I have been playing this game far longer than you have, and I recognize the slippery slope you're trying to lead me down. If I follow you, it will be a lot more than my tongue between your legs by the end of the night."

"Would that be such a bad thing?" I asked.

I meant the question to sound teasing, but it came out soft and a little vulnerable, and something inside me clenched, bracing for a rejection. His eyes met mine in the mirror again, and he trailed his fingers up my throat to stroke the side of my face. "No," he said quietly. "It wouldn't."

He slipped my hand down the front of my underwear again, using his fingers to curl my smaller digits inward. I moaned again as he used my own hand to finger fuck me, and together we found a steady rhythm. The pleasure coiling between my legs built, and I pushed my hips into our joined hands mindlessly, seeking release. But although it felt incredibly good, something about the angle wasn't quite right. I couldn't get myself there.

But then I felt pressure on my clit, a light flick at first, and then harder, as if a phantom tongue was licking me. "There you go," Maximillian purred as my head fell back against his shoulder and my legs began to shake. He used his magic to increase the pressure while he guided my hand with his. "I've got you, Kitten. All you have to do is let go."

He bit down on the same spot on my shoulder he'd fed from earlier, this time with his fangs retracted. A burst of pleasure shot from the spot and straight into my core, and the sensation combined with my fingers inside me and his magic working my clit shoved me straight over the edge. Maximillian clapped his other hand over my mouth as I came, muffling my scream, and my body quaked as I came apart in his arms. The pleasure rattled me from the inside out, all my pent-up tension exploding out of me and leaving mindless bliss in its wake. It was the most intense orgasm I'd experienced in... well... maybe ever.

"That was incredible," Maximillian murmured in my ear as I sagged against him. As the last of the pleasure faded away, exhaustion trickled in, and I struggled to keep my eyes open. I felt more than saw Maximillian swing me up into his arms, cradling my head against his chest. "You're the most perfect creature I've ever seen."

"There's nothing perfect about me," I said, but I couldn't help laughing a little. "I'm a mess."

"Then you're a magnificent mess." He dropped a kiss on my forehead. "Now go to sleep. The first feed is always the most..."

I didn't hear whatever else he was about to say. I was already out.

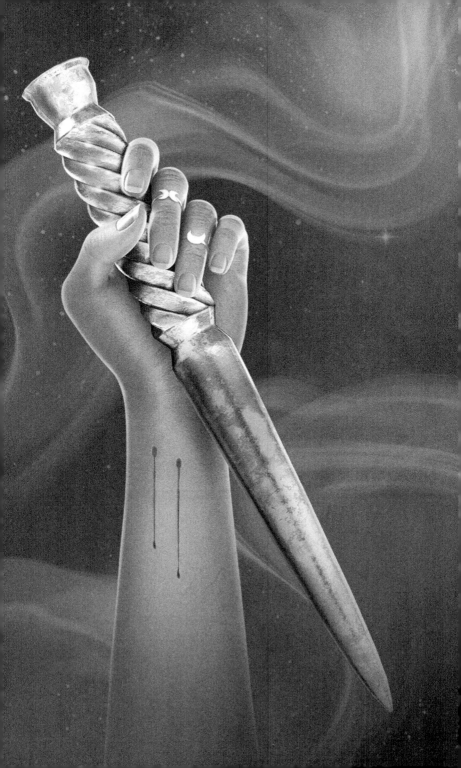

35

Kitana

"You look stunning," Marisse gushed as she adjusted the folds of my gown. "Whoever designed this dress outdid themselves."

"They really did," I agreed, looking at my reflection in the mirror. I'd woken up to find myself in my bedroom, alone, with this gown hanging on the back of my door. It was a deep indigo —not quite blue, not quite purple—velvet that hugged my figure like a second skin, with gold beading stitched into the fabric to form a spider-web pattern that flowed down the bodice and over the wide, a-line skirt.

A note had been pinned to the gown's skirt, and I'd read it, memorizing the words before tossing it into the fireplace. *We have much to talk about, but no time today,* Maximillian had written in a bold scrawl. *I had this dress made for your big night, and it has a few surprises in it. Check them when you are alone, and stick to the plan. I'll be counting down the hours until I can see you in this.*

I had no idea how a simple note could make my heart flutter

and my stomach fill with dread at the same, but somehow, the insufferable vampire had managed it. 'We have much to talk about' could refer to either the incredibly sexy moment we'd shared last night, or the events in the arena a few hours before. 'Your big night' was an obvious reference to the assassination. And the extra surprises...

"Marisse," I said after the thrall arranged my hair in an artful fishtail braid that draped over my right shoulder, "Would you mind giving me a moment before we head down?"

She frowned. "Is everything all right?"

"Yes. It's just... this is my last night as a human. I'm feeling a little nervous about it."

Marisse's expression softened, and she patted my shoulder. "Of course. I'll be right outside. Just don't take too long, all right? You have a strange habit of disappearing on me."

I was pretty sure it was Marisse who liked to disappear on me, but I bit my tongue and waited for her to leave the room. As soon as she shut the door behind her, I dragged my trunk out of the closet and threw open the lid to dig out the stakes and armored corset hidden inside. Quickly, I slipped my stakes into hidden pockets cleverly sewn into the wide skirt—six total—then conjured a few shadow tendrils to undo the back of my gown so I could slide my armored corset on underneath. Maximillian had thought of everything—he'd had the dress designed to leave just enough room for me to wear it underneath, and the neckline and back were high enough that the metal wouldn't peek through. He'd also added a slit in the skirt to allow ease of movement, so that I wouldn't tangle myself up in it if I had to run.

Finished, I used my shadows to lace everything back up, then dissolved them. Taking one more moment to brace myself, I crossed to the window and looked up at the full moon. Hecate's face peaked out from between two of the spires, and I could have sworn I saw the ghost of a smile pass across her silvery surface.

That, or it was just a cloud.

Either way, I was as ready as I was ever going to be. Armed and armored, with a full tank of magic humming in my veins. As long as I stuck to the plan, Vladimir would be dead by the end of the night, and Valentaera would be free.

As Marisse and I headed to the ballroom, I tried not to let my nerves rise to the surface. I had prepared for this moment as best I could, and there was nothing left to do except execute the plan.

But what would the rest of my life look like after this? There was no question that I still wanted my revenge against Sebastian, but what else did I want? Killing the emperor wouldn't rid Heliaris of the vampires who had taken over. Did I want to join forces with the rebels and help them retake their lands? It's something I liked to think my mother would have done. And what of Maximillian? He said he would help me with Sebastian, but would he support my efforts to push the vampires out of Heliaris, or would he become my enemy once more?

The idea of having to fight Maximillian after all we'd shared caused my stomach to twist into knots. I didn't know how I'd be able to kill him, after all the kindness he'd shown me. And there was also Lucius, Sparrow, and Nyra to consider. They'd all taught me so much—the last thing I wanted to do was repay that by driving a stake through their hearts.

One thing at a time, I told myself. I was getting myself all worked up over something that hadn't even come to pass.

"Oh, it's lovely," Marisse breathed as we walked into the ballroom. It felt as though we had walked into the celestial heavens, everything decorated in shades of midnight blue, black, and silver to echo the starry night visible through the floor-to-ceiling windows.

The ceiling was adorned with a magnificent mural, featuring constellations and celestial phenomena associated with Astellion and his pantheon. Crystal chandeliers, like stars captured in glass, bathed the room in a soft, otherworldly glow. Each table bore a centerpiece that featured the emblems of all four houses: the astral eye of Psychoros, the blood-red rose of Sanguis Noctis, the iron sword of Invictus, and the flaming orb of Stellaris, all intertwined with white flowers. The blend of house symbols amidst the starry theme was clearly meant to create an atmosphere of unity under the night sky, which was what the summit attempted to foster each year.

I had deliberately chosen to come late, so the ball was already in full swing. Vampires twirled atop a vast dance floor in the center of the ballroom, the glossy dark floors reflecting the chandelier lights beneath their heeled shoes. The women were dressed in dark jewel tones—deep garnet, sparkling amethyst, verdant emerald, and more, and the men were equally resplendent in their jackets and waistcoats. Bloodwine flowed freely and inhibitions were low, but everyone seemed to genuinely be having a good time. I even spotted Lazarus spinning Sarai from House Invictus across the floor, her skirts sparkling as they swirled about her feet, his white teeth flashing as he let out a genuine laugh.

They had no idea how drastically their lives were about to change.

Maximillian stood off to the side, in conversation with Stesha, but he broke free as he saw me enter the ballroom. My pulse quickened as he approached, his starfire eyes shining with approval as they swept over my figure in a way that made my toes curl. Before I could fully catch my breath, he was before me, scooping my hand up and brushing his lips across my knuckles.

"You are utterly bewitching," he said, glancing at me through lowered lashes. My body warmed beneath the heat of his gaze, and I blushed as I glanced at our joined hands, remembering what they had done together last night.

"Thank you," I said, hoping I didn't sound too awkward. I wasn't used to direct compliments about my looks. Compliments on my blade work or weapons? That was one thing. But telling me I looked beautiful? I had no clue how to handle that. "You... umm..." I took in his appearance, noting that he had dressed in all black, with a single jeweled gold and sapphire pin on his breast to signify his house and ranking. "You look really good."

Maximillian chuckled as he led me onto the dance floor. "Are you ready?" he asked, sliding one hand against the small of my back and clasping my other one with his right hand. The touch reminded me of how he'd braced my back last night, right before he'd bitten me, and heat pooled in my veins as I remembered how out of control I'd been.

"I am," I told him as we began to dance, hoping that I wasn't blushing too hard. I definitely hadn't been in my right mind when I'd all but begged Maximillian to fuck me last night, but even though I was a little embarrassed about my brazen behavior, I didn't regret anything that happened. "Thank you for the dress, by the way. It fits everything I need."

"Good." He lifted our hands overhead, spinning me out and then pulling me in so that my back was against his chest. He dipped his head so that his mouth brushed my ear, then whispered, "I can still taste you on my tongue, you know."

His voice was low and wicked and full of dark promise, and the space between my thighs turned molten. "Are you trying to distract me from my nerves?" I said, my voice coming out more breathless than I intended.

"Perhaps," he said, turning me to face him again. "Is it working?"

A crooked smile played on his lips, and I wondered how he would react if I leaned in and caught his lower lip with my teeth.

Then wondered how in all the hells I'd tumbled down this rabbit hole of lust, and whether I would ever surface again.

"It's working," I confirmed. "So well, in fact, I'm tempted to forget this entire plan and drag you to some dark alcove to see what other tricks you can perform."

"Well, we can't have that." But his smile widened. "I believe I'm not the only one with magic tricks up their sleeve. You pulled a very interesting one in the Summit Hall a few days ago."

I laughed a little, shaking my head. I couldn't believe I'd forgotten that I'd used shadow magic to grab his balls in the middle of a summit session. "That wouldn't have happened if you hadn't gotten all weird and jealous."

"Oh, I'm not complaining," he said, his thumb tracing patterns along my ribcage as we danced. "I'm looking forward to seeing what else you and your little shadow friends can do."

But despite the sexually charged banter between us, neither of us made any move to leave the dance floor. We couldn't—not when we had worked so hard for this moment, when we were mere minutes from everything falling into place. So we simply danced, losing ourselves in the music drifting through the midnight air, in the feeling of being in each other's arms, two separate universes that were never meant to collide connecting.

But all too soon, the moment came to an end. Maximillian's gaze slid over my shoulder to where Vladimir sat. A cool determination slid over his face, wiping away all traces of tenderness.

"It's time," he murmured.

I nodded as he stepped past me, and drifted over to one of the pillars near the windows, stepping into the pool of shadows behind it. The plan was for Maximillian to beg a private audience with the emperor. There was a private room just across the hall with an adjoining chamber, so all I had to do was enter the next room, then wait until the right moment to walk in through the connecting doors. We had agreed to do it later in the evening, when most of the simpering courtiers that gathered around Vladimir to curry favor finally dissipated to join the festivities, and were drunk enough on bloodwine that they were least likely to kick up a fuss or notice anything amiss.

I watched from the darkness as Maximillian bowed before the emperor, then requested the audience. The emperor frowned, probably annoyed at the idea of being pulled from the festivities, but whatever Maximillian said must have convinced him. He got to his feet, and Maximillian followed along with three guards.

I waited until they had disappeared, then waited a little while more before stepping out from behind the pillar to follow. It might raise suspicion if I was seen leaving immediately after they did. But I only made it a few steps before that familiar tug started up in my chest again—only this time, it was a vicious sensation, as if someone had reached into my guts and was now trying to yank them out of my abdomen. It was so painful that I nearly doubled over in agony, and I had to clutch a nearby table to stay upright.

What in the ever-loving hells is going on?

I swept the ballroom for any sign of Casimir, who was the only possible source for this pain. I didn't see him anywhere, but the excruciating tug pointed me to a window in the far corner that turned out to be a set of double doors leading onto a stone balcony. I didn't want to go out there, not when Maximillian was waiting for me with the emperor, but as I moved toward the door, I noticed that the pain lessened with each step I took.

Muttering every foul curse I knew under my breath, I opened the double doors and slipped out into the freezing night that I was absolutely not dressed for. A wide veranda stretched the length of the ballroom, but although there were a few couples out here sharing glasses of bloodwine or necking like young lovers, none of them were the crown prince.

I'm going to murder him when I find him, I swore, descending a set of steps that led from the veranda to the stone garden on the south side of the Iron Spire. I'd briefly explored them on my second day here—it was a beautiful place that, as the name suggested, was carved entirely from stone. Sculpted trees, their branches frozen in an eternal dance, lined the pathways, stone benches nestled among carved flowers and grasses, and a central fountain, its water replaced by swirling stone waves, stood in the center. The moonlight played off the polished surfaces, creating the illusion of movement, and I wondered if, before the Eternal Night, there had been a living garden here that looked like this one.

Casimir stood by the fountain, his hands braced against the stone basin, chest heaving as though he were about to vomit into it. He stiffened at my approach, and the pulsing in my chest grew stronger, pulling me toward him with a force I was powerless to resist.

His head snapped up as I approached, and I sucked in a breath as our eyes clashed. His irises were a strange silvery white, no trace of their usual citrine color to be seen.

"What in the hells are you doing here?" he barked, baring his fangs at me. "Didn't I tell you to stay the fuck away from me?"

"I would if it wasn't literally killing me not to!" I snapped back, all the anger I'd built up toward him finally boiling over. I was fucking sick of this shit, sick of him constantly snapping at me as if this strange thing between us was *my* fault, when *he* was the one out here messing up all my carefully laid plans. "I don't know what the fuck is going on either, but I'm ending this. Right now."

Casimir's eyes widened as I closed the distance between us. "No, wait—" he started, but I pressed my hand against the center of his chest, right where I felt the tug in mine. The action was guided by pure instinct, but as soon as I touched him, the nagging sensation vanished, and I felt a distinct *click*, like a deadbolt sliding free.

But whatever relief I felt was not echoed by Casimir. The flesh under my hand grew burning hot, and he gasped as light began to pulse at the center of his chest. As the light brushed against my skin, I felt a familiar, welcoming warmth, like the kiss of moonlight on my face. Or the blessing of my goddess.

The realization of what was happening crashed into me with such force, I nearly fell to my knees.

"Casimir!" I grabbed his shoulders, forcing him to look at me. "We need to get you out of here. Is there someplace we can go to, a wooded area or a hidden field, where nobody lives?"

"There's the Bramblewood Forest," Casimir panted, pointing northwest. "But it's miles from here. I don't think I can walk more than five paces."

Fuck. The light in his chest grew brighter with every pulse, spreading across his skin in increments. It was only a matter of time before that power unleashed itself, and when it did, there wasn't a single person around for miles who wouldn't see it.

"I don't understand this," Casimir groaned, clutching his chest. "What is happening to me? Why am I burning up on the inside?"

Gods dammit! There was no time. "Don't make me regret this," I snarled, tightening my grip on him.

Casimir looked up just in time to see a wave of shadow ribbons explode out of me. He roared in confusion as they wrapped us in a cocoon of darkness, but my shadows held him fast, defying his immortal strength. Shutting out his enraged shouts, I squeezed my eyes shut and visualized the forest Casimir had mentioned, willing the world to dissolve around us. I hadn't attempted to shadow travel since the night Sebastian had imprisoned me, but I had to get Casimir away from this place before someone saw him.

As I focused on our destination, the pressure of gravity vanished, replaced by the eerie weightlessness that always accompanied shadow travel, as if we were no longer on the continent, but drifting between the stars. The shadow cocoon warbled around us as we traveled through time and space, and then with a sudden jolt, gravity reclaimed us.

The shadow ribbons unraveled around us to reveal the skeletal branches of a dead forest.

And not a moment too soon.

"Fuck!" Casimir screamed, collapsing to his knees as he went supernova. I threw up a shadow shield between us, pouring every scrap of magical energy I had left to protect myself from the tempestuous storm of light he unleashed. The lunar energy tore through the forest like a cataclysmic wave, disintegrating the trees around us and annihilating any animals who had tried to scrape out an existence in this deadened wood. Even through the shield, I could feel the searing heat, and I hissed as my exposed flesh stung beneath the onslaught.

Just when I thought I wouldn't be able to take any more of this, the tsunami ceased, its pummeling force receding into gentle waves of energy that lapped against my shield like a surf. Sighing in relief, I dissolved the shield to find Casimir on his hands and knees, sucking in great lungfuls of air. The hairs on my arms rose at the expanse of barren land around us—by the looks of things, he'd incinerated an entire square mile of forest.

But even though the missing woods would undoubtedly draw attention, that was the least of our worries.

"I don't understand," Casimir said, his face ashen as he held out a hand in front of him. Tiny glimmers of light danced across his skin, casting an ethereal glow around him. "What in Tenebros's name *is* this? And how did you bring me here?"

I shook my head, getting to my feet so I could walk over to him. "Not Tenebros's name," I said as I crouched in front of him.

"Hecate's name. That's the goddess's energy you're holding in your hands."

"What?" Casimir croaked.

I pressed my palm against his, letting my wisps of shadow come out. They wove between his sparks of light, the two twining into an age-old dance that made my magic sing.

The memory I'd dreamed of that first night in Maximillian's tower rose to the surface of my mind, knife bright. "*He is the other half of my heart. I thought I could leave him behind for her sake, Elna, I really did. But if I don't go back for him, his fate will haunt me forever. And I will never be whole.*"

"I always thought she was talking about my father," I said as the pieces fell into place.

"Who?" Casimir demanded.

"My mother." I dropped my hand into my lap. "She left me when I was eight years old to go back to the vampire who'd gotten her pregnant, and I thought it was because she'd been in love with him." I laughed softly, looking at Casimir in wonder. "But it wasn't my father she came back for. It was you."

"Me?" Casimir scowled, shaking his head violently as if trying to clear something from his ears. "Why would your mother have come looking for me?"

"Because she's your mother, too." I sucked in a breath, then exhaled in a rush as I allowed the truth to spill from my lips. "My mother was a Nocturne witch, Casimir. You and I are the two halves of her heart—the two facets of Nocturne power."

"Nocturne power..." Casimir trailed off as he struggled to put the pieces together. "You're saying this is witchcraft?" he asked, sounding horrified.

"Yes. You're half witch, half-vampire, just like I am." I grabbed his hand again, and his magic surged to meet mine, two halves of a whole that were never meant to be parted. This was the reason I'd never been able to use lunar magic, no matter how hard I prayed to the goddess to grant it to me. "I'm not your *amorte*, Casimir. I'm your *twin*."

"Twins?" he asked, aghast. "But that would make your father..."

"Vladimir Invictus," I said grimly. The vampire king of Noxalis, and self-proclaimed emperor of Valentaera.

And now I needed to get Casimir on my side if I wanted to defeat him.

To be continued...

Kitana's journey will continue in *The Bloodline's Deceit*, Book Two in *Empire of Eternal Night*. You can pre-order it on Amazon, or sign up for Jasmine's mailing list at www.JasmineWalt.com so you can be notified when it's released!

P.S. Did you enjoy this book? Please consider leaving a review. Reviews help authors sell books, which means they can continue writing sequels for you to read. Plus, they make the author feel warm and fuzzy inside, and who doesn't want that?

ABOUT THE AUTHOR

NYT bestseller **JASMINE WALT** is obsessed with books, chocolate, and sharp objects. Somehow, those three things melded together in her head and transformed into a desire to write, usually fantastical stuff with a healthy dose of action and romance. She also writes under Jada Storm.

Her characters are a little (okay, a lot) on the snarky side, and they swear, but they mean well. Even the villains sometimes. When Jasmine isn't chained to her keyboard, you can find her practicing her triangle choke on the mats, spending time with her family, or binge-watching superhero shows. Drop her a line anytime at jasmine@jasminewalt.com, or visit her at www.jasminewalt.com.

ALSO BY JASMINE WALT

Of Dragons and Fae

Promised in Fire

Forged in Frost

Caged in Shadow

The Baine Chronicles Series:

Burned by Magic

Bound by Magic

Hunted by Magic

Marked by Magic

Betrayed by Magic

Deceived by Magic

Scorched by Magic

Fugitive by Magic

Claimed by Magic

Saved by Magic

Taken by Magic

The Baine Chronicles (Novellas)

Tested by Magic (Novella)

Forsaken by Magic (Novella)

Called by Magic (Novella)

Dragon Riders of Elantia

Call of the Dragon

Flight of the Dragon

Might of the Dragon

War of the Dragon

Test of the Dragon

Secret of the Dragon

Her Dark Protectors

Written under Jada Storm, with Emily Goodwin

Cursed by Night

Kissed by Night

Hidden by Night

Broken by Night

The Dragon's Gift Trilogy

Written under Jada Storm

Dragon's Gift

Dragon's Blood

Dragon's Curse